KING OF THE HILLS

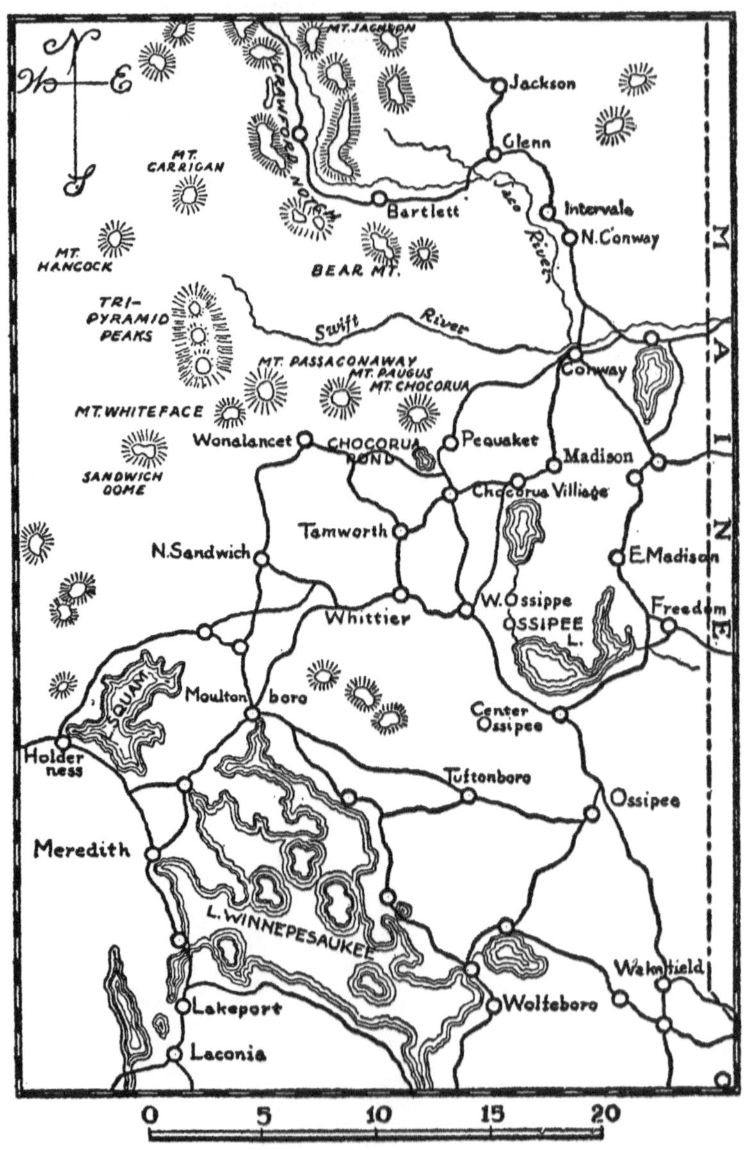

N
E
W
S
MT. JACKSON
Jackson
Glenn
CRAWFORD NOTCH
MT. CARRIGAN
Intervale
Bartlett
N. Conway
MT. HANCOCK
BEAR MT.
Saco River
TRI-PYRAMID PEAKS
Swift River
MT. PASSACONAWAY
MT. PAUGUS
MT. CHOCORUA
Conway
MT. WHITEFACE
Wonalancet
CHOCORUA POND
Pequaket
Madison
SANDWICH DOME
Chocorua Village
Tamworth
E. Madison
N. Sandwich
W. Ossippe
Freedom
Whittier
OSSIPEE L.
SQUAM
Moultonboro
Center Ossipee
Holderness
Tuftonboro
Ossipee
Meredith
L. WINNEPESAUKEE
Wakefield
Lakeport
Wolfeboro
Laconia
MAINE
0   5   10   15   20

King of the Hills

BY STEPHEN W. MEADER

ILLUSTRATED BY LEE TOWNSEND

ISBN 978-1-931177- 82-5 cloth
ISBN 978-1-931177- 83-2 paperback

LITTLE ROCK, ARKANSAS
www.southernskies.com

Dedication

The republication of this book is dedicated with love to Griffin Jerome Henry Kidd by his Papa, Jerry Atchley

ILLUSTRATIONS

I

THE boy in the smart little black roadster leaned back behind the wheel and drew half a dozen deep, tingling breaths of mountain air. Then he laughed, long and loud. There was no one within a mile to hear him but he kept on chuckling as he stepped on the accelerator and skipped up the next hill. What amused him was the idea of all the other fellows plugging away at school while he rolled off, free as air, for a fortnight in the woods. Not a worry in the world, and Boston already a hundred miles behind!

Steadily the smooth, gray breadth of the road unwound before him. The speedometer pointer left its customary 50 and crept up to 55—to 60. Then of a sudden the boy's eye lit on a roadside sign ahead and his foot jumped to the brake. It was not a speed warning he had seen but a crudely lettered board that read, "Fried Clams." It stood in front of an unpainted shack, and shared the desolate dooryard with a gasoline pump.

Breck Townsend uncoiled his rangy length from be-

3

hind the wheel and stretched gratefully. The proprietor was talking to two men beside a big coupe, a hundred feet up the road. At Breck's cheerful toot of the horn he broke away hurriedly and shuffled back to the pump. A little, mean-faced man he was, and badly in need of a shave.

"One dozen of your very best clams," said the boy, "and five gallons of gas in the tank, please."

While the fellow went inside for the clams, Breck had leisure to observe the coupe more closely. It was a powerful and expensive car finished in a light tan shade. Breck remembered having seen it twice before, that day. Once was in Rochester, where he had beaten it on the get-away after a traffic stop. The second time was just below Wakefield, where the big coupe had shot past him, purring a smooth seventy.

The two men who now lolled against it were hunters up for the deer season, judging from their dress. One was big and burly and the other slighter in build but both wore the regulation high-laced boots and leather jackets. Apparently Breck's stare was unwelcome. The big man's brows contracted in a scowl and he nudged his companion furtively. With an unhurried movement the other turned his lean, sharp-featured face in the boy's direction and gave him an appraising look, then swung away with a shrug.

It was about that time that the gas-station owner reappeared with a paper bag full of clams and Breck proceeded to give them his undivided attention. He had an eighteen-year-old appetite, sharpened by three hours in the November air, and fried clams were among his special weaknesses. These he found crisp, hot and succulent, evidently just out of the pan. He was in the act of demolishing his ninth, when the roar of a motor sounded from up the road, and a big truck hove in view. It hauled up short with grinding brakes just opposite the coupe, and there was a low-voiced hail from the driver. At once the larger man crossed the road, spoke for a few moments with the truck pilot and was turning away when the fellow hauled a gun from behind the seat and handed it down to him, butt first.

Breck paused with a clam halfway to his mouth. For though the man in hunter's clothes partially concealed the weapon as he hastened across to the coupe, the boy had enough of a glimpse to be pretty certain it was a 30-30 rifle. And he knew the New Hampshire game laws forbade hunting deer with anything but a shotgun.

The hard-visaged native had finished filling the roadster's tank and now sullenly accepted the money Breck held out to him. "Wait a bit," the boy said. "What do you suppose is in that truck—stowed away so tight under those tarpaulins?"

The man's little rat-eyes shifted, and he spat before he answered. "Dunno's it's any o' my business, or yours either," was his muttered reply.

"Bootleggers, eh?" said Breck, opening the rumble-seat of the Ford. The cushion had been removed and he had stowed the compartment full of duffel that morning, in preparation for his trip. There were blankets and a suitcase and knapsack and, on top, the searchlight and batteries that he had rigged with care the week before. He pulled a spare sweater out of the heap and closed the deck again.

"Huh!" grunted the man at his elbow. "I guess *you* know what they got in that truck!"

There was a sneer in his voice that Breck didn't like. "Just what do you mean by that?" he asked.

The fellow merely nodded in the direction of the rumble seat and moved away with an ugly chuckle.

Puzzled, Breck stood a moment looking after him, then got into the car. "Must have gone goofy, living up here by himself," he decided, and with that he let in the clutch and put the whole matter out of his thoughts.

But twenty minutes later he was given a sharp reminder. He had passed Ossipee Village, and was rolling merrily up the next hill when the drone of a powerful motor grew loud in his ears. Up alongside ranged the long hood of the tan coupe.

"Oh, I'll admit you can trim me, out on the road!" he laughed gayly.

But this time the coupe did not shoot past. When its swanky radiator-cap was two or three feet beyond the Ford's, the big car began edging closer.

As both machines had been traveling at fifty miles an hour when this maneuver started, Breck had little time to think. The shoulder of the concrete was perilously close to his outside tires, and the coupe had already crowded within inches of his fender. Grim-faced, the boy planted his foot on the brake and gripped the wheel.

With less momentum to overcome, the light car had the advantage. To his left, Breck saw the rear of the coupe sliding past—and this in spite of the fact that he could hear the shivery squeal of its brakes. He jerked the nose of the Ford away from the road-edge, just grazing the coupe's rear bumper. And at that instant the other driver swerved viciously to the right, evidently thinking he still had the boy boxed.

Breck had his opening then, and took it. He pressed the button clear to the floor and the roadster leaped out to the left like a bronco under the spur. Behind him, the big car's right wheels were off the road. It swayed crazily as the tires bumped over rough ground, but Breck neither paused nor turned his head. He kept the Ford at sixty all the way into West Ossipee, and when he made his turn to the left off Route 16, the coupe had not yet come in sight.

After that he slowed down a bit and breathed easier. He had no idea what sort of mistaken grudge these men held against him. But even if they meant to make another attempt to ditch him, the chances were they would expect to find him on the main highway.

Breck was in familiar country now—country he had fished and camped and hiked and driven over for three long summer vacations. The thought of being pursued by enemies in that setting of friendly peace and grandeur was so ridiculous that he couldn't repress a grin.

Up there to his right was the bold, rugged peak of Chocorua, its snow-covered sides gleaming bright in the level sunset light. Away to the west the dim, purple bulk of Sandwich Dome stood against the sky. And rolling across the northern horizon were the timber-crested billows of the Sandwich Range. Paugus—Passaconaway—Whiteface—the Tri-Pyramid Peaks—he knew them all —their forests and ledges and hidden valleys. It was towards their spruce-clad knees that he was moving now.

He crossed the level intervale of the Bear Camp River and swung up through Tamworth, then northwestward again along a rough little country road, twisting over the hills.

It was growing dusk when he reached Wonalancet, and lights twinkled in the farm-houses that made up the tiny hamlet. Only two more miles now and he would

reach John Turner's house. He drove more slowly, sniff-ing the balsam-scented evening, looking eagerly to right and left for familiar landmarks. Soon he was rolling up the entrance road between tall trunks of the white pine

grove, and there before him were the long verandas of
the house.

John Turner had chosen well when he picked this spot.
It was high enough on the slope of Whiteface to look out
over forty miles of forest to the south and west. Yet its
rear was sheltered from the bitter northern gales by the
shaggy wall of the mountain range. Here he had built a
long, rambling house of two comfortable stories, with
accommodation for forty or fifty guests. And as the popu-
larity of the place had grown he had added twenty snug
cabins, strung along the wooded mountainside.

Breck brought the roadster to a stop before the doorway and beat a tattoo on his horn. A light was switched
on in the hall but before the door could be flung open
there was a swift rustle of feet along the frozen ground
and a huge, furry shape appeared at Breck's elbow. The
great round head of an Arctic sled-dog raised itself above
the car door, and a pair of tawny-circled yellow eyes
stared into the boy's own. So they stayed for a second and
then, with a gruff whimper, the dog lunged eagerly forward to lick his face.

Laughing, Breck got out and mauled the husky affec-
tionately. Then he turned to greet the lanky, gray-
bearded man who had come out of the house.

"Well, Breck Townsend!" roared John Turner. "I
couldn't hardly believe it, when your wire come! I fig-

gered you was still down at the Academy, ketchin' forward passes. How are ye, anyhow?"

"Never felt better in my life," Breck laughed. "That
doctor must be just a friend of mine, that's all. I got a
couple of ribs cracked in the game with Dartmouth Fresh,
along in October. And after they healed up I couldn't get
my weight back. A week ago the doctor told Dad I needed
some mountain air and exercise to build me up. And here
I am!"

"Well," said the gaunt mountaineer, "it's sure a treat
to see ye. An' this time o' year, too, when we ain't too
busy to play 'round a bit. Never been here in the Fall or
Winter, hev ye?"

"Never," Breck replied. "That's what makes it twice
as much fun."

They set his luggage inside the door and took the Ford
back to the barn. Breck locked the rumble-seat. "I've got
some stuff in there I don't want to lose," he said. "My
new camera and the searchlight I've fixed up."

"Searchlight?" queried John Turner, looking puzzled.

"Sure," said Breck. "Do you know what I want to do
more than anything else, while I'm up here? Get a picture of that big buck over on Passaconaway—the one
they call 'the King.' "

Turner gave a long whistle. "Old Scar-back, eh?" he
said. "Two weeks don't seem any too long fer that job.

I know hunters that have tried to git him every November fer six years, an' never seen him closer'n half a mile off. Supper won't be ready fer twenty minutes. I'd like to have a look at this light o' yours."

Breck was glad to display his handiwork. He took the contrivance out of the car and held it up proudly. "Here's the light," he said, "—an old motorcycle headlight I picked up cheap. It's got a first-rate reflector and I put in clear glass instead of the lens. Then this knapsack arrangement holds six dry cells, wired up to the light. That fits on my back with a couple of straps over the shoulders, and the light is in front, just about over my belt buckle. That gives me room to manage the camera above it, and of course my hands are free."

"Hm—pretty slick," commented Turner. "That's better'n the old carbide hat lamps some o' the boys used to use jackin' deer."

"Jacking?" asked Breck. "What's that?"

"Same thing you plan to do, only with a gun instead of a camera," the mountain man replied. "The easiest way to find a deer is to shine his eyes with a jack-light at night. He stands still, sort o' dazzled, an' you aim below his eyes an' left or right, dependin' how he's standin'. It's against the law, o' course, but most of us have done it, one time or another when we needed meat. The wardens have always let us pretty much alone, knowin' we didn't kill many deer. But the last two or three years a mess o' pot-hunters from outside have been jackin' deer by the hundreds an' sellin' 'em. An' that's bad—bad fer the deer an' bad fer us."

"Where can they sell them?" Breck inquired.

"Most o' the deer are bought by New York an' Boston hunters that don't have no luck themselves," said Turner. "They pay fancy prices fer a buck that they can take home with 'em. Then some are smuggled out o' the state an' sold to hotels and restaurants in the cities. There's a lot o' money in it, an' it's turned into a reg'lar racket, run by a few hard-boiled gunmen."

Turner shut the barn-door and they crossed the pine-shadowed space to the veranda. As they mounted the steps the big sled-dog trotted up and nuzzled Breck's hand, then vanished again into the dark.

"I thought you generally kept Duff tied up at night," the boy remarked.

"We've been lettin' him run loose the last couple o' nights," said the backwoodsman. "Been some funny doin's up this way lately."

Duff was a full-grown Labrador husky, one of Walden's famous dogs, bred in the neighboring village of Wonalancet. An ancestor of his had been with Peary at the Pole; his sire with Byrd in the Antarctic. Brought to Turner's, two summers before, as a gangling puppy,

Duff had grown up as the playmate of Breck and the other lads who spent their vacations at the camp. Though he had never worked in harness he had the build and the fighting spirit of a lead-dog. And the mountain was given a wide berth by prowlers who knew of his presence there.

Breck took his bag up to his room, washed and came down to supper. There were only four other guests in the house—two elderly ladies and a middle-aged married couple from Boston, friends of the Turners. He found them all gathered in the big living-room before a log-fire, chatting as they awaited the call to supper.

"It happened last night—" the Boston man was saying, "down on a cross-road near Tamworth. This farmer was driving home when he saw a big car stopped ahead of him. The headlights were on full and nearly blinded him, but he hauled up alongside and asked if there was anything he could do for them. It was a touring-car with the top down and three men in it. One of them shoved a rifle-barrel over the side and told him to get away from there fast and mind his own business."

"Must have been some o' those jackers," said Turner. "I know that road. The deer cross there to drink at the brook." He frowned. "I don't like that. If these fellers try their gangster methods up here there'll be trouble sure. Our folks won't stand fer it."

A red-cheeked Nova Scotian girl appeared just then

and summoned them to the dining-room. Old Jeannie, the cook, had evidently outdone herself in Breck's honor, for there were half a dozen of his favorite delicacies on the table in addition to the huge baked ham that made its centerpiece. The boy was not backward in showing his appreciation. Only when he had consumed eight of her fluffy biscuits and a third helping of gooseberry jam did he allow his plate to be removed. And then there was a mighty wedge of apple pie to be eaten.

Afterward he took a worn copy of "Monte Cristo" over to the settle by the fire. By ten o'clock he was drowsy, and saying good night to the others, he made his way up to bed. Before he turned in, he opened the front window of his room and stood a moment drinking in the keen air. It was a windless night, frosty and still. The sky was overcast and the woods shrouded in blackness. From away over on the next mountain came the lonesomest of sounds—the faint, far music of a hound-dog's baying.

"Feels like snow," Breck murmured to himself. "Ought to be some good tracking in the morning." And burying himself under the cozy warmth of three blankets and a down comforter he went instantly to sleep.

II

THE dawn came cold. When Breck opened his eyes it was to see his breath rising in a white cloud. He sprang out of bed and closed the window, thrilling to see the level blanket of snow that cloaked the landscape. He took a cold shower and rubbed his body to a glow, then dressed in heavy flannel shirt, army breeches and high laced moccasins.

There were sounds of bustle in the kitchen but Breck knew none of the other guests would be down for another half hour. He pulled on a sheep-lined jacket and went outside. About two inches of snow had fallen in the night but now the air was clear and sparkling. The sunrise threw a delicate rosy light along the upper slopes of the mountains, and the new snow pointed the spruce forests with a million flecks of white. The wooded ridges looked as if a great mantle of silver fox skins had been thrown over them. Breck turned from these poetic fancies to throw a hastily packed snowball at Duff, as the big, solemn wolf-dog trotted around the corner of the house. The next instant they were rolling in the snow, tangled in a furious tussle. And then came John Turner's hearty voice calling the boy to breakfast.

The two sat down at the table together and started on their grapefruit. "These fancy breakfasts sort of appeal to me, now I'm used to 'em," said the mountaineer. "Fer years I wouldn't have no truck with 'em—ate my doughnuts an' pertaters an' baked beans an' pie, an' drunk my coffee, good old country style. But I finally give in, an' took what the guests had, an' it ain't a mite bad. Even the finger-bowls are real useful."

Breck laughed. "I've always told people you had the best meals north of Boston," he said, "and it's not just a woods appetite that does it, either."

A platter of meat, a stack of steaming hot cakes and a jug of maple syrup were set before them. Breck took a piece of the meat. It looked like a boned lamb chop— crisp and brown. When he cut it he found it tender and fine-grained, a trifle dry but delicious in flavor.

"Hm!" he remarked, as he relished a mouthful, "what date does the deer season open?"

John Turner smiled disarmingly. "Fifteenth o' November, here in Carroll County," he answered. "That's tomorrow, if I ain't mistook."

"This meat is mighty good," said Breck, trying to suppress a grin.

" 'Tis good," Turner agreed heartily. "Mountain veal. We sometimes git it this time o' year, an' Jeannie knows how to cook it jest right."

When Breck had stowed away a monumental breakfast he pulled on his jacket and gloves and went outdoors. He was just whistling for Duff when he heard the chug of a motor coming in the entrance road.

A sturdy old touring car rattled up and stopped in front of the steps. The man at the wheel wore an old fur cap and mackinaw. He looked like any backwoods farmer of the district, but Breck sensed a difference in him. There was a certain grimness about the mouth under the close-cropped iron-gray mustache. And the level gaze of the blue eyes seemed to bore straight through the boy.

The silence made Breck feel uncomfortable. "Good morning," he said. "I guess you want to see Mr. Turner."

For a moment the man continued to study him calmly. Then he nodded. " 'Morning," he said, "I'm the game warden."

The words startled Breck, and he took an involuntary backward step. That venison they had had for breakfast! Hastily he collected his wits.

"I don't know just where Mr. Turner went," he began.

"It isn't Mr. Turner I'm lookin' for," the warden interrupted him.

"Oh," said Breck, relieved, "who was it you wanted
to see?"

The man in the car was still maddeningly deliberate.
"Why," he replied at length, "I reckon you're the feller."

The boy threw back his head and laughed. "Me?" he
said. "What do you want with me?"

It was at that moment that John Turner came around
the corner of the house.

"Hello, Jim!" he greeted the new-comer cordially.
"Lookin' fer law-breakers?"

The warden looked a trifle embarrassed as he got out
of the car. "Well, I'll tell ye, John," he said. "I got a tip
last night about a jacker in a Ford roadster with a Massachusetts license, an' they told me in West Ossipee there
was such a car headed up this way. The description fitted
this young chap, so I—"

"Here," Turner broke in, "let me introduce you two.
Mr. James McArdle—Mr. Breckenridge Townsend.
Now, Jim, I think mebbe I kin explain this business.
Who give ye the tip?"

"It was a 'phone call from Dingy Rowe, the feller that
runs that gas station this side o' Wakefield," said Mr.
McArdle. "He told me a young feller stopped there that
had a brand-new jack-light rig in the back of his car."

"An' you took the word o' that good-fer-nothin' rat?"
asked John Turner, contemptuously.

"Well, you see," the other went on, "I've had Dingy under suspicion for some time. I'm pretty sure he's in cahoots with the jackers some way or other. An' I figgered he was tryin' to square himself with me, an' so his information might be worth following up. 'Course, if Mr. Townsend ain't got any light, that's all there is to it, an' I'm ready to apologize."

"I've got the light, all right," said Breck, "but I don't own a gun, and I've no intention of killing any deer, legally or illegally. All I am is a camera hunter." He explained his purpose in building the contrivance, and took the warden out to the barn to show it to him.

"The boy's ambitious," John Turner chuckled. "He aims to get a portrait of ol' Scar-back himself!"

Mr. McArdle smiled and shook his head. "You *have* bit off a job fer yourself," said he. "All the years I've been goin' 'round these mountains, I've never laid eyes on the buck myself. Young Sam, my boy, has seen him an' knows his ways. Sam's jest about your age, son. You two ought to git together."

"I'd like to talk to him," Breck replied eagerly. "If he's going to be home tomorrow, I'll drive down."

McArdle told him how to find their house in West Ossipee, and was climbing back into his car when Breck had an idea.

"That fellow, Rowe, who told you about my light,"

he said, "—do you know who the deer-jackers are that have dealings with him?"

"I'm not sure yet," answered the warden. "I've been told there's a couple o' fellers in a big car that stop there sometimes."

"A big tan coupe?" Breck asked. "That's the car that tried to run me off the road yesterday!" And he told the story of the tarpaulin-covered truck, the rifle, and the attempt to ditch his roadster.

"No doubt about it," McArdle agreed. "They must have been either jackers or liquor-runners. Sounds more like jackers to me. The only reason they'd have had it in fer you would be Rowe's tellin' 'em about that light in your car. They don't like strangers breakin' in on their racket. What did these two men look like?"

Breck did his best to describe them. "One was big and stocky," he said, "—must have weighed 190 or so. He had a hard, square sort of face and looked about forty years old. The other chap was younger and smaller—dark, like a foreigner, and thin-faced. They both had on hunting clothes."

McArdle shook his head. "Strangers to me," said he. "Mebbe they belong to the gang that's been workin' up in Coos County. The season starts two weeks earlier up there, an' the warden's had his hands full with jackers this Fall."

He got into the car and went rattling off down the road. John Turner frowned as he watched him go. "A mighty good man—Jim McArdle," he mused. "I hope he don't git hurt, tanglin' with these tough gangsters. He ain't used to their kind o' fightin'. You was lucky to come off whole yerself, Breck. That snake, Rowe, must have called him up after the jackers lost your trail. Well, I believe we'd all better keep our eyes peeled. Looks like we might have trouble."

After lunch that day, Breck took the Northwest Trail, with Duff trotting by his side. There was no beaten path, but he himself had helped to cut the blazes, and the way was almost as familiar to him as his street at home.

The trail cut gradually up the side of Whiteface, then forked, one branch leading off toward the West Spur, the other striking up hill through the thick spruce bush. Breck chose the northerly fork. He swung along quietly through the light snow, with only an occasional low-voiced word to the dog. Ahead of them, small denizens of the wilderness scuttled to cover at the warning call of the jays, but their tracks were everywhere—squirrel and partridge and rabbit prints, dotting the white floor of the forest with paper-lace patterns.

Once, when they were threading a clump of scrub pines, they almost stumbled into a flock of partridges that had been sunning themselves by a fallen log. The sudden thunder of their wings startled Breck and sent the big husky flying after them in a frenzied rush. Even then Duff did not bark. True to his wolf ancestry, he rarely voiced his feelings like an ordinary dog. Sometimes, when the moon was full, he howled mournfully, and occasion-

ally he growled or whined, but as a rule he was silent.

There were other tracks besides those of the small and helpless woodfolk. Once they found a tiny patch of blood in the snow and the abrupt ending of a rabbit trail. There were marks around the spot that looked as if the snow had been brushed with a whisk-broom, and one deep print of a big bird's foot, long-taloned and sinister. As plainly as if he had been present, Breck could read the record of that hunt—the silent swoop of the great white owl, the brief struggle, the dying scream of the victim.

Half a mile farther up the mountain Duff sniffed at

the foot of a gnarled old sugar maple and Breck saw a line of slim, long prints, like miniature bear tracks, leading to a hole between two roots. He knew the dainty trail for that of a raccoon which had been out taking a final stroll before denning up for the winter.

Beyond, the trail dipped steeply into a narrow ravine. Among the rocks at its bottom, a tiny stream tumbled between fringes of ice. And here they made a real find. Clustered thick along the brook bank were deer tracks cleanly dented in the snow. Breck stooped eagerly to read the signs. Sharply pointed toes, held close together—these were the arrowy prints of does' feet. A few, of smaller size, had been made by a half-grown fawn. But apparently there was no buck with the herd.

Casting about carefully, Breck came on the trail the deer had made when they left the drinking place. It followed the bed of the ravine to a point a few hundred feet above, where it swerved abruptly up the west slope.

The boy took a look at the sun and made sure he still had several hours of daylight. Then he turned up the bank. "Come on, Duff," he said. "I'd like to know where this bunch went to."

They followed the clearly marked trail to the top of the ridge, then northward toward the blueberry ledges. It was hard work, for while the deer always chose good footing they frequently moved through thickets so dense that Breck had to bend almost double, and even Duff plowed his way with a series of crashing plunges.

Once or twice they came to places where the herd had paused to browse. The tender bark was stripped off the twigs and the tracks milled about in leisurely fashion. Then the trail led on, always to higher levels. After a mile or more of rough going they passed the timber line, and Breck looked upward at a snowy waste of dwarf juniper and blueberry bushes. Here the path of the deer became still harder to follow. In many places the boy had to make a laborious circuit around a spreading juniper clump and pick it up again on the other side.

He was on the point of turning back more than once, but his curiosity about where the trail would lead kept him going. And he got his reward. As he toiled up a slippery knoll, his eye fell on a new track that came in from the west and joined that of the does. No ordinary deer could have left a print like that. It was long and broad and blunt—the toe-tips worn off by years of pawing. The two points of the hoof were widely separated, after the manner of all buck-tracks, and the dewclaws spread outward and back a good four inches from the tip of the toes. Here was the signature of such a stag as Breck had never seen. As he looked into those deep, firm prints he could imagine the patriarch that had left them—tall, broad-chested, thick-necked, with a proud head and many-branching antlers. Instinctively the boy supplied one more detail of the picture—a white scar running up across the withers. For he knew there was only one buck in the mountains big enough to make that track—"the King!"

In the pocket of his jacket Breck found a stub of pencil and on the back of an envelope he sketched the clearest of the prints, measuring it with a stick to be sure of the dimensions. When he had an accurate drawing he pushed on up the hillside. But a hundred yards beyond the spot where the buck had joined the herd, the trail ended. A bare, smooth ledge of granite skirted the crown of the mountain. There was no snow on its steep surface but there must have been foothold for a deer, for the tracks went directly to the edge of the naked rock and disappeared.

"Smart old fellow!" murmured Breck admiringly. "He knows this snow has made it easy to follow his trail. He must have let the does go down to drink while he watched up here. Then he took them straight to that ledge. And from there they could travel half a mile either way without leaving a trace. Yes, sir, Scar-back, you'll be hard to catch!"

With that the boy turned and took the back trail. A red sunset blazed across the hills and already the deeper valleys were filling with shadow. Breck hurdled a juniper and went tearing down the rough slope, side-stepping the bushes that loomed up like tacklers in a broken field.

"Come on, Duff, boy!" he called. "Four miles to supper! I'll race you home!"

III

THE last mile of the trail to Turner's was made in the deepening dusk, and the lights of the house sent a welcoming glow across the snow. Breck stamped the clinging crystals off his moccasins and went in, to find John Turner standing in front of the fire.

"Got back jest in time," grinned the bearded woodsman. "'Nother fifteen minutes an' I was goin' to start a search party."

"You can't lose me on these mountains," the boy replied. "I had luck. Look here!" And he produced the scrap of paper on which he had drawn the big buck-track.

Turner's eyebrows went up. "Whew!" he exclaimed, "that *is* an old he-one, an' no mistake! Sure ye didn't exaggerate jest a mite?"

"No, sir!" said Breck proudly. "That's exact size. I found it way up near the top of Whiteface. There were four or five does and a fawn in the herd, too. I lost the trail on the ledges."

"An o' course you figger it's the Passaconaway stag," Turner opined with a twinkle.

"Well," Breck returned, "how many deer are there around here that could make a track like that?"

The other nodded. "I shouldn't wonder if you're right," he said, "though the buck ain't been sighted this side o' the ridge in years. Even so, seein' his track is one thing, an' takin' his picture is another."

That night Breck turned in early. There was a comfortable weariness in his legs, and he wanted to be up in time for an eight o'clock start to West Ossipee.

He woke to another bright morning, crisp and still. As soon as breakfast was over he ran the roadster out of the barn and warmed up the motor. Then on second thought he got his camera and knapsack and packed them in the rumble. There was no telling what chances might come to use them on this excursion.

Half an hour later he rolled into the village. McArdle's home was not hard to find. It was a pleasant, low, white house in an elm-shaded yard, just across the road from the general store. Breck drove in and was about to lift the iron knocker on the front door when a sandy-haired, freckle-faced lad stuck his head around the corner.

"Come back this way," he grinned. "That's just for company. We generally use the side door."

"You're Breck Townsend, aren't you?" he continued,

as he led his guest inside. "I'm Sam McArdle. Pop told me you'd likely pay us a call today."

In the sunny kitchen Breck was greeted by a plump, cheerful woman in a starched apron, her bare arms deep in a mountain of dough.

"This is Ma's baking day," Sam explained when the introductions were over. "Kitchen's no place for us until those pies are done. S'pose we go in the living-room for a spell."

Within five minutes Breck felt as much at ease with his new acquaintance as if they had been chums for years. He had liked the boy from the start—liked his sparkling blue eyes and droll good humor. And as they talked he discovered they had dozens of interests in common. Sam wanted to be a civil engineer. He had finished high school the previous June and had been working with a survey-or's gang on the county roads. With the coming of win-ter that job was done, but he was studying at home and trying to save enough money to enter Massachusetts Tech next Fall.

"Pop says you're up here for a rest," he chuckled, "but you don't look very tired to me."

Laughing, Breck told of his hike to the top of White-face the day before. "The fact is," he said, "I never felt quite so fine in my life. Ready for anything. Did your father tell you what sort of job I've cut out for myself while I'm here?"

"Yep," said Sam seriously. "And it's not so plumb foolish as it sounds. Two winters ago I saw the old King Buck, myself—so close I could have hit him with a snowball. That was the second time, too. The first was up on Chocorua Mountain, one spring. His horns were in velvet then, and I only got a glimpse of him through some bushes. But this other time I was coming down the path, to the south of Swift River, and almost ran into him. He was leading a couple of does down to drink. The wind was from him to me, and I just froze in my tracks. He must have heard some sound I'd made, for he stood there, head up and ears working for a second, and then he was gone like a shot. I had a good view of his horns right against the sky, but I was too excited to try to count the points. Near as I can remember how they looked, though, there were six on one antler and five on the other."

"Golly!" said Breck. "An eleven-pointer! Maybe he's grown the twelfth by now."

"Yep," Sam nodded, "—if he's still alive, that is. A lot of hunters have been after him."

Breck leaned forward earnestly. "I believe he's still alive," he said, "and more than that, he's up there back of Tri-Pyramid right now. I found some tracks yesterday, and I measured the biggest ones. Here's how they looked."

Sam stared at the sketched foot-print with wide eyes.

"That's him," he said emphatically. "Sure as you're born that's old Scar-back! I went and examined his tracks that last time I saw him. And this looks just like 'em."

For half an hour the boys discussed the big stag—his mighty strength and uncanny wisdom—his range and his habits. Sam had heard a score of legends of the buck's prowess, for there was hardly a hunter in the district who had not matched wits with the King and come off second best. Only once had the great deer ever been hit.

"That was ten or eleven years ago, when he was just a youngster," said Sam. "Old Furry Hanson did it. He was an old-timer who lived in a shack in the woods up near Crawford's. Long hair—bushy gray beard—regular old scarecrow. Folks from the hotels used to ride miles to see his camp, with the bear and bob-cat hides on the walls. He was a dead shot with that long muzzle-loader of his.

"One day Furry stalked a herd of four deer and crawled through the brush, up-wind, till he had 'em in plain sight, a couple of hundred yards off. That was about the limit of his old rifle's range, but he laid her across a stump and drew a bead on the big young buck that was on guard. He was trying for the heart shot, but just as he got set, the buck lifted his head and whistled. He'd heard him cock the hammer of the gun. Furry fired anyway, but the buck was starting a sidewise jump and the bullet plowed up along his back behind the shoulder. The deer were all a good way off before the old fellow could load, of course. He found blood on the snow, and trailed 'em till dark, but the buck didn't seem to be tiring, and there were no more blood spots. Furry gave up in disgust and went back to camp. He never told the story of missing that shot until years later, when the hunters began talking about a whale of a big stag with a white scar on his back. The old man died two winters ago. A big snow-slide buried him in his cabin."

The warden's son looked at Breck quizzically. "Pop says you don't aim to hunt with a gun," he said. "That's all right with me. I've got too much respect for the old stag to want to kill him—even though it would make me famous. Anybody smart enough to get within picture-taking range of Scar-back deserves just as much credit as if he shot him."

Breck nodded. "It may be a wild-goose chase," he replied, "but at any rate I'm going to try it, and I'll be mighty glad to have your help. I've got a good camera—high-speed lens and shutter—and super-sensitive film. I've even made fair pictures with ordinary indoor daylight. There's a telescope attachment if I want to use it, but what I'm hoping to do is get a close-range shot at night, shining his eyes with a portable searchlight."

"Jacking, eh?" laughed Sam. "I heard from Pop how close he came to arresting you."

"I don't blame him," Breck said. "With a light like that in my possession, it certainly looked as if I was going into the racket in a big way. I've got it out in the car now. Want to take a look at it?"

They went out to the side yard, where the roadster was parked, and Breck was about to lift the rear deck when a hail came from the road. Two cars had stopped in front of the house, and each held three or four men in expensive-looking hunting clothes. "Hey, Buddy," called one of the gunners in the forward sedan, "is the warden around?"

"Not this morning," Sam replied. "He's down to Ossipee. Anything I can do for you?"

He went over to the sedan and Breck waited while he talked with the hunters. A stream of similar cars was moving up the highway—red hunting caps flashing—gun-cases and duffel-bags showing through the windows. It was the opening day of the deer season and nimrods from the big towns to the south were pouring into Carroll County by the hundred.

Several cars had stopped at the general store, across the street, for supplies. As he watched them idly, Breck's eye fell on a coupe, parked in a narrow dirt road at the side of the store-building. It was a big tan-colored car, its license plate so coated with mud and dust as to be unreadable.

The boy thought he would have recognized that coupe

in China, but he wanted a closer view to make sure. Pulling his cap down over his eyes, he strolled across the road and leaned against the porch of the store. Yes, it was the same car that had figured in his adventure two days before. He could see from the scars on fenders and body that it had been driven hard and carelessly. But these scars were different from the dents and bumps of traffic. They had been made by scraping branches in the woods.

The huge, oversize tires caught Breck's attention. From where he stood he could see those on the hind wheels plainly. The one on the left was of a popular make, worn almost smooth. But the right rear tire was more noticeable. It was practically new, and had the sharp, hexagonal markings of an unusual brand—a Dalton Deep-Tred.

Sam had finished his conversation with the hunters, and as the cars moved off, he crossed over to join Breck.

"What's up?" he asked, glancing at the tan coupe.

Breck's answer was a hurried shake of the head. For just at that moment the store door had opened and a man appeared carrying an arm-load of provisions. He was a smallish fellow—dark—fox-faced—one of the pair Breck had seen at the fried-clam stand.

As he passed the two boys, the man shot a keen glance in their direction. But if he recognized Breck he gave no sign of it. Swiftly he piled his bundles inside the coupe and slipped in behind the wheel. There was a whirr of the starter and the big car backed smoothly out to the concrete. A moment later it was speeding northward on the main road.

"Well!" said Sam, whose curiosity was aroused. "What's all the shushing about?"

"That chap was one of the two who tried to run me off the road, day before yesterday," Breck replied. "Can you imagine that two-ton bus, with a couple of hard-boiled jackers in it, squeezing over against your left fender?"

"Doesn't sound so good!" Sam admitted. "So that's the car, eh? Pop told me about it. He expects to get a line on them in the next day or two."

They recrossed the highway and Breck took his photographic equipment out of the car. Sam, who shared his interest in things mechanical, was delighted with the compact efficiency of the camera and the arrangement of the searchlight.

"Listen here," he said after a few moments. "I've got a little shack up on the Passaconaway Road. Why don't we pack up a few blankets and some grub and run up there tonight? It's right in the middle of old Scar-back's range, and even if we don't pick up his trail we may get a chance to try out the light."

Breck's eyes lit up. "That sounds great," he answered. "I'm all set to start. All I have to do is call up Turner's and let them know I won't be back for a day or so."

While he was telephoning, Sam collected three or four army blankets, an ax, a few cooking utensils and an armful of provisions and added them to the load in the rumble-seat. Last of all he brought out the pride of his heart —a 12-gauge, double-barreled shotgun of a good make— and a box of shells.

"I'm taking some buckshot," he told Breck, "and some

smaller stuff for rabbits and birds if we get hungry. And say—speaking of getting hungry, I smell hot apple pie!"

Mrs. McArdle had not only finished her baking but prepared an excellent dinner, which was even then being put on the table. When they had eaten all they could hold, the boys got into their outdoor clothes and made ready to start.

"Wait a bit," said Sam, looking at Breck's gray cap. "You're likely to get taken for a deer and peppered by some nervous hunter if you wear that. I've got a red hat of my own but we'd better sew a strip of red calico on that topper of yours."

By two o'clock they were rolling up the highway through Pequaket, with the peak of Chocorua towering high in the west. At Conway they swung to the left on a little-used country road that followed the rocky valley of Swift River. Ruts and ledges made the going rough and Breck drove slowly for the next ten miles. It was well along in the afternoon when they reached the little hill farm that marked the end of the road. Here Sam arranged with the farmer—an old friend of his—to leave the roadster in his barn. And loading themselves with all the duffel they could carry, the two boys started up the mountainside.

The first quarter mile of the path led through a steep, stony pasture, dotted with bushes and young pines. Then they crossed a ramshackle stonewall and were in the thick woods. Sam had blazed a trail and trimmed some of the worst of the underbrush when he built his shack, two years before. The light snow made the footing bad, and it took them a full half hour to climb the remaining mile to the camp.

The shack was a three-sided lean-to of poles and bark. It stood on a little cleared knoll with its back against a big spruce tree. There was a stone fire-place in the hollow of a bowlder facing the open side of the cabin. And Sam had built a rough cupboard high up between two saplings at the right.

"I keep a few staple provisions stowed away there all the time," he was saying, as he advanced toward the cupboard. "A little flour and sugar and salt-pork—say—look at here—somebody's been robbing my stores!"

IV

IT was true enough. A corner of the crude cupboard
door had been cut away as if with a dull knife, and
it hung ajar, swinging open at a touch of Sam's hand.
Inside, everything was as bare as Mother Hubbard's
famous storage-closet.

"Wait a minute," said Breck, dumping his pack under
the lean-to and approaching the cupboard. "Maybe these
fellows have left a clue." He looked closely at the corner
of the door and grinned. "I believe I've found one already."

Stooping down, he carefully brushed away the snow
under the saplings. A scattering of white chips and a torn
flour-bag came into view. "Ever see a two-legged robber
that bit a hole in a flour-sack and ate it on the ground?"
he asked.

Sam gave a snort. "You're right!" he laughed. "Noth-
ing but a hungry old porcupine! Well, it's no great loss.
I brought a box of pancake flour and half a side of bacon.
We'll make out first rate."

Both boys were at home in the woods and they went about making camp in businesslike fashion. While Sam stowed the duffel and made beds of balsam tips, Breck was cutting fire-wood. By the time it began to grow dark there was a good-sized pile of four-foot logs for the night fire and plenty of small, dry limbs for cooking.

"Here's the spring," said Sam, "right down at the foot of this ledge," and he led Breck around the side of the knoll to a neatly hollowed basin where a trickle of clear water came out of the rock. They brought a kettle of water and soon had a hot blaze of crackling sticks under the old sheet-iron top that covered the fireplace. Sam set a coffee-pot to boil and proceeded to heat up a can of beans for supper.

They ate them with round, crunchy disks of pilot-biscuit in the approved backwoods manner, and topped the meal off with cups of coffee and apple turnovers, baked by Mrs. McArdle that morning.

When the dishes were washed, they laid a huge back-log opposite the entrance of the lean-to and built a roaring fire to combat the chill of the frosty evening. Breck tinkered with his searchlight and got it perfectly focused, while Sam drew cheerful music from a battered mouth-organ he dug out of his duffel-bag. They had decided not to take the light and camera out that night.

"We'll pick up some tracks tomorrow," said Sam, "and

41

if we don't come across the big buck's trail we can locate a good spot on a deer-path and wait for 'em to come along. The best thing we can do right now is get a good night's sleep."

For a while they sat there enjoying the comfort of the fire. Its light transformed the little open space on the knoll into a mysterious but cozy room—tapestried with flecks of shifting color—walled with the silent dark. Breck spoke to Sam about it. "Ever notice how a camp-fire cuts down the size of everything—makes the woods seem sort of small and homey?" he asked.

"Sure," the warden's son replied. "And when you wake up cold before dawn, and the fire's out—boy, what a big drafty, lonesome place it turns out to be!"

They piled a huge chunk of maple on the blaze and rolled up in their blankets for the night. The fir-bough bed was soft and fragrant.

"Well," chuckled Sam, "call me at nine, and have my bath hot."

Breck's murmured "Yeah?" ended in a luxurious yawn, and that, in turn, in a snore. They were both asleep.

It was perhaps two hours later that something woke Breck. For several minutes he lay listening before he heard anything more than the small noises of the night. Then came a sudden sound that he recognized instantly

—the sharp *spang* of a rifle, somewhere in the valley below.

Quietly, to avoid waking Sam, he unwound himself from the blankets and stepped outside the lean-to. The fire had dwindled to a heap of ruddy embers, and there were bleak, long vistas through the gray woods. In one of these, slanting down the hillside, he saw a sudden flash of light. It disappeared, then returned, less brightly. He could see its wedge-shaped beam shooting among the trees. It seemed to swing, very slowly, to the left. At length he heard the distant, muffled roar of a motor being started, and the light moved off eastward, to be lost after a moment behind a fold of the hill.

Shivering, Breck returned to the shack, threw some wood on the fire, and huddled under the blankets once more. But it was some time before he could get to sleep.

When next he opened his eyes a bright morning sun glistened on the snow-tipped spruces. Rolling over lazily he saw Sam busy over the breakfast fire. "Fry mine on both sides, and have the cantaloupe iced," he called, then ducked under the blankets just in time to escape a well-directed snow-ball.

"What kind of a hunter do you think you are?" chided Sam, as Breck came over to the fire. "Here it is eight o'clock. Been asleep half the morning!"

Breck gave him a superior smile. "That's the privilege

of the faithful sentinel," he replied. "Who was it that guarded the camp through all the excitement of the night watches?"

"Excitement!" laughed Sam. "What was it—a chipmunk attacking us?"

Breck shook his head tantalizingly and went down to the spring to wash. By the time he came back he could see that Sam's curiosity was fully aroused. "No," he said casually, "it wasn't a chipmunk—just a bunch of jackers killing deer." And he told the astonished warden's son what he had seen and heard.

"We-e-ll!" exclaimed Sam when the recital was finished.

"Maybe we'd better go down there and investigate—though they're probably twenty miles away by now." He was silent and thoughtful while he flipped the next two pancakes. "Wish there was some way to get word to Pop," he said at length, "but the nearest telephone is five miles down the valley."

Breck offered to drive down but Sam was doubtful if his father could be reached. "He's mighty busy all through the deer season and especially the first few days," he explained. "We may as well go ahead as we planned."

They finished their breakfast and tidied the camp. Then Sam put some lunch in the knapsack and shouldered his gun, while Breck took his camera and a canteen

A WEDGE-SHAPED BEAM SHOOTING AMONG
THE TREES

of water. Heading westward along the rough slope they worked their way around spruce thickets and through clumps of birch and maple and came after half an hour to the edge of a wide ravine.

"This is a dry brook," said Sam. "It only flows when the snow melts in the spring. But I've seen deer-paths along the bottom there, and they may still use it."

Sure enough, just before they reached the dry gully of the stream-bed, they came on a foot-wide path dented with hundreds of pointed tracks. It must have been a regular high-road of the deer, for under the snow the earth had been worn deep by their passing hoofs.

"Hm," mused Sam. "Must lead to some place they visit pretty regular. Most likely it goes clear down to Swift River. They don't eat snow as long as they can find good water, and there's still some old grass in the meadows along the intervale."

"Where do you suppose the trail starts?" Breck asked. "Up above, I mean. Let's follow it awhile. Maybe where the tracks aren't so jumbled up we can see whether the old buck has been this way."

They went up to the head of the ravine and there the deer-path forked. One branch came down from the east, around the base of Paugus Mountain; the other from the higher slopes to the west. But though the tracks were sparser and easier to distinguish along these branch trails, there was no sign anywhere of the huge splay-toed print that Breck sought. Other bucks had been up and down the paths, as they could see, but theirs were daintier tracks.

"The old King's too smart to travel the easy trails," said Sam. "He keeps his herd off by themselves. What do you say? Shall we head down the other way?"

For nearly an hour they followed the deer-path northward down the winding little valley. At one place there was a tiny spring in the rocks, and here the snow was trampled for several yards around. The trail below was less deeply marked but the boys kept on till the trees thinned ahead and they knew they were nearing the Swift River road.

"Don't know as it's any use to go on across," said Sam. "We passed some good thickets up above where we can hide and wait for 'em to come down tonight. We'll have to find out which way the wind is, after sunset, and— hello! What's that patch in the snow?"

In a hollow, a few yards ahead, there was a deep red stain beside the deer-path. As they approached, they saw the snow had been trodden by men. The red patch was unmistakably blood, and there were other flecks of blood along the trail that led out to the road. Breck knelt to examine the snow where the tracks were clearly marked. "Two men," he announced. "One had on heavy leather boots. What would you call these others—lumberjack's rubbers?"

"Yes, or rubber-soled hunting boots," Sam replied. "Look—here's where they dragged the deer a rod or two. Then here they picked it up and carried it."

While the narrow road was little traveled, too many cars and wagons had passed to make the tracks of the hunters' tires distinguishable.

"They were probably using their headlights, or a special jack mounted in the car, and they shot from the road," Sam suggested. "In that case they may have turned around a little farther up."

The two boys moved westward along the rutted lane, watching carefully for new signs. They had not far to look. At the foot of some bushes on the north side of the road was another tell-tale red spot.

"A doe!" said Sam excitedly. "See her tracks? Heading for the river. They shot her while she was crossing the road, but she didn't drop. Here's where she took off in a big jump. Come on!"

Following the trail of the wounded deer was not difficult. Though she had gone in frenzied leaps, there were red splashes dotting the spaces between her gathered hoof-prints. Straight into a thick clump of spruces the trail ran, and out the other side—mute evidence of the doe's blind, reckless dash.

"Think she got away?" asked Breck.

"No," answered his companion, "it'll be soon now. Look—here are the hunters' tracks coming in. They must have cut through the woods straight from the car. Same pair as before—hob-nailed leather boots and rubber soles."

Hurrying on in silence, they stumbled through a fringing thicket of alders and came suddenly out on the edge of a narrow river. Below, the bank pitched steeply and the thin shell of ice along the margin was broken by a single patch of black water.

"Gosh," murmured Sam. "She went right in, and I bet the current carried her under. It's deep here, and fast. See where the men's tracks go down to the edge? But here's where they climbed up again and if they'd been dragging a deer there'd be some sign of it."

The trail of the two hunters went off again in the direction of the road, but Breck and Sam did not follow it immediately.

"Just above here there's a shallow place where the deer sometimes drink," Sam explained. "They keep it open until the ice gets too thick to break with their feet. Let's take a look."

They tramped up the shore in single file and came soon to a bend where the river ran under shadowy pines. The new ice, clear as glass, had been swept free of snow by the wind, and through it the boys could see the current flowing swift and smooth over golden gravel. Under the south bank was a narrow semi-circle of open water, and the frozen mud at the edge showed dozens of tracks of deer.

Breck looked in vain for a print of the big stag among them. "I guess you're right, Sam," he said. "The old fellow must keep off by himself. He probably has his own secret drinking places. Say, I'm getting hungry. It's after twelve, too. What do you say to some lunch?"

They sat down on the dry pine needles by the riverbank and ate their hard-tack and cheese, washing it down with clear water from the stream. When the meal was over Sam picked up his gun and hitched the strap of the knapsack over his shoulder.

"Well, we covered about six miles this morning," he observed. "Don't want to get too tired, or we'll be going to sleep on the job tonight. Let's have another look along the road and then cut back to camp."

They returned to the place where the hunters had left the river and followed their trail back through the brush. Breck was in the lead when they came out at the edge of the road. "Here we are, Sam—look at this!" he exclaimed, and dropped on one knee, pointing to a tire track in the clean snow.

A car had turned around in the narrow roadway, backing almost into the bushes on the north side. The left tire was smooth. But the right one had left an unmistakable imprint. The hexagonal knobs of its tread were cut clear and deep in the snow—the mark of a Dalton tire.

"Well, we know it now for certain," said Sam. "It's the tan coupe. And there isn't much doubt your friends were up here last night. It was their rifles you heard and their jack-lights you saw. That'll give us some real news to pass on to Pop."

They spend another hour or two exploring the woods farther to the west, then made a bee-line for the lean-to. Sam had cruised that part of the country so often that he knew every forest path and pasture fence. Once, as they passed a pine-thicket near the camp, a covey of partridges whirred up, and Sam's gun was at his shoulder instantly.

He fired twice and his second shot dropped one of the birds.

"Nice and plump," said he, picking it up. "We'll have a partridge stew for supper."

At the shack Breck built a cooking-fire while Sam dressed the bird. "Wish we had an onion to put in this," he said, "but I'll guarantee it'll be good. Ought to be done by dusk. Then we can eat, an' get out to the deer-path before they start coming down."

In another fifteen minutes the pot was boiling merrily. But the boys never tasted that partridge stew. Just before sunset there was a hail from the woods below and a farm-lad of ten or twelve came hurrying up the knoll.

"Sam," he panted, "yer pa's been in a smash-up an' he's hurt. They 'phoned to Baker's an' wanted to git word to you. You better start right away."

V

SAM McARDLE was hard hit by the news, but he kept his head. He shot one question at the boy. "Tell me," he said, "how bad is he hurt—did they say?" But the youngster didn't know. "It was Wash Baker rode up horseback with the message," he said. "That's all he told me—that your pa's car was smashed an' he got hurt."

The boys wasted no more words but collected their equipment and made ready to start. In five minutes the duffel was packed. Sam kicked snow on the fire and looked regretfully at the steaming pot. "Here, Bud," he said, "thanks for coming up to tell us, and take this home for your supper. All it needs is a little more cooking and maybe a slice of onion."

He and Breck shouldered their packs and went down the hill. Dark was falling when they reached the barn. Quickly they loaded the roadster and got in. Breck opened the choke, shoved his foot on the accelerator and never took it off except when the tough little car slithered down some stony hill or careened around a breath-taking turn.

Only when they had reached the main road at Conway and were racing south, did Sam break silence.

"You're a driver," he said with admiration. "I guess you know I'm anxious to get there. They may have been keeping something back—folks do, sometimes."

And Breck answered by pushing a deeper dent into the floor-board. Luckily there were no State Police on the road, for they covered the seventeen miles from Conway to West Ossipee in a shade under sixteen minutes.

There was another car under the elms when they sped into the door-yard—a car with a doctor's cross above the license plate. They ran to the kitchen door and tiptoed in. But as soon as they crossed the threshold their fears were set at rest, for sitting in a chair in the middle of a chatting group was the warden himself. The doctor was there, as well as Sam's mother and a neighbor or two. Aside from the thick bandage that covered his head and a swollen cut under the stubble on his cheek the patient looked healthy enough.

"Well, you boys made good time," cried Mrs. McArdle. "When I telephoned this afternoon I was afraid they wouldn't find you."

The doctor snapped his surgical case shut and picked up his hat. "Now, folks," he cautioned, "don't bother him with too much talk. He ought to be in bed now. I'll call 'round in the morning."

He motioned Sam aside as he was going out. "Nothing serious, I think," he said. "He had a slight concussion, but he's come around all right. Keep him quiet tomorrow."

When the neighbors had taken their departure Jim McArdle gave the boys a wry smile. "Second day o' the deer season!" he sighed. "A fine time to git laid out this way!"

"What happened?" asked Sam eagerly, but his mother interposed her capable bulk.

"No, Sam, not tonight," she said. "Your father's going straight to bed now." And she helped the warden to his feet. "There's some supper I kept warm in the oven. You boys help yourselves."

When she returned, twenty minutes later, they heard as much as she knew about the accident.

"It was up on the main road, between Conway and North Conway," Mrs. McArdle told them. "Your father said he was following a car with some men in it he thought were jackers. He pulled ahead of them and motioned them to stop. When they slowed up at the side of the road he cut in close in front of them to keep them from starting off. He was just opening the door to get out when he heard a noise and looked around. There was a big truck coming—right on top of him—and that's all he remembers except the crash.

"A man was driving down from North Conway a few minutes later and saw him lying there under the running-board. The fenders on the left side of our car were ripped

off and the front wheel was smashed. There was no sign of the other car or the truck. They'd both driven off—the skunks! The man recognized your father and rushed him down here to Dr. Moffat. It was half an hour more before he came to. The doctor says it's a wonder he wasn't killed, but there were no bones broken—only a few bad bruises and that awful blow on the head."

Sam was glowering, his supper forgotten. "I'm going to get those rotters if it takes all winter," he said huskily.

"Right!" Breck agreed. "But let's make it quicker than that. I've only got two weeks up here. What I'd like to know is more about the car he stopped. Did he tell you what it looked like, Mrs. McArdle?"

She shook her head. "No," she replied, "the doctor wouldn't let him talk much, and I didn't think to ask. Don't you boys do anything foolish, now. The sheriff and the chief warden are both coming tomorrow and they'll take charge of whatever's to be done."

Breck shared Sam's bed that night and they lay awake for hours discussing how they could bring the hit-and-run truck driver and the occupants of the other car to justice.

"One thing's as plain as day," Sam concluded. "It wasn't an accident—it was intentional. That truck belonged to the same gang of jackers as the car. They must have been traveling together, and when Pa stopped 'em they signaled the truck to pile into him. Boy—if I ever get my hands on those cold-blooded devils!"

Shortly after breakfast next morning the sheriff drove into the yard and before he had been in the house five minutes another car appeared, bearing a state official license. Chief Warden Sanborn was a tall man, loose-jointed and slow of speech—a marked contrast to the thick-set, active little sheriff of Carroll County, Jeff King.

As soon as the doctor pronounced McArdle able to see them, the two officers were ushered into his bedroom and remained there in conversation for some time.

Sam was impatient for action. He paced up and down the living-room, too perturbed to talk, while the boys waited for the conference to end. After a while the sheriff opened the door and looked out.

"Guess we need you chaps in here," he grinned, and Sam and Breck entered with alacrity.

"Boys," said the chief warden, clearing his throat, "you may as well know that we figure this wasn't an accident. It must have been deliberately planned. McArdle's description of the car he stopped tallies with one we've had trouble with before. It sounds like the car that was used by some deer-jackers in Coos County, just after the season opened up there. It's a big, powerful car—a coupe —sort of a light brown color."

Sam shot a look at Breck and would have spoken, but Mr. Sanborn was continuing. "Now," said he, "I understand young Townsend, here, had a good look at the men who were driving such a car a few days ago. I've got a couple of pictures I want to show you."

Breck took the two small photographs he held out, and studied them a moment.

"Yes," he said, "I recognize them all right. The big man looked like this, only a little older, and he hadn't any mustache. The other one I'm positive is the same, because I saw him again yesterday. Look, Sam!"

"Sure—that's the fellow," the other boy cried. "He

came out of the store with a lot of provisions and drove off in the coupe."

Sanborn nodded. "I guess that's the answer, Jeff," said he, addressing the sheriff. "Chink Durfee and Saranac Slim—a bad pair to fool with. These are Rogues' Gallery photos," he explained to the boys. "Chink Durfee served time once for smuggling Chinamen over the line from Canada. That's where he got his nickname. The picture's ten years old, so he's changed, naturally. The other fellow's an Italian, wanted for liquor-running in northern New York State. Saranac Slim, he's called. The Coos County warden caught them last week with an illegally killed deer and they pulled out a roll of bills as thick as your arm to pay the fine."

"Maybe they're bootlegging and this is just a sideline," suggested Sheriff King.

"Not right now," the chief warden replied. "More money in deer, the way they work it. Up on the stretch of road between Milan and Errol, this gang was killing twenty or thirty a night before we got deputies on guard. The deer bring anywhere from twenty-five dollars apiece up to a hundred from the city sports."

"All right, Chief," said McArdle, moving restlessly in the bed. "Doc says I'll be fit to work tomorrow, an' I'm r'arin' to go."

"You'll go, and no mistake, Jim," Sanborn answered

gruffly, "if you don't have some help on this job. I'm not leaving here till I've sworn in four or five good deputy wardens. We've got to step on these gangsters and step on 'em hard."

"I hate to admit I can't handle the county alone," said McArdle, "but I reckon you're right. An' I know three men that'd make crackerjacks fer the job—all of 'em ready to work right away."

"Good!" the chief warden nodded. "Let's get 'em sworn in before noon. I bet one of 'em is Abe Randall down in East Wakefield."

"Yes," said McArdle, "I had him in mind. He could work in the south end o' the county. Then there's Otis Hanks, that lives in Tamworth. First-class woodsman, an' knows that country over toward Sandwich an' down 'round the Lake like a book. An' the third one I thought of is Mike Kilday. Remember him? Used to be a lumber-camp foreman. If there's goin' to be some fightin' we can sure use that black Irishman. He's got a car, an' so have the others. I figger Mike could handle the north end an' the Notches."

"They all sound good," said Sanborn. "But that's not enough men. To cover the county right, we need at least one more."

"That's me," Sam put in quickly.

His father shook his head. "Too likely to be trouble," he said. "Besides, what could you do without a car?"

Eagerly Breck interrupted. "Why not swear us both in, and let us work together?" he asked. "We could use my Ford. I think maybe we can take care of ourselves in a rough-house, too," he grinned at Sam.

The older men hesitated and Sam hastened to press home their advantage. "We can get around fast—act as sort of roving centers on this team," he urged. "And when it comes to tracking in the woods, Breck's a regular old Leatherstocking!"

"What do you say, Jim?" smiled the chief warden. "I'm satisfied if you are."

"Good enough," McArdle agreed. "Their first job can be to round up Kilday. We can reach the other two by telephone."

Fifteen minutes later Breck was an officer of the State of New Hampshire, duly sworn in. He had an impressive-looking badge pinned under his jacket and the comfortable weight of an automatic lay against his hip.

The weapon had been pressed on him by the sheriff in spite of his protests. "Don't go brandishin' it around," the doughty little officer told him. "But it's a good thing to have when you're in a tight place."

"You both know the game laws," Mr. Sanborn said, as the boys prepared to start on their errand. "You have a right to stop any car on suspicion, examine any hunter's license. Just remember to be courteous and you'll find most people are glad to coöperate. Don't threaten, but if you're sure of your ground, don't weaken. Watch for rifles and jacklights. And if you see that tan coupe, don't fool with it. Call up your father or the sheriff and let them bring reënforcements."

The boys stopped at the nearest gasoline station and filled the roadster's tank. Then they took the road to the north in high spirits.

"For once," Breck laughed, "I don't have to worry about gray uniforms and motorcycles when I speed her up."

"That's a fact," said Sam. "We're officers of the law! Boy, this is going to be fun!"

They drove straight through to Jackson, thirty miles up the highway. And after asking the postmaster where Mike Kilday might be found, they located him at the blacksmith shop. The big Irishman heard their proposition with unconcealed pleasure.

"Shure an' I'll come," he said. "It's just the sort o' job I've been lookin' for. Give me half an hour to git me stuff in the car an' I'll follow ye down. How's the old man? I heard about him gittin' smashed up."

Briefly Sam gave him the details of the accident. "Father'll be as good as ever in a day or two," he said, "but the gang that did it is still loose. If we don't hit them hard and break up their racket they'll slaughter half the deer in the county."

"Good!" chuckled Kilday. "I'd take the job fer nothin'. Tell 'em I'll be there as fast as me old tires'll bring me."

He was as good as his word. By three o'clock that afternoon all the deputies had been assembled and sworn in. Chief Warden Sanborn, Sheriff King and the local sergeant of the State Police gathered in council and laid out a plan of campaign. Then each man was given his orders and sent back to his territory. Abe Randall, lean and taciturn, was to cover the country south from Ossipee to the county line at Union. Otis Hanks took over the patrol of the western section, from Lake Winnepesaukee north to Wonalancet. He was a chunky, grizzled man with a fund of dry backwoods humor.

Mike Kilday was made responsible for the north end of the county—the rugged mountain region that lay between North Conway and Pinkham Notch and ran far up Crawford Notch to the westward. The central section, from Ossipee to Conway, was left in charge of Warden McArdle, whose home would serve as headquarters for the force. And Breck and Sam were assigned to help the warden in any way he might see fit.

It was sun-down when the various officers took their departure.

"You better sleep here with Sam," the warden told Breck. "No tellin' when one o' the deputies may 'phone in, an' we've got to be ready to move fast."

The doctor came just before supper-time and seemed satisfied with his patient's progress. "Considering the kind of day he's had," he said, "Jim's in fine shape. Get him to sleep now and don't give him anything more to worry about."

At eight-thirty both Mr. and Mrs. McArdle had retired and Sam had gone across the road to buy cartridges for the automatics. Breck sat alone with a book in the living-room. Suddenly the stillness of the house was broken by the ringing of the telephone. The boy picked up the receiver, his heart pounding with excitement.

"Hello," he said, and waited, for there was no reply at first. Then a muffled voice came snarling over the wire. "Listen, McArdle," it said, "we know about your deputies. We advise you to keep their noses out of our business or somebody'll get hurt."

There was a pause. "Who is this speaking?" asked Breck, his voice as steady as he could make it. But no answer came. Instead, a sharp click at the other end of the wire told him the man had hung up.

VI

BRECK stood a moment, still holding the receiver, and collected his wits. Then hurriedly he jiggled the hook. Two or three times he repeated this before the sleepy voice of a night operator came back to him—"Number, please!"

Breck's own voice was tense. "This is Warden McArdle's house," he said. "That call that was on here just now—can you trace it?"

"I don't know," answered the operator. "I'll try, but it may take a little time. Was it State business?"

"It was a threat," said Breck, "—a threat against the warden by some gang of crooks. Do your best and call back as soon as you can."

He was just turning from the telephone when Sam came in.

"I got 'em!" said the warden's son gleefully. "The last two boxes they had in this size." Then he caught sight of the other's sober face. "What's up?" he asked.

Word for word, Breck repeated the jacker's message.

66

· "Gee," murmured Sam. "They heard about today's doings quick enough, didn't they? Any idea who the man was, or where he was calling from?"

"No," said Breck. "It was a deep, raspy sort of voice —might have been Chink Durfee. I asked the operator to trace it and she's going to let us know. I didn't wake your father. No use worrying him tonight."

For nearly an hour they waited and then Breck called the telephone central again. "Yes," the operator told him, "we just got word on that call. It was from a pay-station in Rainey's Hotel at North Conway. The clerk couldn't tell us who made it. He says the booth is out of sight of the desk."

"Well," said Sam, when Breck gave him the news, "that doesn't tell us much. We may as well go to bed, because I have a hunch we'll be busy tomorrow."

The boys rose at dawn and got their own breakfast. It was just as they were clearing away the dishes that Mrs. McArdle bustled into the kitchen. "Your father's awake, and feeling fine," she told Sam. "He had a good night. You'd better go in and see him before you go out. He may have some special orders for you deputies," she chuckled.

They found the warden sitting up in bed, a bath-robe around his broad shoulders.

"Well, boys," he said briskly, "glad you're ready fer

an early start. I aim to be on the job tomorrow myself. First thing you do, Sam, I wish you'd go to Rideau's Garage, an' make sure the car'll be fixed up today. Then you'd better start right out on patrol. Cover the roads as far over as Freedom and up to Conway. Look over all the huntin' parties you see in the woods, and keep an eye peeled fer out-o'-the-way places where the jackers might be sellin' deer. That's all, I guess. I don't look fer any trouble from the gang—not fer a few days anyhow."

Sam glanced at Breck and shook his head warningly. "Okeh, Boss," he grinned. "We'll obey orders and be back here for a big, hot supper. The game laws are safe while we're on the job."

It was a gray, overcast morning outside. They ran the roadster out of the McArdles' barn and drove half a mile up the road to the garage where the old touring-car was being repaired. Joe Rideau, the smiling French Canadian who owned the place, assured them that the car would be "good lak new" by afternoon. And with this errand discharged, Breck swung the roadster's nose south and east.

They loafed along at twenty, stopping occasionally to explore a side road or to question a carful of hunters. There were many such along the highway. Sometimes the damp wind would bring the sound of a far-away shot down to them from the woods. And once, when Sam thought he heard dogs running a deer, they tramped half a mile into the brush without finding anything.

"We don't have the trouble with dogs we used to have," the warden's son remarked. "None o' the outsiders bring 'em in these days. When you do find a hound on a deer-track it's usually one that's strayed off from a farm somewhere."

Cruising slowly they rounded the southern shore of Ossipee Lake and followed the Portland road through Freedom to the Maine State line. There they turned and took the back road to the north. It was a few minutes past noon when they pulled into a pasture lane below East Madison and prepared to eat their lunch. They had just opened a box of sandwiches and a thermos bottle of coffee when two Massachusetts cars stopped in the road a few yards from where they were sitting. There was a pair of hunters in each—typical city men, dressed in gunning clothes that still had the store creases in them.

The driver of the forward car looked the boys over for a moment before he spoke. "Any luck, Bud?" he asked.

Sam shook his head. "Haven't seen a deer today," he grinned. "How about you?"

"Naw," the stranger replied. "This is our second day and we've only had one shot. Got to go back tonight. How is it up above Conway?"

"They say there's plenty of deer around Conway

Pond," Sam answered, "but a lot of hunters have been going in there."

The man in the car seemed to hesitate, and turned to exchange a few words with his companion. Then he looked around cautiously and addressed the boys again.

"Know where we could pick up a deer or two?" he asked, his tone confidential.

Sam stiffened but kept his smile. "No," said he, "I can't tell you a thing about that."

"That's all right," nodded the other. "Thought maybe you were on the inside." And he started his motor. As the cars moved on up the road, Sam went back to his sandwich with a frown. "I don't like that guy," he said. "He's the kind that makes this jacking racket profitable. Still, you can't arrest 'em just for asking."

A few minutes later they resumed their patrol. Once, on the narrow road between Snowville and Conway, a whiff of blue wood-smoke drifted out of the woods to the east. Breck stopped the car.

"Look," he said, "there's a heap of smoke in there to come from an ordinary camp-fire."

"Come on," said Sam, and led the way into the brush. The smoke grew thicker as they advanced, and an ominous crackling sound became audible. A hundred yards in from the road they plowed, coughing, through the heavy fumes and came on a broad circle of fire. It was perhaps thirty feet across and was eating its way briskly into the tangled undergrowth. Both boys seized long sticks and set to work beating out the flames. For ten minutes they fought the blaze before the last sparks were extinguished.

"Wow!" panted Sam, as they rested from their labors.

"It's a good thing we weren't any later. That would have been a real forest fire in another half hour. Look here, in the middle of the ring—some duffer ate dinner here and left his cook-fire burning!"

There were the charred remains of papers and egg-shells, as well as a tin can or two.

"That's another thing I've got against these town hunters," Sam observed on the way back to the car. "Not more than one in ten of 'em knows the first thing about how to act in the woods."

At Conway Village the young deputy wardens turned south on the highway. The gray afternoon was turning into dusk when they passed Iona Lake and saw the stark outline of Chocorua Peak towering ahead. But there was still light enough for Breck's quick eye to recognize the two cars jolting slowly down, out of a rocky side road.

"Sa-a-y!" he exclaimed. "Those chaps must have worked fast. Look at the deer they've got in the cars!"

With a twist of the wheel he ran the roadster across the mouth of the narrow lane and stopped, blocking the way.

"Hey, you! What's the idea?" yelled one of the hunters angrily.

The boys got out and went together to the first car. "Let's see your hunting licenses," said Sam briskly.

"What the—" the driver began, but at the flash of

Sam's badge his jaw dropped. The consternation of the pair was almost comical as they fumbled for their papers.

"I—I never guessed you were wardens!" stammered the driver. He finally produced a non-resident hunter's license, as did his companion.

"Okeh," said Sam, handing them back. "Now let's see these deer you got."

There was a carcass tied on each rear fender and the boys examined them carefully, while the hunters stood anxiously by. Both deer had the license coupons properly attached. Sam studied the pitifully glazed eyes and open mouth of the buck on his side of the car.

"How long ago did you shoot this one?" he asked, straightening up.

"Oh—about an hour—two hours." The spokesman turned to his partner. "When was it, Joe?"

"I dunno," the other replied. "They stiffen up quick in the cold."

"Yeah," said Sam, drily. "Your luck seems to have come all in a bunch. Didn't follow my tip about Conway Pond, did you?"

"Why, no," the hunter answered, and made a vague gesture with his arm. "We got these up in the woods to the north, here."

There were two more deer hanging on the other car.

Again the boys made their inspection and found all the forms in order.

Sam asked more questions but was able to get no very satisfactory answers from the hunters. On the other hand he had no definite proof that they were lying.

"All right," he said, at length, "sorry to have kept you waiting."

He made a note of the names and license numbers, and Breck drove out of the way so that the cars could pass. When they had gone the boys held a hurried council.

"They bought those deer, sure as shooting!" Breck exclaimed. "I'll bet they'd been dead forty-eight hours. And say—did you notice the wound in that doe on the first car? A hole you could put your fist in."

"Yes," Sam nodded. "It might have been from a charge of buckshot at awfully close range."

"Looked to me like the hole a rifle bullet makes on the way out," answered Breck. "I did my best to feel under the other side but the deer was tied down tight. Well, that's all past history. What I'd like to find is the hideout where they bought their game. Let's take a ride up this road and take a look around."

"Right," said Sam. "Wait till I unlimber this gat and make sure it's loaded. I don't expect to shoot it, but this looks like a hot trail to me."

The road was hardly more than a woods-track, twist-

ing up the hillside over rocks and threading between birch
saplings where the slim boughs scraped the windshield.
They drove slowly and in silence save for an occasional
murmured warning from Sam. After half a mile of this
rough going the path crossed a sharp ridge and leveled

out suddenly in the door-yard of an abandoned farm-
house.

The house itself was a tiny affair of battered gray
shingles, its two broken windows staring blankly like
sightless eyes and its mossy roof caved in at one end.
Beyond, and partly hidden by the house, was a dilapidated barn, built with its rear wall half buried in the
hillside.

The tracks of several cars passed the corner of the
house, and the snow in front of the barn was cut by zigzag curves where the machines had backed to turn. Breck

drove forward cautiously till they could see all of the yard—empty.

"There may be somebody inside the barn," he whispered. "The door's shut tight. Keep that gun out o' sight, and if they're here we'll ask first if they've got any deer to sell."

They got out of the car and went together to the barn door. Breck was breathing fast with excitement as he lifted his mittened hand to knock. He could see Sam's face, pale and set.

Rap! Rap! Rap! Then deep silence. They waited for what seemed a long time and finally the warden's son gave a hail. "Hello—inside, there!"

Still no answer came and Breck rattled the door. A tug at its flimsy edge sent it creaking open a foot or two. In the deepening dusk the interior looked forbiddingly dark.

"Gee," muttered Sam, "I wish we had a flash. I'll put one in the car tomorrow. See if you can open it any wider."

He stood alert while Breck thrust his shoulder hard against the door. It gave slowly, sliding on its rusty track. Now they could see the inside of the structure more plainly. A floor of worn planks, littered with old hay, stretched back to the gloom of the rear wall. There was a row of gaping stalls along one side and a loft built over them. At the back of the barn, against the board wall, lay a dirty heap of old lumber and a worn-out sleigh.

The boys stepped gingerly inside and looked into all the corners. The chill silence echoed hollowly to the clumping of their feet. Sam climbed the ladder and peered around the loft. To his relief it was as empty as the floor.

"Nobody here, that's certain," he said, brushing his hands as he returned to Breck's side. "And yet I'd swear those hunters got their deer right in this barn."

"Wait a jiff," Breck answered. "If this place has been used to store deer there must be some sign of it. Got a match?"

Sam produced three or four matches—his entire store —and lit one, shielding the uncertain flame with his hand. Slowly they moved back and forth across the floor.

In a few places the planks had been brushed clean of chaff, and once Sam found a reddish-gray hair that he was sure had come from a deer. But it was not till the last match was partly burned that they came on a real clue. There on the floor, a few feet from the entrance, was a brown smear of dried blood. No film of dust lay over it. It had been made perhaps that afternoon—certainly within twenty-four hours.

"Thunder!" growled Sam, as the match burned out. "I guess that finishes our sleuthing for tonight. Those deer we saw came from here, and it stands to reason there must be more, if we could find 'em."

It was too dark for any further search. They went around to the front of the house, but there were no tracks in the snow on the door-stone. Slowly they got into the Ford and drove down the rocky road, still speculating on the whereabouts of the *cache*.

"There might be a trap-door in the floor or something," said Breck. "If we'd had a flash—" but his sentence went unfinished.

From the woods at the right of the trail came the crack of a rifle, near and sudden. And at the same instant there was a ripping sound in the roadster's top.

"Step on it!" gasped Sam. "They're shooting at *us!*"

VII

BRECK needed no urging. He gave the car all she would take and went flying down the rutted hill at breakneck speed. There were no more shots and no sign of pursuit. But it was not until they were well down the main road that they stopped to look at the damage.

A clean, half-inch hole had been drilled in the top fabric not six inches from Sam's head, and the bullet had cut through the rear curtain just above the glass on the way out. The shot had not been fired merely to frighten them, that was sure. There had been murder in its aim.

"Well," said Sam, "we're not doing any good here. Let's get home and report it."

Their experience had not spoiled their appetites. Supper was on the table when they reached the McArdle house, and they ate it cheerfully enough. The warden sat in his usual place, his head still bandaged, but feeling, as he put it, "fit to lick his weight in wildcats."

"How'd you make out today, Sam?" he asked, after a few minutes.

"Oh, fair enough," the boy replied casually. "Didn't make any arrests, but I think we got a line on one of the jackers' storage-places. A barn up on a road I never even saw before—over north of Pequaket. We got shot at as we were leaving, so I'm pretty sure the place belongs to them."

"Shot at!" exclaimed McArdle. "You mean you just heard a shot?"

"No," said Sam, "it was a rifle—fired at us. The bullet went right through the car."

Frowning, the warden sat back and drummed with his fingers on the table. "That," he said quietly, "sounds pretty bad. I'll take one o' the men an' go up there to-morrow. An' you boys'll have to stick to the main roads. No more scoutin' trips unless I give you orders."

Next morning when it was barely light enough to see, Mike Kilday's old car came rattling into the yard. The boys were already up but the family had not yet sat down to breakfast. The air was full of small, stinging particles of snow when Breck opened the door to welcome the big deputy.

"Come in here, Mike," called McArdle, "and wrap yourself around some sausages and coffee!"

The Irishman shook the snow off his mackinaw and entered, grinning his broadest.

"Sure an' it's good they'll do me," he chuckled. "I was

out till all hours skirmishin' wid th' enemy, an' niver got to bed till the roosters was crowin'."

When Kilday was established at the breakfast table, with his napkin tucked well into the collar of his flannel shirt, he enlightened them further.

"I took the car out after supper," he said, "figgerin' there might be some funny business up above the Glen. When I got close to the county line, a couple o' miles this side o' Pinkham Notch, there was lights flashin' at the far side of a pasture. I left the car an' took my shotgun an' cut up through the bushes. 'Fore long I could see the jackers—three of 'em—movin' along in the edge o' the pines. One had a big light that he'd turn on every little bit. The other two was carryin' guns.

"When I was maybe a hundred yards away I saw a couple o' does step out into the beam o' the light. An' before they could shoot I let out a yell an' started runnin' towards 'em.

"First thing I knew the light was turned square on me an' there was a shot. A rifle bullet come scorchin' past, so close I could hear it whistle. I stopped then an' dropped down behind a rock. 'Lay down yer guns,' I hollers. 'You're under arrest!'

"The three o' them started to run back, along the fence. An' at that I jumped up an' ran after 'em. I fired in the air tryin' to stop 'em but all I got was another shot back. They had a tourin' car hid in a lane, an' before I could git close enough to say any more they were tearin' out to the road.

"That wasn't all, either. On their way past that old

coupe o' mine, one o' the divils drills me rear tire clean as a whistle. I was till after midnight gittin' it fixed an' drivin' home."

Warden McArdle had laid down his knife and fork as Kilday's recital proceeded. At the end he gulped down his coffee and got to his feet. "This business of shootin' at wardens has gone too far," he said grimly. "I'm goin' to call Concord right now."

After ten minutes at the telephone he came back to the kitchen with his hat and leather coat on. "I got the Chief Warden," he said. "He's goin' to see the Commissioner, an' the Governor if necessary. We'll have our orders before noon. Now, boys, I'm goin' to let you take patrol again. Try an' keep out o' trouble. Mike an' I'll go up an' look over that barn o' yours."

Sam gave the two older men directions for finding the abandoned farm and they set forth in McArdle's rejuvenated touring-car. A few minutes later the boys, too, were on their way. The light, driving snow kept most of the traffic off the roads, and they went for miles in some places without seeing a car. This time their route lay northward, through Kilday's regular territory. At the Glen fork they swung to the west and drove into the jaws of Crawford Notch, where the black woods went up to right and left and lost themselves in the swirling gray.

It was on the trip back, rolling slowly along above Intervale, that they had their only adventure of the morning. The spruce bush came down dense and dark to the edge of the road. Out of this thick cover, not fifty yards ahead, there suddenly stepped a big reddish animal. As many times as Breck had seen deer, his first impulsive thought was "big dog!" Then in a flash he corrected himself and silently threw out the clutch. The roadster rolled smoothly nearer and still the doe had not sensed their approach, for the southeast wind was blowing up the road from her to them. At last, when they were a bare ten yards away, her great ears went up in a startled V and

she gave one fleeting look at the car. In the twinkling of an eye her slim legs had gathered under her and she cleared the road in a graceful, sailing leap. Barely touching the snow she sprang again and her white flag of a tail flew high as she vanished into the woods.

"Boy, wasn't that pretty?" breathed Breck. "A little more and I was going to jump right out and grab her."

"You'd have had some trouble, at that," laughed Sam. "They can fight like the dickens. Pop says he's seen a doe lick the living daylights out of a bob-cat that tried to get her fawn."

The snow had stopped by noon, when they returned to West Ossipee. Not more than two inches had fallen, for the storm had never been heavy. And with the clouds breaking as the wind backed into the west there was promise of fair weather.

"As long as we're here, and it's time to eat," said Sam, "we may as well stop at the house for dinner."

In the living-room they found quite a crowd assembled. The warden and Kilday had returned from their expedition, and the other two deputies had been called in for a council of war.

"I'm glad you're here, boys," said McArdle. "I think we can give you a real job tonight. We're going to take this fight right to the jackers."

The early morning call to Concord had produced action. From the State Fish and Game Commissioner at the capital a telegram had already arrived. Breck and Sam read it with a thrill. What it said was:

"Instruct all wardens and deputy wardens when fired upon by game law violators they are to shoot to kill."

"Understand," McArdle told them, "this ruling means self-defense. You've got the same rights as any citizen to protect yourself. When you're doing your duty an' a jacker takes a deliberate shot at you, don't waste powder in the air. Shoot straight."

Other news had been telephoned by the Chief Warden. It was definitely established that the gang of deer-jackers operating in Carroll County was the same that had played havoc in the woods of Coos two weeks earlier. According to the warden of the big northern county, the "mob" consisted of six or seven notorious gangsters, led by Durfee and "Saranac Slim" Pasquale. Two of the members drove the trucks that transported illegally killed deer to the cities. And four or five others, with two fast cars, rifles and jack-lights, did the shooting and sold the game from their local hide-outs.

One other item interested the boys. It was that Saranac Slim still had a Federal indictment hanging over him, and that a reward of $1000 had recently been posted for his capture.

"What did you find at the barn, Pop?" Sam asked.

"There wasn't a soul around," replied the warden. "An' I don't reckon anybody had been back there since your visit yesterday. But there's been deer stored there sure. We searched the barn pretty careful, an' the house, too. They haven't used the house. It's full of cobwebs an' thick with dust. But I'm still suspicious o' the barn. There's no trap in the floor that we could find, an' nothin' in the loft or the stalls. Just the same, I believe there's venison hid around there this minute."

A cheerful call came from the kitchen at that moment, and the forces of game protection trooped out to the table.

"My lands," laughed the buxom warden's wife, "it looks like a crew of threshers at harvest time! Well, I hope I've given you enough to eat. There's two whole pots o' beans and a big roast o' side meat. Set right down now and do your worst."

When the meal was finished Warden McArdle outlined the campaign for the rest of the day. The deputies were to go back on their regular patrol through the afternoon. At seven o'clock Hanks and Randall were to meet at Tamworth and hold themselves in readiness there to follow instructions. Likewise the warden and Kilday would get together in Conway at the same hour.

Breck and Sam, meanwhile, were to take the battery searchlight to the top of Mt. Chocorua. From the summit they would have an unimpeded view to the north, east and south, and would be able to pick up the flash of a jack-light almost anywhere within ten miles. As soon as they were sure that jackers were at work, the plan was for the boys to signal whichever post was nearer the scene and give the waiting officers the word to move.

The villages of Tamworth and Conway had been

chosen because both commanded a view of Chocorua Peak. The signals were to be flashed with the searchlight and it was agreed that anything of importance the boys had to tell should be repeated three times to make sure it was received.

Both Randall and Hanks had some familiarity with Morse code, and Mike Kilday had been a telegraph operator at one period in his checkered career. To make sure that each of the men could receive his signals properly, Breck flashed two or three test messages with a pocketlight.

"All right, boys," said McArdle, "take a little something to eat, an' be sure you're dressed warm. You'll find it sort o' chilly up there on the peak. Better get goin' before too late, for it's a long, hard climb. If this plan works we'll have some jackers by breakfast-time."

Sam found an extra sweater for Breck to wear under his jacket and also a pair of heavy woolen mittens. They packed a light knapsack with food, tested the searchlight to make sure it was in working order, and bought a couple of spare dry cells for emergency use. The last thing before they left the house, Breck slipped a good supply of matches in his pocket. And mindful of their experience in the deserted barn, Sam took along a flashlight.

By two-thirty they were driving out of the yard. The sun was shining now, but the weather had turned colder and a wind blew briskly out of the west. Twenty minutes on the highway brought them to a rough little country road that climbed and twisted along the flank of the mountain. In many places it was so steep and stony that Breck put the car in second and even in low gear.

"Where does this go to?" the Massachusetts boy asked after a while. "You might think we were coming to the jumping-off place!"

"Don't worry," laughed Sam. "We're making head-way, or at least holding our own. We'll have to get out and walk all too soon."

At the end of another mile the road, now no more than a pair of ancient wheel-ruts, came to an abrupt stop at a broken-down gate.

"Here we are," Sam announced. "Head of navigation. From now on we depend on our legs." They left the Ford partly sheltered by a jack-pine, and loaded the search-light and duffel on their backs.

"Golly," murmured Breck, as they tramped up across a bushy pasture, "I'm glad we don't have to pack blankets, too. But I'll bet before we get through up there we'll wish we had 'em."

"Don't want to get too comfortable," Sam replied. "This is one night we've got to keep wide awake."

They climbed in silence for an hour. The sun had gone down and the ruddy west was fading to gray when they

LEE TOWNSEND

tackled the last wicked pitch to the summit. The snow
was slippery on the rocks and Breck's whole body ached
with weariness as he scrambled upward.

"Come on," called Sam, from somewhere above.
"We're just about on top now and, boy, is it breezy up
here!"

When Breck gained the crest he was ready to agree.
A cutting wind swept the bare crag. Nevertheless, as he
laid down the precious searchlight and batteries he felt
a thrill at the panorama that stretched around him. Fold
on fold of dark forest, broken by tiny patches of farm-
land, rolled away to the south where the broad sheet of

Lake Winnepesaukee lay pale in the deepening dusk. To the west and north the great ranges lifted like a tossing sea, with the white peak of Washington still catching the last glow in the sky. Here and there in the valleys the lights of villages were appearing. And automobiles made bright, crawling dots along the roads.

"Yes," Sam said, joining him, "it's grand, all right. But if we stand here watching it much longer we'll freeze solid. Let's see what we can do about building a fire."

There was little fuel visible anywhere on the summit. They searched for twenty minutes and finally gathered a scant armful of weather-beaten juniper sticks. Sam looked at the result of their efforts and shook his head. "That won't do," he said. "I'll take the camp-ax and go down below timber line for some real wood. Meanwhile you can be taking our stuff over back of that bowlder. There's a sort of natural fireplace there, sheltered from the wind."

Breck found the place without difficulty. It was a deep niche split out of the granite ledge. Its walls rose four or five feet in a narrow wedge-shaped opening, and with the flashlight he could see charred bits of wood left from earlier fires. The bowlder Sam had mentioned half screened the opening so that when Breck crouched down he no longer felt the biting force of the wind.

Nearly half an hour passed before the warden's son returned. He was staggering under a heavy armful of wood. "Br-r-r!" he growled, through chattering teeth, "we're going to earn our pay tonight!"

VIII

SAM flung down his load of fuel and began chopping shavings with the camp-ax.

"Hold on a minute," said Breck. "Won't we give warning to every jacker in forty miles if we build a fire up here?"

Sam looked about. "Not if we keep it small," he argued. "There's only one direction where it could be seen and that's off here to the west. Mighty few hunters ever go up that side of the mountain. It's too hard to get to."

Dexterously the boy built a little pyramid of sticks with a heap of spruce shavings and a bit of paper beneath. Then while he sheltered it with his jacket spread wide, Breck applied the match. They were lucky. The shavings caught almost instantly, and in three or four minutes there was real warmth coming from the blaze.

"Six o'clock," said Sam. "Let's see about a little supper." He rigged a tin kettle over the fire on two crotched sticks, and filled it with chips of ice. When it was melted he made coffee. With some meat sandwiches and doughnuts, produced from the knapsack, they were able to make a very satisfactory meal.

"There," said Breck, "I feel more like a man. Let me have the flashlight and the ax. It's my turn to go for wood."

In the scrub growth half a mile down the mountain he collected an armful of dry sticks and topped it off with three or four solid chunks that would give lasting heat.

When he got back to the peak, he found Sam standing on the wind-swept ledge above their niche and looking southward over the dark country.

"Thought I saw a light," the warden's son explained after a moment, "but I guess it was only a car on the Whittier road. What we'll have to do is take regular watches, Breck. Half an hour's about all we'll be able to stand, up there in the wind. One can watch while the other keeps warm and tends the fire. I'll take the first go. Call me at eight o'clock."

It was a monotonous business. Breck squatted with his back against the stone wall of the crevice, and fed bits of wood sparingly to the fire. Occasionally, when Sam's sentry-beat brought him close, they tried to converse, but it was difficult in the whistling wind.

At the end of thirty minutes Breck was glad enough to take his turn outside.

"I'll help you get your bearings," shivered Sam, thrashing his numb arms. "Over there is Tamworth. This is Pequaket, down here. West Ossipee is over beyond, and up this way you can see some of the lights in Conway."

Breck turned up the collar of his jacket, pulled his cap over his ears, and began his vigil. Back and forth across the bleak summit he paced, varying the monotony occasionally by running a few steps or flailing his arms. By keeping up a good circulation he did not actually suffer much. Despite the wind, the temperature was only a few degrees below freezing. And he found a fascination in watching the winking lights below. He wondered just how a jack-light would appear if he saw it. Once or twice he paused to watch lights that seemed to flash on and off in the woods. But each time they turned out to be head-lamps moving along distant roads where the trees obscured them from time to time.

It was not until Sam's fourth turn on watch that anything happened. About eleven, when Breck was sitting drowsily in the warmth of the fire, the other boy's voice came back to him, half-smothered by a gust of wind. Breck sprang up at once and ran out on the ledge.

Sam was pointing eagerly downward. "Look!" he said. "Right below here under our noses! See that light in the woods beside the pond? There's no road there. They've been moving along, slow, for the last five minutes, but I wanted to make sure."

Even as he spoke there was a faint red flash beside the light and five or six seconds later they heard the faint crack of a rifle.

Both boys jumped into action. In no time at all they had the searchlight pointed south towards Tamworth. Breck brought the knapsack, which they had agreed to use for breaking the flashes, and they turned on the beam.

"Give 'em half a minute or so, to be sure they see it," said Sam. "Then we'll begin shooting the message. All we need to say is 'Northwest shore Chocorua Pond.' I'll give you the letters so you can concentrate on your dots and dashes. All right, let's start—N."

Crouching beside the light, Breck held the empty knapsack in both hands and dropped it momentarily over the lens. Then he began shooting short flashes and long ones, at Sam's dictation.

"Good!" cried Sam when the phrase was finished. "Wait just a jiffy and we'll let 'em have it again."

"Won't the jackers see it?" asked Breck.

"If they were watching they might," the warden's son answered. "But they're busy down there, and they're way below the line of the light. All ready for the second signal?"

Breck ran through the message again, and as he flashed

the final letter Sam pointed excitedly southward. On the road from Tamworth to Chocorua Village the lights of a car were darting swiftly toward them.

"I'll bet that's Abe Randall's Buick!" said Sam. "Look at 'em come—sixty-five an hour, and that road's none too good!"

"Still," Breck put in, "it might possibly be somebody else—Chink Durfee, himself, for instance. I'm going to repeat once more, just for luck."

Slowly he spelled out the message for the third time, while Sam danced with excitement. He had lost sight of the speeding car for a moment but as Breck straightened up he let out a whoop.

"There they are!" he cried. "This side of Chocorua, on the main road. They'll cut in by the pond in a minute. And the jackers are still down here—still working the flash."

As if to confirm his words the rifle spoke once more in the woods at the mountain's foot. A minute passed—two minutes—and they saw the headlights of a car come up the dirt road past Chocorua Pond. It slowed down and suddenly its lights were extinguished.

"Good!" Sam exclaimed. "That's Abe, sure. They'll come in on foot and catch 'em red-handed. Randall and Hanks know those woods-trails blindfolded. And look— the jack-light's going again!"

He crossed the rocky crest to the niche and was glad to see smoke still curling past on the wind. He placed two or three sticks on the fire and was rounding the bowlder on the farther side of the summit when something caught his eye in the broad valley to the north. It was a light, blinking through the woods, three or four miles away. That was where Swift River lay—the stream where he and Sam had found blood in the snow.

The light moved, it seemed to the boy, as slowly as the hands of a clock. Too slowly for a car, even at that distance. It was extinguished for a moment or two, then flashed on again, and this time it was less brilliant, as if it had been turned in a different direction. That was enough for Breck. He dashed back to the other side, shouting Sam's name, and found his chum still intently watching the woods below.

"They must be near there by now," Sam said. "I haven't seen the light for a couple of minutes. Hope they don't start shooting."

"But there's another one over here!" Breck cried. " 'Way back on Swift River, it looks like."

"Another one!" gasped Sam. "Are you sure?"

"Come look for yourself," Breck yelled over his shoulder. He was already half way across the summit, carrying the searchlight. Sam joined him, as he was setting it in place. "Isn't that about where Swift River would lie?"

Breck asked, pointing to the north. "It's not shining now, but—no—look—there it is!"

Sam stood silent, staring hard at the light for a full minute. "I believe you're right!" he said, at length. "It's too far off to hear any shots, but that slow way it's moving—yes, it's jackers. Come on, Breck, we've got to let Pop know, over in Conway. Let's see—'Swift River road, five miles west'—that ought to be about right."

Once more Breck was signaling. Up and down went the knapsack, flashing and obscuring the light in carefully timed intervals.

The Conway end of the valley road was hidden by low, wooded hills, and Breck had no way of telling whether his message had been caught by the watchers. Chilled to the marrow by the wind that blew hardest on that side of the peak, he spelled out the words, painstakingly, a second and third time. Then he turned off the light and sprinted across to see what was happening down by Chocorua Pond.

"No news," said Sam glumly. "I haven't seen a thing for five minutes. The jack-light's out, too. I'm afraid the gang has sighted 'em and they may get shot at."

More minutes of anxious waiting went by. Then at last the boys saw the headlights of the deputies' car flash on again. After a moment it moved ahead slowly and made another stop, a quarter of a mile farther up the road. There the lights of a second car joined it, and after backing around, the two automobiles went crawling eastward, one close behind the other.

"I believe they got 'em!" cried Sam in jubilation. "That was the jackers' car, hid up the road a piece. Say, we've had sort of a busy night, once things got going! Let's see what Pop and Kilday are up to."

But the northern valley was dark and still. No headlamps moved on the little-used Swift River road, and the jack-light, if such it was, had ceased to flash. Breck picked up his signaling equipment and carried it back to the shelter of the cleft in the rock. Sam joined him there a minute later.

"I don't see as there's much more we can do tonight," he said, between a shiver and a yawn. "Wish I had a warm bed to crawl into."

Breck threw more wood on the fire. "Oh, I don't know," he answered. "You've been out on top too long. It's really pretty snug in here now that the rocks have heated up. Curl up over there beside the fire and toast your toes."

They lay for a while basking in the warmth and saying little. Sam pulled out his ever-present harmonica and played tune after tune. He started with the jigging rhythm of "Turkey in the Straw" and "Arkansaw Traveler" and drifted gradually into more pensive strains—

"Swing Low," "Darling Nellie Gray" and "Old Black Joe."

"I suppose," said Breck, "we'd better stay awake a bit longer and take a look around once in a while." He went outside and surveyed the sleeping woods around the

mountain. The lights in the farm-houses were out now, and only one or two cars moved on the dozen miles of highway that his eyes commanded. The wind had gone down in the last hour, he was sure. Slowly he returned along the northern side of the summit and was just rounding the bowlder at the entrance to their cubby-hole when a faint sound came up the mountain. It was hardly more than the click of a pebble, and listen as hard as he might, he did not hear it repeated. When he had stood there several minutes he decided he might have dislodged a stone with his foot and sent it rolling down the snow to strike some outcropping below.

At any rate he said nothing about it to Sam. Placing a long-burning chunk of wood on the fire, he made himself as comfortable as he could and pillowed his head on the knapsack.

"Going to bed, eh?" yawned Sam. "I'm with you!" And he, too, got ready for sleep.

Breck had the delicious sensation of drowsing off. In another moment he would have been deep in sleep, had not some sound reached his straying senses and brought him back to reality with a jerk. He struggled to a sitting posture, rubbing his eyes, and saw a man standing at the entrance of the cleft. In the dim glow of the fire he looked seven feet tall, and in the crook of his arm he carried a gun.

When he spoke at last, his low voice had a crisp ring in it.

"Well," he said, "who are you and what are you doing up here?"

IX

AT the sound of the stranger's words Sam stirred and sat up, blinking sleepily. All Breck could do was stare, as the man came a stride closer.

His actual height must have been over six-feet-three, and his shoulders were broad in proportion. Covering his raw-boned bigness was a dark blanket-cloth jacket and army breeches, tucked into high-laced moccasins. On his head was a battered old campaign hat. His age might have been anywhere from twenty-five to forty, but his curly black hair showed no gray. In the flicker of the fire-light his weather-tanned face looked gaunt and stern.

Sam found his tongue first. "We're deputy game wardens of this county," he said, a trifle truculently, "up here on official business. Who wants to know?"

The grim look departed from the stranger's mouth, and he laughed, showing a lot of big, even teeth.

"Guess I shouldn't have barged in without knocking," he said, "but I figured you for something different. I'm Jim Borden—ranger—White Mountain National Forest.

I was six or seven miles away, over beyond Hedgehog
Mountain, when I saw a fire burning up here. First I

thought some hikers might be stranded on the mountain.
Then I got some flashes of a light of some kind, and decided you were either boy scouts or bootleggers. And in

either case I guessed I'd better drift over and see what was going on."

Sam rose, grinning. "I'll admit you gave us a scare," he answered. "We've had some trouble with the jackers, you know, and right off the bat I thought you were one of the gang, up here to wipe out our signal nest. I've heard Dad speak of you, Mr. Borden. He's Warden McArdle—I guess you know him."

Breck was properly introduced and the giant forest ranger sat down for a chat. The boys told him about the plan for flashing warnings of the jackers' operations, and about its apparent success.

"Great!" chuckled Borden. "I got most of your message on this side. What was it—'Swift River road—something west'?"

"Yes," said Breck. "You didn't see anything of the gang yourself, did you?"

The ranger shook his head. "No," he said, "but I've run across 'em once or twice up around Crawford Notch. A hard bunch of *hombres*. I hope you clean 'em out of here quick, and I'll be glad to give you any tips I pick up."

For half an hour Borden regaled them with accounts of the lonely life of a government ranger. He had seen service in the Cœur d'Alene and other western forests before coming to New Hampshire. "I'm just as busy here," he said, "but there aren't quite as many thrills. The bears, for instance. These black chaps won't even stay and talk to me when I meet 'em on the trail. There used to be some fun in running slap into a thousand-pound grizzly. I've had to take to the trees more than once, out in Idaho.

"Of course, I see more folks here, particularly in the Summer, and they keep me busier because they start more fires. Then there are plenty of deer around and they're some company for me. That's one reason I get pretty sore when I see a crew of gunmen with jack-lights shoot down a dozen friends of mine in an hour or so."

"Where's your headquarters?" Sam asked.

"My shack's close to the foot of Mt. Hancock, on the upper stretch of Sawyer's River," the tall ranger answered. "In July and August there are a few campers up there, but after frost the nearest neighbors I've got are seven or eight miles away. I don't get lonesome, though. There's a fairly big territory to cover once or twice a week. And I have a lot of visitors—deer and porcupines mostly.

"One night last winter there was a heavy snow—one of those deep, still snows that falls without any wind and piles up a yard thick on the roof. Along about daybreak I woke and heard a noise outside. It sounded extra loud coming out of that dead, white silence. And half asleep as I was, all I could think of was some one sweeping a straw carpet with a broom—*whoosh—whoosh!*

"Then I got my brain clear and knew it was a deer snorting. Earlier in the winter I'd tied a block of rock salt to a stump out behind the shack, and the deer had been coming there to lick it. Well, I shuffled over to the back window and peeked out the top, where the glass wasn't covered with snow. And the whole clearing was full of deer. There must have been fourteen or fifteen does and part-grown youngsters. And right by the place where I'd put the salt was the old daddy o' the herd—the biggest white-tail I ever saw. He stood there, belly-deep in a drift, with his head high, sniffing, looking, listening. Maybe he'd heard a floor-board creak in the cabin. I stayed perfectly still and he seemed to be satisfied finally. Down went his head and he blew so hard into the snow that a white cloud hid him for a minute. That was the whistling I'd heard. Another puff or two and he was down to the salt. All the rest of the herd came crowding around then, and the old buck stepped off to one side, sort of scornful. Man, he was a beauty!"

The ranger paused to pull a battered briar pipe out of his pocket and fill it from a leather pouch.

Breck leaned forward eagerly. "You got a good close look at him!" said he. "Which side was toward you? Was it the big deer they call Scar-back?"

Borden made no reply till he had the pipe going. Then he nodded between puffs. "Yes," he said slowly. "It was the Passaconaway stag. There was sort of a white streak up across his left shoulder. Why—are you after his scalp, too?"

"Not me!" laughed Breck. "All I want is his portrait. I've heard him talked about, all the way from Boston to Colebrook. And I've seen his tracks right over here on Whiteface Mountain. Soon as we've got the jackers cleaned out, Sam and I are going to stalk him in earnest."

He went on to tell the ranger his plan for getting a night picture with the searchlight. Borden shook his head at that. "Not that buck!" he chuckled. "He'd never have lived to grow that pair of antlers if he was an ordinary deer. I reckon he must have been hunted with jack-lights fifty times. Why, it was just last week an old-timer told me he was out one night after meat and flashed his light on two does and a big stag. The does stood and looked, but the buck went out of sight as if he had wings, and before the hunter could shoot he'd got the does to follow him. It was the Passaconaway stag, he was pretty sure. Why, that old deer just knows lights are poison! You'll have to figure out another way."

The big ranger picked up his gun and unfolded his long body. "I've got sixteen miles to hike," he said, "and it's 'most one o'clock. Well, I wish you boys luck in your war with the jackers. Come over and see me some time."

"Hold on!" cried Sam, starting to his feet. "We kept you out of bed with this fire of ours. Now it's only fair to let us take you home. What do you say, Breck?"

"Perfectly right!" Breck answered. "It won't take five minutes to pack up this stuff, and the car's just down here a couple of miles."

Sam was already gathering their belongings. They doused the fire with snow and the three went sliding down the mountainside. It took them only half as long to reach the roadster as it had to scale the peak. And Breck drove up the deserted highway to Sawyer's River in less than an hour. From there a logging-road took them steeply upward along the flanks of Mt. Carrigan and Mt. Hancock.

It was just two-thirty when they reached the end of the road, and Borden explained that his cabin lay only a few hundred yards away, up the mountain. He thanked them heartily and again urged them to visit him. "Call me up as soon as you've cleaned up this job," he grinned. "I've got a special telephone line to my shack. Maybe I can help you track the big stag. I don't promise we'll find him, but I cover a lot of this country on foot, and I often cross his trail."

"Good enough," said Breck, "that's a bargain!"

As the tall ranger tramped away up the path, the boys turned the car homeward. Before they reached West Ossipee, clouds had blown up to obscure the stars, and the yard of the warden's house lay pitch-black under the elms.

"Well, Pop got home," Sam remarked. "His car's in the barn. Say—what's that! Turn your lights on again."

A bright beam from the roadster's headlamps lit up the front of the barn once more. The door was open a foot or so, and the fender of the warden's automobile showed inside. For several seconds the boys sat staring at the brightly illuminated building.

"What did you see?" whispered Breck.

"Thought I saw a man move, there by the door, just after you turned the lights out," the other boy replied. "Come on—got your gun?"

Watching the barn narrowly, they climbed out, one on each side, and moved forward. Two or three steps from the door, Sam stopped and raised his automatic.

"Walk out here," he said, "and come with your hands over your head."

They waited in tense silence. At length Sam motioned to Breck to open the door while he stepped a little to the right, out of the direct glare of the lamps. As Breck rolled the wide door slowly back, the whole interior showed up in sharp light and shadow. There was no intruder there unless he was crouching inside the car, and Breck quickly satisfied himself on that score. But as he returned to the doorway he found Sam peering at a small scrap of paper pinned to the cover of the car's spare tire.

"There *was* somebody here!" the warden's son exclaimed. "Look at this!"

The paper was a dirty leaf torn from a pocket notebook. On it, in pencil, was scrawled a brief message.

"*You had your warning*," Breck read. "*Now look out.*"

"He was in here when we drove up," the boy gasped. "And he was afraid we might come to the barn, so he ducked out the second I switched off the lights! Must have run back this way, around the house. Come on, Sam!"

"Wait!" his chum checked him. "The fellow's had time to get a block away by now. Let's take the car."

But before they could climb back into the Ford, the roar of an engine came from far down the road. Swiftly the sound diminished as the powerful motor sped away in the darkness.

"No use," said Sam. "Even if we could catch him, he's probably got his gang along. What we'd better do is turn in."

They locked the searchlight and the rest of the duffel in the rumble of the roadster and Sam opened the kitchen door with his key. Quietly, so as not to disturb the sleeping house, they made their way to Sam's room. Both boys were too tired to talk if they had wanted to. They pulled off their clothes, scrambled into bed, and fell instantly asleep.

Thanks to Mrs. McArdle's motherly care there were no noises in the house that morning to interfere with their slumber. It was after eight when Breck finally rolled over and found his eyes dazzled by the high sun. He poked Sam in the ribs and they tumbled out.

"Gee," mumbled the warden's son, "I wonder if Pop's left yet. We've got to tell him about that warning note."

He struggled into his breeches and went to the door. In reply to his call, his father came in, already dressed for outdoors.

"Well!" laughed the older man. "You boys sure did your stuff last night. We made a good haul when Abe and Otis brought in the Chocorua Pond gang. There were three jackers, an' they had six deer. They're locked up now an' they'll pay $1200 fine down at Ossipee this mornin'."

"How about you and Mike?" asked Sam. "Did you get our signal?"

"Sure thing," McArdle answered. "We didn't catch 'em though. I guess maybe they saw the flashes, too, for they put out o' there fast. When we were about four miles up the Swift River Road, two cars come over a rise, right on top of us, an' they were flyin', I can tell you. Lucky we didn't crash, head-on, but they pulled out on the side an' went bangin' by without tippin' over. We had to back twice to get turned 'round, an' by the time we got goin' the other way we'd lost sight of 'em. How long did you stay on the mountain?"

"Till about one o'clock," said Sam. "We had a visitor." And briefly he recounted their experience with the Forest Ranger. "We got home around three-thirty, and—" he hesitated, "have you been out to the barn?"

"Only to feed the hens," his father answered.

"Well," Sam went on, "when you look at the car, you'll find a piece of paper on the tire cover. A message from Chink Durfee, I reckon. We pretty near caught the fellow that left it."

The boys had finished dressing now, and the three crossed the yard to the barn. McArdle frowned as he studied the scrawled note.

"All right," he said, finally, "we'll be lookin' out. But they can't scare me that easy. We got under their hides last night. Twelve hundred is real money, even to a racketeer. Too bad the law won't let us put 'em in jail fer a spell."

Breck, meanwhile, had found the tracks of rubber-soled boots leading around the corner of the barn and off across the empty garden patch. Once out of sight, the man had run and kept on running. They followed the trail several hundred yards southward, behind neighboring houses, and traced it to the edge of the highway. There it vanished on the bare concrete.

"Remember the tracks we saw up on Swift River?" said Breck. "This is the small one—Saranac Slim is my guess."

The boys ate a hasty breakfast and accompanied the warden to Ossipee, where the three jackers were given their hearing. The matter was quickly settled. Judge Glendon heard the evidence, imposed maximum fines of $200 for each deer killed, and the total was paid with as much nonchalance as if the gangsters were buying subway tickets. Two of them were smallish men with the hard, expressionless faces of the city underworld. The third was a big French Canadian known to the judge from previous wrong-doing—a typical renegade lumberjack. He swaggered a little in front of the wardens, and gave a sneering laugh as he counted off the yellow-backs from his roll.

"More money than you ever saw before, isn't it, Du-Bois?" observed McArdle mildly.

"Oh, yeah!" returned the Frenchman. "An' plenty more where she come from!"

Without hurry, the three jackers strolled out of the little courthouse and entered the powerful touring-car that stood by the road. To Breck's surprise, they turned south instead of north.

"That's just to throw us off," said McArdle, as he watched them roll away. "They know we've got warrants out fer Durfee an' Slim an' we might try to follow 'em. What they'll likely do is drive down to Wolfeboro an' up around the lake. Then they'll sneak back into the county through Crawford Notch."

The warden went to the telephone and conferred with the State Police for a few minutes. When he came back he was smiling grimly. "All right, boys," he said, "we all may as well go back to work. The sergeant says he'll have a man trail 'em from Wolfeboro on a motorcycle. Soon as they sight him they'll know better'n to go near Durfee, but it may serve to keep 'em out o' mischief a day or two."

McArdle gave Hanks and Randall their orders for the day and then started back with the boys to West Ossipee. "Right after dinner," he said, "you'd better take a ride up the Swift River road an' look around a little. I've got a hunch those fellers hauled out so quick last night they may have left a deer or two in the woods."

The boys got away shortly after their noon meal and covered the route to Conway slowly, stopping several times to check up on hunters who had deer in their cars. About four o'clock they swung into the narrow road running up the Swift River valley. Sam watched the mileage on the dash and spoke up when they had gone three miles and a half.

"Take it easy, Breck," he said. "We must be close to the place where they met Pop coming out."

"Just ahead there, isn't it?" asked Breck. "Golly— look where they went! Right over that stump!"

They stopped the roadster and got out to marvel at the tracks of the two cars. "How they ever made it without tipping over is past me," Sam exclaimed. "And say, isn't that a Dalton tread on the far side?"

Closer inspection proved him right. The brown coupe of the gang leaders had gone careening over that spot. The boys drove slowly on up the road, and two or three miles farther on their careful search of the roadside was rewarded. Tracks, pulling off into the edge of the brush, showed where the two cars had been parked, and the trail of several men led into the woods on the left.

Half an hour of easy tracking brought the two deputies to a shallow ravine. The snow was trampled there for several feet around, and Sam, pointing to the bottom of the gully, discovered the reason. A well-marked deer-path followed the empty water-course. "They stood here with their light," said the boy. "This is where we saw it, too. The woods are thinner, off to the south, and Chocorua Mountain's right over there. Look, you can see the peak if you stoop a little."

There were no foot-prints going down into the ravine, and no sign that a deer had been killed. Instead they found the tracks of the jackers leading back toward the road.

"Hurrying," Breck observed. "Long steps—looks as if they were scared. I guess your father was right about their seeing our signals."

Daylight was beginning to fade when they got back to the car.

"What's the use of going home?" Sam asked. "We're only a little way from the shack. And we've got supplies. I can borrow blankets up here at the farm, and we'll stop at Bakers' and 'phone Pop."

The idea appealed to Breck, who had thoroughly enjoyed his previous visit to the lean-to. They reached camp about dusk and soon had a fire going. Supper was a simple but satisfying affair of canned beef-stew and biscuits. One thing they lacked was coffee.

"Huh!" snorted Sam, when he discovered it was missing. "We don't need it tonight but tomorrow's breakfast'll be mighty flat without a cup. There's a general store about four miles down the road. If you want to lend me the car-keys, I'll go get some coffee this evening. That'll let me out of doing dishes," he grinned.

"Fair enough," Breck agreed. "I've been wanting to try this searchlight on the deer-path. You'll find me up there with a whole herd of deer hypnotized when you get back."

Sam went whistling down the trail and Breck started tidying up the camp. At a few minutes after eight he strapped the searchlight and batteries over his shoulders. He knew that if the deer came down their path that night it would probably be soon. To guide him through the woods he took a hand flash and started uphill along the trail he had followed with Sam a few days before.

He struck the deer track about a mile from camp. There was a convenient hemlock thicket close to the path and he took his station there, testing the wind first, to make sure it was blowing down the mountain toward him. He did not have long to wait.

Against the pale snow he saw two shadowy shapes approaching along the trail. There was absolutely no sound.

The deer moved leisurely, stopping now and then to browse or to listen. When they were thirty yards away, Breck's trembling fingers touched the switch of the

searchlight, and the strong beam shot up the glade. The deer stood motionless, their heads high, their great eyes pools of light. Both were does.

Breck remained perfectly still, wondering how long he could hold them thus. And suddenly the night was split by a crashing sound—the report of a rifle—not ten feet from Breck's side. The foremost doe stumbled to her knees, and the other fled at a bound into the forest.

"Stick up your hands," said a cold voice, and Breck spun around to find himself looking into the muzzle of a rifle.

X

THE searchlight strapped to Breck's chest swung in a half-circle as he turned, and its powerful rays flashed in the faces of two men. He recognized one of them instantly as Chink Durfee. The other was shorter, of a squat, broad build, and it was this one who held the rifle.

"Turn out that light!" snarled Durfee, shielding his eyes from the glare. Breck snapped off the switch, and the figures of the men were blotted out, while the boy himself was still illumined by the bright beam of a flashlight held in Durfee's fist.

"Well, kid!" said the big gangster in surprise. "Seen you before, ain't I? Tryin' to horn in on our territory?"

Breck said nothing. He was thinking fast. The automatic was in the side pocket of his jacket. If he could get at it—

"Keep those hands up!" Durfee snapped as if reading his thoughts. "What did you do with yer rifle?"

"I didn't have any," said the boy quietly.

"Don't try to kid me, youngster," the jacker replied. "Hold the bead on him, Bunk. I'm goin' to frisk him."

While the unwavering muzzle covered him, Breck felt Durfee's expert hands patting his clothes.

"Hm," muttered the gang leader. "Packin' a gat, eh?" He flipped the automatic into his own pocket. "We-l-l! What's this?" His exploring fingers had encountered the warden's badge pinned under Breck's jacket. He turned the flash on it and read it with a scowl.

Then he stood back and looked at the boy, an ugly grin overspreading his face.

"So-o," he remarked. "An officer o' the law, eh? How long they been usin' kids like you?" Then his voice became hard and grating. "Listen, feller," he said. "You know too much. We gotta fix you so you won't make trouble."

He turned to his companion. "Go get the deer, Bunk," he ordered. "We'll let the deputy carry it for us."

Five minutes later Breck was staggering toward the road with a 120-pound doe over his shoulders. Behind him marched his captors with the flashlight and the rifle. The boy had to stop to rest twice before he had traversed the mile of woods. At last he saw the lights of a standing car shining through the trees. It was a big touring car with a searchlight mounted on the right of the windshield. The man lolling at the wheel had his collar turned high and his hat-brim pulled down, but Breck thought he had a familiar look. When they were stowing the deer in the rear seat the light of the flash crossed his face for a second and Breck knew at once that it was Saranac Slim.

Two other men appeared from across the road, carrying a dead buck between them. One wore a light somewhat similar to Breck's and the other had a rifle in his hand. There was a whispered conversation between Durfee, Slim and the two new arrivals, while the man called Bunk kept the boy covered.

"All right," said the slender Italian finally. "Chink an' me will take care of him in the other car. You boys go ahead an' get all you can. We'll meet you at the place in the morning."

As he spoke, Slim climbed out of the car and walked over to Breck. He looked at the boy a moment with a satisfied smile, then produced a piece of quarter-inch manila rope from his overcoat pocket. "Turn around—hands behind you," he said, in a matter-of-fact tone. And with amazing speed he whipped half a dozen loops of the rope around Breck's crossed wrists.

"Now then, got a handkerchief, kid?" he asked.

Breck nodded. "In my right breeches pocket," he replied. The jacker took it out, folded it smoothly on the diagonal and bound it fast over the boy's eyes.

For perhaps three minutes Breck stood there in the

road, helpless and sightless. He could hear snatches of talk from the gangsters. An occasional whiff of cigarette smoke reached his nose. Then there was the sound of a car approaching. It stopped close by and a hand under his arm steered him to the running board. As he stumbled up and into the automobile, he couldn't help wondering if he would get out of it alive. From what he had heard of Saranac Slim and his partner, he believed them perfectly capable of "taking him for a ride."

"Sit close here," commanded Durfee's voice. "There's three of us." And Breck was roughly squeezed into a seat between two men. From this he figured he must be in the coupe. The door closed with a click and the car glided into motion.

Since they had blindfolded him, Breck argued, the two jackers didn't want him to know where he was being taken. Perhaps that was a hopeful sign. There was no conversation as they whirled along, and Breck resolved to concentrate on guessing at the route they traveled. He was a good judge of motor speeds, and of time. From the sway of his body on the curves he was able to tell which way they were turning.

After several minutes of fairly fast going, Breck felt the coupe slow down slightly and swing to the right. They were meeting another car—a Ford, he was sure from the sound of its motor as it passed. Perhaps it was

Sam, returning to camp! He wondered how long it would be before his chum followed up his tracks and guessed what had happened. If the other four jackers returned to the deer-path it was quite possible Sam, too, might get into trouble.

A few minutes later the rough road gave way to a hard surface and smooth going. Breck heard the horns of other cars and knew they must be in the village of Conway. The turn here was important. Which way would it be? Durfee, who was driving, took it very slowly and there was no sensation of side sway. But the big jacker's arm brushed Breck as he swung the wheel, and the boy knew they were heading north.

He sensed each hamlet as they came to it. First there was the "Y," where Route 18 came in from Fryeburg. Then they passed through North Conway, and afterward Intervale. Breck tried to keep track of the curves and figure the general direction of the road they were traveling. At Glen, he knew, they would either turn north, toward Berlin, or go straight through in the direction of Crawford Notch. The miles went by and he could feel no slackening of speed, no sharp swerve to the right. They must have passed the turn-off, he was sure, and further proof came a moment later when the car rumbled across a bridge. That would be the upper Saco River span.

To Breck's surprise, Saranac Slim spoke up, just after

the bridge crossing. "In Maine now, ain't we?" he remarked. The tone was casual—too casual. The boy was surer than ever that they were on the Notch Road, heading straight away from the state line.

After perhaps fifteen minutes the car slowed down and swung abruptly to the right, bumping over the ruts of a country road. Breck knew they were going up hill at first. Then they dipped sharply into a hollow and climbed a second hill.

The car made another turn, this time to the left, and moved slowly. Now for the first time on the trip, Chink Durfee spoke. "I'll stop by the front door an' you can take him in," he said. "Put him in that back room in the attic. He won't be tryin' to jump from there."

Saranac Slim took hold of Breck's arm, when the car stopped, and guided him as he got out. The boy heard the door close and the coupe moved off. Then the gangster pushed him forward until he stubbed his toe against a wooden step.

"Here," said Saranac, "this won't do. You'll be fallin' on that perfectly good jack-light." And he proceeded to unstrap the light from Breck's shoulders.

They went on up the steps then—four steps that felt shaky under Breck's feet—and through a door that had already been opened by some one inside. There was warmth in the house, and a stale odor of boiled cabbage.

No word was spoken but Breck heard breathing and knew he was passing some one, in a narrow hall. Seven short paces and they were climbing stairs. Up one flight, then a right turn along an upper hall and a second right turn at the foot of another flight of stairs.

A yard or two beyond the top of the staircase, Saranac Slim paused, turned the knob of a door and shoved Breck inside. "All right, Buddy," he said softly, "here's where we take off your eye-shade."

As the boy stood blinking in the middle of the room, a door closed behind him and he heard a key turning in the lock. He was in a slant-ceilinged attic chamber with one small window. On a rickety table an oil lamp burned smokily. The only other furnishing was a straw tick on the floor in one corner.

Breck waited till he heard the footsteps of the gangster die away on the stairs below. Then he drew a breath of relief. "Well, kid," he whispered to himself, "you're not going to be bumped off tonight, anyhow."

He tried to figure out what time it was—his strap-watch being out of sight behind him—and decided at least an hour and a half must have passed since he left the shack. That would make it 9:30 or later. Any attempt to escape was out of the question for that night. All he could do was try to make himself comfortable, and that would not be easy with his hands tied. He knelt awkwardly on the mattress and dropped over on his side. It was a cramped position and the light prevented his falling asleep. Nothing for it but to rise and blow out the lamp. He got to his feet and went to the table, and there an idea struck him. By backing up to the lamp and bending over he might get his wrists above the flame and burn the cord in two.

He turned and lifted his bound hands as high as he could, moving back and forth gingerly to find the lamp-chimney. *Ouch!* The instant his wrists passed over the top of the chimney, scorching heat singed his skin. It was no good. He would be almost sure to burn himself seriously before he could hope to sever the rope.

He blew out the light and felt his way back to the makeshift bed. The boy was too weary to care about discomfort. He tumbled face down on the musty-smelling tick and closed his eyes. In a moment he had lost consciousness.

To say that Breck slept till morning would be an exaggeration. The chafing of his bonds woke him at intervals all night long. But in spite of an ache in his arms he felt as if the partial rest had done him good when the sun came in his window.

The room was unheated, of course, and even his outdoor garments had not kept him from growing stiff with cold. Shivering and stumbling, he managed to get to his feet. For five minutes he tramped up and down the floor, forcing the circulation into his numb feet. By that time he realized that he was ready for breakfast. Below in the house he could hear people moving about and an occasional faint clink of dishes. He even imagined a smell of frying bacon.

Waiting impatiently, Breck watched the sun climb higher up the sky, and after a while he began to realize that no breakfast was coming his way. There was nothing to do but sit there and make the best of it. He crouched on the floor beside the low window and considered some possible way of escape. First he tried to wriggle his fingers around to get at the knot that held his wrists. He kept at it until there were cramps in his sides and arms from the strain. He might break the lamp-chimney and attempt to sever the cord with a piece of broken glass. But even if he could get his hands free there was still a stoutly locked door on one side and a twenty-foot drop into the yard on the other.

This yard began to take on a look of activity as the morning wore along. Partly hidden by the corner of the house he could see the big touring-car that had been up Swift River the night before. And several of the jackers were in evidence, moving here and there around the place. About mid-forenoon a sedan drove up beside the house. After a brief conversation with one of the gang the driver accompanied him to the door of a shed, connected with the rear of the building. They went inside and emerged a few minutes later carrying a dead buck. This deer and a second one were loaded on the car, the hunter slipped some bills into the gangster's hand, and the sedan departed.

From time to time other cars came on similar business. Breck saw seven deer sold to the "sports" in this way, and began to appreciate why men of the type of Durfee and Pasquale had left rum-running for the jacking racket. Inwardly he raged at his helplessness to interfere. If he ever got out of here, he would have evidence enough to make real trouble for these deer-slaughterers.

Noon passed and still there was no food brought up to the attic. Breck kicked the straw pallet over to the window and sat there looking out, bored and weary and very hungry. As nearly as he could keep track of the time it was about 2:30 when the loud hum of a motor caused him to look out. Into the yard shot a huge tan coupe and stopped just below with a squeak and a jerk. Out of the car he saw Chink Durfee jump, and a moment later there was a sound of commotion on the ground floor.

Two jackers ran out of the house and opened the shed-door. A big truck came roaring up the road, swerved to avoid the coupe and brought up with its open rear opposite the shed. And in another minute the men were passing deer out of the hiding place and piling them on the truck. Nearly twenty carcasses were packed in, and a tarpaulin was pulled tightly over them. Then the truck backed around and started out. For the first time its right flank was turned to Breck and he got a quick glimpse of a crumpled front fender and a broken headlight on that side. The truck that had crashed into Warden McArdle's car!

But before the boy had time to speculate on this clue, he was interrupted by a hurried pounding of feet on the stairs. The key was turned, and Saranac Slim darted in.

"Get up here, kid!" he barked. "We gotta be movin'."

In an instant the bandage was made fast around Breck's eyes and he was being hustled down the narrow stairway.

SARANAC SLIM DARTED IN

<h1 style="text-align:center">XI</h1>

IN the lower hall, Breck felt a draft of cold air. The front door must be open. The next moment Saranac was dragging him down the steps. He heard the low chug of an idling motor close by, and then he was bundled inside the coupe. Slim reached over and pulled the boy's cap down to hide the blindfold, then piled in beside him and slammed the door. "All right—give it to her, Chink!" he panted and they went off with a jerk that threw Breck's head back.

There had been panic in the gangster's voice. Breck sensed it and wondered what had happened. Certainly the jackers were abandoning their hide-out with every indication of haste.

They went careering down the rough hill road so fast that Breck was scared and breathless. At the foot, the car swung to the left on two wheels and straightened out on the hard surface with a smooth rush. When the jackers spoke it was in monosyllables that gave no hint as to the cause of their flight.

135

The road curved so often that Breck lost track of direction. He only knew they must have been traveling at a breakneck pace for fifteen or twenty minutes when Durfee jammed on his brakes and spun the wheel to the right. There followed several miles of bumpy road which they took more slowly. At length the car came to a stop.

"This far enough?" asked Chink.

"Hm-m, sure, I guess," the Italian replied. "Come on, now, punk, an' step fast."

Breck was hauled out of the coupe and one of the gangsters took each of his elbows. Then they set off briskly over rough, brush-covered ground. There was a sighing of pine boughs overhead and now and then a twig whipped across Breck's face. He could feel something cold on his neck and wrists. It was snowing. Part of the way they climbed, stumbling over bushes and windfalls. Then the ground seemed more level but still wooded. So they must have gone for more than half an hour, until Breck's weary legs would hardly hold him up.

Even the wiry Pasquale was breathing hard when they finally paused, and Durfee, with his heavy build, was gasping. The two drew aside for a moment and talked in jerky whispers, too low for Breck to hear.

"All right, youngster," said Chink, at last. "This is where you're stoppin'. Don't try to follow us. You might get a leg full of lead. Just make yourself at home."

There was a crackling of brush that gradually grew fainter as they moved off. After three or four minutes Breck could hear no sound but the steady rustle and swish of falling snow. It was coming down fast, now, in big soft flakes.

The boy pulled himself together. At least he was out in the open. He had a chance to fight his way to freedom. But before he could accomplish anything he must be able to see. Slowly and carefully he walked sidewise, feeling his way with feet and shoulders. It seemed a long distance that he moved before he encountered anything.

"Gosh," he said with a grin, "if I wasn't hunting for a tree I'd probably bump my head on one in two steps."

At last his moccasin struck a root and he brushed bark with his elbow. It was the work of but a moment to scrape the bandage off against the tree, and he stood blinking at a world of whirling white. The woods around him might have been anywhere in the mountains. There were no land-marks—nothing he recognized as having seen before.

His first thought was to free his wrists from the cord that had cramped and chafed them for twenty hours. He looked around till he discovered a split bowlder with a sharp, rough edge. Backing up to it, he laid the stout manila against the angle of the rock and began to rub methodically up and down—up and down.

It took time, and he had no way of telling what progress he was making. At the end of five minutes he had to rest. He had been without food or water for a whole day now and the effort of rubbing told on him. After sawing away steadily for another five-minute period, he heard a snap and felt some of the tension give, at his wrists. With a mighty tug he pulled his hands free.

Breck had been trying to quench his thirst while he worked, by tilting his mouth to catch the snow flakes. Now he scooped up a handful of snow and stuffed it between his cracked lips. It was hardly as satisfying as a drink but he had no time to do more. The daylight was nearly gone and it would soon be too dark to see.

With renewed eagerness he started to follow the tracks of the jackers out to the road. But where were they? Breck stood staring in dismay at the inch-thick blanket of new snow that lay light and smooth over the ground. Vainly he tried to remember the direction from which he had approached the place. There were no broken twigs to give him a hint. He picked up his cap from where it had fallen when he scraped off the blindfold, shook the snow out of it and put it on his head.

The flakes had nearly ceased falling but dusk was already deep in the woods. Common sense told him that if he struck out blindly he would probably wander all night.

Better to save what strength he had and try to rest and keep warm till daylight returned.

He felt in his pockets. His knife was there, and a handful of matches. With a spruce bough he swept away the snow for a space of several feet in the lee of a big rock. Then he collected an armful of dead twigs and larger branches. From a clump of birches he tore strips of bark, peeling off the dry, papery layers and tearing them in shreds. In a moment he had a good brisk fire going.

There was plenty of dead wood lying about and he proceeded to collect a big pile of it. Food seemed to be out of the question, but at least he resolved to have water to drink. Going to the biggest of the birch trees, he chose a section of the trunk where there were no knots or blemishes and carefully cut away a foot-wide circle of bark. This he folded at the ends and fashioned into an oblong basket, held securely in shape by wooden skewers. It was roughly the shape of a two-quart berry box. He filled it with snow and thrust a green stick through both sides. Then he held it over the fire, close enough so that plenty of heat struck it but too far off to burn. And in five minutes he had melted enough snow for a big, thirst-quenching drink.

By the light of the fire Breck looked around till he found a clump of balsam fir, and cut an armful of soft springy tips. These he placed in overlapping layers a little way from the blaze. At last he was ready to lay his tired body on the bough bed and stretch out his feet to the grateful warmth.

The snow had stopped and overhead he could see a star or two between the tree-tops. Lying there, he wondered about the jackers. Would they come back? It didn't seem likely. If they had wanted to put him out of the way permanently, they had had plenty of chances. He had an idea they were too busy moving their hide-out to want the bother of a prisoner. At any rate he determined to be up and off before dawn so that if they did return they would find nothing but a cold trail. With this firm resolve he threw more wood on the fire, curled up and went to sleep.

Twice in the night he woke twitching from dreams of horror, and sat up listening till the quiet woods and the companionable glow of the fire had reassured him. The third time he was awakened it was by a real sound—a quick, hoarse whistle, startling in its loudness. Without moving, Breck opened his eyes. A faint gray light was stealing among the trees. The fire was reduced to a heap of ashes and a drifting wisp of smoke. He waited, tense with expectation, but the sound was not repeated. It had come, he thought, from somewhere behind him. Inch by inch, the boy moved his chilled body till he could turn his head. And there, not ten yards away, stood a tremendous buck. The deer was still as a statue, one fore-foot poised, great ears upstretched, eyes wide with curiosity. Only the moist, black muzzle worked delicately, searching the

wind. Crowning the stag's proud head were such antlers as no museum held—a pair of rugged butternut boles, big as a man's wrist, sweeping up and out to a dozen points of polished ivory.

For an instant the boy and the buck stared into each other's eyes. Then there was a quiver in the big beast's haunches and he departed in a long, skimming leap that

carried him behind a spruce clump and out of sight. But
as he went he left an unforgettable picture in Breck's
memory. The long, tawny body sailing upward in a graceful arc—the magnificent head and curving neck—and
high between saddle and shoulder the clean white flash
of a scar.

The boy drew a deep breath and clambered stiffly to
his feet. His eyes were shining with a thrill that made
up for the empty ache in his belly, the discomfort of the
cold. Even before he rebuilt the fire he staggered over to
the spot where the great buck had stood and gloated over
the deep, clear tracks. Beyond question they were the
same as the ones he had seen on Whiteface Mountain.

Still in a haze of excitement, Breck returned and kindled a flame with dry sticks from the pile he had collected the night before. By the time he had his patented
snow melter working he had come down to practical
thoughts about his own predicament. It was already light
enough to start, and he figured that whatever direction
he took he must soon come to some hill which would
command a view of the countryside.

Hurriedly he drank as much snow water as he wanted,
and made ready for the trail. It was a simple matter. He
had no duffel, no gun to carry. All he did was pull his
belt a notch tighter around his lean midriff and set forth.
Without having the slightest idea in which direction the

main road lay, he took his bearings by the brightening horizon and headed northwestward. Not even a dimple showed in the clean, new blanket of snow. Once he came to a series of blurred depressions that he thought might be men's foot-prints, but they wandered so aimlessly that he decided they must have been made by a hopping rabbit shortly before the snowfall ceased.

The ground was irregular and the woods apparently endless. There was no definite slope to indicate that a hill was near. Weak as he had felt when he started, Breck seemed to gain in strength as he plodded on. The mounting sun raised his spirits. It wouldn't be long now, he told himself, till he would know where he was.

Since no hills hove in sight he began looking about for a tall tree that might be climbable. Most of those he saw were bare of branches for twenty or thirty feet from the ground and too large to give him a leg-hold. Finally, however, he came on a big spruce standing alone among small hardwood saplings. Its thick limbs grew down to a point just above Breck's head. In a moment he had swung himself into the lower branches and was working his way upward.

So dense were the needle-clad limbs that he could see neither up nor down as he progressed. All he was able to do was worm his body between the close-set boughs and wait for a glimpse of blue sky now and then.

Sixty feet or more above the ground, he reached a place where the branches thinned a little. He rested a while, then went on, finding the climbing easier above. At last, when he had gone so high that the main trunk was small enough to span with both hands, he was able to look around in all directions.

To the north he saw towering peaks, and likewise to the west and south. But none of them had a familiar look. A few miles southeastward a ridge of wooded hills hid the skyline. Bewildered he sat still in the crotch of a limb and studied the profile of the ranges. Possibly he had only seen them from the other side.

Had the jackers driven him northward, then? That was the only part of the county he did not know thoroughly.

For several minutes he strained his eyes to the southward, hoping to discover some sign of a house or a road. But what he finally saw was something wholly different —a white feather of smoke that rose out of the woods, miles away. He waited long enough to make sure that it was moving and then started quickly down the tree. He had seen the morning train puffing up the valley.

Once on the ground, Breck took a bee-line to the south. It was not hard to keep his bearings, for the morning stayed clear and the sun bright. Now that he had a definite objective he settled into a steady, swinging stride and plugged along without thought of his hunger or his aching feet. It was only when he topped a rise and saw a wood-road stretching in front of him that these things made themselves felt. A sudden weakness came over him and he sat down on a stump to rest.

His wrist-watch had stopped for lack of winding while his hands were tied, but he figured it was about ten o'clock when he finally came in sight of a village and a railroad station in the valley below him. Down he went. There was a queer aimlessness about his legs and he felt a bit light-headed, but somehow he made the village street. The sign on the station building said "GLEN." Of course! The place where the gangsters had marooned him must have been somewhere in the woods to the east of Jackson. But his attention did not rest long on the station. Across the road was an ancient railroad coach, transformed by yellow paint into a lunch-car. And the pleasantest sight that Breck's eyes had rested on for a long time was the blackboard outside, that read:

"HAM AND EGGS . . . 30¢"

XII

BRECK felt through his pockets. His billfold, with $7.00 in it, had been neatly extracted by Chink Durfee in the process of searching him. However, in the breast pocket of his shirt he came on a folded dollar-bill, kept for emergencies. If he got a double order of ham and eggs and a cup of coffee, he would still have enough left to call up the warden.

He entered the warm, steamy interior of the diner, fragrant with the smell of hamburg and onions, and established himself on a stool at the counter. A cheerful little Greek, with sweeping mustachios, ducked out from behind the coffee-urn and wiped his hands on his apron.

Breck grinned happily. "Ham—and, twice," said he, "and a nice big cup of coffee."

While the big slab of pink meat was sizzling odorously in the pan, the boy looked around for a telephone. There was no booth to be seen, but an old-fashioned wall 'phone hung by the provision closet back of the counter.

The proprietor made no objection to his using it, and

he was soon calling McArdle's house in West Ossipee. Mrs. McArdle's voice answered.

"Why, Breck Townsend!" she cried delightedly. "I declare, I thought you was lost for keeps. My, but Sam an' the warden'll be glad to hear you're safe. They're out somewhere lookin' for you right now. Where did you say? Glen? Well, just as soon as I can locate one o' the men, they'll come an' get you. Stay right where you be, an' I'll be throwin' a meal together."

"Thanks," laughed Breck. "Don't worry about food. I'm having breakfast now. But if you'd like to do me a real good turn, you might have some water heating. I've had these clothes on for two straight days and nights and I'd sure appreciate a bath."

He ate slowly, relishing every mouthful, and by the time he had finished the last of four fried eggs and sipped the final drop of coffee from the tall, thick mug, he felt completely revived.

He paid his bill and went out to sit on the steps in the sunshine. And before he had been there ten minutes, a familiar-looking old coupe came chugging up the road. Mike Kilday got out from behind the wheel, grinning from ear to ear.

"The return o' the prodigal!" said he, seizing Breck's hand. "Boy, it's glad I am to see yer face ag'in. Pile in here an' we'll snatch ye back to McArdle's."

As they drove down the highway he explained that the warden's wife had reached him by telephone in North Conway a few minutes after Breck had called her. All the deputies, the sheriff and the State Police had been hunting him for the last twenty-four hours, he said. From the time Sam found his tracks and those of the jackers and gave the alarm, the whole county had been aroused. The news of his capture had even reached the Boston papers, and there was a telegram from his father waiting at West Ossipee.

"A lot o' folks seemed to think you'd been bumped off," the big Irishman said. "But not me. These gangsters know it's bad business to wipe out a policeman. Or even a deputy game warden," he chuckled.

As soon as they got to the warden's house, Breck sent off a wire to his father. "Reports exaggerated," he telegraphed. "Don't worry about me. Back safe and sound. Feeling like a king. Could use twenty-five dollars. Home next week, as planned."

While the boy was taking his bath and changing into some of Sam's clothes, Kilday set off to round up the other wardens and notify the police of Breck's return. Before noontime the cars of the searchers began pouring into the yard, and Breck was the center of an excited crowd. Sam and his father were the last to arrive. They had been all the way to Laconia that morning on a tip that the tan coupe had traveled that road.

Sam let out a wild whoop when he saw his chum standing in the yard. "Old Leatherstocking!" he cried. "Where'd they take you? What happened? Tell us about it!"

"It was Chink and Slim got me," Breck answered. "But you knew that from the tracks. I was blindfolded, but near as I can figure they had me in a house somewhere north of the Notch Road, just above Bartlett. It was a regular hang-out. They were selling deer there like hot cakes. Then yesterday afternoon they moved out—scared, it looked like—and they left me in the middle of the woods with my hands tied. I got down to Glen this morning, and here I am. But listen—I wouldn't have missed it. I saw old Scar-back himself, so close I could almost have touched him!"

The warden nodded appreciatively. "I'd like to see that sight myself," he said. "We're goin' to need you for just about one more day, if our plans work out, and then you and Sam can trail the big stag to your hearts' content. Now let's see if dinner's ready. We've got a plenty to do this afternoon."

Immediately after the meal the sheriff arrived. He had some questions to put to Breck. "You saw these gang fellers plain enough to identify 'em?" he asked.

"Yes," said Breck, positively.

"An' they threatened you with fire-arms?"

"They did," Breck replied, "and they kept me a prisoner in a locked room with my hands bound."

The sheriff nodded his satisfaction. "That's plenty to go on," he said. "Kidnaping an officer o' the law. That's how my warrants read. I've got one apiece for Durfee an' Pasquale, an' three blank warrants fer other members o' the gang."

"All right, Sheriff," said McArdle. "Now I think we'd better tell the lad our plan. It's not one o'clock yet, an' we might be able to work it this afternoon. Here's the way things are, Breck. We've got pretty straight information that hunters are getting tipped off where to buy deer by the clerks at Rainey's Hotel, up at North Conway. Remember? That's the place that 'phone call came from, the night after I was hurt. Sam told me about it yesterday. Durfee and Slim have been seen 'round the hotel a couple of times. Now, all of us are known in North Conway. They'd shut up like clams if we tried to find out anything. But they don't know you. What we'd like to do is dress you up like a regular Boston sport, give you some luggage an' a gun in a case, an' let you drive up there an' register. Then you'll see if you can get the clerk to tip you off about jackers' hide-outs. An' when you report back to us we'll round 'em up. What do you think of it?"

"Fine!" said Breck. "It ought to work, and I'll enjoy doing it."

In fifteen minutes the boy had been equipped with a suit-case and an old shotgun. He packed a few shoes and other odds and ends in the bag so that it would not be suspiciously light. And he discarded his red-trimmed hunting cap for a felt hat, tipped at a rakish angle.

Sam bellowed with mirth. "Boy!" he laughed, "you look like the greenest tenderfoot that ever strayed off Boston Common!"

"One thing more," the warden said. "You'll want to flash some money, so the hotel fellers'll think you mean business. Here's a roll—mostly 'ones' to make it bulky. There's $36.00 there. I don't need to tell you to take good care of it."

"Right," Breck answered. "If I register, and leave the bag in my room, I shan't have to spend more than a dollar or two. But if we can spare an hour first, I'd like to run up Bartlett way and find that house where they had me hidden. We might strike some good clues there."

McArdle readily agreed, and it was decided that Breck, Sam and Mike Kilday should make the trip. They went in two cars, Breck and Sam leading the way in the Ford. Sam drove, and after they passed Conway, Breck sat with his eyes closed, trying to recall each turn and hill from his blindfold ride. They took the left fork at Glen and crossed the Saco bridge with the same rumble he remembered. And ten minutes later, just beyond Bartlett, a narrow road appeared, going sharply up the hill. Breck signaled Kilday's car, behind him, and they swung up the rough track.

Half a mile in from the highway the rutted lane led up to a bare, unpainted house. There were wooden steps at the front—four of them. Breck jumped out and went up to the door, testing the steps under his feet. He knew instantly from the feel of them that this was the house, but the windows looked blank and forbidding, and he was not surprised when his knocking brought no answer. Again he pounded on the door and thought he heard a faint creak inside. Then he tried it with his shoulder but found it locked fast.

"Come on," he called to the others, "let's take a look at the shed."

They went around into the side yard and discovered that the shed door was standing slightly open. There were brown stains of blood on the sill and more of it on the floor, inside. And Kilday plucked a tuft of grayish hair from behind a splinter on the door-frame.

"Faith," he cried, "I've evidence enough here to search the place. We'll break in the doors an' see fer ourselves."

"Careful," warned Breck. "I thought I heard some-body move in the house. Better have your gun handy."

The kitchen door, at the side, was fastened only by a loose hasp, and Sam pulled it open with one good tug. There was a fire in the stove, and the place was full of the same stale smell of cooking that Breck remembered. Cautiously they moved through the dirty rooms. In the dark, narrow hallway Breck heard a sniffling sound and made out a figure crouched by the front door, fumbling with the lock.

"Who's there?" snapped Kilday sharply. And a slat-ternly, sullen-faced woman turned toward them.

The big Irishman ordered her out into the light. "Now," he said, "where's the rest o' the gang?"

She shook her head. "Gone," she whined. "Honest, Mister, I ain't seen a one of 'em since yestiddy."

"What!" shouted Mike with a threatening scowl. "You stand there an' tell me Chink Durfee ain't been back here?"

"Not since yestiddy afternoon," she whimpered, "—I mean—who'd you say? I never heard of him!"

Kilday nodded grimly. "Caught ye that time," said he.

"So this was Chink's hang-out, eh?" He looked around at the bare walls while the woman cowered abjectly in a corner.

"I swear I don't know nothin' about it," she blubbered, wiping her eyes with a dirty apron.

Mike turned away from her in disgust. "All right, lads," he called. "Let's get goin'."

The boys had been exploring the upper floors and now reappeared. Breck had found his searchlight and batteries in a deserted bedroom, but otherwise there was nothing of interest in the place.

Kilday winked at Sam solemnly and jerked his head in the female's direction. "Got the hand-cuffs there, deputy?" he asked. "We might's well take her along."

There was a scared pause in the woman's sobbing. "Listen!" Kilday shot at her suddenly. "Where'd they go? Come on, now, tell us the truth."

"Cross my heart, they never told me!" she screamed. "I ain't lyin'—I don't know!" And no amount of questioning could get any more from her.

"Well," remarked Kilday at last, "we've wasted enough time here. What d'ye say, boys?"

They went out, leaving the terrified housekeeper drying her eyes in a corner. When they reached the cars, Breck entered the roadster alone, ready for his visit to the suspected hotel. Sam was to accompany Kilday back to West Ossipee, and they agreed to keep the cars well separated to avoid recognition. It was about three o'clock when the Massachusetts boy drove into the parking place alongside "Rainey's Mountain Inn," as the sign over the porch proclaimed it. There were half a dozen other auto-

mobiles in the yard, but none that Breck remembered seeing before.

A bit self-consciously he took his bag and gun-case and strode up the steps into the lobby. It was a long, low room, showily finished in hunting-camp style, with

155

stained rafters and two or three mounted buck heads on the walls. A little knot of loafers lolled in chairs at the front and eyed Breck lazily as he entered. He went back to the desk and set down his luggage with a thump. A sleek-haired youth took a pen from behind his ear and shoved the small register-book toward him.

"Got a good single room for me?" asked Breck, leaning his elbow on the desk with a bit of a swagger. "Something with running water and a couple o' windows? I like fresh air."

The clerk seemed impressed. "Pretty full in deer-season," he replied, "but I'll try to fix you up. How long you here for?"

"Oh, I don't know," said Breck airily. "I want to do some hunting. Two or three days, maybe."

"O.K.," the clerk answered. "Sign here."

Breck remembered just in time that his name had been in the papers the day before. He pretended to be testing the point of the pen while he thought quickly. Then he wrote the first name that came into his head, "H. Carlton Jennings, Boston."

"By the way," he said, as he finished, "I haven't had much luck getting a deer, so far." He leaned forward confidentially. "Are they—er—fairly thick around here?"

The clerk assumed a polite mask. "Oh, yes," he replied. "Hunters stopping here have killed ten or eleven this season."

"Hm-m-m," said Breck, dropping his voice still lower, "I thought maybe you could tell me where I could—er—get one."

The young man looked at him narrowly. "Why, I shouldn't wonder," he answered. "If you're goin' to be with us several days," he added, pointedly. "Ask me about it tomorrow." And he came around the counter to pick up Breck's bag.

"That's fine," said the boy, as they went up the stairs. "How much?"

"The room? Three dollars," answered the clerk.

"No, the deer," murmured Breck.

"Oh, say fifty—maybe seventy-five for a good buck," the other replied. "Here you are, Mr. Jennings. Back corner room with two windows. Suit you?"

"Yes, this ought to do very nicely," said Breck, looking around critically. And with some ostentation he peeled a dollar-bill off his roll and pressed it in the clerk's palm.

As soon as the door had closed, the boy's face lost its confident smile. He sensed a hitch in the proceedings. McArdle had hoped for a show-down that afternoon, and the clerk's cautiousness made Breck doubt whether he could push matters so fast. He didn't want to arouse suspicion by asking more questions right away.

Frowning over the problem, he washed, brushed his hair at the bureau, thumbed through an old magazine. After ten minutes he wandered restlessly to the window and looked down into the parking place. In the row of four cars his little khaki-topped roadster stood third from the end. Next to it was a big black coupe. He looked at it idly, speculating on what was obviously a home-made paint job. Hasty brush-strokes showed on the top, and the finish on hood and fenders was far from the glossy smoothness one would expect in a car of that make and price.

"That chap must have wanted to go into mourning in a hurry," thought Breck. "Or maybe he was painting against time, trying to win a bet. Looks like about two coats of quick-dry enamel."

Just then the door of the coupe opened and Breck gave a gasp. The man who got out was Saranac Slim.

XIII

BRECK looked again at the black coupe and realized instantly that it was the same car the jackers had been using. It had been repainted overnight. He saw Pasquale step around the rear of the coupe, start toward the side door of the hotel, and pause. Under his low-turned hat-brim the gangster's eyes were studying Breck's Ford. He passed it slowly with a second glance at the rear license plate, then looked quickly up at the hotel windows. The boy had barely time to duck back out of sight. And when he looked again, Saranac had disappeared.

Breck was in a quandary now. He dared not show himself downstairs for fear he might encounter one of the jackers and give the play away. There was no telephone nearer than the lobby or he might have called McArdle. As it was, he saw no course but to sit in his room and wait till the coast was clear.

For a quarter of an hour he fidgeted in his chair and tried to read the magazine. Then he went to look out the window once more. Another instant and he would have been too late to see Chink Durfee open the door of the black coupe and climb in. He was followed immediately by Saranac Slim, who came hurrying out of the hotel, pulling on his overcoat. The big car backed out of the line and swung off down the road to the south.

Breck drew a deep breath. He must take a chance now and work fast. He got into his jacket and hat, snatched up the shotgun and locked his room-door. His heart was pounding with excitement, and he had to wait a moment to steady himself.

"Come on, you nervous ass—keep cool now," he muttered between shut teeth, and sauntered down the stairs, with as much jaunty unconcern as he could put into his bearing.

The clerk looked up at his approach, then appeared suddenly to be busy sorting letters. Breck rested his arms on the counter and forced an affable grin.

"Say," he began in a low voice. "I think I'll go out and get that deer this afternoon. I've got nothing to do and it's still early. I ought to be back here by supper-time, if it isn't very far. Where is this place anyhow?"

The clerk had glanced up now and there was a veiled, mocking look in his shifty eyes.

"Sure, you can get back for supper easy," he replied readily. "Tell you where to go." His voice dropped lower and he leaned close. "You know the road to Madison—

south o' Conway? Three or four miles on that road an' you'll see a wood-trail to the left that goes up between steep banks. It's just beyond a big pine tree, right at the edge o' the road. Follow that trail a quarter of a mile an' you'll see a shack in the woods. That's the place. Tell 'em I sent you an' you'll get what you're lookin' for, all right."

Did Breck imagine it or was there a hint of malice in that last remark? He kept on smiling but he looked steadily into the other's face. The clerk's eyes dropped and he turned back to his mail.

"Thanks," said Breck. "I'll do that."

One or two of the loungers stared at him as he walked out, but he paid no attention to them. In the yard, he had a feeling he was being watched. And sure enough, as he climbed into the roadster he caught a glimpse of the clerk's pasty face at a window. It disappeared instantly, and Breck gave no sign that he had seen it. He backed the car out carefully, turned south, and drove away at a leisurely pace.

Once out of sight of the hotel he speeded up. His first job was to call McArdle and give him the news. At Conway he looked for a telephone sign and found one on a drug-store. There were no customers in the place, and the proprietor sat sleepily behind a counter at the other end of the room from the 'phone booth. Breck nodded to him and entered the stuffy little box, closing the door behind him. In another moment he had the warden on the wire. Briefly he told what had happened and mentioned the inopportune arrival of the gangsters.

"Think they saw you?" asked McArdle, anxiously.

"No, but I'm pretty sure Slim recognized the car," said Breck. "And if he talked to that sneak of a clerk he must have got a description of me. I signed a fake name on the register, of course."

"What about these directions he gave you?" inquired the warden. "Bogus, do you think?"

"Well, no," the boy answered after a second's thought. "But I've got a hunch it's a trap. I tell you I wouldn't trust the clerk an inch. He's framed something on me with Chink and his crowd. They're probably waiting for me to show up now."

"Good!" exclaimed McArdle. "If Durfee and Slim are there themselves, so much the better. I've got the sheriff and two State Police, besides our crew o' deputies. I wouldn't drive along that road alone, if I was you. Tell you what. You come on to Chocorua Village an' we'll meet there an' take the back road up through Madison. Our bunch'll be at Chocorua in twenty minutes, an' that's about what it'll take you to drive down. So long!"

Breck was waiting by the side of the road when the cavalcade of cars appeared from the south. It made a fairly imposing array—McArdle, Sam and Sheriff Jeff King in the warden's car, the two soldierly-looking State Police in a purring gray roadster, Mike Kilday alone in his old coupe, and Hanks and Randall bringing up the rear with a fourth machine.

The warden beckoned Breck to come on and turned his car into the Silver Lake road. After passing Madison he came to a stop and signaled the others to do likewise. When all the cars had pulled out at the roadside and the men had assembled, McArdle turned to the sheriff. "All right, Jeff," said he, "you want to give 'em the lay-out?"

King nodded. "We don't know whether we'll find any-body up here," he began, "but if they're here at all they're likely hid, waitin' to give us a surprise. This wood-road where they're supposed to have a hang-out is just a couple o' hundred yards ahead. I'm goin' to take Corporal Brent with me an' go in on foot from the other side. Sergeant Godfrey and Mike Kilday will do the same thing from here. Give us five minutes to get up near the shack. Then the rest of you'll get in a car an' drive up the wood-road. Everybody got it?"

There was a minute or two of low-voiced consultation, and then the sheriff and one police officer drove on to the top of the next rise, beyond the big pine. When they had parked their car they waved to the others and entered the woods. At once the other policeman and Kilday followed suit.

It was a sober group that waited under the trees. The warden studied his watch and spoke an occasional word to his henchmen. "You haven't got a gun, have you, Breck? Well, I don't figger there'll be any close-range fightin'." He frowned. "I sort o' hate to take you boys into this. Still, I know you wouldn't miss it, if we really find 'em."

There was a pause, while Randall and Hanks slipped cartridges into the magazines of their rifles, and Sam whispered eagerly with Breck.

"Another minute to go," said McArdle. "Better get in the car." The two boys and Abe Randall climbed into the rear seat, and Otis Hanks took his station in front, his Winchester cradled in his arm.

That final minute seemed interminable to Breck. He could feel Sam tense with excitement beside him. At last the warden started the motor and they moved slowly up the road. The old touring-car was far from quiet as it chugged along between the banks of a steep ravine, following the ruts of the woods-trail.

"Gives 'em a fine chance fer a pot-shot—this gully," muttered Randall. "An' they sure can hear us comin'."

"The shack's close now," McArdle said. "Keep your eyes open."

A broad ledge of granite, ten or twelve feet above the road, jutted from the hillside just ahead. Suddenly over the rim of the rock a head appeared, and the wicked blue nose of a rifle.

"Stop right there!" roared Chink Durfee's deep voice. "An', you with the gun, don't make a move or I'll drill you."

The car halted in its own length, not a dozen yards from the foot of the ledge. Two other men showed themselves beside Durfee now, and the three stood up, keeping their rifles trained on the warden and his crew.

"You, McArdle," growled the big jacker menacingly, "you don't seem to take a hint. I've told you twice, an' I'm tellin' you again. You're goin' to lay off of us, see? Now leave your guns in that ice-wagon an' hoof it down the road. Get goin'!"

He punctuated this final command with a shot that blew out one of the front tires of the car. Breck jumped, startled at the report, but the warden sat calm behind the wheel.

"I'll tell you, Durfee," he said slowly, "I'm willin' to admit that right now you've got the better of the argument. We'll go, but you'll see us again. It won't do any good to threaten, because we're goin' to keep right on your trail, an' some day you'll slip."

The gang leader scowled and pumped another cart-

ridge into the chamber. He was just opening his mouth
to retort, when a cool voice spoke behind him. It was the
sheriff.

"Drop those guns," he said, "and put up your hands!"

One of the jackers obeyed. Durfee and the other
whirled about, dumbfounded, to face the covering guns
of the two officers. And at once three rifles in the car were
pointed at the law-breakers.

"It's no use, Durfee, we've got you surrounded," the
sheriff continued. "You're goin' to jail, an' there's no
point in wastin' time."

He slipped a pair of handcuffs on the burly jacker's
wrists. "Yes," he said, "you others are comin' along, too.
March down there, now."

There was no fight left in the gang. They went obedi-
ently down the slope to the road, with Jeff King close
behind them. Bringing up the rear came Corporal Brent
with the confiscated guns.

McArdle and the others had dismounted from the car
and Sam was starting to take off the spare tire when the
sheriff interrupted him.

"Wait a bit," he said. "We'll let the prisoners do that
job," and he motioned the two jackers whose hands were
free to get to work. They grumbled a little but there was
no chance for argument, with the sheriff's Winchester a
few feet from their ribs.

On the opposite bank of the ravine Sergeant Godfrey and Mike Kilday now came into view.

"I see you've got 'em," the policeman grinned. "All right, Mike and I'll go on up to the shack and see what we can find."

They went off through the woods along the top of the

bank, and McArdle and Hanks walked up the road to join them. It was just as the latter pair had disappeared over the rise that Breck heard the whirr of a motor, and a second later the sharp crack of a rifle. With Sam he started at a run up the narrow track in the direction of the sounds.

"Must have been some more of 'em waiting at the shack," Sam panted. "Here, you haven't any gun. Better stay back of me."

They went over a little ridge and saw a low, bark-roofed building just ahead. In front of it stood a truck, empty. The driver was on the ground, facing the leveled guns of the officers, his hands well above his head. Breck needed no second glance to tell him the truck was the one he had seen at the jackers' hang-out in Bartlett. And the driver was the man called "Bunk," who had been with Durfee the night of his kidnaping.

As the truck stood, its right side was away from the group and towards the shack. Breck beckoned to Sam, and the two boys went around the rear of the vehicle. There was no need for explanation. Breck merely pointed to the fender and Sam let out a whistle. "Hey, Pop!" he called. "Ever see this truck before? Take a look at this side. He's crumpled up a front fender on somebody's car, and I'll bet it was yours."

The warden looked and nodded grimly. "That's the truck!" he said. "We'll hold this feller on a hit-an'-run charge. Too bad Saranac Slim got away. He jumped in a black car over there just as we came in sight. Kilday fired at his tire an' missed. This road goes on over the hill to-wards Eaton Center, an' he must be pretty near out there by now. You boys might's well drive the truck down where the others are. We can carry 'em out in that."

Breck hopped up to the driver's seat and started the motor. He had never driven a truck before and there was

a thrill in handling its powerful bulk. By the time he had
it turned around the tire had been replaced on the car and
the posse was ready to start.

Breck drove the truck, with Sam beside him, and the
four prisoners, guarded by Sheriff King and the State
Policemen, occupied the rear. At the road, all the cars
were collected and the triumphant procession set out for
the county seat.

By seven o'clock, when the boys had seen their captives
safely lodged in Ossipee jail, they began to realize they
were tired and hungry.

"Well," chuckled Warden McArdle, coming out of
the sheriff's office, "I guess that settles the Durfee gang.
Chink is due fer about five years in State's Prison, an' the
others won't git off much easier. After what happened
today I don't think we'll see much o' Saranac Slim,
either. He'll leave here in a hurry."

"Guess that means we're out of a job, Breck," grinned
Sam. "Well, we'll have a week's pay coming to us, anyhow."

"And a chance to trail the old King Buck," Breck put
in. "How about it? Ready to start tomorrow?"

"I'll be with you, all right," said Sam. "But what I
want most of all at the present moment is a plate of Ma's
baked beans and a slab of brown-bread. Did you know
this was Saturday night? Let's go!"

THAT evening, when the boys had feasted well on the beans and brown-bread Sam had promised, Breck put through a telephone call to Jim Borden's cabin. The forest ranger was at home and his voice boomed cheerily over the wire.

"Deer-tracking? Sure—I'd enjoy a day of it!" he said. "I came across the big buck's trail only this morning. It was in an old, grown-up pasture on Sabbaday Brook west of Passaconaway Mountain. You say you're comin' up to Wonalancet, first? Well, that'll work out fine. You know the trail over the saddle to the north of Whiteface? Well, there's a spring, down this side a way, right beside the trail. I'll meet you there at four o'clock tomorrow afternoon and we'll make camp and be ready for an early start Monday. Bring along a few provisions and something to cook with, and blankets."

Breck thanked him, and hung up. "Well, that's settled," he said, turning to Sam. "Now we've got to figure out how to build some sort of a flash reflector to take the place of that searchlight of mine. If what Borden says is true, we'll never get a picture of old Scar-back without using flash powder."

Sam's face lit up suddenly. "I've got it!" he exclaimed. "This morning when we were down at Laconia, I stopped in a drug-store to ask if they'd seen Durfee's coupe. While I was waiting I noticed something new at the counter where they sold photographic supplies. You know these big flash bulbs the electric companies are making? Well, they had 'em for sale, and what's more they had 'em rigged up in the head of a regular three-cell light with a big reflector. I've never seen one used but they say they're more efficient than powder. And out in the woods, with wind or maybe rain to bother us, we'd have an awful time lighting an ordinary powder flash."

"Say, I hadn't thought of that," said Breck. "It sounds like just the thing—easy to carry, too. Let's see, how far is it to Laconia? Thirty-five miles? We can get down there and back in two hours tomorrow, and then go right on up to John Turner's for dinner."

Breck was still behind with his sleep and he was ready for bed early that night. Next morning he and Sam made their preparations. They took along two knapsacks filled with food supplies, a few cooking utensils, a camp-ax and a double blanket apiece. Sam had his shotgun and a supply of shells. And of course Breck took his precious camera.

They filled the roadster up with gas and oil and set out for Laconia. Traffic was light, the day fine, and they made good time down through Moultonboro, Meredith and the Weirs. At the store Sam pointed out, Breck bought one of the special three-cell flashes and two extra magnesium-foil bulbs.

"These'll give you plenty of light for a fiftieth-second exposure," the clerk explained. "You have your camera set up and focused, then just open the shutter and leave it open till after the flash."

"Good," said Breck. "It sounds like just what I want. How much range would you say it would give me, out-doors?"

"You ought to get a fairly clear picture at thirty or forty feet, with a good camera," the salesman answered. "You see the reflector throws all the light just where you need it."

The boys returned to the car. "Well," Sam observed as they started north, "looks like we've got to be pretty skillful hunters to get close enough for that snapshot."

Breck nodded. "I've been that close," he chuckled, "only then it was the buck that was stalking me. Yes, it's going to take some time and patience."

At Moultonboro they took the left-hand road to Sandwich and Wonalancet, and reached John Turner's house a little after noon. The big mountaineer gave them a royal welcome.

"We ain't seen as much of you as we'd expected, Breck," he laughed. "But I reckon you've had a good time from all accounts. Must ha' got quite a kick out o' catchin' those guys yesterday, didn't ye? You boys are on the way to bein' famous!"

"Shucks," said Sam, "don't count me in. This fellow's made the front-page headlines for three straight days now. He has to hide in the woods to keep from being pestered by reporters."

Following one of Jeannie's best dinners the boys went up to Breck's room, where he got a change of socks and a fresh shirt to put in his knapsack. "All right," he said, "I guess we've got everything. Salt? Matches? Coffee? We'd better get started now, because it'll take us a couple of hours to cross the saddle."

Duff, the big sled dog, had kept close to the boys from the time they arrived. And when they appeared on the porch with their packs, he trotted up eagerly.

"Hold on, old fellow," laughed Breck. "This isn't your kind of a hike. You'd scare every deer in miles, and it would take a transport wagon to carry provisions for you. No, sir, you've got to stay home this trip."

But Duff was hard to convince. Twice Breck had to

send him back with harsh words, and finally he dragged him inside the house and asked Turner to keep him shut up.

The trail up the mountain had not been traveled since the snow fell, but it was carefully blazed and clear of brush. The boys hit a steady gait of three miles an hour up the first part of the slope. When they reached the steeper climbing they were forced to take it more slowly. Fortunately both were in the best of condition. They made the crest of the saddle in an hour and a half and went on without resting.

"From what Borden said, that spring ought to be about a mile or so over this side," Breck remarked, as they plunged down the northwest slope. "It's close to four o'clock now, so we'll probably see him waiting right on the trail."

He was wrong in that. What they did see was a series of big, broad moccasin tracks in the snow and a twig beside the trail, cut half through and bent to the left. A dozen yards in that direction they found the spring, bubbling dark and clear from under a snow-covered rock. But the moccasin tracks had turned off to the right through the woods.

"That's clear enough," speculated Sam. "He got here ahead of us and cut the stick to show where the spring was. Then he had some business over east there. I figure he wants us to wait for him."

"Sounds reasonable," Breck replied. "We may as well start making camp while we're waiting."

They found an old fire-place of stones, built by other campers, close by the spring. Opposite it, and partly sheltered by a thick-branched spruce, they laid a deep bed of fir tips, broad enough for three. Firewood came next, and they got a good-sized pile of it together before the early winter dusk descended.

"Don't want to start supper till we know when he'll be here," said Sam. "Say, where do you suppose that big moose is? It'll be dark in a few minutes. Maybe we'd better build the fire up, so he can find his way back."

"I wouldn't worry about that lad," Breck chuckled. "If ever I saw a fellow that could take care of himself in the woods, it's Borden."

Nevertheless, Sam kindled the fire and soon had a bright tower of flame lighting up the snowy slope. Then they sat down on the bough bed to wait. It was perhaps twenty minutes later that a voice startled them.

"Looks like a football celebration," it said. "What's the bonfire about?"

For a moment they looked around in vain for the speaker. Then suddenly the big ranger stood right before them. He had slipped up from the other side of the fire, screened by the bright flame.

"That's an old trick," he laughed quietly. "More than one tenderfoot has been shot from behind a big fire like yours. That's one o' the six reasons why an Indian on the trail never builds a fire much bigger than his hand."

"I know," Sam nodded in embarrassment. "I don't do it usually, but—well, we wanted to light you into camp."

"That's right good o' you," the ranger grinned. "You didn't need to, though, because it has to be almighty dark before I lose my own back-trail. What have you got for supper?"

"Bacon and johnny-cake, if that suits you," Sam replied. "I'll start it right now."

The boys had brought along a light wire grid which they proceeded to set over the fire, while Borden slung off his pack and stretched his huge shoulders.

"I've been moving pretty steady since sun-up," he explained. "Feels good to take the harness off. I'd have waited here for you, but I got here so early I decided to hike over north a bit. Wanted to see how the young pine was doing in that burnt-over patch. By the way," he added, looking at the corn-meal batter Sam was mixing, "could I have a spoonful o' that? I've got a little friend here that may be hungry."

Out of the loose breast of his mackinaw he carefully

drew a bundle of gray-brown feathers. It was a rumpled little hen-grouse. He held her gently in his huge hands and the boys could see her beady eyes blink in the fire-light.

"See that wing?" said the ranger. "It's broke. And worse'n that would have happened to her if I hadn't come along. She'd gone to roost in a little jack-pine, and a fox sneaked up on her. I came in sight just as he made his jump. He'd pulled her down and was tryin' to get a fresh grip with his jaws, to carry her off, when I hollered. 'Course, he dropped her then and skipped out. If I can get her home safe I'll make a pet of her. Maybe she'll raise me a brood o' little chicks."

Holding a bit of moist corn-meal between thumb and finger he placed it at the end of the bird's bill and talked to her soothingly. After a little, she opened her beak for a tentative nibble. When she had been persuaded to eat several mouthfuls he wrapped her carefully in his ban-danna and placed her on the balsam bed.

"You're pretty good friends with the animals, aren't you?" said Breck, who had watched the feeding with in-terest.

"Some," Borden smiled. "I don't have much time for the ones that make trouble—the 'varmints' as the old-timers call 'em. My friends are mostly the ones that need friendship. I keep a gun loaded at the cabin for weasels an' foxes an' such-like."

"Come an' get it!" called Sam, and they came. Bacon and johnny-cake on bark plates and tea in tin cups took up their attention for the next few minutes. But when the meal was finished Breck turned the conversation back to animals. He liked to hear the giant woodsman talk.

"They say the deer are coming back, here in the White Mountains," the boy suggested. "What do you think?"

Borden nodded and sat back contentedly against a tree. "That's true," he said, pulling out his old black pipe and tobacco pouch. "Not just 'round here but all through the East. I was raised in Pennsylvania an' didn't go out to Idaho till fifteen years ago. When I went away there were mighty few deer left in my home county, an' I got a great kick out o' seein' herds of blacktail an' even elk in the Rockies."

He paused to strike a light for his briar. "When I was sent back East," he said between puffs, "I went to spend a month with my folks. That was three years ago. An' I found the Poconos so full o' deer that you couldn't drive ten miles after sunset without seein' a dozen of 'em. Tame, too. They come right down to the villages some-times. Last year the State estimated there was close to a million deer in Pennsylvania."

"It's the same here in New England," Sam put in.

"Pop says there are more deer now than any time since he's been warden. They come down to the abandoned farms in the Summer and Fall, before the hunting starts. You can see 'em any time around dusk, stealing along in the edges of the old meadows and orchards, eating the wild hay and windfall apples."

"Yes, but where did they go to when they were so scarce, and why are they coming back now?" asked Breck.

"I reckon they weren't any place," Borden chuckled. "They were killed off, all but a few, an' those were driven back into the deep woods. The market hunters used to shoot 'em all year 'round in the old days. Freighted the venison, dried an' salted, to the towns by wagon-loads. It was cheaper'n beef or mutton—poor folks' meat. That was before the game laws were so strict or so well en-forced. I sometimes think it's a miracle the deer didn't follow the buffalo and the passenger-pigeons right out o' the picture.

"Well, what happened was a survival o' the fittest. An' the deer won. They hung on an' the market hunters died out. If you wardens can keep the jackers licked, there's no reason why the herds shouldn't be just as plentiful as they ever were, in a few more years."

"Gee, do you honestly think so?" asked Breck.

Sam was smiling and shaking his head. "According to old accounts I've read," said the warden's son, "the pioneers in colonial times claimed they found 'em as thick as leaves on the trees. I don't believe they'll ever be that plenty. Look at the number of hunters that come up here to kill deer legally every year. Won't they keep the herds down?"

"Wait a bit," Borden replied. "What would you say there are—seven or eight thousand hunters in the White Mountains in a good year? Suppose five thousand of 'em get their deer—one apiece, killed accordin' to law. That's all done in November, an' only grown animals are taken. Then allow there's five thousand more killed for meat by the backwoodsmen, an' a few by the farmers when they're damagin' crops. That's about all, isn't it? The young fawns an' their mothers aren't molested much in Spring an' Summer.

"Now remember that in those days when they were 'thick as leaves,' there were six or seven thousand Indians in this section, livin' on deer-meat most o' the year. An' the Indians didn't begin to kill as many as the wolves an' panthers an' lynxes did. All those natural enemies are wiped out now. A few bob-cats in the mountains still, but they wouldn't tackle anything bigger'n a baby fawn away from its mother. Why shouldn't the deer multiply nowadays?"

"It does sound reasonable," Sam admitted.

"You mean there were a lot of wolves right here in

New Hampshire?" asked Breck. "How long ago was that?"

"There were still some, seventy years ago," said Sam. "I remember hearing Granddad tell how he shot one

when he was a boy. It was trying to break into the sheep-pen."

"Yes," nodded the ranger. "An' I reckon before that they were a regular scourge. They'd travel in pairs or little packs of four or five an' run the deer to death. Then in the winter, when they'd find a herd yarded up in the deep snow, they'd slaughter 'em by the dozen."

"I wonder if the wolves mightn't come back, too," Breck mused, "when the deer get plentiful enough."

"It's not likely," said Borden with a smile. "Though they've been havin' trouble with 'em over the line in Quebec. Every Winter I hear some story about a timber-wolf bein' seen, but usually when you trace it down you find the chap that saw it had been takin' a drop too much, or he's not sure but what it was a stray police dog. With the cruisin' I do around this part o' the forest, I guess I'd be liable to run across a wolf about as quick as any-body."

"Well," yawned Sam, "wolf or no wolf, I'm going to turn in. And I think it's going to be cold tonight, so I fend the middle o' the bed!"

As he was already leaping for the coveted spot when he made this last announcement, there was not much chance for argument. Breck laughingly took his blanket to the east side of the bed, and Borden, when he had knocked the ashes out of his pipe, lay down on the west. For a while there was murmured conversation across the fir tips. One or another of the trio would roll over to get his blanket snugged around him and be advised in no uncertain terms to shut up and lie still. At last they were all too comfortable to move and too drowsy to talk. A gentle bass snore came from the ranger's end of the couch. Sam was the next to succumb, and the last thing Breck remembered was the sound of their deep breathing, min-gled with the soft crackle of the fire.

He had no idea what time it was when he awoke, nor what had roused him. Yet there he lay, tensely alert, his ears straining for some sound. The fire was out and the woods looked chill and ghostly when Breck lifted his head to peer around. At first he saw nothing but black tree-boles and pale snow. Then something moved—something big and dark and furry, that slipped noiselessly among the spruce clumps twenty yards away. With the cold prickles running up his spine, Breck reached for the flashlight that lay between him and Sam. His fingers clutched it—fumbled with the switch. The beam of light swept in a quick arc through the woods and came to rest, reflected in a pair of close-set, slanting, yellow eyes.

XV

WAKENING in the middle of the night to see that prowling shape so near had shaken Breck's nerves. The flashlight trembled a little in his hand but the unblinking yellow eyes in the brush never wavered. They were a good two feet above the ground—those eyes. And gradually the staring boy began to make out the outline of the beast behind them—the square, furry head and pointed ears.

A sudden certainty darted through Breck's mind. "Wolf!" He almost cried the word aloud. But three seconds later he was sheepishly glad he had not uttered it. With a quick movement the animal left the cover of the spruces and came straight toward him. And in the full beam of the light he saw instantly that it was Duff! The big sled dog uttered no sound but he was grinning from ear to ear with satisfaction as he trotted to Breck's side.

"Why, you old son-of-a-gun!" whispered the boy. "Come here, now, and lie down. No, stay off that bed.

Don't you dare wake anybody else. Curl up right here, and keep me warm on this side."

After a few damp caresses applied indiscriminately to Breck's face and hands, the husky turned himself around three times and flopped down in the snow in a tight wound ball of fur. And so they slept till morning.

When Breck opened his eyes again Sam was still comfortably snoozing at his side, but Borden was already going quietly about the breakfast preparations. A clean, hot fire was blazing under the grid and water was heating for coffee. Duff, it appeared, had investigated the tall stranger and approved his presence. He sat now with head cocked on one side, watching the stirring of the pancake batter.

Breck stood up and stretched, breathing deep of the brisk air of morning. "I see you and Duff don't have to be introduced," he said, walking over to Borden, by the stone stove.

"No," laughed the big ranger. "He looked me over pretty careful before he'd let me build the fire, but we're pals now. Your dog?"

Breck explained the sled dog's unexpected appearance and told of his own fright in the night. Borden was amused but not unsympathetic. "I've been fooled that way myself," he nodded. "Once, out West, I shinned up a tree to get away from a bull elk I thought was chargin'

me, an' it turned out to be a stray heifer. What with all
that talk about wolves before we went to bed, it's a mercy
you didn't shoot the dog."

"I believe I would have, if I'd had a gun in reach,"
said Breck. "But the thing that's worrying me now is
what to do with him. It's half a day's hiking from here
to Turner's and back."

"Pshaw!" Borden replied. "Don't worry about him.
Take him along. He won't be any trouble unless you get
right close to the deer an' you can always tie him up to
a tree."

Since Sam showed no signs of rousing, they woke him
by the old approved method of jerking up one edge of
his blanket and rolling him out. And by the time he
and Breck were done tussling in the snow, Borden called
them to breakfast.

They were ready for the trail by eight o'clock. The
ranger fed his hen-partridge a few crumbs of flap-jack
and placed her tenderly in the breast of his mackinaw.
Then he strode out in the lead, his weather-worn knapsack on his back.

"We have to leave the regular trail just below here,
an' cut north towards Potash Mountain," the big woodsman announced. "The old meadow where I saw the
buck's trail is half a mile to the west o' the hill. Holler
out if I get movin' too fast."

If he was intentionally slowing his pace it was not obvious to his companions. Those long legs of his swung along in a four-foot stride that had the boys puffing within half a mile. They followed the crest of a northward sloping ridge that dropped gradually toward the valley of a little stream.

"Downes Brook," said Borden laconically. "There's Hedgehog over on the right." He pointed to a steep, heavily-timbered little mountain a couple of miles to the eastward. They crossed the brook and climbed a wooded spur that ran down from the Sleepers. At the top the ranger paused and looked back at his companions with a grin.

"Thought I'd hear a yelp from you fellers before this," he said. "I've been hittin' it up a bit, I admit, though this is about the gait I generally travel when I'm alone."

Breck and Sam were red-faced but undaunted. "I'm ready to sit down for a minute," gasped the warden's son, and suited the action to the word.

"It's only a mile or so further," said Borden. "Better get your wind now, because you'll want to keep pushin' when we come on the deer-tracks."

When they started again it was down hill and the ranger went at a more leisurely pace. They struck straight west to a blazed trail that followed the course of Sabbaday Brook, and turned to the right. Soon the woods began to open up ahead. The spruce and hemlock gave way to scattered birch-clumps and jack-pines, and finally they came out on a tiny intervale a hundred yards across.

"Here's the place," said Borden, "an' here are my tracks, two days old. Over by that old apple-tree we'll see the deer-trail. I reckon this must have been a farm, fifty or sixty years ago."

Duff was trotting ahead as they crossed the open meadow. Suddenly he stopped and sniffed the snow. "I didn't know you had a huntin' dog," said Borden jokingly. "Let's see what he's found. By cracky, it's deer-tracks, an' they're fresh!"

There they were—the prints of three or four does threading the snow in a slender line. And woven into the dainty pattern were the big, bold tracks of a giant buck.

"If I was a Blackfoot hunter," said the ranger, "I could tell you just how many hours old these are—whether they were made last night or early this morning. It's a cinch they haven't been here more'n twelve or fourteen hours, though. See how the snow has sifted into those tracks of mine a little? But there isn't a bit of it in these. The last time the wind blew strong was yesterday afternoon."

Breck studied the great buck's trail with the same heart-pounding thrill he had felt that day on the Whiteface Ledges. He stood up and shifted his pack for greater comfort. "All right," he said, "Let's go!"

At the lower end of the meadow they found a trampled space where the little herd had paused to browse among feathery tufts of wild hay. "Come on," cried Sam. "Every time they stop, it puts us closer to 'em!"

The deer had gone on with short, unhurried steps, following the eastern slope of the valley down toward Swift River. This country they were in now was several miles west of Sam's shack and beyond the end of the river road. The woods ran down unbroken to the edge of a steep ravine with the frozen stream at its bottom. The trackers had traversed something over five miles since breakfast and descended a good two thousand feet.

"Well," remarked Borden, "if that ice held old Scarback I reckon it'll hold us. He must weigh close to 350 pounds."

They slid down the bank and tested the snow-covered surface. It was firm enough, and they followed the deer-trail to the opposite shore. There the tracks bore northwestward, skirting the base of a rounded hill.

"Heading for the Deer Ponds, I'll bet a cooky!" Sam exclaimed.

"What are they?" asked Breck.

"You'll see in a few minutes," the warden's son answered. "They're a couple of little ponds at the head of

a swamp where there's a lot of alder and blueberry bushes
—good deer feed. They lie right on the county line between Carroll and Grafton."

But before they reached the Deer Ponds they found
something that changed their course. In the middle of a
spruce thicket on a high knoll the herd had lain down
to rest. Four smoothly pressed hollows in the snow
showed where the does had couched. Duff sniffed eagerly
at each place, and Borden knelt to look closely into the
packed forms. "These are so fresh they're almost warm,"
he announced, after a moment's inspection. "Here's a
green-briar shoot that hasn't sprung back yet. They
haven't been gone twenty minutes!"

"Do you suppose they caught our scent when we were
coming up from the river?" Breck asked. "You see the
King didn't lie down at all. Here are his tracks circling
around the thicket as if he was anxious about something."

"They did get wind of us, sure as shooting," called
Sam, from the far edge of the spruce clump. "When the
does left here every one of 'em jumped clear over to the
other side o' that log to break the trail. Gosh, what a
jump! It's better than twenty feet. I just happened to
strike the tracks over there or I'd have been hunting
yet."

"But the buck didn't jump with them," Breck put in.
"Look at this! He went off up the hill here, but he wasn't

in any hurry. See—he stopped twice to look back. You might almost think he wanted to leave an extra plain trail."

"Sure he did," said Borden. "If he found the herd was being followed, his first idea would be to get rid of the does and have us trail him. He knows all the tricks, this old feller! Now we have our choice. We can stick with the herd and likely catch up with 'em before dark. There's a chance he may cut back an' join 'em tonight. Or we can take out after the stag an' try to wear him down. Which do you want to do?"

Breck thrilled to the challenge of the big buck's strategy. "If it was left to me," he said, "I'd follow Scarback."

"Me, too," nodded Sam.

"All right," the ranger answered. "It means no dinner, an' maybe ten or fifteen miles of tough hiking. But if you're game to try, there ought to be some fun in it. Come on!"

That was an afternoon to test the boys' courage. Again Borden set the pace and there was no easing up in his stride. The buck had traveled slowly for the first two miles. Then, on a high spur they found where he had stopped, watching his back track. And after that the trail went away in long bounds, hard to follow through the brush of the cut-over country. Down into the next valley it led, and across the rusty track of an old lumber railroad. Then north toward Sawyer River and the white, towering summit of Mt. Carrigain.

"A couple more miles an' he'll be walkin' right in my front door," chuckled Borden. But the big deer had no intention of leading the ranger home. A few minutes later they found what seemed to be the end of the trail, in front of a heap of brush. Sam went around the pile, supposing the buck had leaped over, but there were no tracks on the other side. Puzzled, they cast about in all directions without finding a trace.

"What in thunder—" blurted Sam. "Did he take off and fly?"

Again they ranged in a widening circle, thirty feet—forty feet from where the tracks ended. "No deer could jump this far," said Breck. "We've got to figure it out some other way." He went back to the last of the hoofprints and stooped low above them. Then he turned and followed them in reverse, examining each one.

"I've got it!" he cried at last. "Look at these tracks again. They're all a little blurred. The dewclaw prints aren't clear. That's because he was back-tracking, stepping in the same spots. And right here"—he pointed—"the old cuss stopped backing up and jumped sidewise. See how the snow is thrown out on the left? I'll bet he lit just over beyond that juniper bush!"

With that the boy took four or five strides to the right and shouted in triumph. There under the sheltering fringe of the juniper were the close-gathered tracks of the buck's landing.

Borden whistled. "I told you he knew some tricks," he said, "but this one beats 'em all. I'll take my hat off to you, Breck, for a real tracker. I'd have been foolin' around here the rest o' the afternoon."

They pulled their belts tighter, settled their packs and took up the trail again. The cunning old stag had swung back at a sharp angle to the east after his startling maneuver. Over a wooded rise it led, and dipped into the valley of a little stream. There the buck had stopped to drink, where the water fell unfrozen over a ledge, and the trailers were glad to do likewise. Through the afternoon they went on, past Sawyer Pond and the steep southern ledges of Owl Cliff, and as they climbed, Borden pointed downward to the trail.

"He's tired," said the ranger. "Short steps, see?"

"I sure hope he is," Sam gasped. "If he's any tireder than I am, he's lyin' down right now."

They were toiling up a hillside at the moment. Ahead of them, on the crest, was a dense thicket of young growth, and suddenly there came a commotion in the midst of it. Breck caught a glimpse of a big reddish-gray form bounding to its feet and dashing away on the other side. The boy hurried forward at a run and reached the summit in time to see the huge buck skimming down the open slope beyond. He went in great sailing leaps, and

his feet seemed barely to touch the snow. Breck, watching that effortless speed, felt his own weariness drag at his limbs like a leaden weight.

"Huh!" he said bitterly. "He's playing with us! How can anybody catch up with a thing like that?"

The others had come up now, and stood in silence watching the buck flit out of sight in the distant woods.

"He was sure going, wasn't he?" muttered Sam.

"Going! He was flying!" Breck growled in reply.

Borden laughed. "You boys aren't going to give up already, are you?" he asked. "I thought you chose to follow old Scar-back because he'd give you a run for your money. Well, he's giving it to you. An' you may not believe it but he's tired this minute—as tired as you are. I don't think you'll get close to him tonight, but another day of steady trailing may do it. Remember, he's scared and nervous. He won't sleep a wink all night. By this time tomorrow he'll be lying up in every thicket he comes to—watching his back trail an' trying to rest."

The tall ranger turned and looked at the sun. "I hate to leave just as the trail's getting hot," he said, "but there's only about an hour more o' daylight an' I'm supposed to be back in camp tonight. I have to 'phone my report in. Good luck, an' don't forget to send me one o' the pictures of the buck when you've taken 'em!"

Breck looked at him quickly, suspecting a jest, but there was only honest friendliness in the big, tanned face. The boy thrust out his hand. "We'll take 'em," he said, "and you bet we'll send you one!"

They said good-by and watched Borden go striding off toward the far blue dome of Mt. Hancock. Then Sam turned to Breck with a grin.

"How d'you feel now?" he asked. "Let's keep on till dark an' then make camp at the first water we come to."

"Sure thing," Breck agreed. "I guess we're not as tired as we thought we were. But these packs do get heavy!"

They settled down doggedly to the trail again. For the next mile or two it was down-hill and easier going. The buck's frightened burst of speed had not lasted long. A hundred yards after he entered the woods he had settled down to a walk, stopping to look back at frequent intervals. At the bottom of the valley the trail crossed another lumber line and a brook, then swerved northward around the rugged side of Bear Mountain. Once, as the boys came puffing to the top of an open ledge, they sighted a party of hunters in a clearing to the north.

"Come on, get out of sight," panted Breck. "We don't want any outsiders following this track."

They ducked hurriedly into the woods and followed the stag's foot-prints in a long curve along the mountainside. The sun had long since dropped below the summit and it was growing dark as they entered the gap between Bear Mountain and Table Mountain. Luck favored them in finding a camping-spot, for hardly had they crossed the saddle when the buck's tracks led to the brink of a good-sized spring. There they slung off their packs and drank. Tired they might be, but they were hungry, too. In twenty minutes Sam was brewing tea and broiling the last of the bacon.

"I don't know what Duff's going to eat," he said, "but

if he's a real husky a little starvation won't hurt him. Here!" and he tossed the bacon rind to the expectant dog.

"We'd better tie him up tonight," Breck suggested, "so he won't go off foraging and be missing in the morning."

They made the big dog fast to a tree with a piece of cord and rolled up in their blankets on an armful of spruce boughs beside the fire.

"Gosh," murmured Breck, "I could lie right here for a week." But there was no one to hear him, for Sam and Duff were both sound asleep.

XVI

"WHAT in tarnation!" Sam was mumbling, when Breck opened his eyes. "Look what that dog has gone and done!"

In the early morning sun the boy stood holding the frayed end of the cord with which they had tied Duff. But the animal himself was nowhere to be seen.

"Skedaddled in the night!" exploded Sam. "Probably be miles away when we want to start."

They tried whistling, without result.

"Oh, well, he'll find his way home," said the warden's son. But Breck did not take it so lightly. "I should have taken him back in the first place," he told Sam. "Duff's a valuable dog, you know, and John Turner would be pretty much cut up if anything happened to him. I think I'll go and see if I can find him while you're getting breakfast."

"All right, but make it snappy," said Sam. "It won't take long with what we've got—a couple of flap-jacks is all there's flour for."

Breck's legs were a bit stiff, but otherwise he felt none the worse for his long day's trailing. He found the big dog's tracks following those of the buck for a short distance down the valley. Then the deer prints ended. Old Scar-back had broken the trail with one of those long jumps of his, and the baffled Duff had wandered off in a zigzag course up the steep flank of Bear Mountain. The boy tracked him for a quarter of a mile, calling and whistling as he went. It was no use. The dog did not appear, and finally, when he paused to listen, he caught Sam's hail from up the valley, faint and distant. Perhaps Duff had returned to camp.

Breck cut back along the hill, and had not gone fifty paces when a strange sight stopped him in his tracks. A good-sized grayish animal scuttled across an opening just in front of him and plunged into the brush. It had exactly the look of a mother cat carrying a kitten in her mouth. The next instant, the boy realized that what he had seen was a big bob-cat with a captured rabbit. But before he could make a move something flashed past him with a rustle of padded feet. A dark-furred thunderbolt charged into the clump of bushes that concealed the lynx, and a second later there was such a babel of yowling and spitting and growling as Breck had never heard before.

"Duff!" yelled the boy, recovering from his surprise. "Get him, boy! Eat him up!"

Out of the brush tumbled a ball of gray fury that seemed all claws and teeth. And right after it sprang the sled-dog, undaunted. Duff's deep fur stood him in good stead now. Without its protection his hide would have been cut to ribbons by the swift-striking claws of the desperate cat. As it was the fight did not last long. With a deep-throated snarl the husky leaped in. His big wolf-jaws snapped shut on the gray beast's back and he jerked the lynx high into the air. That ended the struggle. In another moment he was worrying at his victim's throat.

Breck pried the bushes apart and found the rabbit lying where the cat had dropped it. It was a full-grown cotton-tail, still warm with the life that had been in it ten minutes before. Whipping out his knife the boy quickly skinned and dressed the rabbit, then called to Duff and took the shortest way back to camp. Before he reached the spring the dog overtook him, trotting with the dignity befitting a victorious and well-fed warrior.

"For Pete's sake!" sputtered Sam. "I thought you were lost, too. Found him, did you? I don't know what he'll have for breakfast unless you want to give him your flap-jack."

Breck grinned. "Don't you worry about the food-supply," said he. "Duff had a whole bob-cat for breakfast. He oughtn't to be hungry again for a week. And what's more, here's our dinner, in case we don't pass a grocery-store." He held up the rabbit before Sam's astounded eyes.

"What in time—how'd you catch him—with your bare hands?"

"Sure," chuckled Breck. "Just ran him down. I'll show you how some time," and between sips of coffee he gave the true account of the morning's adventure.

When the meager breakfast was disposed of they got under their packs once more and made a start.

"Here I've been lugging this gun all over two counties and haven't fired a shot yet," Sam grumbled. "And if you keep on bringing in game, I might just as well have left it home."

"You've no cause to grouch," returned Breck. "My camera's getting heavy, too, and unless we get a move on and come up with the King it's not going to be much use to us."

Two or three minutes' searching showed them where the buck had landed after his side-leap, and to their joy the trail led on southward.

"He's heading back to his old stamping-ground around Swift River and the Passaconaway range," Sam declared.

"We know that country 'most as well as he does, and we'll have a better chance to outguess him."

When they had covered a little more than a mile the tiny water-course which the tracks had been following dipped steeply into a narrow valley, and at the bottom they saw a road and a larger stream.

"What did I tell you?" asked Sam triumphantly. "There's Swift River now. We'll find where he swung west towards Paugus as soon as we get across."

But instead, the big stag's trail continued southeast. It climbed through a second-growth slashing and rounded a rugged hill, and on the heights above Hobbs Brook they came on the thicket where Scar-back had made his bed for the night. From the much-trampled snow around the form they judged that he had done little sleeping.

"Come on," urged Breck. "He's worried, just as Jim Borden said. I wouldn't be surprised to see him jump up almost anywhere ahead of us, now. I'm going to get the camera ready and try a quick-exposure shot, if he does."

The buck had crossed the brook a little way above, and skirting the eastern edge of the swamp had gone on southward. As they descended the next ridge they could see the State Road straight ahead and hardly a mile away.

"This isn't so good," said Sam, with a frown. "If he

keeps on this way, we'll be chasing him right into some
fool hunter."

"Maybe," admitted Breck. "But I'll bet on the King.
He's been trailed before, and I reckon he won't be out-
smarted by any city sport."

Ten minutes later they crossed a broken-down stone
wall and found themselves standing in an old wood-road.
The deer had jumped from beyond the wall and it took
them a moment of hunting to discover where he had
landed. It was Breck's eye that first spotted the tracks,
far over at the edge of the brush on the opposite side.
But just as he was about to announce his find he saw
something else that took his breath away. Close to the
print of the stag's foot ran the track of an automobile
tire, and at that particular place it was clearly marked.

"Look here, Sam!" he whispered. "The car that made
that track went through here last night or this morning,
and it's Saranac Slim's coupe, as sure as you're born.
I've got so I'd know that Dalton tread in my sleep."

Sam studied the track, then turned suddenly and
stared down the road. His face wore a funny look. "Do
you know where we are?" he asked.

"No. Why?" said Breck.

"We're right up behind that old barn you and I found,
the night we were shot at," the warden's son answered.

"I knew we were close to it, and I'll bet this lane leads right down into the farm-yard."

"Well, it shouldn't take us long to go and see," said Breck. "Come on!"

They had gone only a few hundred yards down the winding wood-road, when they came in sight of a weather-worn roof and a chimney. That was the house. The barn, backed up under the hill, was not visible until they had come out of the woods into an unkempt pasture.

"Careful, now," said Sam, "if the gang is still using this place as a hide-out we want to be mighty sure they don't see us. Better let me go ahead. They don't know me, and with this gun I can pass as a hunter. You keep the dog here."

Breck took hold of the short length of cord still tied to Duff's neck and waited while Sam went cautiously down to the door-yard. After a few minutes he reappeared, beckoning his chum to come on.

"There's nobody here now," Sam reported, "but they've been here within a day or two. There's some fairly fresh tire tracks in the yard."

They opened the barn door a foot or two and slipped inside. As on their previous visit the place was empty. And yet as Breck looked about he could have sworn the dust had been recently disturbed. Though it lay thick on the beams and rafters, the floor was brushed clean in many places.

"No use staying here any longer," said Sam. "We'd better get back on Scar-back's trail."

They started out the door and were about to close it when Breck missed the dog. He looked around the yard and whistled once or twice, then peered inside the barn again. Back at the rear of the dimly lit floor he heard a snuffing and growling.

"Come here, Duff, you sap!" he called, impatiently, but the husky only growled the louder. Both boys went back to the pile of old lumber, from which the noise came. Behind the broken-down sleigh Duff was crouching, his nose pressed to a crack in the boards.

"Here, get out your flashlight and let's look at this," said Breck.

In the beam of the light they saw a section of boarding, about four feet square, which had been sawed out of the back wall and then carefully replaced. In the semi-darkness behind the sleigh, it was so well concealed that they had completely missed it before.

Breck got his fingers under the bottom and felt it give a little as he pulled. At the second tug the section came neatly out in his hands. He stood it to one side and bent to look into the hole.

"Whew!" he coughed. "It smells like a butcher shop!"

And at that moment Duff tried to rush past him through the opening.

"Here—hold him!" cried Sam. "It's full of deer carcasses in there. Look at 'em! Hung up in rows!"

The earth of the hillside, against which the back of the barn was built, had been dug out for a distance of perhaps fifteen feet, leaving a deep, narrow vault. It was higher than Breck's head when he stood inside, and the roof was shored up with stout timbers. From beams along the two sides hung the bodies of nearly a score of deer.

"Let's get out of here quick, and find a telephone!" urged Sam. "This'll be the biggest haul yet. But if they catch us here, somebody'll get shot!"

Breck replaced the door of the cave as rapidly as possible and they hurried out into the yard, pulling Duff with them. The coast was still clear. They took no chances on being seen from the entrance road and made a wide detour through the woods to the east.

"There's some houses up the highway, between here and Lord's Mill," panted Sam as they pushed along. "We'll come out about a quarter of a mile above the wood-road, if we keep on this way."

There was a farm in sight, when they emerged on the main road, and to their relief there were telephone wires running up to the house. A brisk little gray-haired woman

FROM BEAMS ALONG THE SIDE HUNG THE BODIES OF SCORE OF DEER

answered their knock at the door, a belligerent expression on her face.

"May I use your 'phone, ma'am?" asked Sam. "It's on State business." And he turned back the lapel of his jacket to show his warden's badge. The woman peered at it through her spectacles, then looked shrewdly at the two boys.

"Indeed you may, young man," she said. "An' I only hope you're goin' to report some o' those hunters. They've druv me wild comin' to the door, all hours, an' askin' fer the Varney place. That's that old farm back in the woods a ways below here. I suspected you was some more of 'em when you come to the door."

Sam went in to the telephone while Breck held the talkative lady in conversation. "Do these hunters ever tell you what they want at the Varney place?" he asked.

"No, can't say they do," she admitted. "But I've got my suspicions." She nodded violently and pursed her lips. "Rum!" she whispered dramatically. "Rum an' beer! I've seen furrin-lookin' fellers drivin' trucks up that road. That's why I gen'rally give 'em the wrong directions when they ask."

Breck was properly sympathetic. "Do you ever see the hunters' cars when they come away from the place?" he asked.

"Not often," said she. "Too drunk to drive, I guess."

The talk was interrupted by Sam's reappearance, his face flushed with excitement. "I was lucky!" he exclaimed. "I got Pop just as he was leaving. He'll be up here in fifteen minutes, with Kilday and Randall. We're to go down and watch the entrance road."

They thanked the woman and departed before she could ask the questions that were evidently on the tip of her voluble tongue. A moment later, as they tramped down the side of the highway, a big open car roared past. The top was down and there were three men in the front seat. A few hundred yards beyond the boys, the car slowed down and turned abruptly into a side road on the right.

"That's the place!" cried Breck. "And that's one of the jackers' cars. Did you get a look at any of those men?"

"No," said Sam, "but I'd know the machine 'most anywhere. We couldn't have timed it better if we'd tried."

They reached the road and were standing there waiting when another car appeared. It was a small sedan, moving slowly. The two men inside wore hunting caps, and there were shot-guns in the rear seat. At the entrance to the Varney place they stopped the car and looked at the boys but asked no questions. Finally the driver said, "This must be the place," and started the sedan up the narrow track.

Hardly had the sound of the engine died away when

Sam pointed down the road. "Here comes the U. S. Cavalry!" he exclaimed gleefully, and waved to the occupants of the ancient McArdle car.

The warden pulled up. "What about it? Have you seen anybody?" he asked, glancing up and down the road. Sam told him about the two cars.

"Good!" nodded his father. "The touring-car sounds like the one that Frenchie, DuBois, was drivin'. The others must have been a couple o' customers. All right, hop in, boys. We'll ride up as if we were in the market for a few deer, ourselves. Keep your guns down but have 'em ready for business."

And as soon as the boys had packed themselves and Duff into the rear seat, the sturdy old car went rumbling up the road.

XVII

THE corner of the dilapidated gray house hid the rear yard and the barn, and the warden's party could see nothing of what might be going on there.

"You'd think they'd have a guard posted," muttered Sam, and eased his shotgun up under his right arm, ready for emergencies.

The car was moving only about ten miles an hour as it crossed the open yard in front of the house, and at the moment they turned the corner there came a shrill, piercing whistle from somewhere inside. That could mean only one thing. The jackers must have had a sentry at one of the windows!

At the sound, McArdle jammed on his brakes and jumped out, lifting his rifle as he reached the ground. The other two deputies were as quick as their chief, and Sam soon followed. The four advanced in open order toward the jackers' touring-car and the small sedan. The barn door stood wide and the city men were just carrying out the carcass of a buck when the raiders appeared. Some of the gangsters were evidently inside the barn for the door began rolling shut.

"Hold that!" barked McArdle. "Come out here, you, and don't start anything!" And under the menacing guns of the law, two of the jackers came sullenly out.

Breck, unarmed, had stayed in the car, holding on to Duff. He had, however, slipped off his pack so as to be able to move fast if the need arose. From his seat he could command both the front and the side of the house. Just as the pair of law-breakers were leaving the barn the boy heard a faint noise at the house door and turned in time to see a third man go scuttling across the front yard.

Breck was out of the car in a bound and the sled-dog was with him. "Go get him, Duff!" he cried, and they tore into the brush on the heels of the fugitive.

The man ran crouched far over and he went with surprising speed. Breck gained on him a little but he was still a dozen yards behind when the flying Duff closed in. The jacker must have heard the big dog behind him, for he half turned and fired an automatic under the crook of his arm. It was too late. The husky was in the air, in the middle of his spring, and the shot went wild.

The next second, a hundred-pound avalanche landed on the gangster's shoulder and felled him sidewise with terrific force. The breath was knocked out of him, and before he could squirm his arm free to shoot again, Breck was on the scene. It was the work of only a moment for the boy to pinion the wrist of his gun-hand and twist the pistol out of his grip. Then, panting but triumphant, Breck rose and hauled Duff off his cowering victim. It was none too soon, for the big dog's fangs had been inches from the jacker's throat.

"Get up here," Breck ordered. And when the man had staggered to his feet—"Now march ahead of me back to the house." Getting a good look at his captive, the boy recognized him as the swaggering Frenchman, DuBois, who had been fined at Conway. There was no nonchalance in his bearing now. The ferocity of Duff's attack had left him scared and shaken.

Sam, who had heard the shot, came hurrying to meet them as they neared the house.

"Hot dog!" he shouted. "Another one! Hey, Pop, Breck's got the Frenchman."

Back in the barn-yard the round-up was complete. Under the surveillance of McArdle and Kilday the jackers were carrying deer out of their hiding-place and loading them into their touring-car. Twelve carcasses were piled in the tonneau and tied on the fenders, and when the car was filled to capacity there were still half a dozen bodies left. The city "sports" had been standing sheepishly by during the raid. Now the warden turned his attention to them for the first time.

"I'm not goin' to arrest you," he said gruffly. "But I'm goin' to commandeer your car for about an hour. We can put the balance o' these deer in there an' get 'em down to Ossipee."

In a few minutes they were ready to start. McArdle, Kilday and Randall took the three prisoners in the warden's car. The hunters followed with their loaded sedan. And Breck and Sam drove the big machine with its freight of contraband venison. It was just noon when they rolled up in front of Ossipee Court House. The business was swiftly handled. Fines amounting to $3600 were imposed on the jackers, and they had less than a thousand among them. In default of payment they were taken up to the jail to think it over. The two shamefaced hunters were dismissed with a reprimand from the magistrate.

Two hours later McArdle and the boys had finished dinner at West Ossipee, and Duff had been rewarded for his part in the day's work with a big juicy steak-bone.

"That winds up the jackin' racket in Carroll County," remarked the warden, as he lit his cigar. "Those fellers were hangin' on, tryin' to cash in on the deer they had hid. But from what we know about 'em this accounts fer the whole batch. You noticed Saranac Slim wasn't around. He skipped out when Durfee was caught, I reckon."

"I'm not so sure he did," said Sam thoughtfully. "We found the tracks of his coupe up there back o' the Varney place, an' they looked as if they'd been made within a day or two. Still, maybe they were older. We haven't had snow since the night Breck was left in the woods."

"What do you boys plan to do about yer camera hunt?" asked McArdle with a twinkle. "Ain't goin' to leave the ol' King Buck in peace now, are ye?"

"No, sir!" said Breck stoutly. "Back on the job this afternoon. Only I'm in favor of going up to Wonalancet first and getting the roadster. You'll be needing your car and we can save a lot of footwork if we have some way to get around fast. Besides, I expect John Turner's wondering about his dog."

They borrowed the warden's machine for the trip and by four o'clock they were in front of the Turner house. Duff bounded out of the car to greet his master on the steps.

"Worried about him?" said the backwoodsman in answer to the boy's query. "No, I figgered he was with you an' safe enough. Soon's I found his tracks follerin' yours I knew where he'd gone."

They told him how Duff had knocked down the gangster that morning and described his battle with the bobcat. The big dog sat by with ears cocked and grinned with satisfaction while they praised him.

"He won't be able to follow us this time," said Breck. "We're going to take the car. So long, Duff, old-timer."

He ran the Ford out of the barn and followed Sam's tail-light down the long hills through the early dark. When they reached the warden's home they held a consultation. Both of them had had enough of sleeping out for the time being, and they decided to stay in West Ossipee for the night.

"We can get a real night's rest an' set the alarm for five o'clock," said Sam. "Then we can be on the stag's trail again before daylight."

It was so arranged. They replenished the provisions in their knapsacks and made ready for an early start. When the alarm clock roused them it was still pitch dark out-

side and the room was chilly enough to prevent any
dawdling over their dressing. They went shivering to the
kitchen and opened up the range fire. And in a few minutes Sam had coffee boiling and eggs frying.

"Eat hearty!" urged the warden's son with a grin.
"This is the last square meal you get till tomorrow afternoon."

"Tomorrow afternoon?" asked Breck. "What makes
you think we'll be back by then? I aim to stay out, this
time, till I get a picture."

"Say—have you forgot what day this is?" Sam
chuckled.

"Wednesday, isn't it—" Breck counted on his fingers,
"the twenty-sixth of November? Why, of course! By
golly, Sam, I'd clean lost track of the calendar! Tomorrow's Thanksgiving!"

"Sure it is," the other replied. "And you'll be insulting
Ma if you aren't right at that table with a napkin tucked
in your collar at three P.M."

When they were well warmed and fed they sallied out
through a white rime of frost. The east was showing a
pale streak at the horizon by the time they got started.
Breck drove up the highway past Chocorua Pond and
turned in at the Varney place. They found the lane leading up from the barn-yard was passable and decided to
take the car as far as they could. It was slow going and

bumpy through the pasture, but as soon as they got into the wood-road it was possible to move faster.

"Hold it!" said Sam, after a moment. "There's the place. See our tracks coming over the wall?"

Breck turned the Ford around and ran it under the thick canopy of a spruce beside the road. "All right," he said, "here's where we put on the harness."

The boys strapped their packs on, took the gun and the camera, and picked up the buck's trail where they had left it twenty hours before. It was harder to follow now than when it had been fresh, because in many places the smaller folk of the wood had criss-crossed it with a maze of assorted tracks. For a short distance only it bore south. Then the buck had turned at an abrupt right angle to the west, heading for higher ground. And at the rugged foot of Nickerson's Ledge he had started a long swing northward.

"I knew it!" said Sam in triumph. "He's cutting back around Chocorua. Remember, the wind was north, yesterday? He was keeping tabs on us with his nose. And when he went off the trail he knew it mighty quick."

The trail led steadily upward toward the saddle between Blue Mountain and the Three Sisters. It was a stiff climb and the boys were glad to rest at the top after two hours of back-breaking work. The sun was well up now and it promised another fine day. Before them stretched a narrow valley, leading down to Swift River, and high on their left they could see the Three Sisters Fire Tower, a slender black frame-work against the sky. To the limit of the horizon there was no other man-made thing in sight.

"Pretty, isn't it?" mused Sam.

"Great!" Breck answered, stirring himself. "But we can't look at it any longer. Don't forget that buck has got a whole day's start on us."

They plunged down the northwest slope and into the green hush of the spruces. And before they had gone a quarter of a mile Sam, who was leading, pulled up short with a sudden exclamation. He looked questioningly at Breck, and pointed to the snow ahead. Directly across the trail they were following cut another, clear and fresh —the tracks of half a dozen deer. They were heading south toward Chocorua. All the tracks but one were those of does. And that one was the huge, unmistakable print of the Passaconaway stag.

"Who said he had a day's start?" cried Sam gleefully. "Not now, he hasn't! This trail is new—made this morning. He thinks he's shaken us off, too, or he'd have been careful not to give us this break."

"I don't know how much of a break we've got," Breck replied. He was down on one knee, bending over another track, two or three yards away and paralleling the line the deer had taken. It was a man's trail—the marks of rubber-soled hunting moccasins sharply printed in the snow.

Sam lost his grin as he stared at the tracks. "Say— that's bad!" he murmured. "Somebody else following the buck!"

"Not just 'somebody else,' either," said Breck. "Unless there's another man wearing shoes exactly like Saranac Slim's, he made those tracks himself."

Sam nodded slowly. "I'd forgotten," he said, "but I'm afraid you're right. It's funny, though, that he'd be hunting in daylight. Seems as if it must be some one else."

"Well, maybe so," Breck admitted. "But anyhow, it's up to us to keep out of sight. Whoever it is, he won't welcome strangers horning in."

"Huh!" snorted Sam. "Who's horning in if he isn't, I'd like to know?"

They went ahead swiftly but with greater caution than before. The deer appeared to have been taking their time, nibbling at alder shoots as they went along. And for the most part the man's tracks moved steadily beside theirs. There was one place, however, where he had knelt on his right knee behind a waist-high screen of bushes. Ahead, the trail lay open for some distance and putting two and two together, the boys decided that their rival must have seen a possible shot and taken aim.

"He didn't shoot, though," Sam declared. "If he had, he'd have reloaded his gun and we'd find the empty shell. Besides, I think we're close enough to hear a shot. The deer must have moved and spoiled his aim."

Breck had been silent and scowling. At last he blurted out what was on his mind. "I don't know how you feel about it," he said fiercely, "but if there's any way to stop his getting a shot at those deer, I'm going to do it. Nobody's going to kill our buck while I'm around."

"Right!" agreed Sam. "But don't get excited. The buck's too smart to let any ordinary hunter get within shotgun range."

"I'm not worried about shotguns!" Breck fumed. "But suppose he's got a high-power rifle?"

"Golly," Sam muttered, taken aback, "that's something I hadn't thought of. And if it's really Slim—say, let's get going!"

They hurried forward along the plainly marked trail, looking ahead constantly for some sign of the hunter. But strangely enough it was the deer that came into view first. The boys were coming over the top of a rocky ridge, bare of trees, when Sam ducked suddenly behind a bowlder and motioned Breck to join him.

"Over in that little meadow, beyond the next valley," he whispered. And when Breck peered around the rock he saw them—half a dozen red-brown spots against white snow and a dark wall of pines.

"Careful," said Sam, "the King'll be watching his back-trail because what wind there is, is coming from the west, and he can't depend on sound or smell."

Crawling almost on their stomachs they moved from rock to rock and finally gained the shelter of the wooded valley below. Hardly were they among the trees when they saw the man's track cutting away diagonally up the mountain to the left.

"What the—" frowned Breck. "Look at that! He was running! Do you see? Getting up to leeward for a shot. Come on, Sam!"

They left the trail of the deer and sped along on the hunter's tracks. He had not run far but the wide-spaced foot-prints showed that he was still moving rapidly. After two or three hundred yards, Sam plucked at Breck's sleeve. "Go easy," he whispered. "We're getting close now. See, he's turned down-hill again."

Breck felt his throat tighten with excitement. He stepped carefully to avoid cracking sticks, and yet some inward urge told him he must hurry. Ahead, he could begin to catch glimpses of sunlit snow. They were nearing the fringe of the woods, and the open meadow lay just beyond.

A dozen strides more, and Breck came to a noiseless

stop, pointing with a hand that trembled in spite of him. Between the trees he had a clear view of two does nibbling the withered grass. They were a scant hundred and fifty yards away—an easy shot with a good rifle. And even as he looked, the great buck moved into view beside them. His mighty head was lifted, tensely watchful, his eyes fixed on the back trail.

At Breck's side, Sam was slipping the pack straps from his shoulders. He laid the knapsack down and held out the shotgun to his companion without a word. Bewildered, Breck took it, and saw Sam creep forward stealthily, one step at a time. Only then did his eyes fall on the gully just in front of them and he gave a startled gasp. Sprawled on the far edge of the depression lay a man. He was facing the meadow and sighting along the barrel of a repeating rifle at the giant stag.

XVIII

FOR a full second, Breck stood paralyzed. Then he saw Sam launch himself in a long dive toward the prone body of the hunter, and he woke to action. Dropping the camera, he hurried forward, holding the shotgun ready for use. Sam's swift and silent attack had caught his adversary unprepared. Landing squarely on his back, the boy knocked the breath out of him. And before he could roll over, Sam had wrenched the rifle out of his grasp.

As the warden's son scrambled to his feet, the man turned, crouching, his face twisted with the snarl of a cornered rat. It was Saranac Slim.

"Tryin' to kill deer with a rifle, eh?" panted Sam. "You're under arrest, Pasquale."

With a quick movement, the gangster's right hand started for his jacket pocket, but Breck forestalled him. "Up with 'em!" he snapped. "Reach for the sky!" And he was looking down the cold, blue length of the shotgun as he spoke.

Sam strode forward. "Keep him covered, Breck," he said. "I'll see if he was bluffing."

In the pocket was a wicked-looking automatic, which the boy promptly confiscated. "You're through, Slim," he smiled triumphantly, "and there's nothing you can do about it. So just walk along ahead of us."

The rage and fear in the jacker's face had given place to a mask of sullen calm. "Okeh," he said softly. "I'll come along. Only I'm tellin' you right now you spoiled a thousan'-dollar shot. I ain't kiddin' you. A rich sport from Boston offered me a grand for that buck's head."

Involuntarily Sam turned to look back at the meadow, and Breck checked a similar impulse just in time. Their prisoner had tensed for a spring. He straightened up again as he met Breck's glance, and gave a silent chuckle.

"Are they still there?" the Massachusetts boy asked. He spoke without taking his eyes off the shifty gangster.

"Yep," Sam answered. "They've moved off a little way, but they didn't see us."

The trio marched back through the woods in silence. Slim went first, followed by Sam with the shotgun, and Breck came last, carrying the camera and rifle. It was a good four miles back to the car by the way they had come. An hour and a half of hiking brought them into the old wood-road. Breck was tired, and he couldn't help wondering why Slim, fresh and unencumbered, didn't make

HIS MIGHTY HEAD WAS LIFTED

a break for freedom. As it was, the gangster went forward peaceably enough. But with the attempted trick stirring in his memory, the boy was wary. He gave a grunt of relief when they reached the car.

"Better put the duffel and guns in the rumble," muttered Sam. "We can sit three abreast in front and I'll keep him covered with the automatic."

They opened the rear deck and thrust the gun and rifle inside. Then, both at once, they began to remove their knapsacks. Breck was just slipping out of the last shoulder strap when he saw Saranac spring like a cat into the front seat. The ignition key! He had left it in the car! There was an instant whirr from the starter and the motor roared. Sam, still struggling with his pack, was powerless to do anything. It was up to Breck, and he had no time to run around to the far side of the car. As it darted away, he caught the back of the rumble-seat with his hands and managed somehow to haul himself aboard. Pasquale must have seen him in the rear-view mirror, for he hurled the tough little car down the trail at breakneck speed. It rocked and plunged like a canoe in white water, and Breck, clambering around to the right running-board, was all but shaken loose. At last he gained his objective. His left hand was on the top of the door, when something struck it a hard blow across the knuckles. A jolt of pain shot up the boy's arm but he hung on, jerked open the door and pulled himself inside, all in one desperate lurch.

He flung his left elbow into the gangster's face and reaching for the switch with his right hand he shut off the ignition and threw the key on the floor. Then they battled for the wheel. It was a brief struggle, breathless, with life and death as the stake. The roadster swerved, poised on two wheels—righted itself by a miracle—and began to lose momentum. In another moment Breck got a grip on the emergency-brake and brought them to a grinding stop. Under him he felt something hard. It was a black-jack—the same weapon that had broken his knuckles the moment before. Without a second's hesitation he crashed the shot-filled leather down on the gangster's head and saw him slump limply over the wheel.

Breck himself was near exhaustion, sick with the pain in his hand. It was two or three minutes before he could sit up, and when he did, it was to see Sam running down the road.

"Gosh," panted the boy, white-faced, as he came abreast of the car, "I was afraid he'd killed you!"

"Better see if I've done for him," answered Breck shakily. "I—I hit him with this thing."

Sam pulled the gangster out of the seat and laid an ear to his chest. "Heart's beating," he announced. "He'll come out of it. Sa-ay! What happened to your hand?"

The back of Breck's left hand was puffed to twice its normal size and an ugly purplish white in color. "Busted, I guess," he answered. "I can't seem to close it any more. I can drive, though."

With his right hand he helped Sam hoist the unconscious jacker into the seat between them, and after collecting the knapsacks, they started for West Ossipee.

Saranac Slim stirred, groaned and opened his eyes just as they drove in under the warden's elms. Sam got out first and kept him covered with the pistol, but there was little need of it now. The gangster managed to climb dizzily out of the car and was led, unprotesting, into McArdles' living-room. A telephone call brought the sheriff to the scene within twenty minutes, and Dr. Moffat arrived immediately after. The medical man examined the prisoner's head and to Breck's relief assured them that his skull was not fractured.

"You did exactly right, my boy," said Sheriff King heartily. "It wasn't any time to fool with him. This chap's as dangerous as a rattlesnake. I've already called up the United States Marshal, an' he'll be up tomorrow. Meanwhile I've got a few scores to settle with Slim, myself, an' I'll see that he's kept mighty safe in Ossipee jail."

The doctor had closed his surgical case and was preparing to go, when Sam stopped him.

"Hold on, Doc," he exclaimed, "we've got another patient here."

Breck had been holding the throbbing hand behind him. "Oh, shucks," he laughed, "this isn't anything. We'll lose those deer if we don't hustle back there."

But Dr. Moffat took one look at the injured member and shook his head. "It's broken, all right," he said. "Two middle bones of the hand, just back of the knuckles. You oughtn't to try to use it for three weeks."

He saw the look of disappointment in Breck's face and smiled. "I don't see why you can't go back in the woods, though, as soon as I get the hand set and properly bandaged. Let's see what we can do right now."

An hour later, the two boys had eaten a hurried lunch and were in the roadster once more. Breck was glad to let Sam do the driving, for his hand, rigidly splinted and swathed in bandages, was still painful.

"Isn't there some way we can get in closer to that meadow with the car?" he asked.

"Yes," said Sam, "I was going to suggest we could drive up the wood-road to Champney Falls. That's only about a mile from the place where we sighted the deer. It'll be twelve or fifteen miles further by road because we'll have to go up to Conway, first. But it'll save a heap of walking."

It was early afternoon when they left the car—locked,

this time—at the head of the Champney trail. Up the rocky slope to the west of the Three Sisters they followed a blazed path made by summer campers, and in half an hour's climbing they came on the tracks of the deer-herd.

"Say," mused Breck, "this is a part of the trail we haven't seen before. Even Slim wasn't following them when they came by here."

"Maybe these tracks aren't as fresh as the ones we found this morning," Sam replied. "They're not heading in the same direction either. Let's follow 'em a little way."

The trail led obliquely down a rocky hillside to a bare ledge, twenty or thirty feet wide and running for a hundred yards along the mountain. Except for a few sheltered patches, the snow had been melted off by the sun, and at the edge of the rock the deer-prints vanished completely.

"Now," said Breck, "if I hadn't spent two days watching that buck's mind work, I'd probably go straight across the ledge and expect to find tracks on the other side. But he came here for a reason, and that was to break the trail, just in case anybody like us was around."

"Correct," Sam nodded. "We'll go in opposite directions from here and holler if we find anything."

Breck turned northward. He knew better than to walk

along the rim of the rock. Instead, he went into the woods below and held his course parallel with the ledge and a dozen yards beyond it.

What he was looking for was a bush or a thicket, screening the rim of the ledge, and when he found it, a

moment later, his eyes went straight to a cluster of deep dots in the snow. The deer had jumped from the rock, just as he figured, and landed beyond the bushes, so that their trail was hidden from above.

"Oh, Sam," he called softly, and when the other lad joined him they followed the tracks southwestward down the mountain. In spite of the descending slope of the ground it was hard going. The tangle of vines and brush grew constantly denser, and bowlders and fallen trees blocked the path. Before them the woods seemed impenetrable.

Sam, stopping to clamber over a ridge of rock, stared in dismay at what lay ahead. "Do you see that hemlock thicket," he asked. "If they went through there we'll have to quit. It's the sort of place where you wriggle on your belly and cut your way with a knife."

But the tracks turned to the left at the edge of the hemlock growth, skirting the thicket to the south. Suddenly the boys stopped in bewilderment. Beside a huge fallen log the tracks joined a maze of others, and half a dozen deer-trails converged at the spot, leading from as many different directions.

"These tracks go both ways," said Sam. "And some of them are days old. Look—here's where old Scar-back came once before. What do you reckon this is—some sort of meeting-place?"

Breck looked around him carefully. "I've got it," he said at last. "Hold on—don't go too near that log. We don't want to leave our scent all over the place."

"Why not?" asked Sam curiously.

"Because we're coming back here, and so are the deer," he answered. "I'll bet you right now that there's a place in the middle of these hemlocks where they sleep. I wouldn't have guessed it, except that I saw a mark in the snow, there on the top of the log. A doe jumped over it and didn't lift her feet quite high enough. One of them flicked the snow off and left a groove. She must have landed or taken off right in the thicket. Lift me up and let me look over on the other side."

Stepping in Sam's cupped hands and steadying himself by a tree, Breck was able to command a view of the brush on the other side of the log. "Yes, sir!" he whispered excitedly, "there's a passage through there, and I can see tracks, a little way in."

The boys withdrew a short distance to discuss their find.

"I think you're right," said Sam. "I've heard o' these hidden 'yards' from some o' the old hunters. The deer don't use 'em every night, but as long as they're in the neighborhood an' don't know they're being chased, they're likely to lie up here. There's only one thing against it to-night. The wind's southwest. And the entrance, if that's it, there behind the log, is on the south side of the thicket. The old King Buck might decide it was too risky to go in unless he could get the scent o' the place first. That's something we'll just have to chance."

"All right, what's your idea?" asked Breck.

"The only way I can see is to burrow our way through, somewhere on the north edge of the hemlocks, an' wait for 'em to come in. The whole thicket isn't more than fifty yards across, and we ought to be close enough for a picture if they get inside without hearing or smelling us."

"Great!" Breck exclaimed. "That's just what I was thinking. It's about three-thirty now, and it'll be dark in two hours. We may have to wait most of the night, but I'm game to try it if you are."

They spent a few moments in a scouting expedition around the northern side of the covert, but found no other deer tracks. Apparently the herd always approached the place from the south.

"Well," said Breck, at length. "It doesn't make much difference where we try to get in as long as it's on this side. It won't be easy anywhere." Crouching on hands and knees they began crawling through the mass of thick-grown bushes and interlacing twigs. Handicapped by his bandaged fist, Breck was content to let Sam go ahead, cutting a path with the camp-ax where it was necessary. At last the warden's son paused in his labors and looked back with a grin. "There's daylight ahead," he panted. "Five minutes more and we'll know what's inside this deer-castle."

XIX

AFTER a brief rest Sam again attacked the stubborn under-growth. It was a matter of hacking out a tunnel as far ahead as his arm would reach, then creeping forward a foot or two and starting afresh. When he had progressed a few more yards he squeezed his body to one side and motioned Breck to come up. They were through the worst of the thicket. Beyond were a few bushy little hemlocks, forming a waist-high screen. And when Breck rose to his knees he could see over their tops.

In the center of the thicket was an irregular open space, nowhere more than thirty feet across, and walled like a room with evergreens and young birches. But it was the floor of this woodland chamber that gave him a thrill. In the middle, the snow was trampled hard and flecked with deer-sign. Even around the nearer edges, hundreds of dainty tracks dotted the white, and every birch twig, from the ground to the height of a man's head and higher, was stripped of its tender bark.

Sam had already had his view of the place. "Breck,

we're in luck," he said, his eyes alight. "You know we'd never have got close enough to take a picture if we'd kept on following the buck. This way, I honestly think we have a chance. It all depends on how suspicious he happens to be, and whether the wind holds."

Breck nodded. "If we're going to stay here and wait," he said, "we'll need room to stretch out in comfort. I'll go back to that last little brook we crossed and get a canteen of water while you're trimming out some more here. We'll have to do without supper, I guess. I wouldn't want to build a fire anywhere near here."

When he returned with the water, Sam had a space about four feet square cleared of brush, and had brought in the gun, camera and duffel. They wrapped their blankets around them and made themselves as comfortable as possible. Breck looked over the camera carefully. "We've got to plan everything while it's still light," he said. "I think I can handle this box. I'll steady it with my arm and open the shutter with my good hand. The flash will be up to you. If you hold it just above those two little hemlocks—so—it ought to light the whole place like a ball-room. I'll be right over here with the camera. You listen hard and when you hear the shutter click open, you'll know I'm ready. Then you'll have to work fast, because old Scar-back'll hear it, too."

They went through the motions two or three times for

practice, then settled down to wait. With the sunset it grew cold in the woods. There was a mournful sighing of wind in the taller evergreens, and through it came the occasional faint chirp of a winter bird going to its roosting place. The boys wrapped themselves closer against the chill and sat there hunched and silent.

Breck's worst fear was that one or both of them might fall asleep. As it grew darker he nudged Sam every little while, and was impatiently nudged back. They knew how silently the deer would come and they were afraid even to whisper, now.

The steady strain of watching the dim, white oval of the clearing made Breck's eyes water and ache. He longed to close them just for a moment but fought off the inclination doggedly. How long they sat there he did not know, for his wrist-watch had been removed to make room for the bandage. The night seemed ages long. Half a dozen times he was on the point of giving up the vigil in disgust, but at last he decided that morning could not be far off. He would stick it out till dawn.

Then he was blinking his eyes in astonishment. For a moment he thought he was dreaming those shadows that drifted so slowly across the open space. A stealthy shove from Sam's elbow told him they were real. Two, three, four—he could count them now—slim, dark creatures with great, inquisitive ears. And then he saw the King.

Without a sound, without even the rustle of a bough, the biggest shadow of them all slipped out of the black wall at the far side of the clearing. It hesitated, took two cautious steps forward and stopped again, testing the traitor wind. Inch by inch Breck brought the camera upward to rest on his knee. He could see nothing through the finder, but he pointed it by touch, making sure the line of vision cleared the hemlock bush at the right. Then, trying to control the trembling in his fingers, he laid them on the shutter release.

"Whoosh!"

With startling loudness the buck had whistled, then moved. He was nearer—poised for a tense instant, right in front of the does. Breck clicked the shutter open. And suddenly the secret place of the deer was illumined by a sheet of white light, brighter than noonday.

It lasted but a fraction of a second—that illumination—and the dark that followed was black as the pit. But whatever the camera had caught, Breck knew the picture he had seen was worth all the toil it had cost. Shaking like a leaf he closed the shutter and sat staring ahead of him. When his eyes were adjusted to the night again the glade was empty.

"Whew!" breathed Sam, at his side. "There was more kick in that than I ever got hunting with a gun! I'm as weak as a cat, now it's over. How'd you make out?"

"All right, I hope," giggled Breck. "If I didn't I'm the prize boob o' the world. Gosh, what a chance he gave us!"

"Yes," interrupted Sam, "an' I thought you were never going to get that camera set. Seemed as if I just couldn't wait any longer, for I was sure he'd jump clean out o' the place any second. I bet he knew something was wrong just as soon as he set foot inside!"

For several minutes after the tension was relaxed they chattered like a pair of magpies. Then Breck rose and stretched his legs. "Well, now we can get home in time for breakfast," he yawned.

"Breakfast!" cried Sam. "Say, what time do you think it is?" He hauled out a pocket flash and pointed it at his watch. It was just five minutes after ten.

Breck's laughter mingled with Sam's and went ringing through the woods. If any one else was on the mountain that night he must surely have thought there were lunatics at large. The boys collected their duffel, crawled out of the thicket and started for home. Sam went ahead with the flashlight and Breck followed, carrying the camera as if it had been a basket of eggs. When they were in the car and headed out to the highway, Breck lay back luxuriously in the seat.

"It's been a grand two weeks," he chuckled. "Probably

not exactly what the doctor ordered, but I never felt better in my life."

He was quiet for a minute. Then, "Do you suppose the big stag will ever come back to that place?" he asked.

"I was just wondering the same thing," said Sam. "Gee, I'd hate to think we'd scared the old boy away for good. Did you ever see a neater hide-away? No wonder he's kept his health all these years!"

"Well, we don't need to worry about him," Breck grinned. "He's probably got a dozen strongholds like that. And if he hasn't, he can find 'em. The mountains are big, and he's wise."

They were at home and in bed before midnight. Next morning Sam was still snoozing peacefully when Breck walloped him with a pillow.

"Hey!" grunted the warden's son. "Don't you know it's Thanksgiving an' a swell morning to sleep?"

"I know it's half-past eight," Breck laughed. "And we've got to rig up a dark-room and do some developing."

"Gee, that's a fact!" said Sam, tossing back the covers. "Go ahead to breakfast and I'll be with you in a jiffy."

Mr. McArdle and his wife were almost as excited as the boys over the success of their expedition, and little else was discussed during the morning meal.

"Now you've taken the buck's photo, Breck, I reckon

you've got all you come up here for—and maybe a little extra," beamed the warden.

"Don't be too sure about the picture," Breck warned them. "It may not show a thing but his feet, or the back side of a bush. Or I may have jiggled the camera. We'll just have to wait and see. Sam and I are going to work on it this morning."

"Fine!" said McArdle. "That'll keep you busy while I do some telephonin'. I may have a surprise for you a little later," he added mysteriously.

The New Hampshire boy had experimented with amateur photography before, and he quickly transformed his mother's big linen closet into a dark-room. They carried in buckets of clean water and a couple of wash-basins, and covered the lens of a hand-flash with four or five thicknesses of red paper to give them light. Then Breck took the film out of his camera, handling it as gingerly as if it had been a tube of radium.

There was a breathless twenty minutes while the film was in the developer. The boys looked, waited, looked again, and Sam burst forth in an excited whisper. "It's there! You got him—every inch of him! Boy, what a shot!"

Breck washed the film carefully and put it in the hypo bath. Then followed another half hour of impatient waiting. When at last it was "fixed," they rushed at top speed to the kitchen. Breck placed a soup-plate in the sink and set the film to wash under a stream of water from the tap.

"How does it look?" inquired Mrs. McArdle eagerly. But Breck shook his head. "You wouldn't be able to tell much from the negative," he said. "In three hours this ought to be dry and then I'll pull half a dozen prints. If I don't do anything to spoil it, I think it'll be quite a picture."

The boys spent the rest of the morning alternately passing a football in the yard and running in to make sure the drying negative was safe.

"Land's sakes!" cried the warden's wife cheerfully. "How many more times are you youngsters goin' to traipse through my kitchen? First thing you know I'll put aprons on you an' set you to work!"

Breck offered to help, but she sent him on his way with a laugh. "No, indeed!" she said. "When I'm gettin' a Thanksgivin' dinner I don't want any men folks under foot."

By one o'clock the film was dry enough to print. And an hour later the boys were proudly bearing the first finished picture into the living-room.

"Pop," Sam grinned, "you told me once you never saw a stag with more than ten points. Well, you're going to see one now! Old Scar-back's got twelve. Count 'em your-self."

The warden took the print in his hand and stared in amazement. "Great jumpin' Jehoshaphats!" he murmured. "Look—at—that!"

It was worth looking at. The camera had caught the buck in clean-cut outline from the frosted tips of his antlers to his black and shining hooves. His head was up—his startled eyes wide—his nostrils distended. Even the white scar on his shoulder showed clear. Close behind him were the huddled shapes of the does, and then the background of white snow and somber forest. It was one of those perfect pictures that camera-hunters dream of.

The warden was still finding details to marvel over when a horn sounded in the yard. From the window they saw two men getting out of a car. One was Sheriff Jeff King. The other was a stranger—a tall, quietly-dressed man with a square jaw and pleasant eyes.

"Howdy, Jim!" cried the sheriff, as McArdle threw wide the door. "I see those young deputies of yours are here. I've brought a gentleman who's anxious to meet 'em. Boys, this is United States Marshal Kent."

The Federal officer shook hands with them, and took the chair Sam pushed forward. "I understand you two are responsible for bringing in Pasquale," he smiled. "I'd like to hear all about it."

There was a moment of embarrassed silence. Then Breck spoke up. "Who told you *we* were responsible?" he asked. "It was Sam that did the capturing. We were following a deer-trail and came out right on top of a man who was lying in the gully getting ready to shoot the buck with a rifle. That's illegal in this State, you know. Anyhow, I didn't even see the fellow till Sam dove at him—the prettiest flying tackle you ever saw! Saranac had a 30-30 rifle and an automatic, but Sam got the jump on him, disarmed him and took him prisoner, and I didn't have any more to do with it than—"

"Hold on, there!" Sam broke in hotly. "How about that scrap in the car, when I'd let him get away? I suppose you busted that hand swatting flies! Listen, Mr. Kent—this boy Breck is the nerviest wildcat I ever saw in a fight. When Slim jumped in the Ford and started, didn't he hang on by his eyeteeth, and climb over the rumble-seat, and stop the car, and crack Slim's head with his own blackjack? He's the fellow that did the real work!"

The Marshal threw back his head and roared with laughter. "Between you," he said, "you make a pretty thrilling yarn out of it. And as long as you can't agree on the main question, I think there's only one way to settle it. I've got a blank government draft here for a thousand dollars' reward. Suppose I make it out to you, Sheriff,

and let you pay these boys five hundred apiece with your
own checks?"

Breck stood up, flushed and earnest. "That's mighty
fine, Mr. Kent," he said, "but I want to explain. In the
first place Sam really did make the capture, and any help
I gave him was afterward. Besides that, I don't need the
money. Of course I'd be tickled to have it. Any boy
would. But my people give me all that's good for me and
maybe more. Sam's trying to save for his college expenses
at Tech. If I refuse to accept any reward, you can't make
me take it, so you might just as well fill Sam's name in
on that draft."

The Marshal looked at the tall boy quizzically, and
saw that he meant what he said.

"Very good," he nodded at length, and drew out his
fountain pen.

Sam slipped over to Breck's side. "You old son-of-a-
gun——" he muttered, and gripped his chum's hand, un-
able to put more of his feelings into words.

"Don't be a sap," said Breck. "I owe you a lot more
than any old reward. Do you think I'd ever have got that
picture if it hadn't been for you?"

As the men got to their feet, a sizzling sound came
from the kitchen, and with it a most enticing odor of
roast turkey. Mrs. McArdle had opened the oven door.

The boys grinned and sniffed the air like a pair of hunt-ing-dogs on a hot scent.

"M-m-m," said the warden heartily. "Smells as if din-ner's ready. An' I sure hope you gentlemen will stay an' help us eat it."

"Thanks a heap, Jim," replied the sheriff, "but we've got a dinner of our own waitin' for us, down Ossipee way." And with cordial good-bys all around, the two offi-cers took their departure.

.   .   .   .

All his life, Breck had been blessed with a healthy appetite. But he never enjoyed a meal more thoroughly than the one the warden's wife gave them that Thanks-giving afternoon. It was served in the old-fashioned way, with everything on the table at once. A tender young turkey, golden-brown and stuffed with savory dressing, occupied the place of honor. Its platter was flanked by dishes of cranberry sauce and fluffy mashed potatoes, golden hubbard squash and succulent creamed onions. There were biscuits, light as feathers, and pats of sweet, home-made butter. And for dessert, great luscious wedges of mince and pumpkin pie.

When the plates had been cleared away, they sat around the fire with bowls of shagbark hickory nuts and a frosty pitcher of ruddy mountain cider.

Breck's eyes met Sam's and he lifted his glass.

"I'll give you a toast," said he. "To the old King Buck
of Passaconaway! May he outwit his enemies, and live
in peace on his hills, and see his fawns grow up as strong
and wise and handsome as himself!"

THE END

獅城情緣（繁體字版）

LOVE IN SINGAPORE (A NOVEL IN TRADITIONAL CHINESE CHARACTERS)

B杜

For my Family

第一章／自身難保

公元14世紀，蘇門答臘的室利佛逝王國王子乘船旅遊，看見岸邊有一頭異獸，當地人告知爲獅子，他認爲這是一個吉兆，決定建設此地並命名"新加坡"（乃梵語"獅城"的諧音）。

車子經過寸土寸金的烏節路，老公説今天下班後會彎到ION ORCHARD 買我愛吃的老曾記咖喱角,問我除了咖喱角之外還想吃些什麼？

老曾記在新加坡無人不知、無人不曉，他家的咖喱角外皮酥而不膩，裏面的咖喱餡綿密中帶著香氣，不似印度咖喱辣舌，很受大衆歡迎。

"什麼都別買，没胃口。"我冷冷地答，將頭轉向車窗外。

這個月我上早班，老公順路載我理所當然。

車子一個轉彎上了Dempsey Hill,我們的醫院就在這片綠意盎然的山頭上。

“鄭醫生早，和夫人鶼鰈情深呀！”

“呦！馮主任，這麼早就來上班？真是憂國憂民、憂國憂民啊！”

我們一下車就和內科馮主任打上照面，他很熱情，老公也不甘示弱，兩人旗鼓相當。我很反感這些，匆匆點個頭便走進醫院大廳。

REQ是新加坡聲名遠播的一家私立醫院，以軟硬體設備先進、收費昂貴著稱，有1/3的患者來自海外，新推出的高級體檢項目尤受中國富豪歡迎。

我到更衣室換上淺綠色的護士服，據說這顏色代表生命與希望，天知道爲了穿上這件制服我吃了多少苦、受了多少累。

想當初仲介說得天花亂墜，一到新加坡月薪翻了不止五倍，有房屋津貼、交通補助、來回機票……等，而最最重要的是工作兩年後即可申請綠卡。

我雖是國內本科畢業生，護士執照註冊時間超過3年，在三甲醫院也工作了三年，但月薪不過五、六千元，在二線城市付完房租及生活費後基本已捉襟見肘，忽聞從天而降的大好機會怎肯錯過？咬咬牙跟貸款公司借了四萬多元付給培訓中心及仲介，又狠狠地惡補了兩個多月的英語，終於過關斬將來到人人稱羨的“花園城市”—新加坡。

來了之後才發現被忽悠，薪水是多了，但也只是翻了兩翻，要做的工作卻多出好多，因爲新加坡的住院病人大小事都要護士效勞，親人向來不幫忙，舉凡洗澡、按摩、餵藥、擦屁股的活兒都得幹，與國內大不相同。有人因心理落差太大，沒待幾天就鎩羽而歸。

我一向逆來順受慣了，既來之則安之，打算忍一忍，等有了海外工作經驗後，以此爲跳板到太平洋彼岸討生活，畢竟美國才是大家趨之若鶩的移民天堂。然而事與願違，在護士長的撮合下，我和REQ的耳鼻咽喉科主治醫師鄭之龍相識、相戀，並進一步結爲夫妻，又在他的大力幫助下，我從公立醫院跳槽到REQ。任誰都知道，私立醫院的薪水多、福利好、一切的一切看似苦盡甘來，可是……

八點鐘有醫護大交班，交班過後，我便得開始一天的工作，諸如：查房、滙報病人一天的病情、與醫生討論下一步的診療和護理計劃、執行醫囑……這些是身爲註冊護士的我應該做的，但一忙起來就不分彼此，甚至連助理護士、護理員的工作也得做，譬如：整理床鋪、準備針劑藥品、餵飯、逐個床位打針輸液……等。

今天一早就有病人按鈴要求處理輸液針口，我在通道裏快速奔走了兩個來回，然後又有病人反映枕頭太薄想要更換，剛拿來新枕頭，隔壁床的老人提出幫忙翻身，接著又有家屬向我詢問病人病情……一個早上我忙得像隻勤勞的小蜜蜂，只有在接到通知（把第三床病人送到手術室）時，才得空坐在電腦前核對醫囑。

"媛媛學姐，吃飯不？"穿藍色護理員制服的寶兒輕敲我敞開的房門問。

"行，妳先去食堂佔位，我馬上到！"我飛快地打字，眼睛盯著屏幕不放。

"還是吃福建麵？"

"不，今天吃雞。"

~

寶兒原本不叫寶兒，她有個很土的名字叫蔡招弟，而且如父母所願真的招了個弟弟，從此便爹不疼娘不愛，成了家裏最礙眼的。

由於從小缺乏關愛，她極想成爲別人眼中的寶貝，所以成年後自行改名蔡寶兒，聽説爲此還鬧過家庭革命。

她的學歷不高，上的是中專的護理學校，一註冊完護士資格就猴急地飄洋過海而來，由於沒有工作經驗，連助理護士都當不了，只能從最低的護理員幹起。

我曾問她爲什麼不在國內積累好經驗再過來，起碼薪水能高一點兒，工作相對也不那麼辛苦。她答前男友想追殺她，她不得不連夜逃跑，因爲是帶笑説，讓人分不清真假。

"給妳點了海南雞飯，媛媛學姐快坐下。"看見我來，寶兒説。

其實我和她只是曾在同一個城市學習過，連校友都談不上，寶兒卻學姐學姐地喊，很多事因此都拉不下臉來説不，好比她想知道內科那個帥到不行的住院醫生是打哪兒來的？有沒有女朋友？能不能吃辣？愛唱歌不？……

我曾建議她自己去問，但寶兒説我是已婚婦女，沒人會對名花有主的人設防，她就不一樣，待字閨中的女人若在愛情上主動，首先就掉價了。

"妳怎麼不吃？"我坐了下來。

寶兒點的是炒粿條，是以甜醬油、黑醬油、蠔油、血蚶爲主要醬料爆炒出來的麵食，嗜辣者還可以配上三峇辣椒醬，使味道鹹甜中帶點兒辣味。

"等妳呀！"她笑咪咪地答。

我們在鬧哄哄的食堂吃飯，我正吃著雞，寶兒忽然提出再幫我叫碗湯，我正想推辭，她已起身離去，沒多久爲我端來一盅薏米冬瓜老鴨湯。

"一共多少錢？"我掏出錢包問。

"不用了，沒多少錢。"

寶兒一個月的薪水不過1050新幣，扣掉與人合租的租金及伙食費，所剩無幾了。

我給了她15新幣，她默默收下，有意無意地喃喃自語："不知新來的員工都住在哪裏？吃些什麼？"

這新來的員工不會是別人，而是……

寶兒看上的醫生長得白白淨淨、瘦高瘦高的，他的名牌上寫著MO Wang, 意即 Medical Officer Wang，代表醫學本科畢業後PGY2, 相當於住院醫生，只是不知道該稱王醫生還是汪醫生？

"那人在內科，和我老公同一層樓，實在不方便過去問。"我答。

"有什麼不方便的？"她嘻皮笑臉，"順便還可以和自己的老公拋拋媚眼、說說情話，何樂而不爲？"

寶兒才來REQ不到三個月，只知我老公是主治醫生，對他完全不熟，然而閃婚的我又何嘗了解他？不過有一點是肯定的，自己的老公控制慾極強、猜疑心又重，我不願在好不容易平靜的湖面上再開機關槍。

之所以說"再"是因爲昨晚一通打錯的電話讓鄭之龍賞了我一巴掌，到現在牙關還疼。

"他爲什麼喊妳Darling ？"

"都說是打錯的，回打過去，那人不也承認了？"我捂著臉，委屈至極。

"告訴妳崔媛媛，別讓我抓到證據，否則……有妳受的！"

醫院裏的員工人種很多，有新加坡本地人、印度人、馬來人、菲律賓人、越南人、大陸人……偏偏鄭之龍是印尼華僑，算是少數中的少數。

"別看他黑黑瘦瘦的，但聰明又多金，在Nassim Road上有棟別墅，其他……能忽略就忽略吧！"護士長當初是這麼說的。

鄭之龍離過一次婚，長得不好看，年紀又大我一輪，剛開始我是不滿意的，所以相過一次親後便沒了下文，但緣份就是這麼神奇，某個大雨滂沱的夜晚，公交車遲遲不來，我正思忖該不該打電話叫出租車，鄭之龍剛好開車經過。

"崔小姐，讓我載妳一程吧！"他搖下車窗說。

爲了表示感謝，那個週末我請他吃長堤海鮮樓的辣椒螃蟹，一來二去，彼此有了好感，兩個月後他在摩天輪上掏出兩克拉鑽戒向我求婚，也許是夜景太璀璨，也或許是累了想找個依靠，我點頭成爲鄭太太。

婚後的蜜月期很短，我們都忙，加上倒三班，有時他前腳剛進門，我後腳就出去，飯都吃不到一塊兒，感情怎麼不會出問題？無怪乎他說想開個私人診所，兩夫妻都朝九晚五，家才像家。

"好不好嘛！小姐姐。"見我不吱聲，寶兒來軟的。

"下午如果不忙，我幫妳問問。"我嘆了口氣說。

她歡呼一聲，說我是她生命中的貴人。

"貴人？我是泥菩薩過江，自身難保呀！"我內心冷哼一聲。

第二章/不祥之兆

我服務的是住院部，和老公的耳鼻咽喉科門診部相隔三、四百米，但我還是在相對不那麼忙的時刻，以送尿檢報告的名義到內科轉轉。

" Miss Cui, are you looking for Dr.Zheng?"一個矮個子的印度裔女子問我是不是在找鄭醫生？

我認出她是五官科的助理護士Alisa，趕緊否認，表明自己是來交尿檢報告的。

" Dr.Zheng is a good man. You're a lucky girl."她對我眨眼睛，説鄭醫生是個好人，而我是那個萬中無一的幸運女孩。

有那麼幾秒鐘我有個錯覺，莫非此鄭醫生非彼鄭醫生？但疑慮很快被打消掉，因爲Alisa接著説Dr.Zheng胃不舒服，到樓下便利店買消化餅乾去了。

老公曾不止一次向我推廣"少量多餐"的好處，把一天原有的食物分量分成六至十餐來吃，不僅不會給胃帶來負擔，同時減少脹氣及水腫，對控制體重也有好處。

"順便還能藉養生的名義休息一下，因爲連續看診是對病患及自己的不負責任。"他補充説明。

原來鄭醫生還是那個鄭醫生，没變。

我謝了Alisa，很快走人。

知道自己的老公不在這一層樓讓我如釋重負，少了窺視的眼睛，我的腳步輕盈許多。

" Excuse me. Is this your pen?"

聽到背後有人説話，我轉過頭去，那人手中的圓珠筆筆桿上有蜘蛛俠的貼紙，是一個來探望奶奶的小男孩執意給我貼的。

" I guess that's my pen. Thanks!"

我以爲他會馬上還我，没想到他卻要我提出證據，證明那支筆是我的。

"上面有我的味道呀！王醫生。"我答，其實不確定他姓王還是汪，我選擇比較普遍的那一個。

他裝模作樣地聞了一下筆桿後還我，不忘提醒以後帶香味的圓珠筆還是少用，因爲香精中大多含有甲醛、苯等有害物質，這種物質很容易揮發，如果長期使用會對身體健康造成影響，嚴重的甚至會損害到人體的血液及神經系統……

我笑説醫生果然都往壞裏想，小小一支筆能有什麼殺傷力？要有，恐怕也比醫院的細菌來得小。

王醫生攤手説自己已盡到告知的義務，聽不聽在我。

"你打哪兒來？"我没忘記此行目的。

"華夏、中夏、諸夏、諸華、神州、中土、禹域、中域、九州、震旦……這些都是古稱，近代稱爲中國，妳呢？"

我答自己沒他那麼有學問，也不擅長把事情複雜化，簡單一句：我是中國人。

"和我想的一樣，這醫院的護士有 1/4 來自中國，尤其妳的身上沒洋味，應該才來不久吧？！"

"快三年了。"我答，心中懊惱三年了還沒入鄉隨俗，讓人一眼就瞧出。

"三年了......"他喃喃自語，"希望三年後我能晉升主治醫生，否則太對不起自己割捨掉的東西，包括在國內已有的主治醫生職位及安逸的生活。"

我問他現在是不是在做MO級別的臨床輪轉並等待通過Post Graduate考試？

"沒錯，內科輪完後，下一個是五官科，全部科室走完一遍才得以參加考試。若有幸通過，我希望將來從事全科醫學或家庭醫生的工作。"他答。

由於醫學院畢業生的養成不易且數量有限，加上爲應對人口增長及打造東南亞醫療中心等原因，新加坡的醫院管理機構MOH HOLDING大量從海外招募低年資的醫生，這也是近年來不少中國醫生前往新加坡工作的一個時代背景。

"那麼祝你早日夢想成真，也好將家鄉的老婆接過來。"我設局。

"我還是單身漢。"

"女朋友也得接呀！"

他反問一天工作16個小時的人配有女朋友嗎？

"愛吃辣嗎？"

"無辣不歡。"

"喜歡唱歌嗎？"

"人稱'北大陳奕迅'。"

"住哪裏？自己開伙嗎?"

"預算不多，目前和朋友租住在政府組屋裏，早餐在家裏吃，午晚餐吃醫院食堂。"

我沈思了一下，將得來的答案在腦中各就各位。

"妳是醫院派來做戶口調查的嗎?"他笑問。

"呵呵！真風趣。"我笑得很尷尬，"算是吧！醫院裏有很多摽梅之年的女護士，我得替她們把把關。"

"妳呢？怎麼没把自己算進去？"

我答自己已婚，老公是耳鼻咽喉科的鄭醫生。

"鄭之龍？那個醫界翹楚?"他睜大眼睛問。

我再度受到驚嚇，不知王醫生是刻意戴高帽還是自己真嫁了個人中蛟龍?

見我點頭承認，他的態度一百八十度大轉變，顯得畢恭畢敬。

"我期待下禮拜向鄭醫生學習，剛才的談話若有冒犯之處請見諒。噢！還有，我姓汪，三點水的汪，汪致遠，此乃出自諸葛亮的《誡子書》—非淡泊無以明志，非寧靜無以致遠。"

輕鬆的談話轉變爲"説明會"，這不是我要的，但又能如何？

"很高興認識你，汪醫生，希望你在REQ有充實的生活及愉快的回憶。"我也跟著嚴肅起來。

～

這個月我上早班，理論上可以和看門診的老公同進退，實際情況卻是只能同進，不能同退，因爲有時交班過後我才發現病歷書没寫完或有突發狀況臨時被留下；老公也一樣，雖然已是主治醫生，難保不加班，所以我們一向各自回家，今天也不例外。

我在醫院門口的公交站牌下等車，寶兒氣喘吁吁地跑向我，嘴裏學姐學姐地喊。

"妳怎麼這個時候下班？"我問。

中午吃飯時，她還唉聲嘆氣地表示今天得連續值12個小時的班。

"還沒下班呢！我特意跑出來找妳，就想問妳……他……他怎麼説？"

他？我想了一下，恍然大悟。

"汪致遠、北大高材生、未婚、沒有女朋友、嗜辣、有好歌喉、住政府組屋、經常吃醫院食堂。"我一一向來者報告。

"住政府組屋？不應該呀！那是窮人住的，他可是高收入的醫生。"

新加坡有80%的人口住組屋，組屋是指由政府建造，擁有獨立廚衛設施的單元房，通常低於市場價，這是政府的德政，讓"居者有其屋"。顯然寶兒並不買單，同時也高估了一個初來乍到、尚未通過認證考試的醫生荷包。

我藉機教育她一番，她很快釋懷："説的也是，男人就是要成家才有動力，努力個幾年也能像妳老公一樣坐擁豪宅，是不？"

這一問把我給問住了，鄭之龍的收入是不錯，但大部份來自薪水以外的灰色地帶，見不得光。

我支支吾吾了半天仍説不出個所以然，還好寶兒並不在乎答案，很快轉了話題。

"妳説邀請他去Party World唱歌好不好？我可喜歡唱了，以前在國內就經常上KTV，大家都説我是小王菲。"

我想起汪致遠説他是"北大陳奕迅"。

"我不知道，也許妳自己問他。"

"怎麼是我？當然是妳問，送佛送上天，好不好嘛！小姐姐。"

什麼？！簡直粘上橡皮糖，甩都甩不掉。不行，事情到此為止，我得抽身……

無奈公交車來了，我被人群簇擁著上車，連開口拒絕的機會都沒有。

"謝了，媛媛學姐，路上小心啊！"寶兒向我揮手。

～

我家在Nassim Road上，鄰近使館區及植物園，是有名的富人區。這個擁有20個單元的別墅群既有新加坡特有的熱帶風情，也有日本頗富禪意的庭園景觀，室內設計採法國的輕奢風格，是Nassim Road上一抹高貴冷豔的風景。

我趿上拖鞋到主臥室換上家居服，然後洗手做羹湯。

結婚前，鄭之龍原雇了個菲律賓女傭，能煮"似是而非"的中國菜；結婚後，女傭想當然爾被解雇，美其名曰更喜歡我煮的菜，其實是為了省下一筆人工費。

老公的"摳門"在婚後顯露無遺，連香皂、衛生紙都算計著用，就別妄想有一天我會像那些有錢太太們一樣，沒事修修指甲、逛逛商場。

我把早上出門前放進水槽解凍的魚拿來熬湯，又把空心菜洗了、豆腐瀝乾。兩菜一湯的菜色即使放在平常人家也稍顯寒磣，但煮多了會被罵，說我不懂得過日子，白白浪費老公辛苦賺來的錢……

天知道我同樣在掙錢，四房兩廳的大房子整理起來也挺累人，但說這些鄭之龍是不會懂的。

～

剛把魚湯端上桌，老公就進門，臉色不太好，大概在外面受了氣。我没說話，默默接過他的公事包。

新加坡的病患和醫護人員平起平坐，得了什麼病、用了什麼藥、做了什麼護理……都要一一告知，若因溝通不良被投訴還得寫報告，這是很煩人的事，所以老公偶爾有壞心情，我能理解。

"妳看起來心情不錯。"他酸溜溜地説。

"有吃住就該高興，你説的，不是嗎？"我冷冷地答。

我們安靜地吃著飯，連牆上掛鐘行走的聲音都聽得一清二楚。

"妳今天去了內科門診部?"老公突然問。

我的心喀噔了一下。

"是的，拿尿檢報告給Dr.Smith。"

"和帥氣醫生談得很開心的樣子嘛！"説完，他將筷子伸向魚頭，一挖，白色魚眼進到他嘴裏。

原來和汪醫生的談話被他發現了，我大呼不妙但仍故作鎮定地解釋："都是中國來的，多聊了兩句，那裏人來人往，要有什麼也不選在醫院。"

"呵呵！要有什麼妳就完了，妳知道'完了'是什麼意思吧？！"

我打了個寒顫，打算以不變應萬變，但老公没放過我，開始抱怨湯太鹹、麻婆豆腐没煮出味道、空心菜全是梗……

"不吃了。"老公推開桌子起身，"幫我按摩，現在！"

見他帶著怒氣走向房間，我有了不祥的預感，心中叫苦連天。

第三章／雙面人

婚後的第一次耳鬢廝磨，我曾推開老公惴惴不安地問：" 怎麼没裝窗簾？"

" 放心，那是單向玻璃，外面看不見裏面，而且多層實心，中間有超彈隔音膜，另外，房門是鋼製的，牆壁內也塞了吸音棉，妳叫再大聲也無人能聽見。"

當我們情投意合時，這樣的談話無疑增加夫妻間的情趣，但當我們關係緊張時，這樣的室內設計無疑將我推向痛苦的深淵。

" 說！"鄭之龍掐住我的脖子，" 和那個奶油小生眉來眼去多久了？"

" 没⋯⋯没有的事⋯⋯今⋯⋯今天第一次⋯⋯真的⋯⋯"

没人比一位醫生更了解人體結構，只要掐對地方，我分分鐘會氣絕身亡。

" 難怪⋯⋯難怪最近陰陽怪氣，説話也冷嘲熱諷，原來找到相好的。"鄭之龍繼續編派我的不是。

“没……我發誓……我拿父母的性命……發誓……”

“切，妳那對吸血鬼父母的命值幾個錢？早死早超生！”

想當初談婚論嫁時，鄭之龍對我父母的態度可不是這樣，他正襟危坐，老實巴交地像個没見過世面的鄉下人，讓父母從不滿意改投贊成票。

“人是乾瘦了點兒，但選老公不選漂亮的，實用最好。”母親説。

“他看著還行，收入高又有大房子，結婚就圖個安穩，妳也算是找對人了。”父親説。

有了父母的加持，我們的戀情火速升溫，秋季還没度完，我就急匆匆地披上嫁衣……

婚後，鄭之龍的狐狸尾巴才露出來，挨了幾次揍後，我忍不住打越洋電話求助，母親是傳統的中國婦女，雖然心疼我，但認爲失婚女子難再嫁，勸我能忍則忍，但這不代表她没有遠慮。

“把錢拿好，哪天……妳也不致於完全没有後路。”

新加坡的華人結婚也給彩禮，但鄭之龍説他是印尼華僑，不時興這個。當時感情好，父母也認爲他們不是賣女兒，所以連房子、車子都没要就嫁過去，事後才後悔，這要是一拍兩散，我豈不是淨身出戶？

亡羊補牢，母親的計劃是把我的薪水以供養父母的名義全留住。礙於情面，鄭之龍没説什麼，時間一久，我的父母便成了他口中貪婪無厭的代表，也有了指責我在家當蛀米蟲的底氣。

“對……對不起……我……我錯了……”鄭之龍的大臉在我眼中漸漸模糊，知道自己快失去意識，我趕緊求饒自保。

老公終於鬆開手，在呼吸到第一口新鮮空氣後，我忍不住痛哭失聲。

"哭？不守婦道的人還有臉哭？"他咆哮。

我哭是因爲婚前沒擦亮眼，遇人不淑（偏偏別人還用羨慕的眼光看我，彷彿我是灰姑娘，一朝飛上枝頭變鳳凰）。

擦乾眼淚後，我討好地說下樓爲他泡杯咖啡。

"別加糖。"他叮囑。

鄭之龍有飯後喝黑咖啡的習慣，這似乎不符合養生之道，但對於接下來還要熬夜讀書的人來說，喝杯提神飲料不爲過。

老公是我見過最刻苦學習的人，即使已是主治醫生，他仍然維持一年發表兩篇學術論文的自我期許，有幾篇甚至被收錄在醫學界最具權威的學術刊物《The Lancet》上，無怪乎連醫院院長都要對他客氣三分。

"你的咖啡。"我將咖啡置於床頭櫃上。

泡的是新加坡最著名的貓頭鷹咖啡，顏色比普通咖啡淡，少了苦酸味，口感更好。

"媛媛，"他的聲音轉爲溫柔，"謝謝妳！"

我點了個頭，默默離去。

總是這樣，言語和肢體施暴後，老公變得格外體貼，不僅口惠，有時還會給我買小禮物，甚至親自下廚煮我愛吃的菜，讓我迷惑不已。也正因如此，我一次次地原諒他的家暴與……變態，甚至反求諸己，認爲是自己的錯，罪有應得。

趁著老公在"學習"，我把家務做了、洗好澡，然後坐在客廳百般無聊地按著電視遙控器，從時事新聞看到綜藝節目，再從華語電視劇看到印度電影，沒有一個頻道讓我的眼光停留超過五分鐘。

"媛媛，睡覺了。"老公站在樓梯口喊。

"你先睡，看完'長女的婚事'我就來。"

“無聊的電視劇也看？”老公還是下樓來，“越看越笨，倒不如省下時間做有用的事。”

我答我沒他有學問，生活中也只剩下看電視這項愛好……

“這怎能算愛好？一沒錢賺、二沒增廣見聞、三沒繼往開來，怎麼說都是浪費時間，還是從從妳老公的愛好，沒看到他爲這個家勞心勞力？”

我皺了皺眉，推說今天不方便。

“妳哪天方便過？”老公的聲音變得粗巴巴，“吃我的、喝我的、住我的，現在是我在養著妳，可別忘了自己應盡的義務。”

我嘆了口氣說知道了，讓他先上樓，自己隨後就到。

“鄭醫生早，和夫人琴瑟和鳴呀！”

“呦！是李醫生，”老公的聲音彷彿浸過蜜似的，“這麼早就來上班？真是憂國憂民、憂國憂民啊！”

我們一下車就和骨科的李醫生打上照面，我匆匆點個頭就鑽進醫院大廳。

“Miss Cui, 八號病房的第五床病人又不吃飯了，妳去搞定他。”護士長下令。

那床病人是個古怪的老頭，只要兒女週末沒來看他，週一他就賭氣不吃飯，屢試不爽。

“好，待會兒就去。”我心不在焉地答。

“媛媛，”護士長忽然叫住我，眼睛盯著我的脖子瞧，“昨晚和鄭醫生打架了？他咬妳一口？”

我下意識用手遮住脖子，窘得不知如何是好。

“没事，熱情點好，愛情才能長保新鮮。”她笑著離開。

我趕緊衝向寄物櫃，還好在角落找到去年冬天遺留在那裏的絲巾，立馬拿來繫在脖子上。

説來真是難以啓齒，老公的性慾非普通人能及，每次都像狂風暴雨般橫掃而過，留下一地狼藉。

“能不能……能不能別每天來？”我問。

“怎麼，妳不喜歡？”

“也不是不喜歡，就是有點兒吃不消。”

老公不同意，他説床頭打床尾和，他需要靠做愛來修復夫妻間的裂痕……

我心想只要不打我、不在精神上折磨我，何來的裂痕？又何需修復？

“媛媛學姐，病人的留置針掉了，妳幫幫我！”寶兒求助。

“好歹妳也是護理學校畢業的，重打不會？”我像吃了炸藥。

“妳……怎麼了？”

寶兒像被一腳踢進河裏的小狗，可憐兮兮地望著我，我才意識到自己把情緒帶進工作裏，很要不得。

“没什麼，病人在哪裏？這次我教妳，妳一定要學起來喔！”我放緩口氣説。

第四章／心痛

打完針，寶兒問我是不是感冒了？

"爲什麼這麼問？"

"因爲妳繫了圍脖。"

"噢！那個……是的，喉嚨痛，怕是感冒了。"

寶兒要我多保重身體，她幫隔壁房的病人做完復健後再來看我……

"不必了。"我説，一擡頭她已走遠。

～

21號病房第二床病人今晨做胃部切除手術，術後兩小時出現出血性休克，醫生判斷是切端有小血管未結紮或縫合不夠緊密所致，很快又推回手術室。

" @&$%#£……"病人的父親用福建話責問我。

我聽不懂，回頭找護士長，然而她開會去了，我斷不可能爲此敲開會議室大門，回頭再看護士站裏的護士們，大概只有我的母語最接近福建話。

"阿伯，我告訴你……"我用普通話説。

那個怒氣沖沖的人仍用福建話轟炸我，正當我無計可施之時……

"病人家屬問爲什麼剛手術完就嘔血？現在推回手術室又是什麼道理？"汪致遠代爲翻譯。

這真讓人左右爲難，據實以告恐給醫院帶來麻煩；隱瞞實情又怕引起更大的誤會……

見我面露難色，汪醫生安撫病人家屬幾句後，交待我帶後者到手術室外等候。

"還是讓手術醫生來解釋比較恰當。"他對我説。

今天午餐吃粥，因爲没什麼胃口。

"我只有減肥時才吃粥，這東西不經餓。"寶兒説，她點的是大碗牛肉麵。

我問她今天還加班不？她答不清楚，要看最後通知，不過她不排斥加班，因爲加班費很豐厚。

"難道妳一輩子就想當護理員？總得唸唸書參加考試，不説註册護士，即使助理護士的薪水也比護理員多得多。"

"知道了啦！書會唸，考試也會去考，妳就別再説了，拜托！"

不知爲什麼，寶兒説話的聲音音量越來越小，而且面色緋紅。

"這裏有人坐嗎？"汪醫生拿著托盤俯視我們。

我看了一眼寶兒，她眼露期待，我遂答：" 没有。"

他坐了下來，我這才發現他點的是紅油抄手，已經火紅一片還加了兩勺辣椒醬。

" 看來你很愛吃辣，四川人？"我問。

" 不，我是混血兒，北京混福建。"他答。

寶兒聽了噗嗤一笑，她說她也是混血兒，峨眉山混武當山。

" 敢情妳是功夫高手的後代，失敬失敬！"

" 什麼功夫高手呦！只差没被抓去當道姑。"

看他們兩人談得很好，我樂得做壁上觀。

没想到話說三巡，那人還是顧及到我，他讚美我的絲巾很漂亮，我謝了他。

" 媛媛學姐感冒了，喉嚨痛。"大嘴巴寶兒主動交待。

" 最 近 有 流 感 疫 情 ， 我 們 醫 護 人 員 都 得 小 心 應 對 。"汪醫生說。

～

我正忙著核對醫囑好完成交班前的工作，汪醫生遞過來一盒口含片，說能對口腔及咽部做局部消炎，舒緩疼痛。

" 不用了，家裏有。"我冷冷地答。

" 哈！也是，妳老公是耳鼻咽喉科的主治醫生，有什麼比貼身醫生做得更到位？"他將口含片收回。

" 不是這個意思，我……我不習慣接受別人的好意。"

汪致遠說那可麻煩了，他很習慣照顧別人，尤其是病人……

" 對不起，我得交班了，Excuse me."没等他說完，我趕緊逃。

知道這很無禮，但我還是將他拒於千里之外，老公已經吃過一次醋，我不想再節外生枝。

~

臨下班接到老公打來的電話，他說今天是太平日，可以準時下班，要我在停車場等他。

我等了半小時才見到人，老公一句解釋也無，很快上車發動引擎。

"想去哪裏吃飯？"他問。

我答隨便。

駕駛盤一轉，車子往Scott Road 的方向駛去，我知道今晚必定是吃蟹。

我極愛吃蟹，同時也是吃蟹高手，連蟹腳內細細的腿肉也不放過；鄭之龍卻相反，他認爲螃蟹是涼性食物，吃多了胃寒，容易引起消化疾病，而且蟹殼硬，不易食用，長相又不討喜，像極了八腳蜘蛛......

然而不愛吃螃蟹的他，今晚卻甘願爲了我跑一趟，夠誠意！

~

"紐頓美食中心"是當地人會去的夜市，用餐環境簡陋但食物一流，我們來到常去的那一家。

一坐下，老公就點了我愛吃的黑胡椒蟹、蒜蓉蝦及魔鬼魚，三道菜花掉一百多新幣，對於摳門的他來說算是大手筆的開銷。

"我打算開個私人診所。"老公舊話重提。

"好呀！你去開。"我忙著吃蟹。

"貸款有點兒多，銀行說若夫妻聯名貸會容易些。"

聯名貸意即一旦還不了款，我也遭殃。

" 診所可以用租的，不一定要買，很多人都這麼做。"我説。

鄭之龍看上的是繁華地段的辦公樓底層，兩百多平米，價格不是普通的貴。

"投資懂不懂？人的眼光要看遠，目光短淺者只能看著別人吃肉而自己只能喝湯。再説，好不容易建立起客戶群，房東若漲租金，搬還是不搬？幾十萬的裝修不要錢嗎？"

賺錢的事我不懂，我只知道鄭之龍要把我們住的別墅拿去抵押，又要我聯名貸，可説是強拉我下水。

見我悶不吭聲，老公開始給我灌迷湯，不外他是新加坡名醫，多少人衝著他的招牌來，如果他會倒，其他人也別想屹立不搖，吧吧拉、吧吧拉……

"讓我考慮一下。"我打算採拖延戰術。

"妳慢慢考慮，"他將剝好的蟹肉放進我盤裏，"噢！不，不能慢，銀行正等我回覆。"

這下子我全然没了胃口。

～

回到家，我把花隨意插進花瓶裏，連水都懶得注。

我們離開"紐頓美食中心"後，老公執意送我一束花，挑了半天，選了我最不喜歡的菊花。雖然菊花的花語代表長壽、吉祥及歡樂，不見得不好，但在我的家鄉只有死了人才用菊花，我不知道他爲什麼非得選它，難道就因爲牌子上寫著30%的折扣？

"媛媛，幫我泡杯咖啡。"老公説。

"……好。"我把委屈吞下肚。

當我把咖啡置於床頭櫃上時，鄭之龍遞過來一個小本子，說是貸款合同，讓我在底頁簽名。

我受夠了這接踵而來的壓力，也厭倦他爲了達到目的刻意的示好，大筆一揮，簽了。

"真是我的好老婆，妳放心，一定會賺，賺了讓妳分紅……"

没等老公説完，我轉身離去，然後躲進廁所嗚嗚嗚地哭泣。

爲什麼……爲什麼自己的命運多舛、所遇非人？難道就因爲耐不住寂寞，得用後半輩子無窮無盡的痛苦來償還？

想至此，我更加悲傷，忍不住淚流成河。

第五章/待宰的羔羊

新加坡的醫院會給病人戴標註了個人信息的手環（包括名字、生日及家人的手機號），有的還會多戴兩個，綠色表示防跌倒，紅色表示過敏，10號病房的劉小弟戴的就是紅色手環。

我看過他的病歷—地中海貧血，這是由常染色體的遺傳性缺陷所引起的珠蛋白鏈合成障礙，除了會出現嚴重的貧血現象外，劉小弟的肝脾還腫大，可說是個可憐的孩子。可喜的是，雖然疾病纏身，但他仍樂觀面對，總是笑嘻嘻的，是醫護人員眼中的開心果。

這一天，護士長把一個新進的助理護士Crisha帶給我，要我關照她兩天，我答沒問題。

"Where are you from?"護士長一走，我問Crisha打哪裏來？

她心不在焉地答菲律賓，然後眼光飄呀飄的，就是不看我。

我告訴她，護士長讓我帶她兩天，所以有問題請發問，我會知無不言、言無不盡。

結果她問的不外加班費有多少？能連著休假嗎？生病給不給薪水？食堂打折不？……

我一一答覆，見她一時沒問題可問，趕緊帶她熟悉環境，遇有特殊病人我還特別提醒，譬如劉小弟不僅是重度地中海貧血患者，同時對堅果過敏，所以"絕對絕對"不能讓他食用乾果或裂果。

Crisha嘴巴Yep,Yep個不停，但眼光四處遊走，所以我也不清楚她到底聽進去了沒？

"崔姐姐，送妳一條紅繩手鏈，可以避邪保平安。"劉小弟說。

前幾天大學生義工到醫院教病患編織紅繩手鏈，說它是好運的象征，送給媽媽能永保青春；送給愛人能心想事成；送給自己則能長命百歲、健健康康……

沒想到劉小弟將其中一條送給我，讓我大受感動。

"謝謝！我會永遠戴在手腕上。"

看他細心地幫我繫上紅繩，我感觸良多。那孩子頭大、眼距寬、前額及兩頰突出，膚色暗黃還有色素斑，完全是一副患兒的模樣，但卻笑容可掬，讓人心底發酸。

" Miss Cui, room 14, 6th bed patient needs blood drawing."肝膽外科Dr.Baker對我說14號病房第六床的病人需要抽血。

我答馬上來，然後要Crisha跟著我去見習。

她聳聳肩，無可無不可地跟在我身後。

～

我和Crisha約了一起吃中飯，順便帶她參觀食堂，臨到約定時間卻遲遲未見人，我急得跳腳。今天事多，中午用餐時間不得不縮短，然而那個吊兒郎當的人卻不把約定當一回事，偏偏我又沒她的手機號，簡直浪費我寶貴的時間！

"媛媛學姐，妳等我？"寶兒扶著一個吊點滴的病人走過來。

"不是，護士長要我帶一個新人，跟她約了吃飯，到現在還不見蹤影，氣死我了！"

"別氣，管她愛吃不吃，幫她是情份，不幫是本份，妳等我一小會兒，我馬上陪妳吃飯哈！"

寶兒說的没錯，我已盡到提攜的情份，没必要再委屈自己，於是等寶兒空出手來，我便與她一起上食堂。

用完餐回到住院部，一切都不一樣了。

在醫院待久後，任何風吹草動、暗潮洶湧都能立馬察覺到，好比現在，護士站裏的護士個個驚慌，幾名醫護人員小跑步而過，在在說明有不尋常的事發生。

" What's happened?"我抓住同爲註册護士的Miss Jones問。

她答10號病房，第三床病人死了。

10號病房第三床......那不是劉小弟嗎？怎......怎麼死了？今天早上他還幫我繫上愛心紅繩呢！

Miss Jones答因爲一位新來護士的失誤，讓孩子誤食了堅果，没想到反應來得如此劇烈，送到搶救室時人已經不行了......

我倒吸一口氣，這個新來的護士不會是別人，我怒氣沖沖地去找"殺人兇手"。

～

Crisha淚眼婆娑地坐在主任辦公室裏，看見我來彷彿看見救命稻草，嘴裏嚷嚷她都照我說的做，絕無過失，不應入她罪......

主任問我這是怎麼回事？我答不清楚，然後那個皮膚黝黑的女人搶著說今天是她第一天正式在REQ上班，護士長安排我照顧她，後來我走了，她還回到病房陪劉小弟說了會兒話，没想到被護理員抓去幫忙送午餐，她完全不知道劉小弟需要食用特別料理，因爲我没告訴她……

"I did. I told you Liu Yong is allergic to walnuts."我揚起聲説自己的確告訴過她。

"No, you didn't."Crisha哭得像個淚人似的。

住院部主任摘下黑框眼鏡揉了揉鼻樑，半天終於下了裁決：**Crisha 停 職 接 受 調 查 ， Miss Cui 照 常 工 作 ， 必 要 時協助調查……**

Crisha聽完憤而起身，聲嘶力竭地喊著不公平，我還想説什麽，被護士長強拉到辦公室外。

"兩害相權取其輕，Crisha受訓期間就很不經心，出事不在意料外，相信我，這是最好的安排。"她説，同時要我閉上嘴巴與醫院同進退，別讓自己處於不利的地位。

天哪！雖然我問心無愧，但讓一個菜鳥獨自頂罪卻不是我的初心……

護士長問我想怎樣？難道讓自己一同背鍋？

我語塞了。

我意氣消沈地回到住院部，看見我來，護士站裏的護士全安靜下來。

真他媽的好極了，我可以想像接下來的一週自己鐵定能上"蜚短流長排行榜"的第一位，更甚者還能成爲"後台硬"的代表人物，妥妥的"不要臉"形象。

"媛媛學姐，"寶兒向我跑來，"妳聽説了没？劉小弟……死了。"

我怎會不知道？我還是劊子手呢！

"寶兒，陪我散心，現在！"我早先一步走向電梯。

"按理說不是妳的錯，所有醫護人員受訓時都被告知病人若戴上紅手環代表有過敏史，這點常識她應該有，妳提不提醒都改變不了她的過失。"我們在醫院外的走道上散步，寶兒替我分析。

"話說得没錯，但……我對劉小弟有愧疚，如果……他不會死。"

寶兒說我的負罪感太重，生死有命，誰也躲不了。

"我難以想像他的父母會有多傷心……"

話剛落音，我看見一對神色慌張的男女疾步而過，他們是劉勇的父母，在國家單位擔任公務員。

與其他國家不同，新加坡的公務人員薪水很高，以符合前總理李光耀的"高薪養廉"理念，這也是劉勇能入住私立醫院的原因。

"我去慰問一下劉小弟的父母吧！"我說。

"這樣好嗎？小心被當沙包。"寶兒一臉的不放心。

我看了一眼手腕上的紅繩手鏈答没事，即使挨打也願意，然而我還是在搶救室外被攔下，住院部主任問我來幹嘛？嫌事少?

"我來安慰劉勇的父母。"

"妳省省吧！現在由醫院全權處理此事，非必要別出現在死者家屬面前，也別亂發言。"

"可是……"

"Miss Cui,若不是看在Dr.Zheng的份上，妳今天很難全身而退，我講得夠清楚了吧？！"

面對主任那張撲克牌老K臉，我點了點頭，默默離去。

"聽說妳今天攤上麻煩了。"晚餐桌上，老公提起。

我嗯了一聲，低頭扒飯。

"爲了這個欠下老余人情債，妳可真會幫倒忙！"

我憋了一整天的氣無從排解，此時正好找到發洩口。

"誰讓你欠著的？大不了説不認識我，讓他將我送往醫療監控部門接受調查……"

話没説完，鄭之龍甩過來一巴掌，打得我眼冒金星。

"誰讓妳没大没小來著？"他虎著眼。

我噙著淚水説他就只會欺負我，算什麼英雄好漢？人渣！

然後一個身影撲了過來，以迅雷不及掩耳的速度一連給我五、六個耳光，打得我找不著北，趁著耳朵還嗡嗡作響，那人抓住我的前襟往樓上跩。

"Help～"我嘶吼著但仍抵不過男人的蠻力。

當上鎖聲響起，我知道大勢已去，等待我的將會是無窮無盡的痛苦與折磨……

第六章/明哲保身

我家備有急救藥箱，裏面不外創可貼、眼藥水、清涼油、紗布、鑷子、剪刀、雙氧水……等，除此之外還有好幾瓶雲南白藥，我曾傻呼呼地問老公爲什麼？

"那是治跌打損傷的，哪天……我能幫妳擦。"他答。

那會兒剛新婚，只覺得無限幸福，自己的老公如此體貼入微，真是前世修來的福氣，然而……

當老公拿出雲南白藥想替我上藥時，我蜷曲在房間角落，拒絕他的示好。

"媛媛，妳受傷了，不擦藥會瘀血腫脹，明天妳怎麼上班？"他好脾氣地說。

我反問他這是拜誰所賜？

"誰讓妳說話不經大腦刺激我？我也不想啊！傷害妳如同傷害我自己。"他眼露哀戚地跪了下來，"乖，讓我幫妳上藥，如果妳不同意，我就長跪不起，直到妳原諒我爲止。"

總是這樣，凶狠過後的他溫馴地如同一隻小貓，喵喵喵地乞求饒恕。

"把藥放下，我自己擦，你現在出去，我想靜一靜。"我氣若如絲地說。

他還想說什麼，話到嘴邊又吞下。

"那好，寶貝兒，我下樓做你愛吃的薄餅，今晚妳沒怎麼吃，剛好當宵夜。"

我將臉撇向一旁。

他在我的臉上小啄一下後，很快下樓。

聽腳步聲遠去，我將今晚挨揍的畫面在腦中倒帶：鄭之龍將我拋向房內地板，緊接著拳頭便像雨點般落下，胸部、腹部、背部……即使我雙手合十求饒，他仍像殺紅了眼，揍得我滿地打滾。

"打死妳這個潑婦！竟敢爬到我頭上？不要命了妳！"他惡狠狠地說。

我甩甩頭，想把這些不好的回憶都甩開。

鄭之龍太聰明了，專挑衣服遮蓋的部位打，即使我已被家暴大半年也無人察覺。

我該怎麼辦？難道永遠如此卑屈、畏首畏尾地度日？

爲了老公，我已經杜絕了所有工作以外的社交活動，生活花費也降到最低，但仍然不能讓"金主"滿意，他總能在雞蛋裏挑出骨頭，然後編派我的各種不是。活了二十多年，我才發現自己竟然如此糟糕，簡直不配在宇宙間生存。

"媛媛，是媽媽打來的電話，妳接聽嗎？"鄭之龍打開房門小聲地問。

這個"媽媽"絕對不是婆婆，鄭之龍稱他的母親"阿母"，而在我們夫妻的日常對話中，他往往以"母后"戲稱。

知道是自己的母親打來，一時百感交集，難道她心電感應到什麼？我的淚水像扭開的水龍頭，嘩嘩嘩地下。

"媽，媛媛在洗澡，我讓她待會兒打給您。"

聽到老公在電話裏回絕了母親，我稍微放下心來，現在這個狀態的確不適合接聽。

"妳看看妳，怎麼還不擦藥？這哪兒行？"他收起手機向我走來。

"別貓哭耗子假慈悲了。"

"妳現在心情不好，我不跟妳吵，"他將我的衣服褪去，然後在手掌內倒入適量的紅棕色液體，"疼告訴我，我再輕點兒。"

那人輕輕地擦了我的背、我的胸、我的小腹，在他的溫柔撫觸下，傷痛漸漸化為煙雲，我甚至覺得他沒那麼令人討厭……

沒想到我剛原諒他，他反倒欺身而上。

"鄭之龍你幹嘛？！"我高喊著。

"對……對不起，忍不住了，我會很快的。"

我想用力推開他，但仍被他強壓在底下。天哪！這是什麼狀況？剛被家暴，緊接著又遭性侵，而這些都發生在"家"的保護殼下。

在老公的前後抽搐中，我的淚水不由自主地滾落下來。

見我遲遲沒回打，母親又主動打來。

"媛媛，最近好嗎？"

"好。"我答，剛哭過的鼻音很重。

“妳怎麼了？”

“没什麼，有點兒感冒。”

母親似乎接受了這個理由，轉而告訴我中國新年想和父親一起飛來看我。

新加坡一年過四次新年，分別爲西洋人的新年（即元旦）、華人的農曆新年、馬來人的新年以及印度人的新年。除了中國新年放兩天假外，其餘放一天。

“我……我不知道，也……也許會和老公出國一趟。”

鄭之龍曾耳提面命過，凡我的娘家人想來訪都得經過他的批准，否則一律謝絕招待。

母親在電話那頭很失望，她説原本打算做紅糖年糕帶給我。

我從小就喜歡吃沾上面糊炸的年糕片，軟軟糯糯還冒著熱氣，那是童年的快樂回憶。

“那……我問問老公，也許度假計劃能改期。”

我和母親又拉拉雜雜地談了些瑣事，因爲鄭之龍就在身邊，我專挑安全的話題講，免得惹禍上身。

“真不心疼錢，講了超過十五分鐘的廢話。”剛放下電話，老公嗤之以鼻。

我很想説又不花他的錢，他也好唸叨？但話終究沒説出口，今晚受夠了，不想再起波瀾。

“丈母娘是不是想過來？”沒想到老公主動提起。

“是，距離上次見面已過了七、八個月，他們想農曆新年飛過來看我。”

老公沈默了一會兒後表示爸媽只有我一個女兒，嫁得又這麼遠，肯定會想念，還是讓他們來吧！

如果不是心裏還有氣，我肯定會給老公一個擁抱，他若能天天如此待我該有多好？！我要的不過是一點點兒的溫柔與理解，在異鄉，這是無依無靠的我僅有的小小願望而已。

1o號病房第三床來了個新病人，劉小弟的個人用品被收了起來，人們好像忘記那張單人床上曾經有個笑臉迎人的患兒，但我沒忘，手腕上的紅繩手鏈時刻提醒著我。

"劉小弟的父母看樣子會起訴醫院，所以非必要請別開口，由醫院統一發言。"護士長提醒我。

新加坡的訴訟費用很高，除非有十足的把握，否則沒人會提告。我衷心希望劉家最後能與醫院達成和解，因爲根據以往的例子，醫院被判有罪少之又少……

"Crisha現在怎樣了？"我問護士長。

"不清楚，妳還是明哲保身吧！"

我能感覺到醫院站在我這邊，明顯想讓Crisha當炮灰，雖然後者的確難辭其咎。

"謝謝！"我説。

"不用謝，"她交給我這週的藥品使用記錄表，"聽説妳老公想開私人診所，連地點都選好了，如果……幫我美言幾句吧！兒子上高中了，我想多點兒時間陪他衝刺。"

私人診所的固定薪水和私立醫院差不多，雖然少了加班費，但不用倒三班，能定時上下班，所以還是有不少人前仆後繼而來。

"好的，我會跟他提。"

現在換護士長跟我道謝。

哎！這是個功利的世界，講得好聽是你幫我，我幫你；講得不好聽就成了利用，偏偏我正需要這樣的保護傘......

" Miss Cui, Dr.Hill needs to speak to you. You haven't handed in PET-CT reports."註册護士Carole對我説。

真是糟糕！昨天答應給Dr.Hill 斷層顯像，一忙竟忘了。

" Coming."我邊答邊衝向放射科。

第七章／約定

寶兒從後掐我一把，像學生時代會有的惡作劇，我哀嚎一聲，摀住後背。

"妳怎麼了？"她一頭霧水。

我怎能告訴她昨晚被老公施暴，身上有大片烏青？

"没……没什麼，下次別這麼做，太幼稚了。"

她顯得無趣，説我没幽默感，假道學……

我轉而問她怎麼來了？現在不是該去整理床鋪及收病人用過的餐具嗎？

"那個可以等一等，"她忽然來勁，"就想問妳屠妖節能不能和我去小印度逛逛？來新加坡好幾個月了，很多地方都還没去過呢！"

屠妖節是印度的一個傳統節日，又稱萬燈節，一般在10月末到11月初舉行。相傳很久以前世界被妖魔所侵擾，天神下凡降魔，降魔後，大地女神爲天神誕下一名男嬰，取名Naraka Suran。没料到男嬰長大後與妖魔爲伍並且強迫百姓不准點燈，天神只好又下凡來與自己的兒子展開對戰，最後邪不勝正。Naraka Suran死後，人民點燈慶祝。

由於新加坡有不少印度人，所以這個傳統節日被正式納爲新加坡的節日。每到這一天，新加坡小印度的大街小巷及各大廟宇都會升起幡帶點亮燈火，歡迎神仙與凡人的到來，好不熱鬧。

"不了，我還有事要忙。"我想起外出總要花費，老公又不喜歡回家看不到我。

"能有什麼事？聽説屠妖節可好玩了，好不好嘛！小姐姐。"她又撒起嬌來。

"別説了，不去就是不去。"

見我還是不答應，寶兒賭氣地説要跟未曾謀面的網友去，如果有什麼三長兩短，請我代她照顧遠在中國的父母……

"妳可別做傻事呀！網上什麼人都有，妳又剛來新加坡不久，小心被賣。"

"那妳陪我去嘛！我們又不玩通宵，逛逛就回來，皆大歡喜。"她再次遊説。

其實我也想出去走走，在那個令人壓抑的家待久了，人會發霉。

"説好了不玩通宵，別到時又食言。"我還是妥協了。

"一定一定，"寶兒點頭如搗蒜，"就知道妳是我的好姐姐！"

看她滿意地走了，我才思忖起該如何跟自己的老公開口。

臨下班接到老公的電話，他要我今晚多煮些菜，余主任和馮主任會來家裏吃飯。

"我四點下班，家裏又沒什麼菜，怎麼不請客人到外面吃？"我說。

"外面吃既貴又不衛生，哪有家裏好？乖，下班後打出租車去買菜，我們大概七點半到，時間上來得及。"

外面餐廳的確貴，衛生程度也沒家裏好，但這些都不是主因，而是飯後他們有密事商討。

"知道了，預算多少？"我問。

"沒預算，妳看著買。"

對於鐵公雞的老公而言，這很不尋常，我突然有了捉狹的念頭，下班後，特地繞到Market Place，它是牛乳集團旗下最高端的超市，蔬果及生鮮食品以有機爲主，還進口不少外國商品，都是頂級的。

我買了大閘蟹、海膽、黃鱔、牛蛙，轉頭看松茸和巴掌大的洋菇不錯，豪氣地各買500克，又在結賬前拿走一瓶法國波爾多紅酒。

明知這一趟採購絕不便宜，但一聽收銀員說一共620元新幣時，還是嚇了一跳，三千多元人民幣一餐，不是普通的貴啊！

~

我把大閘蟹放進蒸籠用大火蒸，再將食材該炒的炒、該煎的煎、該燉的燉，終於在老公和客人進門前把五菜一湯端上桌，順便將冰鎮過的酒開瓶。

"鄭醫生真有福氣，弟妹會煮菜，天天山珍海味，難怪一下班就往家裏跑。"我的直屬上司余主任首先表揚。

"沒錯，連赤霞珠干紅都捨得請，老鄭呀！這該不會是場鴻門宴吧？！"內科馮主任接棒。

老公乾笑著否認，眼光卻凌厲地打在我身上，讓人很不舒服，我藉盛飯的名義走開。

酒足飯飽後，三人上樓密談，以主臥室的隔音程度而言，我不可能偷聽到，遂到廚房洗堆積如山的碗盤。

兩小時後，老公站在樓梯口喊：「媛媛，幫余主任和馮主任叫出租車。」

我噢了一聲，拿起手機撥號。

送走兩個略有醉意的人後，鄭之龍劈頭就問今晚的晚餐花了多少錢？

「620元。」我答。

「妳有病是不？錢是大風刮來的嗎？」老公揚起聲。

我將責任撇清，說是他讓我看著買，沒預算。

「說妳傻還真傻，花的可是辛苦錢，我讓妳別看電視劇怎麼不見妳照做？」

「聽你的不對，不聽你的也不對，你到底要我怎麼做？」

看老公氣得臉色發青，我有種莫名的快感，就該這樣，讓他大出血一次好讓我受傷的心得到些許的平衡。

大概知道覆水難收，老公最後也只能接受既定事實，但仍不忘亡羊補牢：「記住了，以後請客只能選便宜的買，超過兩百我大刑侍候。」

也只有老公會把家暴說得如此自然且毫無愧疚感。

我撇撇嘴，默默走開。

"媛媛學姐，別忘了今晚的約會，我還特地帶來新買的裙子，就等著下班跟妳一起狂歡。"寶兒一遇見我就嚷嚷。

糟糕！昨晚一忙就忘了跟老公提這件事，加上昨天買貴了菜，今晨老公仍是一副冷冰冰的臉孔，我不認爲他會大發慈悲讓我出門。

"寶兒，我還沒跟老公說，我看……算了吧！"

"妳怎能這樣？都說好了的。"寶兒急得踱腳，"現在就跟鄭醫生說，何難之有？"

我根本不想蹬釘子，多一事不如少一事，何況屠妖節也不是非去不可。

"不行就是不行，妳找別人吧！"我將洗腸器交給她，"8號病房第五床已經很久沒排便了，妳帶他到廁所灌腸。"

我走了，還能感覺到背後不友善的眼光刺得我千瘡百孔。

我以爲寶兒這會兒一定恨死我了，沒想到一踏進食堂又聽見她熱絡的呼喊聲。

"媛媛學姐，這裏，幫妳佔好位子了。"她向我招手。

我勉爲其難地走過去，她馬上問我想吃什麼？她去買。

"隨便，清淡點兒。"我答。

結果她幫我買來飄著濃濃藥材味的肉骨茶套餐和薏米水。

" Guess what?"寶兒閃著狡點的大眼睛要我猜。

"What?"我咬下排骨肉，根本懶得猜，

"鄭醫生說我們可以去參觀屠妖節燈會，而且他負責接送。"

我嚇得拿不穩湯勺，問她這是怎麼回事？

原來寶兒在我這裏得到No的答案後，決定直搗黃龍，趁著護士長不在，偷溜到耳鼻咽喉科。

"妳没説妳老公是這麼藹可親的人，他聽完我的陳述後説妳太閉塞了，總是宅在家裏，他還巴不得妳出去走走，心情會愉快一些。"

我不懷疑寶兒説的，因爲鄭之龍就是條變色龍，見人説人話，見鬼説鬼話，對女生還特別和顏悦色，難怪在醫院裏的評價頗高，想當初我就是這麼給騙來的。

"噢！是嗎？我希望他不要忘了自己説過的話才好。"我一語雙關。

"不會忘的，他還跟我約了4:2o在停車場見。"寶兒胸有成竹地答。

第八章/不期而遇

我和寶兒在下午4:15抵達停車場，老公已在那裏等候。

"學姐夫，你真準時。"寶兒説。

我看了她一眼，什麼時候鄭醫生變成了"學姐夫"？而且改口改得如此自然，一點兒忸怩也没有。

"當然，有這份榮幸替美女服務怎能遲到?"

親耳聽自己的老公講風話也是頭一遭，不知道的人還以爲鄭之龍和寶兒才是一對。

"還是開車吧！估計很多人趕著去看燈會，再不走肯定堵在路上。"我面無表情地説。

車子一發動，寶兒便戴起高帽，説她好羨慕我，嫁了個好老公，有大房子住還能坐好車，真是前世修來的福氣……

老公呵呵呵地笑，顯然很吃這一套，還説原來自己的老婆有這麼一位聰明伶俐的學妹，早知道就把她挖來耳鼻咽喉科當助理護士。

“寶兒還只是個護理員。”我冷冷地説。

“考個試不難的，何況她還這麼……這麼的聰明伶俐。”鄭之龍不忘回頭對後座的寶兒微笑。

我能想像那個涉世未深的小女孩肯定心中小鹿亂撞，得到一位名醫的賞識是多麼至高無上的光榮，果然……

“學姐夫你放心，我一定能通過考試，到時爲你效犬馬之勞。”她説。

這馬屁算是拍對了，耳朵再次傳來鄭之龍呵呵呵的笑聲，我趕緊潑冷水：“那可不成，住院部缺人手，護士長還説想從別的部門調人手過來，怎麼可能放人？再説了，Alisa做得好好的，對鄭醫生又多所讚揚，妳若過去了，Alisa怎麼辦？總不能讓人回家吃土吧？！”

那兩個一廂情願的人這才沈默下來，大概也察覺到現實沒想像中豐滿。我轉了話題，問老公是不是與我們一起看燈會？

“當然囉！人不是機器，我也需要娛樂。”他答。

然而人算不如天算，五分鐘後醫院來電要老公回去值急診班，因爲某位醫生的因故缺席。

“ No, I can't. I'm not available tonight.”

儘管老公在電話裏再三推辭仍抵不過人事的一聲令下。

“抱歉，不能陪兩位美女共遊，今晚我得工作到午夜，哎！連續值班16個小時也沒那個誰了。”

寶兒安慰他幾句，不外仁心仁術、救死扶傷、杏林春暖……等，把鄭之龍哄得很開心。

“病患的確需要醫生，我不入地獄誰入地獄？總得有人犧牲小我完成大我才是。”

這時的老公已化爲正義使者，大有“捨我其誰”的氣概。

老公在實龍崗路放我們下車，交待幾句後，風塵僕僕地趕回醫院。

"這就是小印度啊！"寶兒望著一片燈海感歎。

1819年，萊佛士爵士的船隻在新加坡靠岸，隨行的隊伍中有很多印度助手及士兵，他們成了新加坡土地上的第一批印度移民，大多聚居在如今的"小印度"地區，加上後來的移民及繁衍，這裏的印度人越來越多，成了新加坡的一道特殊風景線。

"是的，錢包看緊一點兒，小心扒手！"我提醒。

由於這是寶兒的"第一次"，我先帶她參觀千燈寺院，裏面保留了不少佛教古文物，最受矚目的是一尊高達15米的大佛像，四周圍點著無數的燈燭，燈火通明，佛座底下還懸掛著記錄佛陀一生事跡的美麗畫布。

"真是大開眼界，若不是學姐帶我來，我還不知道這寺內別有洞天，連壁畫都那麼豐富。"

寶兒嘴甜的功夫真令人無法招架，被灌迷湯後的我緊接著又帶她參觀新加坡最大、最豪華的印度教神廟—維拉瑪卡里亞曼興都廟。它建於1881年，供俸的是擁有力量和勇氣的卡里女神，其特殊的彩繪門樓是典型的南印度建築風格，塔樓上堆砌著許多神祇、聖牛及戰士的雕像，色彩鮮豔、栩栩如生。

"媛媛學姐，妳有沒有聞到什麼味道？"寶兒忽然問我。

不用她說，整個小印度充斥著辣椒、咖喱和香料的味道，想"找不到地"都有困難，基本不需要問路。

寶兒答她不是指這個，而是聞到消毒水的味道了。

我順著她的眼光望過去，果然看到熟悉的人影，他正對著五彩燈光猛按快門。

“妳的鼻子真靈，趁他還沒發現我們，趕緊走！。”

然而寶兒耳聾了，她不理會我，逕自走上前去。

汪致遠很訝異會在此處遇見同事，話沒說兩句，我看見寶兒回過頭指著我，大概說的是與我同行。

不是我多疑，汪醫生看我的眼神是有那麼點兒戒備。

“Guess what?”寶兒把人帶過來，邀功似地說明，“今晚急診室脫逃的醫生在此，他就是害學姐夫趕回去補位的罪魁禍首。”

“噢！是嗎？爲什麼？”我問那個一臉通紅的人。

“因爲……心情不好。”

我等著他解釋爲什麼心情不好，但他悶不吭聲。

“哎呀！肚子好餓，能不能找個地方吃飯？”寶兒出手化解尷尬。

那個原本沈默的人此時開口了，他說來時路上經過一個菜市場，裏面有很多吃的，問我們要不要試試印度菜？

我對印度菜一直不感冒，來新加坡快三年了還沒有勇氣嘗試，但寶兒不一樣，她一臉興奮地表示很想嚐嚐正宗的印度菜。爲了“合群”，我只好跟著一同走進一家貌似只有印度人會去的餐廳，簡陋到連菜單也無，只提供兩種套餐—咖喱羊肉飯和咖喱雞肉飯。

服務員問我們需不需要刀叉？寶兒搶著答不需要，於是生平第一次我嘗試用手抓飯吃。

天知道這要怎麼吃？我們三人像初學吃飯的小孩，吃得桌上“一片狼藉”，坐在對面的印度大叔看不下去，主動教我們如何吃，原來要用中間的3個手指挖飯，再用大拇指壓住送入口中。

入鄉隨俗的結果是飯後即使洗了手，上面的咖喱味依舊不散，噁心死了！

帶著一身異味，我們來到拱廊旁的甘貝爾巷，巷裏有張燈結彩的店鋪出售豐富多彩的印度特色物品，是個人氣頗爲旺盛的市集。走走停停，經過一家音樂行時，寶兒突然提到受室友所托，今晚她得買幾張印度梵樂CD回去交差，然後留我和汪致遠在比肩接踵的人流裏對望。

“我不知道鄭醫生今晚值急診班，我……不是故意的。”

汪致遠舊事重提且極力撇清自己的任性行爲具針對性，讓我很迷惑。

“臨時翹班，人事會抓狂，對臨危受命的人來說也不公平。”

“我知道，但最近壓力太大，如果不開小差，我怕自己會崩潰。”

我聽說有剛來的中國醫生因英語不好加上水土不服得了抑鬱症，但我以爲汪醫生不會，他可是北大的高材生，而且看著很陽光。

他解釋自己的確沒那麽糟糕，而是太害怕會栽在五官科裏過不了關，一時想不開，所以任性而爲……

“你的意思是我老公給你小鞋穿？”

他抿抿嘴，點頭承認。

這下子我聽明白了，鄭之龍公報私仇，對“假想敵”加以打壓，汪醫生受不了才“出走”，沒想到回馬槍打在老公身上。

“恐怕鄭醫生現在對我更有意見了，妳能不能幫我解釋一下？我真的不知道人事會找他代班。”

想起老公醋勁大，我還是繞道而行爲佳。

面對我的不願介入，汪致遠很氣餒，一副天要塌下來的模樣。

"怎麼了？"寶兒買完CD走出店家，一眼就看到那個陰鬱的人。

"没什麽，"他努力擠出一絲笑容，"我送妳們回家，時候不早了。"

～

洗完澡再把襯衫燙好，老公這才推門進來，時間：○○:35。

"屠妖節好玩嗎？"他問。

"還行。"我接過他的公事包。

鄭之龍鬆開領帶，趿上拖鞋，一坐下來就抱怨："今天被中國來的醫生擺一道，也不想想需要我評分，竟敢欺負到我頭上，哼！"

我倒了杯開水給他，有意無意地説菜鳥還不致於使壞，這中間可能有誤會……

"妳怎麽知道是隻菜鳥？"鄭之龍的聲音透著冷冷的殺氣。

"因……因爲你説……説需要評分，所以……"

老公直挺挺地看著我，讓人不寒而栗。

"我去幫你放洗澡水。"我趕緊找藉口離開。

～

睡到一半，有人壓在我身上。

"晚上妳遇見誰了？"老公問。

"誰？"我丈二和尚摸不著頭腦。

"妳晚上一定遇到什麽人了，我有預感。"

我頓時嚇出一身冷汗，指天發誓只和寶兒在一起，看完燈會就回家，誰也沒遇著……

"是嗎？"他伸出舌頭開始舔我，口水糊了我一身。

"別……我想睡覺。"

"做完再睡。"他呢喃著。

第九章/藥商代表

隔天一到醫院，我馬不停蹄地找人。

“ 原來妳在這裏。”我氣喘吁吁地說。

寶兒正在給一位得了膽囊炎的患者餵飯，那老人吃得很慢，每一口都咀嚼半天。

“ 還能在哪裏？想到我的青春都耗在這裏，連活下去的勇氣都沒有了。”她無限感嘆。

“ 那就趕緊自立自強，書讀了沒？”我問。

她擡起頭來，反問：“ 如果我答好久沒蹝書了，妳會不會殺了我？”

我現在已經沒力氣殺人，先求自保要緊。

“ 到樓梯間講話，我有重要事交待。”我轉身先行一步。

“ 什麼事？”一關上樓梯間的消防門，寶兒迫不及待地問。

"如果……如果我老公問起昨晚我們有沒有遇見認識的人，請答沒有。"

"認識的人？……妳指汪醫生？……爲什麼？我們沒做壞事呀！"她睜著無邪的大眼睛問。

我答當然沒做壞事，只是……只是鄭之龍對汪醫生有成見，我若和他見面，不論爲了什麼，老公都會不開心。

"沒想到鄭醫生這麼古板，都是同事，擡頭不見低頭見，怎麼可能不虛應一下？"她做沈思狀，"看來我得好好教育他一番……"

"不，不，不，絕對不可以，這會出人命，千萬千萬別說昨晚我們和汪醫生見過面，拜托了，我的好妹妹！"

寶兒聽完噗嗤一笑，因爲很少看我這麼低聲下氣。

"好啦！又不是世界末日，瞧妳緊張的……"

見寶兒答應，我半吊的心終於能放下。

"記住了，一定不能說，知道不？"離去前我又再次叮嚀。

今天早上有兩床病人動手術，都送入手術室後，我回到護士站，剛喝了一口水，外科護士就跑過來說麻醉醫生不見了，要我陪著找人。

"我剛剛還看見他在手術室裏準備藥品和器械。"我答。

"問題系而家佢唔見啦！"

還好有一陣子迷港劇，簡單的廣東話還是聽得懂的。

"怒，我知咗。"我說。

麻醉醫生是保障病人術中安全的天使，沒有他，手術只能停擺，無奈之下我只好跟著找人。

我一間一間病房地找去，連廚房間、醫護人員的休息床也没放過，可惜依舊没人，等回到護士站，我才聽説麻醉醫生昏倒在廁所裏，被緊急送往搶救室。

"可別又猝死了，幾個月前才死了一個。"我聽到護士間的閒言碎語。

俗語説"內科出事幾天，外科出事幾小時，麻醉出事幾分鐘"，人命關天，醫生（尤其麻醉科醫生）的工作強度及壓力之大可見一斑。

面對突發事件，我没有消沈很久，因爲接下來得替6號病房第一床的病人打營養針，他術後無法正常進食......

別怪我冷血，在醫院待久了，很容易對生死反應麻木，逝者已矣，生者如斯，人只能活在當下。

～

風風火火地工作一上午，好不容易到了午餐時間卻不見寶兒來喚我，心中不免犯嘀咕。

我獨自走進食堂買加東叻沙吃，它的湯頭以咖哩汁混合椰漿，口味甜、鹹、辣兼有，加上新鮮的蛤、蝦、魚餅等，很是開胃。

" Is this seat available?"有人問我能坐下否？

我擡頭望著問話的人，一時迷惑該答Yes 或No.

" I guess the answer is yes."説完，那人坐了下來，順便把手中的果汁放在桌上。

老公曾經不止一次告誡我要遠離Dr.Davies，但食堂不是我開的，他不請自來，我啥辦法也没有。

彼此沈默幾秒後，還是Dr.Davies先開口，他要我轉告老公低調點兒，有人反映他開的藥品太貴......

“ You can speak to him yourself.”我說。

孰料他卻答以爲我會對藥商代表感興趣，看來他多慮了。

我問這是什麼意思？他笑了笑没回答，端起果汁走人。

是這樣的，同樣一款藥，藥效其實差不多，醫生用A藥或B藥全憑個人喜好，於是藥商便得出動代表與醫生保持好的“合作”關係，男醫生用上美人計，各種巧笑情兮；女醫生則攻心，各種體貼關懷，私下有没有交易行爲不清楚，但鄭之龍肯定有，證據是我們的蜜月之旅全程有人買單，逢年過節更是禮物收不完，平常還有免費的加油券及超市禮券，明眼人一瞧就知道是怎麼回事。

Dr.Davies 屬於醫院的保守派，可説是“紀律委員會”的“義工”，難怪被老公列入黑名單。

“他提到‘藥商代表’到底是什麼意思？難道有我不知道的部份？”我心想。

懷著忐忑不安的心回到住院部，護士長提醒我佈置交誼廳，下午有中學生到醫院義演，劇目是《阿姆雷特》。

我點了點頭，往交誼廳的方向走去。

～

剛把米下鍋，老公便來電，他要我馬上整理行李，今晚他飛北海道。

“ Why ？之前没聽你提起過。”

“ 臨時被派去札幌醫科大學做交流，我也是剛剛才知道。”他答。

這實在太不尋常了，哪有這麼趕鴨子上架的？

我想起中午與Dr.Davies的對話，心中隱隱感到不安，遂説自已没去過北海道，今年的休假也還没用完，若跟人事説一聲，也許能放行……

"妳趕什麽熱鬧？我這是去工作，不是去玩，難不成妳打算留在酒店裏度過三天？"

我還想説什麽，被老公搶了先，他答自己正忙著，要我趕緊打包，兩個小時後他回家取，然後很没禮貌地掛斷。

～

老公拿上行李就出門，話懶得説一句。

五分鐘後我也跟著出門，知道他坐的是日本航空，我直搗黄龍。

在check in 櫃台前，我終於看到行單影隻的鄭之龍，頓時放下心來。真是的，竟然懷疑起自己的老公，吃飽了撐著！然而我没有開心很久，因爲……

"Honey～"一位長髮披肩的摩登女郎拖著行李箱快步走來。

鄭之龍給了她一個熊抱，還摸了人家屁股一把，兩人像連體嬰似地進入安檢口。

這是什麽狀況？我彷彿被雷擊中，人徹底懵了。

待我能再度思考，已是好幾分鐘以後的事，趕忙翻出手機打給老公，鈴聲響了五、六聲後被掛斷，再打時對方已關機。

"鄭之龍，你怎能這樣？我待你還不夠好嗎？"我欲哭無淚，感覺心已死。

第十章／不醉不歸

"Dr.Brown 懷疑我們的VIP病人聲帶長息肉，打了幾次電話到耳鼻咽喉科，接電話的汪醫生一會兒說妳老公上廁所；一會兒又說他有事外出，能不能麻煩妳轉告一下？"護士長説。

我冷冷地答鄭之龍有事到北海道了。

"怎……怎麼汪醫生不講實話？"

我回答不知道，但內心想說的是—大概兩人狼狽爲奸吧！

"真是糟糕！我們的VIP病人不能等，但他又指定要名醫動刀。"

"這簡單，要嘛等我老公從北海道回來，要嘛轉院，兩者選其一。"

護士長想了想說也只能這樣了，要我去問病人做何選擇？

"爲什麼是我？"我没好氣地問。

"難不成是我？"護士長也發飆，"崔媛媛，妳是不是大姨媽來了？別忘記我可是妳的頂頭上司。"

把氣發在上司身上的確不智，我只能摸摸鼻子走人，誰讓我是卑微的下屬？

～

這位VIP病人是國際知名的聲樂家，最近唱歌有音域變窄、發聲受限的現象，伴隨呼吸困難及喘鳴。

溝通的結果是他願意等鄭醫生回來，但仍希望先做個確診。

耳鼻咽喉科有三位門診醫生，鄭醫生去了北海道，Dr.Robinson請事假，唯一的Dr.Thompson則忙得焦頭爛額，門診室外大排長龍。

"看來只能由你出馬了，喉鏡檢查會不會？"我問。

"別忘了我在國內是認證過的主治醫生。"汪致遠有些惱怒地答。

"那好，我把病人帶過來。"

～

汪醫生細心地詢問病人的生活習慣，譬如抽不抽煙？喝不喝酒？吃不吃辛辣食物？又問最近有無上呼吸道感染？唱歌頻率多少？……

病人一一答覆後，汪醫生開始做喉鏡檢查，先噴麻藥再下管，檢查的結果在聲門下腔發現單側的帶蒂息肉，還好不大，用喉顯微技術即可切除。爲了安撫病人的情緒，他還特別強調這種手術的創傷小，疼痛感也少，加上鄭醫生又是名醫，大可放心……

他的說明讓病人感到滿意，我看見後者交待秘書給汪醫生兩張音樂會的入場券作爲答謝，汪醫生遲疑片刻，還是收下。

總是這樣，護士只能當配角，病人並不認爲也得給辛苦的護士來點兒獎勵。

我將不平一把揉碎，帶聲樂家回VIP病房後，很快投入一天繁複的工作裏。

"媛媛學姐～"我正給病人換第二瓶點滴，寶兒探頭進來。

"又什麼事？"

"今天是我的生日。"

我轉頭問她是真是假？她答千真萬確，她是愛恨分明的天蠍座。

"那麼……Happy Birthday to you."

寶兒說光口頭祝福不夠，還得來點兒實際的，今晚上她家吃飯，再到KTV唱通宵。

我答吃飯可以，唱通宵就免了，老公不喜歡……

"鄭醫生不是上北海道了嗎？妳有什麼好顧慮的？"

我停下手中動作問她聽誰說的？

"聽護士站裏的護士說的，好像鄭醫生走得很匆忙，讓耳鼻咽喉科雞飛狗跳的。"

Shit! 流言的速度還真快，到底還有沒有隱私可言？

"鄭醫生因公出差，兩、三天就回來，耳鼻咽喉科還有其他醫生在，說雞飛狗跳太誇張了。"我趕緊澄清。

寶兒答既然老公不在，何不Happy兩天？她等了很久才等來這個機會，汪醫生應該不會好意思說不……

"等等，妳該不會讓我去邀請汪致遠參加妳的生日派對吧？！"我問。

寶兒笑得一臉燦爛，說我不愧是她的好姐姐，一眼就瞧出她的心思。

“對不起，時間不對、心情也不對，改天我送妳生日禮物，今晚就不出去了，我想在家靜一靜。”

老公出軌的傷害還在，我的心亂糟糟的，連上班都心神不寧。

“那……中午一起吃飯總可以吧？！妳買個蛋撻請我吃，算是祝我生日快樂。”

壽星的要求不過份，我點頭同意。

中午時分，我隨寶兒到食堂吃飯，只是沒料到汪醫生也在場，而且點了一桌子的菜，包括葡式蛋撻。

“生日快樂！”他對我說。

我一時迷糊，這是什麼跟什麼？

“媛媛學姐，我跟汪醫生說今天是妳……的生日，鄭醫生剛好不在，一個人過生日多可憐！他馬上表示和我們一同慶祝，菜和蛋撻都是他買的，妳看汪醫生多有心！”

聽完我氣炸了，立即用眼神向寶兒抗議，她傳來乞求的訊號，我在心裏咒罵一句，但……看情形也只能幫她圓謊了。

“小生日，你們也太慎重其事了。”我坐了下來。

一頓普通的午餐成了我的生日宴席，真是莫名其妙得可以。

“鄭醫生因公出差，是一個人去的嗎？”不明就裏的寶兒突然哪壺不開提哪壺。

我還沒想到怎麼回答，汪致遠代勞了：“當然是一個人，不然還會有誰？呵呵！”

他說得那樣急，讓我不禁懷疑鄭之龍的“偷吃”，他是知情的，搞不好還從中幫忙過，這可不，早上護士長問他鄭醫生在哪兒，他不也遮遮掩掩的？

想至此，我怒火中燒。

"我老公不是一個人，他和一位長髮披肩的……醫生一起出差，這個人汪醫生也認識。"

"長髮披肩的醫生？"寶兒皺起眉頭，"誰啊？"

"是……是其他醫院的醫生。"那個一臉窘迫的男人答。

"就說嘛！我們醫院的女醫生都是短髮的，哪來的長髮披肩？"寶兒鬆了口氣。

汪致遠的回答讓我更確信他是知情人。

"來，"我舉起果汁，"祝我29歲生日快樂！"

面對那兩人的祝福，我突然感覺人生如戲，糊里糊塗成了壽星，也沒那個誰了。

吃完中飯，我主動邀請汪醫生今晚到寶兒家狂歡。

"你應該嚐嚐她的好手藝，還有，她的歌喉賽王菲，你也見識見識。"我說。

"妳呢？去嗎？"汪醫生問。

我答今晚有事不去。

"那……我也不去，手上還有essay要寫。"

看到寶兒失望的神情，我再一次被同情俘虜。

"如果我去，你去還是不去？"我問。

汪醫生答我若要他去，他就去。

這是啥意思？好像我左右他的決定似的。

"妳煮個飯要多久時間？"我轉頭問寶兒。

"七點能上桌。"她很快地答。

那夠了，我打算利用這短暫的兩、三個小時打聽出小三的來路，所謂"知己知彼，百戰百勝"。

"寶兒，下班後妳回家準備，我和汪醫生去選瓶好酒慶生，咱們來個不醉不歸！"我說。

第十一章／戀曲1990

寶兒對組屋有意見，認爲外型醜，也没游泳池、桑拿、健身房……等公共設施，加上無保安，任何人都可以進入，等於門戶洞開，可偏偏她的收入只能租組屋，而且還是老式那一種，不免氣結。

"到時你們從中峇魯路轉進來，我住在茂源台。"寶兒説。

"這麼巧？"汪醫生很驚訝，"我住在忠坡路上。"

原來他們兩人都住在中峇魯市場附近的舊式組屋住宅區內，這下好了，近水樓台先得月。

~

我和汪致遠約了下班後在醫院大廳見，他脱下白大褂，我則脱了綠色護士服，但彼此身上仍有去除不掉的藥水味。

"到哪個超市買酒？"他問。

我答附近就有好酒賣，要他隨我來。

我們的醫院座落在美麗的Dempsey Hill上，四十多年前這裏還是英軍駐紮的軍營，誰能料到如今成了新加坡的"小清新"，擁有多家酒吧、風味餐廳、咖啡座、精品屋、古董家俱店、畫廊以及藝術展廳等，是文青們和小資派鍾愛的休閒場所。

左拐右繞後，我帶他來到"Jack's"，店內除了有純正咖啡及新鮮出爐的糕點外，還能買到高品質的外國食品，比如法國黑松露、地中海海鹽、意大利黑醋、印度茶葉、自然健康的蜂蜜和果醬、還有上百種芝士及各國美酒，即便是挑剔的大廚也會感到滿意。

"不是買酒嗎？"汪醫生見我坐下，忍不住問。

"酒當然要買，一分鐘的事，咖啡也要喝，我們若太早去寶兒家，等於給她壓力，何不坐下來小憩片刻？"

汪致遠只得無奈坐下。

我在"劈頭直問"及"循序漸進"中游移，等點餐的服務員一走，我決定來軟的，希望他大發慈悲，提供一些有利的線索。

"我從國內二線城市來到新加坡當註冊護士，初期的水土不服以及'獨在異鄉爲異客'的孤獨感只有親身體驗過才會知道，所以當一個男人對我好，哪怕只是杯水車薪也會像荒漠甘泉般滋潤早已枯竭的心，我不想失去這份安定，因爲除了安定，我一無所有......"我語重心長地說。

"妳的安定若由他人給予，注定一輩子也無法安定。"

"那麽......請告訴我是誰破壞了這個表面上的安定，總不能讓我死不瞑目吧？！"

面對我的哀求，汪致遠看著很糾結，眼睛直盯著遠方不言語。

"好歹......好歹我們同文同種，搞不好遠古時代還是一家親，你不幫我，誰能幫我？"說完，我梨花帶雨。

" Miss Cui, 妳別……這不是叫我爲難嗎？"

我因此哭得越發不可收拾，成功引來幾道注目的眼光。

"好，好，好，我説，妳別哭了。"他終於投降。

原來那個長髮披肩的女郎叫Lucy，是大衆藥品的藥商代表，經常在醫院裏走動。汪致遠蹓過她幾次，但由於自己只是小小的MO，決定不了生殺大權，所以Lucy的眼睛總放在頭頂上，對他視若無睹。

也是湊巧，因爲没完成鄭之龍交待的工作，昨天中午用餐過後，他急忙往門診室跑，就這麼撞見Lucy與我老公坐在診療床上嬉戲，衣衫倒是整齊的。

他説了句Sorry後，退了出去。

没多久，Lucy走了出來，指責他是不懂得敲門的內地人，鄉巴佬！

汪致遠也來氣："鄉巴佬總比站街女強，鄭醫生是有家室的人，妻子也在這所醫院工作，請低調點兒，省得成了過街老鼠。"

"哼！我偏要高調，看你們能把我怎麼了？"Lucy答。

然後的然後，鄭醫生在下班前向人事告假三天，後面的事我也知道了。

聽完，我沈默良久，一旦猜測成了事實，我反倒没那麼心浮氣躁了。

"也許……也許妳的傷痛還是我造成的，但……請相信那是無心之過。"他説。

"別把罪過攬在身上，會偷腥的貓擋也擋不住。"

"很抱歉在妳生日時發生這樣的事，晚幾天也好……"

我遂告訴他今天不是我過生日，而是寶兒，她爲了能與他有更進一步的接觸，撒了個謊。

"爲……爲什麼？"

"大概是少女的矜持吧！待會兒你可別揭穿她。"我提醒。

喝完咖啡，我隨便拿了兩瓶紅葡萄酒，汪致遠主動到櫃台買單，然後我們叫了部出租車到中峇魯。

茂源台位於中峇魯南，那裏的老房子俗稱"五層樓"，建成一個馬蹄形，聽說底層是廢棄已久的防空壕。

"這是英國人設計的老房子，建得銅牆鐵壁、堅硬非常，連根釘子都釘不進去。即使大戰期間，炸彈也只是打穿一個小洞，底層拿來做防空壕再合適不過。"汪致遠介紹。

我問他是怎麼知道的？

"齊天宮的顧問説的，他是中峇魯的地方領袖，也是本活字典。"他答。

大概爲了安穩人心，寺廟在組屋群裏很常見，汪醫生因此結識顧問也就不足爲奇。

走進老式組屋，每層都有一條長長的開放式走廊，兩邊住著多戶人家，安靜且乾淨，只是濃濃的咖喱味有點兒讓人倒胃口。

"別告訴我今晚妳煮印度餐。"寶兒一開門，我衝口而出。

"没有的事，隔壁鄰居是印度人，連夜裏11、12點也煮，讓人很受不了。"她答。

寶兒租的是三居室其中一間，房東是新加坡人，有個還在讀高中的兒子。我們匆忙打過招呼後躲進房間內，小小的矮几上有個電磁爐，看來今晚吃火鍋。

"知道你們愛吃辣，我特地準備了毛肚火鍋。"寶兒邀功似地説明。

我能吃小辣，但不是非辣不歡，這個寶兒也知道，顯然她把汪醫生的口味擺在第一位。

“ 水滾了，讓我先將牛脊髓放入火鍋內，很快就能吃，你們快坐下。”寶兒説。

由於心情不好，我喝得多、吃得少，汪致遠也是，我喝幾杯，他也跟著喝，只有寶兒滴酒未沾。

“ 不喝酒的人生多乏味呀！”我感嘆。

“ 妳以爲我不願意？但一想到會起酒疹，只得禁口。”她答。

酒足飯飽後，寶兒提議到Party World飆歌，我答不去，她説我不可以如此掃興，硬是押著我一同出門。

在K歌房裏，我才見識到什麼是好歌喉。寶兒已經不得了，汪致遠的歌聲更勝天籟，他們兩人不當歌手太可惜了。

“ 唱首失戀的歌給我聽，快！”趁著幾分醉意，我對那個男人提要求。

汪致遠説爲我唱歌可以，但他想唱快歌，因爲不想看到有人流淚……

“ 唱！”我拿起寶特瓶指向他，“ 不唱我斃了你。”

“ 唱吧！我想聽羅大佑的《戀曲1990》。”寶兒站在我這邊。

盛情難卻，汪致遠喝了一大口水後，像下定某種決心，他拿起麥克風開唱。

……

人生難得再次尋覓相知的伴侶，

生命終究難捨藍藍的白雲天。

……

. . .

不知爲什麼，聽到這兩句我感慨萬千，淚水嘩嘩嘩地流。

"媛媛學姐，妳怎麼了？"寶兒輕撫我後背，"没這麼感動吧？！太誇張了。"

"我來，"姓汪的丟了麥克風向我走來，一把推開寶兒擁我入懷，"没事了，乖，没事。"

他親了親我的髮，我腦子一熱，將嘴湊上去，兩人就這麼擁吻起來，直到寶兒氣急敗壞地將我們拉開。

"有完没完？"她咆哮著，"你們是真醉還是藉酒裝瘋？"

"醉了，回家！"汪致遠率先起身，但走没幾步就一頭撞上牆壁，發出好大的聲響。

我呵呵呵地笑著，問他撞傻了没？没傻我們一起去酒店開房......

寶兒隨即怒甩我一耳光，罵我不要臉！

"我哪裏不......不要臉了？不要臉的在......在北海道......"我支支吾吾地答。

未曾想下一秒突然傳來寶兒的呼喊聲，那聲音忽遠忽近，忽近忽遠，我的視線也越來越模糊，最終成了白茫茫一片，醒來已是隔天一早的事。

第十二章／意外

手機響了好幾聲，我翻了個身，不理。它卻像揮之不去的夢魘，一聲接著一聲，非常的有毅力，我不得不伸手去接。

" Hello."我閉著眼睛說。

" 妳在哪裏？Miss Cui."護士長的聲音兇巴巴的。

我答在家。

" 都早上十點多了還在家？"

我一聽嚇壞了，睜眼一看更是徹底懵了，這是哪裏？

" 我……我……馬上到！"

掛上手機，我才發現不止護士長打給我，連老公也打給我了，而且不下數十通，我是怎麼了？睡死了？

跳下床，我拉開窗簾往外瞧，Party World K 歌坊所在的亮閣購物中心近在咫尺，難不成是寶兒送我來的？人呢？

懷著不安的心，我很快梳洗一下，然後到前台退房，意外發現房費已付，看來待會兒得還寶兒錢。

～

即使打出租車，回到醫院也近中午，護士長大動肝火，我像個孫子似地拼命賠不是。

"人手已經嚴重不足，妳和寶兒還玩失蹤，到底有沒有敬業精神？"

"寶……寶兒不見了？"我嚇得闔不攏嘴。

"誰說不是？她最好有個好理由，否則我肯定給她一個警告。"護士長氣呼呼地走了。

昨晚醉酒以後的事，我怎麼也想不起來，虧寶兒有心，送我到酒店住宿，可她人呢？

由於遲到，做完該做的，我晚了一個半鐘頭才到食堂吃飯，踫巧聽到離座的人講的話屑子，原來汪醫生今天也無故缺席了。

難道昨晚那一撞撞得不輕？

我翻出手機分別打給那兩人，可惜任憑鈴聲怎麼響都無人接聽，這是怎麼回事？

"嘟……嘟嘟嘟……"剛掛上手機就有來電，我趕緊接聽。

"妳到哪兒去了？我打了無數通電話給妳，還差點兒報警！"

聽到老公的抱怨，我幾乎要像從前一樣縮頭縮尾地道歉，還好今天腦子夠清楚，沒做"割地賠款"的事。

"還活著，有什麼事？"我冷冷地答。

"我……"他有些錯愕，大概沒料到我是這種反應，"就想告訴妳，我在北海道交流得很好，得到不少經驗和收獲。"

呵呵！交流得很好？得到不少經驗和收獲？怎麼聽起來像污言穢語？

"Congratulations. 還有事嗎？"我問。

"我明晚回家吃晚餐。"

"知道了。"

掛上電話我趕緊吃麵，這麼一耽擱，麵都糊了。

下午三點多接到寶兒打來的電話，她要我跟人事告假。

"都這個點了才想起來要請假？醫院是妳家開的？"我沒好氣地問。

她答醫院不是她家開的，但睡死了有什麼辦法？昨晚把汪致遠送往醫院，又馬不停蹄夥同KTV的服務人員將我送往就近的酒店，她已經筋疲力竭，更別說觀察期一過，還得連夜把那個高大的男人送回家，還好汪致遠能走兩步，否則再怎麼著她也無法背一個150斤的男子上樓……

"妳現在在哪兒？"

"汪致遠家。"

"汪致遠在哪裏？"

"床上，額頭腫了個大包。"

雖然很想問她昨晚睡哪裏？但還是忍住沒問。

"知道了。"我答。

掛上手機，我往人事處走去。

下班後，我上汪致遠家探望那兩人。寶兒說他們已經餓了一整天，問我能不能順路上中峇魯市場帶兩份外賣？她沒力氣煮飯了。

中峇魯市場是一個建於50年代的菜市場，它不像牛車水那樣專門接待各國遊客，反倒像是當地人會去的地方，樓下賣菜，樓上提供美食，用餐環境非常乾淨、明亮。

我上二樓轉了一圈，買了菜頭粿、星洲炒米粉、娘惹粽、馬來烤麵包、燒鵝及豆花水，肉骨茶雖然看起來不錯，但隊伍排得太長，果斷放棄。

別看現在的中峇魯屬於老街區，二戰之前，這兒可是新加坡的富人區，普通人是住不起的。瞧！圓陽台、平房頂、螺旋樓梯、隨處可見的椰子樹⋯⋯當時屬於新式住宅，也吸引了不少文人墨客前往居住，比如作家郁達夫、畫家劉海粟等。

汪致遠住在中峇魯路一轉進來的忠坡路上，那裏有很多"飛機樓"（長長的樓身兩翼對稱，彷彿一架架即將起飛的飛機，這是英國殖民政府興建的第一批公共住房）。

我走進其中一架"飛機"內，是寶兒開的門。

"妳終於來了，我已經餓得前胸貼後背！"她接過外賣往廚房走去。

這是個有些陰暗的單元房，窗戶很小，只有兩張攤開的報紙大，如果改成落地窗，採光會好很多。

"Hi."那個額頭上有明顯血腫的男人向我打招呼。

"嘖嘖嘖⋯⋯冷敷了沒？"我問。

"嗯！頭顱CT也做了，沒事。"他答。

我說那就好，醫院少了他們兩人，一整天都雞飛狗跳的⋯⋯

"真的？"汪醫生一本正經地問。

"假的，"寶兒端來四盤吃食，"像我們這種小螺絲釘，可有可無。"

汪致遠說此話差矣，螺絲釘雖小，缺了可不行，他明天就上班……

"額頭腫成那樣，還是休息兩天吧！"寶兒關心地說。

我也站在她那邊，留得青山在，不怕沒柴燒，何況鄭醫生很快就會回來，能緩解耳鼻咽喉科的看診壓力……

"學姐夫什麼時候回來？"寶兒問。

"明天晚上。"

"這下好了，小別勝新婚，一切又回歸正常了。"寶兒面帶喜色。

如果回歸正常代表我又得像個小媳婦兒似地窩窩囊囊活著，那我寧願"不正常"。

"吃吧！再不吃就涼了。"我先下箸，他們二位也跟著吃起來。

吃完飯沒多久，汪醫生的兩位室友就陸續回家，我們也不好多停留，很快起身告辭。

"去哪兒？"寶兒問。

"回家。"

"妳家在哪兒？能不能讓我見識見識？我還沒參觀過新加坡的豪宅呢！"她眼露期待地問。

我答也就那樣，沒啥稀奇的。

"拜托啦！小姐姐，就看一下下，看完就走，絕不食言。"

如果鄭之龍在，我肯定不會帶外人回家，偏偏他明天晚上才到，讓我失去了最好的藉口。

"好吧！看在昨晚的汗馬功勞上，我就滿足一下妳的好奇心，可別回頭又跟別人說嘴去。"

"一定，一定。"寶兒忙不疊點頭。

第十三章/離婚挽歌

"哇！好漂亮啊！我若住在這棟房子裏，肯定每天笑著醒來。"寶兒站在玄關處睜大眼睛説。

"行了！也就住的前幾天會開心，審美也有疲勞的時候。"

寶兒説我是人在福中不知福，如果她有這麼一棟大房子，絕對天天開派對，不像我，小氣得很！

我想起鄭之龍，除了必要的客人外，輕易不肯讓人進入他的私人領域，遑論開Party, 那是犯大忌。

"妳隨便看看哈！我泡壺茶，龍井還是香片？"我問。

寶兒答隨便，然後像劉姥姥進大觀園似地走開。

～

"媛媛學姐，我越來越羨慕妳了，人生開掛指的就是妳這種人。"

我們喝了多久的茶，寶兒就讚美了多久，連一塊瓷磚、一片玻璃，在她看來都美得無懈可擊。

"如果我說家裏没請女傭，我得將上班以外的大部份時間都耗在維持這個家的乾淨、整齊上，妳還會羨慕我嗎？"我問。

"請個阿姨也就一千多新幣，對你們這種家庭來說，不貴的。"

寶兒不知道我家每月的開銷得控制在一千新幣上下，多了老公會過問。

"呵呵！是不貴，"我打起哈哈，"平常少運動，剛好做做家務活動一下筋骨，妳説是吧？！"

我們又聊了些無關痛癢的八卦，寶兒忽然提到汪醫生，説感覺那人不排斥她，她還是有希望的。

"何以見得？"我太好奇了。

"他不介意我用他的電腦上網，而且吃我削好的蘋果……"

"這……不是很尋常嗎？"

寶兒説我不懂，使用電腦、吃她遞上的蘋果的確没什麼，但汪致遠不僅把電腦密碼告訴她，還用含情脈脈的眼神看她削蘋果，所以她認爲未來可期。

含情脈脈的眼神？這不是戲劇裏才會有的情節？難不成汪醫生也來這一套？他看起來不像會做戲的人呀！

我想起自己索來的吻，也許別人會認爲醉酒做的事不算數，但只有自己心裏清楚，我是三分醉意，七分清醒，換個尖嘴猴腮讓我試試，我肯定掩面而逃，更別説打啵兒了？然而……爲什麼汪致遠不拒絕？

"醫院裏那麼多醫生，爲啥妳獨看中姓汪的？"我問起寶兒這個重要的問題。

她答"非我族類，其心必異"，雖然新加坡的華人居多，好幾代以前也來自中國，但畢竟受過不同文化的洗禮，話都講不到一塊兒去，還是選國內來的人爲妥，況且汪致遠的長相好，帶出去特有面子，不像鄭……

看寶兒捂住嘴巴，我知道她指的是鄭之龍。

"我知道自己的老公長得醜，但我也不是沈魚落雁之姿，所以彼此彼此。"

"對不起，我不是有意的。"她吐了吐舌頭。

"沒事，"我起身去拿錢包，翻出幾張票子遞給她，"這是昨晚的酒店錢，謝謝妳送我上酒店。"

寶兒默默收下，然後說時候不早了，她得趕最後一班公交。

我没挽留她，陪她走到大街上。

即便是醜老公，也不保證安全，外面的鶯鶯燕燕看的不是皮囊而是鈔票，偏偏老公有很多很多的鈔票，這是很大的閃光點。

此時的我也感到壓力山大，他是逢場做戲還是來真的？我該如何面對歸來的老公？是假裝不知情還是河東獅吼？

就在心煩意亂中，我將三道菜端上桌，老公進門時，我正面對還冒著熱氣的晚餐發愣。

"老公回來了，怎麼不拿雙拖鞋過來？非得我喊？"鄭之龍站在玄關處發火，即使拖鞋就在他腳邊不遠處。

我噢了一聲，勉爲其難地走過去。

"真不知妳成天都在想些什麼？"他一臉輕蔑。

我把到嘴的話壓下去，崔媛媛，耐心點兒，還不到攤牌的時候。

鄭之龍穿上我遞過去的拖鞋後，轉身走向洗手間。總是這樣，他認爲外面髒，進門一定得先洗手。

"就吃這些？"剛坐下他就抱怨，"好歹顏色也均勻些，怎麼感覺血淋淋的？"

我猛一瞧，西紅柿炒雞蛋、糖醋魚、酸辣白菜，三道菜都紅火一片，難道潛意識當中我認爲今晚會刀光血影？

"Shit."老公將嘴巴裏的食物吐出，"不是讓妳別在西紅柿炒雞蛋裏加糖？"

我加了嗎？也許迷迷糊糊當中錯把糖當鹽了。

鄭之龍接著將筷子伸向糖醋魚，很不確定地戳了戳，再夾一片白菜入口，咀嚼幾下後很快下結論："魚肉底層是生的，只有酸辣白菜還可以吃，妳是怎麼了？傻了還是笨了？"

"是傻了、笨了，"我冷冷地答，"自己選的老公在外面偷腥，回來還趾高氣昂，我……我受夠了！"

"偷腥？神經病！誰偷腥來著？說話得有憑有據！"

好呀！不到黃河心不死，到現在還想耍賴？我遂把尾隨他到機場，看見他摸一位長髮披肩女人的屁股一事說出。

"So? 這只能證明我有鹹豬手，不能證明我出軌，完全兩碼子事。"他毫無愧色地答。

啥？簡直睜眼說瞎話，我氣不打一處來，反問他若我和別的男人親嘴，是否只能證明我作風海派，不能證明我浪蕩？

"妳跟男人親嘴了？"他虎著眼。

我想起與汪致遠的激吻，一分神，沒及時否認。

"果然親了，妳這個不要臉的爛貨！"

他伸手想打我，被我躲掉，讓他更加憤怒，撲上來就是一頓好打。如果我沒反抗，情況也許會好些，偏偏我反擊了，所以被揍得更慘，而且連臉也遭殃，因爲跌倒時撞上桌角，額頭起了個大包，還因大聲呼救又死不上樓，嘴巴被老公強行塞入抹布，拉扯中，嘴角裂開一個口子……

“説！跟妳親嘴的是哪個不要命的？”

此時的我頭髮凌亂、傷痕累累，即使抹布被拿開，我也沒力氣喊叫。

“没有，没有人和我親嘴。”我氣若如絲地答。

“崔媛媛，妳肚子裏有幾條蛔蟲我會不知道？妳肯定親了，還是承認吧！坦白從寬、抗拒從嚴。”

我問他要不要也坦白從寬、抗拒從嚴？人事説他請的是事假，壓根兒不是出公差，這作何解釋？

他答生意上的事，説了我也不懂，要不是怕我誤會，他也不會撒謊，又説男人在外工作多辛苦，女人在家就得多體諒，哪有趁老公不在和別的男人勾勾搭搭的？這在古代會被行木馬刑，即在木馬背上豎起一根大拇指粗的尖木椿，直刺女犯的下身，隨著木馬的前行，那根尖木椿也一伸一縮，讓女犯鮮血直流、痛不欲生……

我知道自己的老公是傳統的大男人，但没想到他的腦子還停留在那麼久遠以前，簡直是食古不化。

“鄭之龍，我受夠了這一切，不管是木馬刑還是五馬分屍，I don't care. 只求你放過我，我們……我們還是離婚吧！”

這是我第一次提“離婚”，老公悶不吭聲地直視我，那樣子像是要把我活剝生吞。

我低下頭去，躲開他眼裏射出的箭。

“告訴我，那個要妳離婚的男人是誰？”

我還能聽見從他牙縫裏發出的聲音，嘶嘶嘶的，像蛇在吐信。

“没有這樣一個人，而是我真的受夠了，再也不想過非人的生活。”

“妳要想清楚，離婚的女人難再嫁，也別想從我這裏撈到一分好處，更別想要綠卡，因爲我會盡一切辦法將妳轟出新加坡，等著瞧！”

提到綠卡，這也是我耿耿於懷的地方。鄭之龍曾信誓旦旦地說婚後會幫我申請護照，拿著新加坡護照，到哪兒，哪兒方便，然而一個月過去了、兩個月過去了、半年過去了……我拿的還是工作簽證。

“我總得觀察觀察妳，很多女人爲了一本新加坡護照假結婚，我得確保自己不是那塊跳板。”他是這麼解釋的。

如今他又以辦綠卡爲談判籌碼，威脅離婚就不給辦，是可忍孰不可忍？

“不論護照還是綠卡，我通通不要，即使遣返回中國也無所謂，只求你在離婚協議書上簽字，我可以淨身出戶。”

沒想到我毫無原則的退讓反倒讓鄭之龍更加確認我做了對不起他的事，否則懦弱的我不會如此決絕……

“沒有……沒有這麼一個男人……是你……是你想出來的，拜托別打我，別打……我疼……”我邊後退邊苦苦哀求。

疼痛每幾分鐘就找上我，這次的下手力道比前幾次都來的凶猛有力，我以爲自己會因此掛了。

也許因爲提到離婚的緣故，家暴過後鄭之龍沒像往常一樣幫我上藥、向我道歉，而是任憑我躺在客廳的冰涼地磚上度過一夜，完全不加理會。

“早餐呢？”老公邊扣鈕扣邊下樓來。

“馬上。”我猛的站起身，馬上感到一陣昏眩，趕緊扶住牆壁。

“別裝了，”他對著玄關的穿衣鏡邊打領帶邊說，“我們的事還沒完，除非妳道歉並且告訴我那人是誰，否則天天有妳罪受。"

我忍住淚水、咬緊牙關，然後像隻戰敗的雞，有氣無力地走向廚房……

第十四章／揚長而去

老公要我在家休息，不是因爲心疼我，而是因爲臉上帶傷，怕引起不必要的關注。

我默默吃粥，不發一語，等鄭之龍前腳一走，我後腳也跟著出門。我的想法很簡單，他怕什麼，我來什麼，偏要讓他臉上無光。

$\sim$

" Miss Cui, what happened?"

運氣好，一踏進醫院就踫見院長，他可是神龍見首不見尾，一年難得見上幾次面。

" My husband beat me last night."我答老公昨晚打我了。

他怔了一下，問我是不是開玩笑？

我沒回答，説了聲："Excuse me."後快步走人。

第二個開口問的是護士長，我依舊回答同樣的答案，她的反應和院長同出一轍，我這才發現鄭之龍的表面功夫做得很到位，至少周邊的同事都不認爲他會打老婆。

"媛媛學姐，"寶兒向我飛奔而來，"我聽説了，妳......怎麽摔的跤？"

原來大家都認爲我是摔跤受的傷，壓根兒不是被家暴。

"半夜起來上廁所，没開燈，摔了一跤。"爲了"順應民意"，我撒了個謊。

"就説嘛！怎麽可能是學姐夫下的手，他是那麽好的一個人。"

原來鄭之龍如此强大，背後有那麽多人支持，想跟他鬥無異以卵擊石。

"妳手上是什麽東西？"我問寶兒。

"九號病房第二床今天早上咯血了，Dr.Jones要我把片子拿給呼吸內科的石醫生看。"

呼吸內科和耳鼻咽喉科相距不到五十米。

"交給我吧！我正好要上內科轉轉。"我説。

～

把片子交給石醫生後，我在內科晃蕩，果不其然，收到好幾雙好奇的眼神，但我假裝没看見。

"呦！這不是鄭夫人？"內科馮主任向我走來。

他的眼光很快落在我臉上，我以爲他會説出什麽驚心動魄的話，但......没有。

"來找鄭醫生？"他很隨意地問起。

我答不是，而是來揭示傷口，我......昨晚被老公打了。

"呵呵！"他笑了，" very funny. 我不知道鄭醫生的老婆如此幽默。”

整個內科歸馮主任管，他與鄭之龍又有著千絲萬縷般的關係，是利益共同體，我斷不可能從他這裏得到任何同情與安慰。

“Excuse me.”他很快與我道別，那樣子像是甩掉一個大包袱。

我繼續在內科閒蕩，直到……

“Miss Cui, 妳怎麼在這裏？”

我轉過頭去，是汪醫生，他的手裏拿著一個銀托盤，上面有針管和藥劑。

“我……”

“妳的臉怎麼了？”他關心地問。

我答跌了個跤。

“是不是……他？”顯然汪致遠並不買單。

“不是，”我看著他，那是一雙清澈無邪的眼睛，“是，我經常被家暴。”

“打女人的男人很不可原諒，我就從來不打女人。”

不知爲什麼，聽完這席話讓我感觸良深，怎麼我就沒那麼好的運氣遇上這麼好的男人？

“別哭，”他看了一眼四周，“這裏是醫院，如果……我會盡綿薄之力。記住，別打草驚蛇，妳有我的電話。”

我們對目相望，盡在不言中。

“知道了，你快走吧！”我還是放走他。

這是在孤苦無援之際，第一次接收到來自血親以外的溫暖，總算有人相信我，也總算有人願意作我的後盾，雖然我不知道他能幫我到什麼程度。

汪醫生説別打草驚蛇，於是我回住院部，讓"任性妄爲"戛然而止，然而不到午餐時間，老公還是上護士站找人。

"媛媛，我不是讓妳在家好好休息嗎？跌傷了還堅持上班，哎！妳就是這麼敬業, 叫我如何説妳好？"他過來牽我的手，"走！我帶妳回家。"

他那一副"好丈夫"的嘴臉真讓人噁心，但護士站裏的護士卻紛紛傳來傾羨的眼神，大概沒過多久，鄭醫生"疼老婆"的事跡會傳遍整個醫院。

我甩開他的手説自己不回去，這裏正忙著。

"回去吧！老公都親自過來帶妳，這樣的好男人，妳打燈籠都找不到。"説話的是Miss Qiu, 來自福建，五十歲上下。

衆所周知，閩南女人的地位普遍低下，那裏的男人又多是"甩手掌櫃"，所以一旦遇到懂得疼惜女人的男人，無不動容。

"媛媛，還是別添亂，快走吧！嗯？"老公對我微笑，讓我想起加菲貓。

就在衆人的催促聲中，我不負所望地答："好，讓我把制服換下。"

人總得識時務，我不想被唾沫星子淹死，遂走向更衣室。

"妳不嫌丟臉嗎？頂著個大花臉上班，還説是被我打的。"一回到家，老公就大發雷霆。

我問他是打人的丟臉還是被打的丟臉？

他惱羞成怒地説就算我昭告天下也沒人會信，他可是醫院裏的表率，王牌中的王牌。

"越是菁英就越可恨，也許大部份的人都會被你的演技所蒙騙，但我相信這世上總有心如明鏡的人存在。"

"呵呵！忘了妳還有個相好的。"

我答這是"欲加之罪何患無辭"，怎麼不談談他的"北海道之旅"？

"不跟妳說了，我趕著上班。"他走沒兩步回過身來，"好好待在家裏打掃衛生，哪兒也別想去，我替妳請假三天。"

"三天？我才不想在家待那麼久！"我喊著。

老公不理會我，將門用力甩上。

我站在工具梯上擦拭挑高的窗戶，一個不小心踩空跌了下去，感覺鼻子一陣劇痛，有熱熱的液體流了出來，用手一抹，原來流鼻血了，我趕緊頭向前傾並用手指捏緊鼻翼根部靜待血止。看著滴在白色地磚上的血花，心裏無來由地感到悲哀，人都被欺負成這個樣子，我還在打掃這棟"冰冷、無愛"的家，圖的是什麼？

等哭完，淚流盡，鼻血也止住了。

我冷靜地上樓打包行李，這個家再也待不下去了。

要出走首先得有錢，我的手上有一張銀行卡及信用卡的副卡，前者的餘額不多，主要用來支付水、電、煤氣、物業管理費……等，後者則依附在老公的主卡之下，每月的限額在2000新幣。

"還好母親英明，將我的薪水全留下，否則現在連出走的本錢也沒有。"我心想。

當初爲了躲過鄭之龍的耳目曾將這筆錢辦了自動轉滙，錢一到賬就滙往中國，爲此老公不止一次地冷嘲熱諷，他説光滙費就去掉收入的5%，真不知我父母是怎麼想的，看過貪心的人，還没看過這麼貪的……

其實滙費問題我早留意到，做戲三個月後，看鄭之龍已不再糾結此事，我忙不疊上銀行中止自動滙款至中國的服務，另外又開了戶頭，所以老公一直不知道我還有個小金庫。

我將手伸進許久不穿的牛仔褲口袋內，摸出一張銀色銀行卡，裏面應該還有兩萬多新幣，夠我支撐一陣子。

鄭之龍的東西我一樣也没帶走，只有無名指上的兩克拉鑽戒讓我躊躇了一會兒，脱了戴，戴了又脱，最後還是戴上。雖然那是個恥辱，讓我簽下了賣身契，但終究是屬於我的，哪天……我可以賣了變現。

等收拾妥當後，我回頭一望這棟讓我的生命耗損十個月的籠子，忽然感覺一陣輕鬆。

“永別了！”我説。

拿上行李，我義無反顧地離去……

第十五章／朋友

我在牛車水附近租了個床位，在異國總不由自主地想和自己的祖國靠近些。

牛車水指的是"唐人街"，早年該地没有自來水，爲了清掃塵土飛揚的街道，每天不得不用牛車運水來沖洗，故得其名。這裏是新加坡華人聚集最多的地方，不僅擁有來自中國各地的小商品及美食，還包括現代購物中心。

" Good afternoon，Miss." 我一進旅舍，前台小哥很熱情地和我打招呼。

我回禮並報上名來，他説我訂的是四人房，有兩人已入住，洗手間和浴室共用，房間內有帶鎖的保險櫃，附早餐，餐室在三樓……

入住背包客旅舍實屬無奈，由於不知這場戰役將持續多久，一分錢不得不掰成兩分用，如果再延長久一點兒，恐怕得另租房子住了。

我的房間在二樓，没有電梯，還好行李不重，一個人扛没問題。

床是上下鋪，每個床頭都有充電插座和燈，挺乾淨的。與兩位室友打過招呼後，我把行李箱塞進床底下，然後爬到上鋪。

窗戶很小，旁邊就是清真寺，還能看見穿白袍的阿拉伯人及賣烤餅的小販。我就這麼望著窗外發呆，直到夕陽西下，然後夜幕降臨……

"嘟……嘟嘟……"果然是鄭之龍的來電，大概回家後發現我不見了。

我將手機調成靜音，這種感覺很奇妙，好像老公在不遠處咒罵我，而我卻一句也聽不見。

約莫半小時後，那人才放棄call我，改發短信，但我沒興趣打開來看。

既然警報解除，我恢復手機鈴聲，沒想到隨即傳來熟悉的嘟嘟聲，不會吧？這麼有毅力？

還好掛斷前我瞄了一眼來電顯示，否則汪致遠就要被我撇在一旁了。

"妳還好吧？"他問。

"很好，我……離家出走了。"

他在電話那頭停頓一會兒後，說："那麼出來吃個飯吧！"

我答行，讓他來牛車水找我。

～

夜市的牛車水燈火輝煌、車水馬龍，像是中國的廟會，吸引著全世界紛至沓來的遊客。

我和汪致遠約在牛車水大廈見面，就在地鐵站出來不遠處，一樓主要賣生活用品，二樓是大排檔，有好吃的肉骨茶、港式點心和魚豆腐等。

由於我住的旅舍離約定的地點很近，我特意晚了十分鐘出門，没想到汪醫生的動作這麼快，他已經站在那裏等候。

"Hi."我努力擠出一張笑臉。

他的目光停留在我臉上一小會兒，問鄭醫生是否"又"打我了？

"没有。"

"那妳的鼻子……"

噢！原來說的是這個。

"做家務時從工作梯上摔了下來。"我解釋。

"算是工傷囉！"

本來想否認，但再一想，自從嫁給鄭之龍以後，我在家一直做著女傭的工作，說是"工傷"也不爲過。

"的確是工傷啊！可恨的是連保險費也拿不到。"面對苦難，我也只能自嘲兼故作瀟灑，"想吃什麼？我請客。"

他答怎能讓女人破費？爲了慶祝我重獲自由身，他請我吃米其林餐廳。

那得多貴？

一路上我再三推辭，等靠近斯密斯街口時，我終於放下心來。

"怎麼知道我愛吃他家的油雞？"我問。

"因爲我接收到妳的心電感應。"他答。

"了凡油雞飯"是全球最便宜的米其林一星餐廳，5-7新幣有一份，不僅雞肉香嫩，雞皮還特別彈Q，把雞汁淋在米飯上，連盤子都能舔得乾乾淨淨。油雞麵也特別，用的是鹹水麵，非常有勁道。

拿號時，服務員告訴我們適逢飯點，得等一個鐘頭以上……

“等不等？”汪致遠轉頭問我。

“等，我現在什麼都沒有，除了時間。”

爲了這句“話中話”，他特意看了我一眼。

由於需要久候，汪致遠提議到外面走走，經過路邊冷飲攤時，他體貼地買了兩杯喝的。

“妳要哪個？”他問。

我要了美祿恐龍，是用美祿調制的冰飲，爲什麼叫“恐龍”呢？因爲表面還撒上一層巧克力粉，看起來很像恐龍的背脊，因而得名。我拿走“恐龍”，汪致遠便只能喝“哥斯拉”，那是在美祿恐龍的基礎上加上一球奶油冰淇淋。

“我喜歡喝美祿，小時候母親經常泡給我喝，她說這是含麥芽的飲品，有多種礦物質和維生素，能讓我既聰明又健康。”

我說他的確聰明，否則怎麼考得上醫學院？身體看著也健康，他父母一定引以爲傲。

“母親應該會，父親……我不知道他是怎麼想的？也許恨我吧！因爲是我將他送進牢房裏。”

話題一下子沈重起來，我問他是怎麼回事？

“家暴，”他像說別人似地說自己，“我父親愛喝酒，酒後便動粗，母親和我沒少挨打過。慘劇發生在一個刮風下雨的夜晚，母親爲了保護我，拿起菜刀和父親拼命，慌亂之中，父親奪刀砍死了母親，我成了唯一的見證人。”

原來陽光青年也有晦暗的過去，而他對我的“義舉”如今看來也其來有自，我的心因此與他靠近許多。

“I am sorry.”我深表同情。

“沒事，都過去了。我當然心疼母親，但如果不是因爲這件事，我也遇不上自己的養父母，他們無私地接納我，還負擔高昂的學費，我希望有朝一日能湧泉相報。"

我感慨地説他總算是守得雲開見月明，而我還不知猴年馬月才能真正脫離苦海……

"我認爲首先妳得去報案留個記錄，同時開具驗傷報告，這樣打起官司對妳才有利。"

想到既要報案又要驗傷，我猶豫了。都説家醜不可外揚，一旦撕破臉，肯定兩敗俱傷，我看……還是先協商再説吧！

他答隨我，如果我等得起的話。

"什麼意思？"我問。

"根據新加坡的法律，結婚三年內不得提離婚，除非一方有重大過失，譬如家暴、刑事犯罪……等。"

"怎麼辦？我的婚姻還不滿一年，若要再等兩年，我恐怕會没命！"

"所以妳得盡快下決定，"他低頭看了一眼腕錶，"快輪到我們了，也許吃完飯妳的思路會清晰一些。"

我點點頭，我們往相反的方向走去。

第十六章/模範夫妻

汪致遠建議我去警局報案留記錄，同時開具驗傷報告，這樣打起官司對我才有利。想到要在陌生人面前一遍又一遍地敍述被老公欺凌的過程，甚至掀開傷口讓人拍照……不，不行，太丟臉了，別人會怎麼看我？如果鄭之龍被激怒，反潑我一身髒水，我要怎麼辦？難道讓雙方互撕直到玉石俱焚？

我搖搖頭，對這步棋投下反對票。

就在混亂的思緒中，我迷迷糊糊走進夢鄉，直到隔天一早被寶兒的來電叫醒。

"媛媛學姐，好點兒了没？聽說妳大後天才上班，怎麼辦？我已經開始想妳了。"

聽到自己被人需要著，我鼻頭一酸，要她多保重，把份內的事做了，同時努力提升自己，將來找個好人嫁了，不像我……

寶兒在手機那端咯咯咯地笑，要我別開玩笑了，她一生最大的願望就是找一個像學姐夫一樣多金又有學識的人嫁了，當然，如果顏質再好一點兒就滿分了。

"不説了，放妳去工作，省得妳被護士長罵。"

話不投機，我想早點兒收線，但寶兒不依，她説我真沈得住氣，自己的老公獲獎了還能處變不驚，她要是我，早……

"獲獎？獲什麼獎？"我問。

"媛媛學姐別裝了，再裝就不像了。我不管，這次妳一定得請客，我想吃André的法式大餐……"

掛上電話，我還能感覺耳朵嗡嗡作響。

得知老公獲獎的消息，雖然有些驚訝，但不感意外。鄭之龍一向自我期許很高，打從認識至今，他没有一天不看書，有時甚至會爲了一件棘手的病症，不辭辛苦地與其他醫生討論及翻閱國際醫學雜誌，就想從中找出相同或類似的病例好借鑒。這樣戰戰兢兢、如履薄冰的敬業精神的確值得表揚，即使我對他的人品並不苟同。

～

旅舍的早餐不外麵包、果醬、麥片、咖啡、牛奶等，自然和五星級酒店的没法兒比，但管吃飽。

我邊吃邊看早報，報上説中國現在有無人超市及ATM機掃臉取款服務，我忽然覺得自己已被時代巨輪輾壓，這還是我認識的祖國嗎？才出國幾年自己竟成了鄉巴佬。

同桌的兩個年輕洋人看我看得入迷，問我報上可有什麼新消息？我將報紙遞過去，告訴他們中國有多現代化，藍眼珠一臉驚訝，反問我中國有電嗎？

我忍俊不禁，告訴他們中國没水没電，到現在女人還裹小腳……

然後黑皮膚彎腰看了我桌面下的雙足後，説還好我不是中國人。

" Sorry, I am Chinese."我驕傲地答我是中國人，然後起身將自己用過的杯盤拿到廚房清洗。

~

用過早餐，本想宅在旅舍一整天，但吸塵器的聲音實在太吵雜，我決定出外走走。當走到哈芝巷時，我不由自主地停下腳步，這是一條曾經遍佈戰前房屋的空蕩街道，如今大批本土設計師和創業者前仆後繼而來，使這條舊巷重獲新生，成了特色小店區。

我之所以佇足不前不是因爲被玻璃窗後的精品時裝或前衛設計所吸引，而是有對新人在拍照，新娘子穿著白紗和新郎倚靠在五彩繽紛的藝術塗鴉牆面上，有種另類的美感。

没有對比就没有傷害，我想到家裏那張掛在主臥室床頭上的36吋婚紗照，背景是假山假水，我和鄭之龍都笑得僵硬，再也没比那張更假、更廉價的了。

" 婚紗照不重要，有就好，還是過日子要緊。"這是老公的解釋。

事實證明儀式感在婚姻當中不可或缺，女人如果連這麼重要的時刻都能馬虎帶過，還有什麼值得珍惜？

這可不？一步錯，步步錯，老公覺得我好打發，連生日禮物挑的都是地攤貨！

爲了避免觸景傷情，我選擇繞路而行，不想再看別人曬幸福。

~

汪致遠打電話來時，我正在逛東南亞最大的書店—紀伊國書屋,就在烏節路的義安購物城內，不單外文書十分齊全，連中文書籍也自成一區，而且版本都很新。

“找妳吃晚飯。”他説。

我答好，就吃路邊攤。

新加坡的“路邊攤”是個地名，在克拉碼頭摩天輪下方，現已改名“新加坡美食滙”，與大食代、美食廣場極爲類似。

“那裏很一般，爲什麼想到那裏吃？”他問。

“因爲想坐摩天輪。”我答。

吃完口味不過不失的海鮮炒麵、煎蠔和蝦餅後，我如願坐上摩天輪。

新加坡的摩天輪高165米相當於42層樓高，比英國倫敦的“千禧眼”還要高出30米。坐在摩天輪裏可把新加坡風光明媚的濱海灣、高聳的摩天大樓以及馬來西亞、印度尼西亞的部份島嶼都盡收眼底，尤其當華燈初上時，五光十色更顯魅力。

“鄭醫生獲得新加坡的杏林醫學獎，主要表彰他在醫學教育及醫藥衛生事業上所做的貢獻。消息一傳來，整個REQ無不振奮，一整天恭賀的電話響個不停，電視台及電台也爭相採訪。”汪致遠説。

“他肯定笑得闔不攏嘴。”我望著遠處的流光溢彩答。

汪醫生説人前的確如此，但喧嘩過後，鄭醫生反倒眉頭緊鎖，看來我的出走帶給他很大的壓力。

“他有什麼好損失的？我走了還會有下一個鄭夫人，這世界多的是不明所以的無腦女人，像我一樣。”

“別自我貶低，人生這麼長，總會遇到幾個人渣，跌倒了再爬起來，没什麼大不了的。”

我收回被窗外夜色吸引的目光，重新打在他那雙清透無暇的眼眸上。

"謝謝！没有你的鼓勵，我恐怕會就此沈淪，走上絕路也不無可能。"

"No, 妳太小看女人的潛力，没有我，妳一樣能自癒，而且風雨過後會更強大。"

"謝謝！"我忍住即將奪眶而出的淚水，"謝謝你……謝謝……"

一整天没接到鄭之龍的電話，我隱隱感到不安。

打開手機，昨天他發來十幾條短信，今天卻只有一條。抵不過好奇心的驅使，我點開閱讀。

和我猜測的一樣，昨天的留言基本是辱罵、威脅加詛咒，一條比一條凶狠，一條比一條歹毒，還説我若午夜之前没回家，不管天涯海角，他一定會逮到我，讓我成爲"人彘"。

彘即豬，人彘是指把人變成豬的一種酷刑（呂后發明的，拿來對付受漢高祖寵愛的戚夫人），手法極爲殘忍，把人的四肢剁掉，使其不良於行；挖出眼睛，使其失明；用銅注入耳朵，使其失聰；割去舌頭，使其不能言語，最後扔到廁所裏任其痛苦死去……

鄭之龍想讓我成爲人彘，可見恨我至深，我不禁心底發毛。

然而今天發來的短信卻又讓我迷惑，內容極短，只有十幾個字：**獲獎，無人分享；心傷，盼妻回；愛妳，全心全意**。

如果昨天的他是殺人不眨眼的魔王，今天的他便是深情款款的羅密歐，我到底該相信哪個？

我陷入痛苦的深淵裏……

又是個陽光普照的好天氣，吃完早餐，我被前台的印度妹

喚住，她問我是否住到今天？我答不是，也許多住一個禮拜。

於是她要我趕緊把床位給定了，看樣子很快會客滿。

我很爽快地付給她一張橘色票子。

“嘟……嘟嘟……”是護士長的來電，我接聽了。

“什麼時候回來上班？”她問。

我答後天一早。

“十二月妳排晚班忘了嗎？我知道妳請了三天假，但因排班的關係，明天下午四點得上班，除非妳想再多請一天假。”

無端少了半天假，我毫無怨言，因爲才休息兩天我就悶得慌，想趕緊投入工作之中。

“好，明天下午到。”我答。

“真奇怪，今天一早我讓鄭醫生轉告妳，他突然發火說没義務當傳聲筒，怎麼，兩夫妻吵架了？”護士長接著問。

“呃……他要我多休息，我不肯，所以……”

那個單純的女人聽了一點兒也沒懷疑，反而説應該頒發“模範夫妻”的獎牌給我們，這狗糧灑得真是“人神共憤”呀！

她大笑兩聲後掛機，而我還在想著到底是活在謊言裏還是面對現實比較幸福？

我……没有答案。

第十七章/地獄使者

雖然付了旅舍一週的床位費，但心中一直籌劃著租一間完全屬於自己的小天地，於是上華新網、獅城論壇以及其他搜房平台查找房源，赫然發現600新幣的月租已成神話，除非我想住在印度人聚集的區域或紅燈區。

新加坡的房屋分為組屋、公寓、排屋或別墅，房間的種類則有主臥、普通房以及傭人房。我不介意與人共用衛浴和廚房，只要位置離REQ不遠，周邊配套設施完善，月租控制在1000新幣以下即可。

考慮再三，若想在短時間內租到合適的房，還得找仲介，雖然因此多出半個月的房費。

約的仲介是一個胖胖的中年大叔叫Jerry，長得有點兒像香港演員鄭則仕，走路很慢，爬樓梯還會氣喘如牛。

看的第一個，房子剛裝修好，有兩間空房，一間已出租出去。房東要求只能輕煮（水煮），衣服晾曬在房間內，水電及網費平均分擔，月租金800新幣。

我有些心動，但仍說要考慮一下，沒想到剛走出巷口Jerry就收到消息—房間出租出去了。

"房東大概不喜歡我吧！"我很氣餒。

"不是的，新加坡的租賃市場就是這樣，條件好點兒的，很快就會出租出去，所謂'手慢無'，妳若看對眼就得趕緊下決定才成。"他答。

第二個是個有些年份的組屋，雖然是帶衛浴的主臥出租，但屋況沒第一個好，還要價1000新幣，果斷放棄。

第三個是個公寓，有漂亮的小區和游泳池，房間很大、很亮敞，還有個不小的陽台，報價1200新幣。我讓1100新幣，沒想到房東在電話中不降反升，現在的月租金是1400新幣。

我很反感臨時加價的房東，一開始心裏就有疙瘩，以後要如何相處？即使後來房東來電維持1200新幣的月租金，我也興趣缺缺。

"這樣吧！我回去再幫妳找找，明天能看房嗎？"Jerry問。

我答下午三點前可以。

～

剛和仲介在巴士站分手就接到寶兒的來電，她問我在哪裏？我答正要上新捷運巴士。

"那正好，妳在武吉巴梳路站下，我們在那裏蹓面。"

我問爲什麼？她答因爲André在那裏。

"寶兒，現在不是吃大餐的時候，何況……"

"何況學姐夫已經同意讓妳請客了。"她將話截去。

啥？這是什麼狀況？

原來寶兒今天獨自上食堂吃飯，没料到鄭之龍也在，兩人便一起用午餐。

“學姐夫真是個大好人，給我叫了大碗叻沙和冬陰功湯，連飯後的酸奶冰淇淋也是他買的。”她説。

老公很摳，但凡請客肯定有目的，我問寶兒吃飯時他們都談了些什麼？

“都是些生活瑣事，雞毛蒜皮的……噢！他問起前陣子他出差到北海道，我有没有約妳出去玩？”

“妳……妳都説了什麼？”我感覺自己正在高空上走鋼索。

“説……哎呀！手機快没電了，媛媛學姐，記住了，我們在餐廳見，不見不……”話没説完，寶兒的手機便罷工了。

我跳上巴士，匆忙往武吉巴梳路前進。

ANDRÉ被評爲米其林二星餐廳，開在一間十九世紀的老式住宅內，室內設計走簡約風格，很有幾分文藝氣息。餐廳主廚來自台灣，他用“獨特、質感、記憶、純淨、風土、鹽、南方和手藝”等“八角哲學”來呈現美食。

早聽過有關這家餐廳的傳説，但一直没機會吃（更確切地説是没預算吃），如今爲了和寶兒見上一面，我不得不硬著頭皮進入。

“放心，咱們不點酒，貴不到哪兒去。”寶兒壓低聲音説。

饒是這樣，晚餐人均也要350新幣起，兩人便要700新幣，我的一個月薪水已去掉1/5。

正餐開始前，先呈上的是幾款鹹味小食，趁寶兒正在大啖野生雜菌塔，我問她有没有跟鄭之龍提起汪醫生的事？

“汪醫生能有什麼事？”她反問我。

“就……就是我們三人上KTV唱歌的事。”

“噢～那件，說了啊！唱歌是很正常的社交活動。”

我哆嗦著繼續追問：“除了唱歌，妳沒講別的吧？！”

“別的？接吻嗎？那個肯定不能主動講，我沒那麼笨！”

聽寶兒這麼一答，我大大鬆了一口氣。

“可是……學姐夫説他有第六感—妳在那段時間出軌了，這讓他痛苦不堪，每天像生活在水深火熱當中。於是我告訴他，那些全是空穴來風，沒有的事，即使學姐和汪醫生接吻了，也是在醉酒的狀態下，我敢作證，除了接吻，你們兩人當天什麼事都沒發生。”

聽完，我煞白了臉。

“媛媛學姐，妳還好吧？！”她問。

“不好，很不好,妳該不會連在屠妖節上遇見汪醫生一事也説了吧？！”

“那個……説溜嘴了，下次……下次肯定記住。”她雙手合十作求饒狀。

完了，全毁了。

見我一副生無可戀的樣子，寶兒説她不明白我爲什麼要如此戒慎惶恐，學姐夫聽了都沒我的反應大，還説早猜到是汪醫生，就差一層窗戶紙了……

“妳聽不出這是暴風雨前的寧靜嗎？”我捂住臉，欲哭無淚，“我該怎麼辦？妳教教我。”

“媛……媛學姐……”寶兒喚我，聲音是飄著的。

我放下手來，赫然發現一個人就立在桌旁。

“太好了，才上到前菜，不介意我加入吧？！”我的老公説。

臨時多加一個人，服務員問是否多來一份套餐？鄭之龍就敢厚著臉皮拒絕，理由是他的老婆胃口小，他吃我的即可。

事實證明的確如此，面對佳餚我完全沒胃口，即使餐後甜點是我愛吃的抹茶冰淇淋，我也味同嚼蠟。

寶兒曾對我投來關心的眼神，但都被鄭之龍截了去，他關心地問她家裏有什麼人？現在住哪裏？來新加坡適應不？對未來有什麼計劃？……

寶兒是人來熟，何況對鄭醫生並不陌生，一來二去，話匣子打開便止不住，兩人相談甚歡。

"我……我上個廁所。"我把膝上的餐巾置於桌面。

"我陪妳去。"老公說。

"那是女廁。"

"没關係，我進男廁。"

實際上鄭之龍就待在女廁外守候，若不是廁所內的窗戶小，我肯定爬窗脫逃。

"告訴妳，"他附在我耳邊低語，"休想逃出我的手掌心。"

鄭之龍把車停在茂源台，我還能看見下車後的寶兒笑得一臉燦爛，她揮手與我們道別。

車子重新上路後，老公問："要不要彎到汪醫生家把妳的隨身用品拿走？"

我答我不住汪致遠家，他怎麼可以有這麼骯髒的想法？

"呵呵！骯髒？妳也知道骯髒？想到妳這張嘴親過那個奶油小生，我噁心到想吐！"

我受不了他的冷嘲熱諷，要求他停車，然而他非但沒有放緩車速反而腳踩油門。我一急，用手去扳車門，他没有猶豫，立馬猛擊我的頭部。

"臭婊子！還輪得到妳撒野？"他罵道，然後拉上車門且上鎖。

我被揍得眼冒金星。

"停……停車，我……我不舒服。"我捂住口，因爲酸水直往外冒。

"忍住，待會兒我幫妳治一治。"他一語雙關。

第十八章／隱去的曙光

一回到家，老公便強押我上樓，在固若金湯的主臥室裏，任憑我怎麼哀嚎也無人聽見。

"不守婦道、做淫亂之事、毀壞我的清譽、最後還好意思離家出走，簡直天理難容......"老公開始控訴我的罪狀，而我已被五花大綁在椅子上。

"我知道我不是個好老婆，是我配不上你行不？讓我們好聚好散吧！"

隨即甩來的耳光，連疼痛的滋味都那麼熟悉。

"妳以爲全身而退那麼簡單？再怎麼著也得折磨折磨妳以洩心頭恨。"鄭之龍憤恨地說。

"折磨吧！不論怎麼折磨我都能忍，但折磨過後請放我走。拜托了，我在這裏一個親人也沒有......"

說完，我的眼淚嘩嘩嘩地流。

"嘖嘖嘖！把我說得像個混世魔王似的。憑良心說，哪次打妳沒有理由？是妳咎由自取，怨不得人。"

鄭之龍有自己的一套邏輯，向來都是別人錯，自己只是替天行道罷了。

我還在哭泣，老公忽然走出房外，很快又回來，手裏拿著一把手術用的彎頭剪刀，此工具多用於剪除瘀肉、血筋、皮、膜等。

"你⋯⋯要幹嘛？！"

"妳說拔哪個好？"老公蹲下身端詳我的腳趾頭。

"不，別拔，求你了，我疼⋯⋯"知道他想幹啥，我害怕極了。

鄭之龍答拔是肯定得拔，好讓我長記性，還問我小趾頭怎樣？面積小癒合快，也沒那麼疼⋯⋯

我拼命搖頭，眼淚像開了閘的洪水。

"沒說話表示默許，我這就拔了，警告妳別試圖抗拒，抗拒一次多拔一個。"

患者會到醫院拔趾甲通常是因爲內裏積血壞死或趾甲長到肉裏面，爲了減輕疼痛，醫生通常會打麻藥，但顯然鄭之龍想跳過那個步驟直接將趾甲硬生生拔下，那得多疼？

我緊閉雙眼、咬緊牙關，果然疼痛像墨水滴入清水裏，很快擴散開來⋯⋯

"我還以爲妳的血是黑的呢！"他站起身來嘲弄我，而我已無力反駁。

～

"對不起，發了幾封郵件，忘了時間。"去而復返的老公低頭看我的傷口，"怎麼腫成這樣？不行，我幫妳擦藥。"

我下意識將腿往內縮，告訴他別貓哭耗子，我不領情！

"別鬧孩子脾氣，若感染了，最後可能得截肢，我可捨不得妳受罪。”

説完，他拿來急救箱爲我消毒再上藥，當然没忘了解開我身上的繩索。

“疼嗎？疼告訴我，我再輕點兒。”他説，像一位極有愛心的醫生。

我告訴他自己很疼，不止腳趾疼，心更疼，問他能否結束這種相互折磨？

“我還不夠愛妳嗎？人要有良心，妳跟那個小白臉眉來眼去我都大度地原諒妳了，妳還想怎樣？要我把心剖開讓妳看嗎？”

不知道的人恐怕要以爲我是“得了便宜還賣乖”的一方。

我斬釘截鐵地表示我們夫妻之間的事與外人無關，結婚以來我的痛苦多過快樂，如果他能放過我，我敬他是條漢子，如果不行……他可以桎梏我的肉體但阻止不了我想飛的心。

“也就是説，不管我對妳如何掏心掏肺，妳都鐵了心要離開，是嗎？”他漲紅了臉問。

知道火上加油會帶來什麼後果，但我把頭伸出去，就等他一刀砍下，大不了一死。

得到答案後，鄭之龍憤而抓住我前襟，眼睛睜得比牛鈴還大，我以爲他會像平常一樣給我一頓好打，然而……

“這次我不打妳，妳還得留著好皮相陪我參加頒獎酒會，但我告訴妳，咱們之間的事還没完，妳若斗膽離開我，那個姓汪的就別想有好日子過，妳自己看著辦！”

想到鄭之龍手操汪致遠的生殺大權，我猶豫了。

自己早對未來没有盼頭，但汪醫生不一樣，他還有大好前程，我不能因爲自己的愛恨情仇毀了他一生，尤其他還是對我伸出過援手的恩人……

"想清楚了就上床！"老公率先一步走向席夢思床，"妳有五分鐘思考時間。"

搶奪、擄掠、破壞、搗毀……我的身體像一座廟宇被橫搶武奪。

"能不能配合點兒？這樣一點兒都不好玩！"老公抱怨，不忘在我的肩胛骨上留下一個血印子。

"去找Lucy吧！她會全力配合。"我冷冷地答。

"告訴過妳，我和Lucy之間沒什麼事，妳要鑽牛角尖請便，但別忘了妳的應盡義務！"

義務通常和權力捆綁在一起，我的義務是"上得了廳堂下得了廚房，上床還得當蕩婦"，那麼我的權力何在？

鄭之龍伸出舌頭邊舔我邊呢喃著："妳的權力就是享受無窮無盡的魚水之歡……"

我厭惡地撇開臉。

仲介問我在哪裏？他等我有一刻鐘了。

"對……對不起，臨時出狀況，我……不租了。"

他又問我是不是價錢的問題？錢的事情好商量……

我答不是，而是找到住處了。

"那也得事先通知我呀！"他揚起聲，"真是的，內地人就是這樣，有幾個錢就隨意指使別人……"

我聽了老大不高興但也無言反駁，自己的確錯了，昨晚至今意外頻發，我怎麼記得住和仲介的約定？臨時爽約，人家不高興也可理解。

掛上電話，我懷著快快的心到牛車水的旅舍辦退房。前台説提早退房只能退押金，房費不給退，政策上寫得很清楚……

我答我了解。

退房後，我找了家咖啡店喝咖啡烏，不加糖和奶，苦澀的滋味如同我現在的心情。生命剛出現曙光馬上又隱去，我內心的抑鬱可想而知，但我没得選，只能繼續活在黑暗之中……

"嘟……嘟嘟……"是寶兒的來電，但我一點兒都不想接聽。

然而在她打來第五通時，我還是接聽了，"不知者無罪"，牽怒她没道理。

" Thank God. 妳總算接電話，要不然我真以爲妳生氣了。"她説。

"妳也知道自己罪惡滔天？我離自由就只差一步。"

寶兒問我這是什麼意思？我才發現自己説溜嘴了，忙答没什麼意思，當我發神經好了。

"學姐怎麼可能發神經？愛説笑！"她在手機那端果真呵呵呵地笑起來，" 就想問妳能不能幫我補習？下個月我有資格考試。"

"恐怕不行，這個月我上晚班。"

如果没記錯，寶兒這個月上大夜班，時間上兩人無交集。

"可不可以……"

"不可以，"我馬上否絕，" 熬夜很傷身，如果再用有限的睡眠時間幫妳補習是自殺行爲，妳只能自求多福了。"

聽得出來寶兒很失望，而且多少埋怨我没有爲朋友兩肋插刀，但我的煩惱事太多，已經無暇他顧。

∽

“ Mɪss Cuɪ，聽説妳請假好幾天了，今天又是滿床，我很怕妳不來。”説話的是晚班護士長，身材矮胖，背地裏我們都喊她“大番薯”。

“ 我這不是來了嗎？醫囑呢？”我問。

她答在護士站的桌上，話鋒一轉她説我一定很驕傲自己的老公獲獎，讓她好生羨慕，不像老胡，多年不思進取，像個打卡的公務員……

“大番薯”的老公是救護車上的急救員，人像樹枝一樣纖細，大概肉都堆到護士長身上了。

“ 我認爲老胡做的是了不起的工作，他是挽救急症患者的先鋒。”我説。

“ 但哪能跟鄭醫生比？”她翻了翻白眼，“ 杏林醫學獎可不是誰想得就能得，院長已經交待下去，明晚的酒會放妳假，記得打扮得美美的，後天一早的頭條新聞肯定有你們夫妻倆。”

原來酒會訂在明晚，難怪老公“捨不得”打我。

我答知道了，轉身到護士站拿醫囑。

第十九章／美豔佳人

醫囑就是醫生根據病情和治療的需要對病人在飲食、用藥、化驗等方面所做的指示，分爲長期醫囑、臨時醫囑和備用醫囑三類。

很多國家已採用智能化管理，讓值班護士可實時上電腦查看醫囑，但不知爲什麽，REQ的某些老醫生仍採取舊式的手寫方式，厚厚的一沓表格，讓人看了眼花繚亂。

" Room 7, 6th bed patient has pneumothorax. MO Wang asked us to watch that guy."我正查看醫囑，Miss Clinton 在邊上說七號病房，第六床病人有氣胸，MO Wang 要我們多留意病人。

MO Wang? 難道是汪致遠？他也值晚班？

讀完醫囑，我趕著去測病人的血壓，又給中風者餵飯，再幫重度低血糖患者注射葡萄糖，等忙完回到護士站，剛坐下就聽到兩位年輕護士的對話。

"汪醫生真可憐，已經連值兩個班好幾天了，鄭醫生真狠心，也不怕出人命！"

"這跟鄭醫生有啥關係？班又不是他排的。"

"聽說鄭醫生不滿意汪醫生，給他的評價極低，原因是英語不行、臨床經驗也不夠，雖然值晚班是汪醫生主動提的，但始作俑者還是鄭醫生。人手不足，人事當然樂見其成，只差沒讓他連大夜班也一塊兒上了。"

"這麼說的確可憐，別的**Medical Officer**都順利到下一個單位實習，只有他還卡在五官科，再這麼拖下去，怕趕不上農曆新年過後的**Post Graduate**考試。"

……

知道鄭之龍開始使出殺手鐧，我感到憤怒與內疚，憤怒是針對老公，內疚則給了汪醫生。

"如果他不淌這渾水就好了。"我心想。

～

我特意到各個病房轉轉，終於在二十號病房發現那人的身影，他正和一位肝癌患者Lisa說話。

老太太的病情我是知道的，乙型肝炎兼肝硬化，肝腹水使她的腹部高高隆起，只能仰面躺著，連護士輕微的蓋被動作都讓她喊疼。

"Am I dying?"病人問醫生自己是不是快死了？

汪致遠避重就輕地答未來還有無限可能，這明顯是白色謊言。

"Miss Cui, am I dying?"沒想到Lisa把同樣的問題甩給站在汪醫生背後的我。

我沒考慮多久便決定和醫生站在同一陣線，要她放寬心，一切都會好的。

隨後汪致遠要我準備白蛋白注射，注射完畢讓Lisa採半臥位，必要時給予氧氣吸入，同時對易出現褥瘡的部位進行按摩……

" Yes, MO Wang."我信心十足地答。

趁汪醫生走出二十號病房，正要進入下一個病房前，我在走廊適時將他攔截。

"聽說你已經連續加班好幾天了。"我説。

"沒辦法，師傅不滿意，我只好採'勤能補拙'的笨方法。"

"對不起……"

他笑了，問我何需抱歉？這事與我無關，還問鄭之龍有沒有找我麻煩？

"沒……沒有，我……回家了。"

汪致遠的嘴巴張得老大，似乎不敢相信耳朵聽到的。

我嘆了口氣説自己是如此軟弱，愧對他的幫助，今後就讓我們各走各路，他……別管我了。

他沈默了一會兒後，問我Lisa有沒有康復的可能？

我答她是肝癌晚期，生命已是倒計時了。

"重回施暴者的懷抱也是生命倒計時，妳要做的是抵抗惡勢力而不是屈服，懂嗎？"

哎～我怎麼不懂？但鄭之龍以他人的職業生涯要挾，叫我如何是好？

"我想……老公還是愛我的，只要不惹他生氣，婚姻還是能繼續，我自己不也缺點一大堆？夫妻就是要互相包容才能走得長遠……"我洋洋灑灑地闡述夫妻相處之道，連自己都差點兒相信了。

"好吧！算我杞人憂天，祝妳和鄭醫生白頭攜老。"說完，他面無表情地跨進二十一號病房。

洗完澡，我輕手輕腳地上床，已是凌晨兩點多，我不想吵醒熟睡的人。

"上完班，妳去哪裏了？"老公翻過身，將我壓在底下，"今天晚了二十分鐘到家。"

我答下班前送來一位剛動完手術的車禍重傷者，因爲住院部滿床，我們只好又將他推回急診觀察室……

"妳最好說實話，別忘了妳老公神通廣大，隨便一查便知有沒有。"

"查吧！在你面前我早已無所遁形。"

接著鄭之龍將鼻子湊近我的臉，像獵犬般嗅著，我問他幹嘛？

"聞妳身上有沒有別的男人的味道。"

"神經！"

我想推開他，手腕反被他銬在床頭的鐵藝欄桿上，銬完一隻再銬另一隻。

"哈哈！網上真的什麼都能買到。"他勝利一笑。

"這是幹嘛？快放了我！"

"做完再放。"他脫下自己的睡褲。

鄭之龍找到新玩法，把我折騰得骨頭都快散了才放我睡

覺，而今晨六點半我照樣得起床為他準備早餐，睡眠時間不到四個小時。

"怎麼搞的？蛋煮老了，"他老大不高興，又用叉子掀開麵包，"說好了Kaya醬要自製，就會買現成的偷懶！"

說起新加坡的"國民早餐"非咖椰吐司莫屬，把調味醬（用雞蛋、糖、椰漿以及香蘭香料製作而成）塗抹在烤好的吐司片上，再加入小塊黃油，同時搭配著吃的還有撒上白胡椒粉及醬油的三分熟養生蛋。

"Kaya醬是在亞坤買的，你不也喜歡他家的東西？"我弱弱地答，感覺自己快昏睡過去。

老公答那是趕時間或沒的選的情況下不得不做出的讓步，我既然有大把時間就該好好做份早餐，也不是很難的事，怎麼這麼不上心？

"拜托！我已經累到兩眼睜不開，想吃好的明天吧！現在我得去睡個回籠覺。"我手揉太陽穴說。

老公提醒我睡完回籠覺好好打扮一下，今晚七點別忘了參加富麗敦酒店的頒獎典禮，還要我把他的禮服準備好放進後車廂內，今天事多，我們直接在酒店踫面。

哎呀！他不說，我還真把這事給忘了。

"我的禮服穿舊的還是買新的？"想起衣櫃裏毫不出彩的衣服，我問。

鄭之龍想了一下答買新的，但別上烏節路買，那裏隨便一件T恤也要好幾張橘色票子。

送走老公，我上樓倒頭就睡。在夢中，我穿著一件Alexander MacQueen設計的米色露背拖地晚禮服，頭髮高高挽起，一舉手一投足，顧盼生姿，美得不可方物......

第二十章/二見LUCY

就因爲做了一場美夢，醒來後我拿上錢包直奔烏節路，把老公的叮囑拋在腦後。

"妳運氣好，這是剛到的貨，昨晚差點兒被方太買去。" Alexander MacQueen工作室的導購邊替我拉開裙襬邊説。

"方太？誰是方太？"我問。

她答就是方淮安的二太太，大老婆長年吃齋唸佛，早已不過問俗事，現在方家的大小事都是二太太張羅，儼然是原配，然而誰不知道上位前她還只是個賭場裏的發牌員……

"方淮安？該不會是那位長期霸佔東南亞製藥公司產業鏈，還有自己研發團隊的隱性富豪吧？"我問。

"可不是，不說新加坡首富了，前五名肯定排得上。"

看著落地鏡中的自己，我喃喃自語："没想到他老婆的審美觀和我相同。"

說來真不可思議，我竟然在Alexander MacQueen工作室找到與夢中一模一樣的晚禮服，連拉低的胸口位置也如出一轍。

“要我説，這種晚禮服就得有對大胸脯才撐得起來，方太的胸像洩了氣的皮球，誰看誰尷尬，難怪後來選了中規中矩的高領禮服，把自己的缺點嚴嚴實實地包起來。”

這也是我擔心的地方，衣服的胸口開得太低，極易走光，回頭還得找個裁縫把它縫上……

導購睜大眼睛，問我是不是在開玩笑？禮服就是要吸人眼球，我把好料藏著掖著，枉費這八千新幣了。

“什麼？！八……八千？”我嚇壞了。

導購沒注意到我的心情起伏，重申我好運氣，還説Alexander MacQueen的禮服很少有這麼好看又便宜的。

美麗是需要付出代價的。

付完八千，我想著大頭都出了，何必在乎小錢？於是上高島屋的 Chez Vous 把頭髮給做了，不僅染了色還梳成夢中的花苞頭。

“我就説紫紅的髮色適合妳，妳現在看起來比泰國人妖還美！”那個嗲聲嗲氣的髮型師Kevin説道。

看過蒂芬妮秀的人都知道泰國人妖比女人還要女人，Kevin所言非貶義詞。

“謝謝！”我没忘記夢裏的配飾，“我還需要珍珠頭飾。”

“Certainly.”

Kevin消失一會兒後，帶著珍珠歸來，那是一串可以從頭繞到頸項的長鏈子，亮白色的珠子顆顆飽滿。

“看過達芬奇的‘戴珍珠頭飾的夫人像’没？這條就是仿的，不貴，五百新幣不到。”他説。

～

六點半，我抵達富麗敦酒店會議廳入口。

"呦！這不是鄭夫人？"內科馮主任看見我，眼前一亮，像饑餓的狼看見油汪汪的肥肉。

我問他有沒有看見我老公？

"剛剛還在，他被幾個商人模樣的人帶走了，怎麼，兩人走丟了？"

"沒有的事，我從家裏過來的。"

馮主任說既然這樣，讓他帶我入場，鄭醫生是今晚的主角，我們夫妻被安排坐大桌。

走進會議廳，原以為會像上大課一樣排排坐，結果觸目所及全是鋪上筆挺桌布的大圓桌。我被帶到前排正中的十人座，同桌的除了REQ的院長及其夫人外，還有另一對看著眼熟的男女，桌上的紅酒已開瓶，他們四人正把酒言歡。

"容我介紹一下，這位是鄭醫生夫人，她同時也是REQ的傑出護士。"馮主任轉而介紹另一方，"REQ的院長及夫人就不多說了，另外這兩位是杏林醫學獎的贊助者及授予方-蔣博士及尹博士。"

我微笑著說"幸會"。

一入座，馮主任立馬為我的高腳杯注入紅色的瓊漿玉液，今晚的他鞍前馬後的，讓人有些招架不住。

"謝謝！"我說。

沒想到那人不僅沒離開，反而緊挨著我坐下，而且眼光直落入我胸口，讓人很不舒服。我趕緊抓來餐巾捂住洞開的口阻止侵略，隨後他找個藉口離開。

"我說這會議廳的冷氣也太強了，鄭夫人穿成這樣會不會太冷？我包裹還有條長絲巾。"說話的是院長夫人，已是當奶奶的年紀。

"年輕人身體好，妳就別多管閒事了。"院長説，樣子有些尷尬。

其實一走進會議廳我就後悔，冷氣彷彿不要錢似的，我的低胸兼露背禮服成了最差勁的選擇，雖然它成功地吸引住所有男人的目光，並且讓我成爲與會女人的公敵。

很快，十人座大桌又來了兩位，據説是政府官員，除了鐵定會來的老公外，另外兩個位置留給誰？

答案在兩分鐘後揭曉，鄭之龍和一對男女走過來入座，那男的一頭花白，身體還算硬朗，女的則年輕許多，身著高領的中式禮服，不過不失。

"讓我介紹一下，企業家方淮安及夫人百忙之中抽空前來參加小弟的頒獎典禮，真是榮幸、榮幸。"老公向同桌者鄭重介紹。

"原來方淮安已是耄耋老人，我還以爲是精壯的中年人……"我心想。

沒想到我在觀察人，別人也在觀察我，方太的眼光沒離開過我的衣裳。

" Alexander MacQueen的新貨。"我主動提起。

"我知道，若不是我的好姐妹説看著很廉價，昨晚我差點兒買了。"她答。

第一次會面就刀光血影，讓我如坐針氈。

"衣服因人而異，穿在公主身上便成了傳奇，反之亦然。"我冷劍出鞘。

方太還想説什麼，但司儀宣佈頒獎典禮開始，她只好硬生生將話吞進肚裏去。

" ......I am really honoured to be presented with this award . Without the help of REQ and my dear wife's unwavering support, I won't be standing here today. Thank you . I love you."

我很慶幸老公的獲獎感言沒有像老太婆的裹腳布一樣又臭又長，相反的，它很精簡，時間控制在三分鐘，恰恰在一般人尚能忍受的範圍內。

"鄭醫生是人中蛟龍，妳一定很爲他驕傲。"方淮安邊鼓掌邊與我低語。

"謝謝！"我對他微笑。

"有没有人説妳笑如春花？"那老人問，很友善的樣子。

我本來想否認，但看見方太不懷好意的眼神，突然改主意，反問他這樣的微笑是否想擁有？

方淮安没料到我會説風話，支支吾吾了半天，方太則鐵青著一張臉。

"方老已經擁有太多，"院長開口圓場，"事業興旺、家庭和睦、方太還明豔動人，再也無人比他擁有更多。"

老公拿獎後回到座位，估計聽到話屑子。

"没錯，方老要風得風要雨得雨，的確羨煞旁人，但他有一樣永遠也得不到，"鄭之龍擁住我，"我的美麗嬌妻。"

酒會開始没多久老公就消失了，讓我像個傀儡似地應付前來道賀的人群。

"鄭醫生呢？"馮主任不知從哪裏又冒出來。

"不知道，也許上廁所了。"

“我幫妳去找。”

美麗果然有魔力，馮主任平常高傲得很，今晚卻像隻勤勞的小蜜蜂，揮都揮不去。

等了十分鐘還不見小蜜蜂飛回來獻殷勤，我知道有事不對勁，拎起拖地的長裙往洗手間走去。

就在角落，我看見馮主任找到另一個落單的女子，兩人正竊竊私語著，等他的眼光和我一銜接，瞬間我全明白了，轉身便往左邊旋轉門走去，只因他的眼睛不由自主地往那邊瞄，很怯生生的樣子，這個細微的動作不巧被我捕捉到，果然……

鄭之龍和Lucy在樓梯下方親親我我，旁若無人的樣子讓人為之氣結。

那女人是藥商代表，這種醫學界的頒獎盛事她肯定知道（也許還是老公告訴她的）。想到此，我感到悲哀，自己做如此精緻打扮為哪樁？老公還不是背著我偷腥？

我踩著高跟鞋回到會議廳，不同的是這回我決定自棄，並且仗著酒醉放浪形骸，就想讓鄭之龍顏面掃地。

當老公拉開我時，我正掛在方淮安身上。

“ Sorry.”我聽見他向對方道歉，但聽不見那老人說了什麼。

一進車內，老公就衝著我發火：“妳就不能給我留點兒面子？大庭廣眾之下跟個糟老頭不清不楚的，可真會選對象！”

“ 不跟糟老頭，跟……跟誰？哈！跟 Lucy 。 ”我呵呵呵地笑著。

鄭之龍說我發酒瘋，他不跟我計較，呵！好個煙霧彈。

～

老公把銀製獎杯放在客廳的顯眼處，轉身對我說：「妳今晚的服裝太難看，坦胸露背的，一看就是不正經的女人。」

「Alexander MacQueen的……新貨，八千新幣呢！」我跌進沙發裏，冷不防打了個酒嗝。

「八……」他氣得臉紅脖子粗，「崔媛媛，妳腦子進水了？」

我答沒進水，與會的男人都因此羨慕他娶了個性感尤物，還有比這個更值的嗎？

鄭之龍還想說什麼，被突來的手機音樂聲給打斷了。

「Hello.」

他一接聽，我便跳起來搶他手機，果然是賤人打來的，我大罵她不要臉，搶人搶到頒獎酒會上……

「有完沒完？」老公過來回搶他的手機，反被我張口一咬，虎口因此留下個血口子。

「崔媛媛，沒想到妳真瘋了！」鄭之龍捂住受傷的手，很氣急敗壞的樣子，「妳等著，等我回來跟妳算賬！」

大門開了又關，然後是車子駛離的聲音。

我舔了舔嘴邊遺留的血漬，發現它竟然是鹹的。

「哈哈！原以爲老公的血會像黃蓮一樣苦。」

我大笑著，然後在沙發上擺個最舒服的姿勢沈沈睡去……

第二十一章/突發事件

醒來已是午後，餐桌上有用過的碗，吃的是麥片，顯然老公草草吃了早飯應付過去。

我在沙發上坐起，約莫十幾分鐘後才總算將昨晚發生的事一一捋清。

"不知老公生氣了沒？"我有些擔心。

一進住院部，"大番薯"便迫不及待地拿出報紙與我分享。

" 没想到妳的身材這麼有料，猛一看還以爲是哪個明星。"

"鄭醫生太瘦了，妳没給他做吃的？"

"方淮安比去年老多了，他太太倒還是一臉精明相。"

……

晚班護士長人不壞，就是喜歡八卦，估計同樣的話題她已經和別人倒帶無數次了。

"妳也認識方淮安？"我邊問邊打卡。

"大番薯"說那自然是，他是REQ的VIP客人，每年都會上這裏做身體檢查，一住就是三天，只有最優秀的護士才能獲得服侍他的機會……

"又不是王公貴族，說得好像是件美差。"我嗤之以鼻。

"怎麼不是？"她附在我耳邊低語，" 去年Miss Zhou拿到不菲的小費，立馬將Honda換成Buick."

Miss Zhou是體檢部的年輕護士，說話輕聲細語，很有小家碧玉的樣子。

"看來今年她能把Buick換成路虎了。"我開著玩笑。

"大番薯"答人家早開上了，服侍完方淮安沒多久，Miss Zhou便離開REQ成了方老闆的私人看護，薪水不知翻了多少倍。

"那倒好，麻雀變鳳凰。"

"大番薯"聽完笑得很神秘，她說不久之後又會有一隻新鳳凰誕生。

我來不及問她什麼意思，一位看著面生的護理員拎著一口黑色大塑料袋前來，話未出口，護士長指著我道：" 這位也是中國來的，有什麼問題問她。"。

待胖胖的身軀離去，那個清湯掛麵的新進人員望了我身上的名牌一眼後，說出驚心動魄的話：" 媛媛學姐，請問醫療廢棄物扔哪裏？"

～

忙完一圈回到護士站，Miss Fan遞過來一個塑料盒，問我吃不吃鴨脖子？

我撿了根醬得紅通通的細長物，邊啃邊問她哪裏來的好東西？

她答牛車水的熟食攤能買到，不過水平參差不齊，她買的這個還行，我若喜歡，下次幫我帶。

"不必了，這東西偶爾吃吃還行，我更喜歡美珍香的豬肉乾。"

"好奇怪！汪醫生也這麽說，你們說好統一口徑了嗎？"她問。

"没有的事，"我吮了吮沾滿醬汁的手指，"汪醫生人呢？"

"早陣亡了，他正在休息室裏睡大覺，但願今晚一夜無事。"

汪醫生已經連續加班好幾天，就算鐵打的身體也會受不住，然而怕什麽來什麽，今天轉院過來的新病人在劇烈咳嗽後突然大咯血，我給他服用鎮咳藥後好了些，没想到才洗個手回來，他又第二次咯血，地板上血跡斑斑。

"我去叫汪醫生。"Miss Fan説。

我要她別去，讓汪醫生多睡會兒，自己會從旁觀察，没事的……

護士小范一走，我讓患者二次服藥，待病人的呼吸漸趨平穩，我拉把椅子坐下，打算至少觀察一個小時。

我被突來的嘔吐及喘息聲吵醒，地板上又有了新的血跡，依據呼吸急促及皮膚發紺等現象，我判斷病人有休克的危險，趕緊按下緊急鈴。

汪醫生趕到時，咯血量已超過500 ml,情況非常危急。

"快！馬上體位引流！"他喊。

我幫著將床尾擡高45度，汪醫生則讓病人側頭，然後輕拍其背部，避免血液流入肺部。

"替病人戴上氧氣罩，我去拿血漿，馬上進行止血和輸血。"他一臉嚴肅地説。

一直到大夜班的醫生和護士接手，我們兩人才像剛跑完馬拉松的選手，累得癱坐在椅子上。

"爲什麼不在第一次咯血時通知我？"汪醫生望著天花板問。

"我……我想讓你多睡會兒。"

没想到他像換了個人似地兇我："妳這是棄病患於不顧，他們是妳的玩偶嗎？妳不知道過度抑制咳嗽中樞會使血液淤積氣道引起窒息嗎？虧妳還是多年的護士，這點常識也無！"

我被他罵得啞口無言。

"是的，我是意氣用事愧對我的護士執照，但説到底還不是爲了你，不想讓你積勞成疾，你不懂嗎？"我拭去不爭氣的眼淚，"算了，就當我熱臉貼冷屁股吧！"

運氣好的話，下班時會有善心同事"順路"載我一程，但顯然今天的運氣不好。

我拿出手機撥號，半夜打車我習慣使用UberX或GrabCar, 因爲零點過後，出租車的附加費會增加50%。

當我站在醫院右側的路燈下等車時，一個瘦高的影子走過來，我趕緊背對他。

"打車嗎？"汪醫生問。

“不用你管。”

“能讓我坐一段嗎？放我在牛車水下即可，我步行回家。”

我答“道不同不相爲謀”，他還是另外叫車吧！

“可是……我的錢包丟了，現在身上一分錢也無。”

剛來REQ時我也丟過錢包，說來很詭異，不過是轉個身，現金連同銀行卡就這麼不翼而飛，讓我不禁懷疑遇上了高級扒手。

我嘆了口氣從皮夾裏掏出二十新幣給他，被他拒絕了。

“其實丟錢一事是假的，就想找個機會跟妳道歉，今晚我太衝動，對不起！”

我還想說什麼，一輛私家車駛過來，駕駛員問我是不是叫車了？我答是。

“上車吧！明天見！”汪致遠替我開了車門。

直到車子離開醫院正門的小圓環，我還能看見那男人屹立在昏黃的路燈下……

一開燈，赫然發現客廳沙發上坐個人，右手掌纏著紗布。

“嚇死我了，”我捂住胸口，“你就不能出點兒聲？”

老公說“不做虧心事，半夜不怕鬼敲門”，由此可證，我鐵定做了不可饒恕的事。

“隨你怎麼說，我累了，今晚有突發狀況，我和汪醫生……”話一落音我就後悔，趕緊踩刹車。

“汪醫生？怎麼又是他？這個點他還在醫院？”

看得出山洪就要爆發，我試圖穩住局面：“還問爲什麼？你不是給人家打低分嗎？汪醫生爲了博你好感，主動加班好幾天了。”

“妳心疼嗎？”

知道老公又在雞蛋裏挑骨頭，我找了個藉口上樓避難。

第二十二章／在劫難逃

送走老公，我把碗盤洗了、地擦了，再把髒衣服丟進洗衣機裏……

在轟隆轟隆的機子運轉聲中，我泡了壺碧螺春，打算看本書小憩一下。

"村上春樹在哪裏？"我在書架前流連。

我是村上春樹迷，他的每一本小說我都有，而且重複閱讀N多遍，每次都有新感覺。今天我想重讀的是《再襲麵包店》，由看似互不相干的6個短篇組成，演繹人入中年的必有光景……

"哈！找到了。"

也許是灑入的陽光剛剛好，也或許是餘光恰巧落在對的地方，找到書的同時我竟然發現久未觸摸的護理考試用書不見了。

望著空了的架子，我的腦海裏開始排列各種的可能性。

"不，不會的，不可能……她不會背叛我。"

我拼命搖頭，但仍拿出手機撥號，寶兒上大夜班，這時肯定睡了。

手機響了五聲後被接聽。

"媛媛學姐，怎麼是妳？我剛要入睡。"

"噢！没什麼事，就想問妳資格考試準備得怎麼樣？"

"考試？很好啊！我有信心能通過助理護士的考試。"

電話中的寶兒表現得很正常，我遂放下心來，要她趕緊上床，我不吵她了......

放下手機，我喃喃自語："崔媛媛啊崔媛媛，妳也太小題大做，簡直成了驚弓之鳥。"

～

一進住院部，整個氛圍詭異極了，像有什麼不安的因子在蠕動著。

"Miss Cui，主任找妳。"晚班護士長説。

"Why？"

她答不清楚，汪醫生也被叫去了。

～

"2號病房，第九床病人今晨過世了，大夜班的程醫生説他是從你們二位的手中接過病人，當時情況還好，没想到後來又咯血，大量的血液進入氣管堵塞了管腔，雖經搶救但仍告不治，你們能還原最初的發病狀況嗎？"住院部余主任問。

知道那位瘦弱的青年病人身亡，我感到無比震驚，我們離開時他的體徵其實已經漸趨平穩，怎麼後來又急轉直下了？

"我……我是在晚上九點多時發現病人咯血，給他服用了鎮咳藥，當第二次咯血時，我……又給鎮咳藥，到了第三次……我按下緊急鈴，汪醫生過來急救……"

余主任憤而拍打桌面，問我鎮咳藥是神仙妙丹嗎？咯血是多麼嚴重的事，我沒通知醫生找病源，反而胡亂給藥，那還要醫生做什麼？

"我……對不起……我錯了……"

"這可不是動動嘴皮子就能解決的事，我會將妳交給醫療監控部門。"

一個多月前的"劉勇事件"記憶猶新，當時余主任讓Crisha獨自頂罪，我還內疚了好一陣子，沒想到風向一轉，一向偏袒我的人這回主動將我推向風口浪尖……

"余主任，"汪醫生開口了，"這件事跟Miss Cui無關，而是我睡著了，要她別吵醒我。"

沒想到汪致遠將過錯一肩扛起，這與事實不符，我趕緊否認。

"真是有趣，"余主任皮笑肉不笑，"你們二位互相爭著擔責任，即使是手足也不見得能做到，這麼可貴的情誼真令人感動啊！"

他的話中有話，但我管不了那麼多，一心要將汪醫生排除在外，他還沒參加Post Graduate的考試，頂多只能算是半吊子的醫生，如果再攤上麻煩事，等於宣告職業生涯的終止。

"汪醫生，"那雙不懷好意的賊眼打在汪致遠的身上，"我就問一句，昨晚當班時你是否睡著了？"

"拜托！說沒有。"我內心祈禱著。

約莫三十秒後……

"是的，我睡著了，這件事和Miss Cui無關。"他答。

從主任辦公室出來，我強拉汪醫生到樓梯間。

"幹嘛說謊？事情根本不是這樣，你知道一旦被送醫療監控部門，小則聲譽受損，大則可能被判刑，你何必替我頂罪？"我質問。

他答雖然沒要求我別吵醒他，但我的出發點是好的，爲了這份心意，他有義務站出來……

"傻瓜，大傻瓜，"我氣不打一處來，"估計被監控部門這麼一調查，你連Post Graduate的考試資格都沒有了，REQ立馬會不要你。"

"不要就不要，大不了回國，我照樣有飯吃。"

他假裝無所謂的樣子讓人更心疼，我決定挽回劣勢。

下午五點，我又回到辦公室，主任正在收拾桌面，看來準備回家。

"余主任，你別爲難汪醫生了，我願意承擔所有的罪過，請你放他一馬。"

" Miss Cui,"他指示我坐下，" 我不明白妳爲何找罪受？一個多月前怎不見妳替Crisha求情？"

"那是……那是因爲……"

"那是因爲汪醫生比鄭醫生年輕、有魅力。"他接話。

我趕緊否認，這是什麼跟什麼？余主任怎麼可以有這種可怕的聯想？太糟糕了！

余主任沒解釋，反而另起爐灶，他說自己沒去參加鄭醫生的頒獎酒會，只能從報上瞻仰其風采，但他的眼光卻不由自主地被照片上的一隻性感小貓所吸引，感慨過去幾年瞎了眼，錯過一親芳澤的機會……

"你……什麼意思？"我沈下臉來。

"没什麼意思，醫院出紕漏的事情何其多，我若要一件一件拿出來計較肯定過勞死，"他摘下黑框眼鏡用領帶擦拭乾淨後重新戴回，"過兩天我到香格里拉酒店開醫學座談會，休息時間也許我們能就這件事商討解決方案。"

什麼？這豈不是公然約炮？我怒不可遏。

"別發火，鄭之龍跟我說過一定要弄走姓汪的，即使汪醫生逃得了這一劫，也逃不過某人的刻意封殺，現在能救他的人也只有我……和妳，明白不？"他説。

第二十三章/不是寶兒

我心情鬱悶地回到工作崗位，做什麼都不帶勁。

"媛媛學姐，"一位身著藍色工作服的護理員很熱情地跟我打招呼。

看到清湯掛麵，我想起她是昨晚見過面的新進員工。

"又見面了，在REQ工作還習慣吧？"我問。

她坦言不太習慣，譬如才剛入職，醫院就讓她連值兩個班，從下午四點到隔天早上八點，要不是加班費多，肯定熬不下去……

我安慰她加班不是常態，剛來那會兒，我也常加班，大概是REQ的傳統吧？！讓新人先吃點兒苦，以後才有"倒吃甘蔗"的幸福感。

"聽妳這麼說我就放心了，"她笑了，"寶兒學姐說的没錯，妳是個大好人。"

寶兒？我問她是否也認識蔡寶兒？

"那當然了，她值大夜班，有什麼不懂的地方我總問她，她有時挺熱心，有時又不理人，大概因爲下個月有資格考試的緣故，她打算抓緊時間復習。”

我藉機鼓勵她，說護理員的薪水低，做的事又雜又多，她也該跟寶兒學學，工作一陣子後準備資格考試，不說別的，工資起碼翻倍……

“好呀！好呀！到時跟妳借考試用書看。”

“妳……怎麼知道我有書？”我太驚訝了。

她笑彎了眼：“我看到了呀！寶兒學姐讀的書就是跟妳借的，封面上有妳的名字。”

上床時，我故意發出很大的聲響，老公嘟嚷兩句，轉個身又沈沈睡去。

望著窗外的月光，我怎麼也睡不著，鄭之龍把我的書給了寶兒，而寶兒一句話也沒吭，他們兩人到底背對我做了什麼？

我努力回想日常的點滴，老公照常六點半起床沐浴，七點吃我煮的早飯，七點半開車上路以便趕上八點鐘的打卡。

正常的情況下，他下午四點能下班，但拖到五點多也正常，這幾天我上晚班，下午三點便得出門，意即我們只能床上見。

至於寶兒，她上大夜班，從零點到早上八點，我看不出他們兩人在時間上有任何交集，除非……除非趁我上班時約了見面。

有這個想法後，我不淡定了，越想越可疑，越想越對號入座，簡直到了草木皆兵的程度。

“我一定得揪出他們在背地裏玩什麼把戲？”我下定決心。

"Miss Cui, 余主任找妳。"

我正在給一位嚴重腹瀉的病人打生理鹽水，晚班護士長走過來傳達命令。

"跟他說我不在。"我頭擡也不擡地說。

待我掛好點滴，發現"大番薯"還杵在那裏。

"What?"我問。

"這句話應該是我問妳，妳是吃了熊心豹子膽了？敢跟主任說不。"

我答沒有的事，而是該做的事太多，我現在要去幫Lisa翻身兼按摩，她長褥瘡了，臀部中間部位已經結成黑痂，周邊總流水……

"妳別管，我找別人代替，妳趕緊去報到。"她輕推我一把。

話都說到這個份上，再不去就說不過去，我只好深呼吸一口氣，走向主任辦公室。

"妳來了，坐。"

我等余主任坐下，自己才挑了個遠點兒的位子坐。

"瞧妳，這對商討解決方案完全沒有幫助。"他欺身過來。

我趕緊跳起，乾脆不坐了，問他有什麼事找我？

"明天我到聖淘沙香格里拉酒店開會三天，中午12點半會回酒店小憩一下，房間號是518。"

果然露出狐狸尾巴了，我語帶威脅地說就當他什麼都沒說，這件事如果被我老公知道了，肯定有他好受……

沒想到余主任笑得好大聲，彷彿就要岔了氣。

"你這是幹嘛？有那麼好笑嗎？"

"當然，鄭之龍玩得可High了，若知道自己的老婆替他守身如玉，絕對大受感動！"

Lucy的事我早知道，老公抵死否認，我也就自欺欺人，顯然余主任也知道此事。

"除非親眼見到Lucy和我老公有不軌的行爲，否則我還是選擇相信他。"

"Lucy？他奶奶的，連Lucy也……"余主任看了我一眼，趕緊換口供，"這個Lucy也太不像話了，回頭我說她去哈！"

離開主任辦公室，我悶悶不樂，非常明顯，除了Lucy之外，老公還和別人不清不楚，是誰？

此時腦海出現一個人。

" Miss Evans, could you tell the head-nurse I am going out for a while?"我抓住其中一位同事，要她轉告護士長我出去一下。

Miss Evans問我去哪兒？我答回家，因爲……後院著火了。

晚上八點多，我繞到後院直接用鑰匙開門，廚房裏一團亂，餐桌上有未收拾的兩個大盤和兩個高腳杯。

樓下很安靜，我輕手輕腳地上樓，主臥室緊閉著，我走上前貼緊房門，可惜靜悄悄的，倒是走廊盡頭的客房內有女人細微的説話聲，分辨不出是誰。

" 崔媛媛，冷靜點兒，稍安勿躁，她不一定是寶兒。"

“不是寶兒也是某個女人，這下子我真的後院起火了。”

“我看算了吧！哪個男人不偷腥？睜一隻眼閉一隻眼，只要他還認這個家。”

“很快家就不是家了，像寶兒這種‘良家婦女’最可怕，她們要的不是幾張鈔票，而是一鍋端走，連湯都不讓妳喝。”

“那能怎麼辦？妳倒是說說。”

……

我像個傻子似地自我對話。

我沒有像其他原配一樣當場捉奸，而是選擇逃跑，大概還心存僥倖，只要不當場戳破，男人玩玩就收手，一切還有挽回的餘地。

“嘟……嘟嘟……”坐在出租車裏，有人打電話給我。

“Hello.”

“媛媛學姐，妳房子著火了嗎？”

聽到寶兒的聲音，我喜極而泣。

“妳怎麼了？別哭，我現在過去找妳！”

我要她別來，自己正在趕回醫院的路上……

“那妳慢點兒，我給妳帶宵夜來了。”

寶兒給我們帶的是“添好運”的叉燒包，與一般的叉燒包不

同，它的外皮比較酥，還帶著甜味，很像香港菠蘿包的味道，吃一個很經餓。

" Miss Cui, 家裏没事吧？ Miss Evans 説妳家後院著火，我還嚇了一跳。"晚班護士長邊吃邊説。

" 我……我以爲忘了關瓦斯，所以……"

" 還好今晚很太平，不然護士們都要亂成一團了。"

她又八卦了一下最新的影視消息後才要大家作鳥獸散，只留下晚到的我及送宵夜的天使。

" 妳今天怎麼提早上班？"我問寶兒。

" 也不是上班，汪醫生説也許……也許有空解答我的模擬試卷難題，所以……"

哎～我差點兒忘了汪致遠才是寶兒的菜。

" 人呢？"我撕下包子皮塞進嘴裏。

" 他正給病人換藥，馬上來。"

我們彼此沈默，直到我的眼光落在自己的書上。

" 寶兒，妳怎麼會有我的書？"我還是問了。

她顯得很詫異，問難道不是我主動借給她的？反正鄭醫生是這麼説的……

" 噢！是，我忘了。"我趕緊跟著圓謊。

寶兒鬆了口氣，轉而讚美我老公是個大好人，不僅答應今晚幫她解題，還請吃飯，可惜後來鄭醫生臨時有事，她只好向汪醫生求助，嘻嘻！没想到男神真答應了。

我喉嚨發乾地問鄭之龍打算在哪裏教她？

" 當然上妳家囉！他還説上課前會親自下廚做印尼炒飯請我吃。"她答。

第二十四章/魔高一丈

第一次上鄭之龍家，他端出的便是印尼炒飯，除了色澤油亮的飯外，還有蝦片及沙爹牛肉串當配菜，很有南洋風味。

我問他飯裏的特殊味道是什麼？他答是用糖、蝦米、辣椒、鹽、酸柑汁、食油、蝦膏等炒出的醬料，叫桑巴醬或馬拉盞。

"没想到你還會做飯，可惜我對印尼菜没研究。"

"没事，以後妳隨便煮煮，只要是中國飯我都愛吃。"

婚後我才知道鄭之龍服膺"君子遠庖廚"，唯一拿得出手的只有印尼炒飯，而每個和他交往過的女人都吃過這一味，原因是會做飯的男人更具魅力，他的外貌已經減分了，不得不以此加分。

如今我的男人也想讓寶兒吃"鴻門宴"，司馬昭之心昭然若揭。

"寶兒，我老公做的飯很難吃，下次……請說不。"我沈下臉來。

没想到她説我太謙虛了，鄭醫生的印尼炒飯在REQ是出了名的，他尤其喜歡請護理員或助理護士吃飯，順便指導她們的功課……

"妳怎麼知道？"

"女人最愛八卦了，妳應該認識Alisa，她原是五官科的助理護士，現在已經升爲註冊護士。她説鄭醫生學富五車，對考題的走向很清楚，如果我也想通過考試，最好找他指導，這已是護士間公開的秘密了。"

我聽了脊背發涼，到底還有多少護士被鄭之龍染指？

"寶兒，相信我，沒有我老公的指導，妳照樣能通過考試，不難的。"

她嗤之以鼻，説自己可不像我一樣頭腦頂呱呱，只要面對考試，她的腦子就不好使，大概是小時候發高燒給燒壞的……

"妳是怎麼了？聽不懂人話嗎？好説歹説，妳還是不撞南牆不回頭，Shit，花癡指的就是妳這種人！"

"媛媛學姐，妳怎麼……"

看寶兒一副受傷的樣子，我才意識到自己説重了，正想低頭道歉，然而她的眼光卻不在我身上，眼淚像斷了線的珍珠，啪啦啪啦地掉……

我轉過身去，赫然發現汪醫生就立在我身後。

"妳也太過份了，大家都是同事，何必呢？"他説。

我正想解釋，寶兒已經衝進汪致遠的懷裏哭成淚人。我抿抿嘴轉身離去，不想看見汪醫生安慰人的樣子。

～

一整晚我都不説話，看誰都討厭，看誰都不給好臉色，好不容易捱到下班時間，我一馬當先走出醫院大門。

新加坡位處熱帶地區，全年皆夏，無明顯的四季之分，只是冬季比較多雨罷了。好比現在，外面正下著傾盆大雨，我走也不是，不走也不是。

"媛媛學姐，"寶兒突然向我奔來，"我的傘借妳。"

我本想接受她的好意，藉此修復關係，没想到汪致遠此時也走出醫院大門，害我拉不下臉來。

"不必！"我冷冷地對寶兒説，然後一頭鑽進大雨裏。

到家時已然成了"落湯雞"。

洗完熱水澡，再把濕漉漉的地板擦乾，上樓時已近凌晨三點。

我原本應該向左走向主臥室，但腳卻不由自主地向右走向走廊盡頭的客房……

這棟別墅有四個房間，全在樓上，除了主臥室之外，其他三個房間基本空著。由於"突發事件"的發生，我認爲有一探究竟的必要。

打開房門後，初看並無異樣，家俱照舊擺放得井然有序、整整齊齊，但我還是在床底下發現用黑色塑料袋裝著的舊床單。

原來這就是鄭之龍玩的把戲，事後鋪上新床單，然後把用過的丟棄，船過水無痕，難怪我一直未發現他帶女人回家共度良宵的痕跡。

我跌坐在床上，一會兒哭一會兒笑，像個瘋子似的。

自從嫁給鄭之龍後，我的人生便一直走下坡路，雖然極力想掉轉車頭，無奈駕駛盤脱落兼刹車失靈，只能眼睜睜看著車子墜落無底深淵……

"我恨你！鄭之龍。"我握緊拳頭，像頭被激怒的母獅子。

~

我重新穿上ALEXANDER MACQUEEN設計的米色露背拖地晚禮服，再將頭髮高高挽起，除了早上因爲沒準時叫醒老公，挨了他一巴掌留下的五爪印外，我仍是那個美得不可方物的崔媛媛。

在臉頰上塗上厚厚的粉後，我琢磨著該塗哪個顏色的唇膏，最後選擇像血一樣的石榴紅。

~

聖淘沙被譽爲新加坡最迷人的度假小島，它曾經只是一個小漁村，後被英國佔領成爲軍事基地，直至1972年才被改造成爲一個悠閒美麗的度假村，島上有各式各樣的娛樂設施和休閒活動區域。

從新加坡本島前往聖淘沙的交通方式有五種，分別是纜車、渡輪、巴士、捷運和出租車。由於身著晚禮服，我選擇搭出租車前往。

當余主任發現我站在518房外時，像中了頭彩似的興奮非常。

"快，請進。"

由於太過激動，他的卡刷了五、六次才成功打開房門。

"吃中飯了沒？"進到房內，他問。

我答沒，待會兒吃他就行。

余主任哼哼哈哈地笑著，我們兩人就這麼尷尬地互望，直到他按耐不住撲上來，我才表明要他立字爲據。

"寫什麼寫？！"他將我遞過去的紙筆扔一旁，"春宵一刻值千金，待會兒再寫。"

我打掉他不安份的手，説不寫就走人，我不被人白玩。

"媽的，真掃興！"他彎腰撿起紙筆，問我寫什麼？

"一、讓汪醫生安穩地待在REQ。二、找個名義弄走鄭之龍。三、把崔嬡嬡調到體檢部。"

他提出抗議，説這是三個要求，未免太多了？

"所以我陪你三天嘛！"我答。

他挑起眉梢，色眯眯地看著我好幾秒後，開始疾筆書寫，一簽完大名及日期後，他跳起來將我撲倒在床。

"妳這個悶騷貨太會撩人了，看我怎麼治妳！"他的髒嘴湊了上來，順便撕下我的乳貼。

在一上一下的起伏中，我轉頭看擱在電視櫃上的包，那裏有個小孔正閃著紅色的光芒......

接下來的兩天，我都準時報到，次次功夫做足，連余主任都誇讚我敬業。

"如果......真想打造個金窩將妳眷養起來。"他在我耳邊低語。

我推開他，把衣服一件件穿回去，然後慢條斯理地説："也不怕你太太河東獅吼，偷吃得適可而止。"

余夫人是個厲害角色，於公於私都大權在握，余主任能坐上這個位子，她功不可沒。

"好端端地提她做什麼？晦氣！"

"不提就不提，"我拿上包，"我走了，別忘了你的承諾。"

余主任似笑非笑地反問我什麼承諾？他可什麼都沒答應呀！

切，早知道他是隻老狐狸，事後會反悔。

我氣定神閒地從包裏拿出一個削筆器大小的黑色塑料物，嘴巴道出一長串地址，那是他老婆上班的地方。

"我警告妳別亂來，那會死人的。"余主任急了。

"知道就好，什麼時候完成三項使命，什麼時候我將小東西給你，裏面的畫面可精彩了，把你的臉孔拍得一清二楚。"

他憤而撲上來搶針孔攝像機，被我巧妙地躲掉。

"我同樣警告你，別讓我做玉石俱焚的事。"我齜牙咧嘴，然後踩著高跟鞋傲睨自若地離去。

第二十五章/宏圖大業

鄭之龍完全没察覺到我的“出軌”，讓我有了“報復”後的小小快感。

“Alisa走了，新來的助理護士糊里糊塗的，讓人很頭疼。”老公邊吃早餐邊說。

“她爲什麽要走？”我明知故問。

他答Alisa通過考試，現在已是註冊護士，被調到腎臟科，所以......

我忍不住酸溜溜地問該不會因爲他的幫忙，Alisa才通過考試吧？

“什麽意思？”鄭之龍停下咀嚼的動作。

“没什麽意思......對了，寶兒說你想請她吃飯，順便指導功課，我告訴她這世界免費的最貴，要她三思而行。”

“有病！同事間互相幫忙很正常，妳別胡亂攪和！”

還不到攤牌的時候，我没回嘴，用筷子戳破蛋黃，讓蛋液四處流竄。

剛進住院部就與從辦公室走出來的余主任踫上面，他很熱情地和我打招呼，像往常一樣。

"昨晚睡得好嗎？"我問。

他答很好，反問我是否也睡得安穩？

"不好，翻來覆去的，因爲想起昨天忘了服避孕藥。"

余主任聽了大驚失色，一把將我跩進辦公室裏。

"妳説過每天吃早餐時會順便吞一片媽富隆，所以我才沒採取任何防護措施，現在……這是怎麼回事？説！"他問，樣子像要殺了我。

我無所謂地答："忘了唄！放心，没那麼好運。"

"好運？那是天崩地裂的災難呀！妳等著，別走開。"

没多久余主任踅回，遞給我一杯水及一個白色藥片。

"吃這個有副作用，我不吃！"我將臉撇向一旁。

那個一臉衰相的人説這事可由不得我，他已經五十歲高齡，不想再當爹。

我答要我吃也行，但鄭之龍得在一個星期內垮台，他一走，汪醫生就安全了，等於一石二鳥。

"崔媛媛，妳乾脆殺了我吧！要弄走一個剛獲得杏林醫學獎的人談何容易？總得讓我坐籌帷幄，好好策劃一下吧！"

"別告訴我，你不知道鄭之龍拿藥商回扣的事；也別告訴我，你不知道他把八成新的醫療器材報銷，然後轉移到即將開幕的私人診所裏。"

余主任聽完在辦公室內很不安地來回踱步，我乘勝追擊，告訴他夜長夢多，我去酒店找他時曾在走廊撞見骨科的李醫生，那人若多嘴，他想全身而退就難了，鄭之龍什麼事都幹得出來……

"知道了，"他停止踱步，"把藥吃了，我……盡快。"

我聽話地服下藥片，然後開門走人。

我沒在酒店走廊踫見李醫生，充其量只是看到他的背影；我也沒有服用避孕藥的習慣，因爲婚後我和老公就積極造人，可惜送子娘娘還是缺席。

你若問我怕不怕懷了余主任的孩子？怕，我當然怕，而且很怕，所以當他要我服用左炔諾孕酮腸溶片時，我求之不得，但緊急避孕藥的副作用實在太大，沒多久我便全身乏力，不僅頭痛，還吐了兩回。

" Miss Cui, 妳不要緊吧 ？ ！"我從廁所出來，"大番薯"很關心地問。

"沒……沒什麼，大概吃壞肚子了。"

"那怎麼成？我叫醫生過來看看。"

我答不必了，自己到休息室的床上躺一下就行。

然而"熱心過度"的晚班護士長還是找來汪醫生，他坐在我身側，問我今天吃了什麼東西？

"培根、炒蛋、豆漿、水餃、酸辣湯……左炔諾孕酮腸溶片。"我答。

身爲醫生，他完全清楚最後一項指的是什麼。

"緊急避孕藥很傷身，妳和鄭醫生應該謹慎一點兒才好。"

我說我知道，但一時沒考慮那麼多，尤其余主任又這麼猴急……

汪醫生聽完像看怪物一樣地看我，讓人很難受。

"我能運用的資源就這麼多，你讓小蝦米如何對付大白鯊？"我弱弱地答。

汪致遠嘆了一口氣，緊接著又嘆第二口氣。

"不用替我擔心，好壞我都能承受，大不了一死。"

"妳不能死，聽到沒？"他揚起聲，"醫院裏每天都有人死去，難道妳沒從中學會什麼嗎？"

没錯，死亡是最不需要趕的，因爲它最終會來到，螻蟻尚且偷生，我又何嘗不是？然而正因不想淪爲俎上肉，我才不得不捨去尊嚴奮力一博，但說這些外人是不會懂的。

"置死地才能後生，有戰死的準備才會奮勇向前，都已經這樣了，我只能順勢走下去。"我試圖說服自己也說服汪醫生。

余主任的動作很快，回到家，我看見老公還没睡。

"快凌晨一點了，怎麼還不睡？"

他答晚上接到內科馮主任打來的緊急電話，有人舉報他收受藥商回扣，還好給的是商場抵用券，會有專人以七折回收，他現在急著刪除與中間人的郵件往來……

知道鄭之龍正在毀滅證據，事不宜遲，我馬上脫光衣服走向他。

"妳……這是怎麼了？"他頗感意外。

"好久没和你一起淋浴，走，我們一塊兒洗白白。"

我不由分說地拉他起身走向浴室，待他放鬆後又以拿香氛爲藉口回到他的電腦前，把即將被刪除的郵件拷貝到U盤上。

～

早餐桌上，老公話多得令人厭煩。

"......我和REQ的醫生、護士們關係都非常好，想不出會有誰扯我後腿。"他仍對"告密"事件耿耿於懷。

我提醒他樹大招風，多的是嫉妒他獲獎的人。

"妳這麼說讓我想起 Dr.Smith，從學生時代起我們就有瑜亮情結，肯定是他在背後搞鬼！"

知道他沒聯想到余主任，我放心了，要他趕緊把早飯吃了好上路，再不出發就趕不上八點鐘打卡。

"今天不去上班了，我得差人把私人診所裏的醫療器材搗毀後扔垃圾場。哎！扔的全是錢，沒辦法，我得防著小人使壞。"

～

當老公指揮工人把醫療器材從尚未開門營業的私人診所移出時，我正在馬路對面的椰子樹後猛按快門，連老公的身影也被我攝入。

"鄭之龍，看你這回往哪裏跑？"我憤恨地想。

成果在五天後顯現，我一進住院部，晚班護士長就拉我到一旁說悄悄話。

"怎麼回事？聽說妳老公辭職開私人診所去了，爲什麼辭？一邊在大醫院任職，一邊開診所才賺錢呢！"

我答他老了，不想太勞累。

"大番薯"睨了我一眼："四十多歲就喊老，你讓REQ那些年過半百的醫生怎麼想？不對，鄭醫生肯定有更長遠的計劃。"

我笑著同意，說鄭之龍有心從政，目標是當上衛生部部長……

"那麼妳就是部長夫人囉！到時可別忘了我們這幫老同事呀！"她說。

哎！燕雀安知鴻鵠之志？我失去那個多，絕不會滿足一個小小的"部長夫人"頭銜，弄走鄭之龍不過是第一步，我的宏圖大業才剛要開始呢！

"當然，到時給老胡安插個急救大隊長的位子哈！"我説。

老胡是"大番薯"的老公，目前是救護車上的急救員。

"急救大隊長？有這個位子嗎？"晚班護士長没聽出我話裏的揶揄。

我大笑著離開。

第二十六章/又一個交易

汪醫生説要給一位急性發作的哮喘病患者輸液及做吸氧治療，我幫著把阿奇黴素的點滴掛上。

"聽説……鄭醫生辭職了。"他邊幫患者戴上氧氣罩邊問。

"你的消息真靈通。"

他苦笑著答怎能不靈通？耳鼻咽喉科只有三位門診醫生，鄭醫生不在，讓Dr.Robinson和Dr.Thompson忙得焦頭爛額，因爲門診室外大排長龍，連他也被抓去看診了。

"很好呀！當上家庭醫生或全科醫生不是你的最終目標嗎？"

"妳忘了我的當前目標是通過Post Graduate考試？我已經待在五官科太久了，再不到其他科實習，連考試的資格都沒有，遑論最終目標。"

哎呀！我怎麼把這個給忘了？

"你放心，給你穿小鞋的人走了，你馬上就能離開五官科到下一個科室報到。"

"但願如此，"他嘆了一口氣，" Dr.Robinson説最近呼吸道感染的情況有擴大的趨勢，加上政策原因，醫院暫停招收從國外引進的Medical Officer，所以除非有新進主治醫生入主五官科，否則短期內我是走不了了。"

哎呀！機關算盡竟沒算上這一步，真是失策！

" 別心急，一定有辦法可以解決，一定的。"我爲他，也爲自己打氣。

一走進辦公室，住院部余主任就給我臉色看。

"又怎麼了？不是把妳老公成功踢出去了嗎？"他虎著眼，完全失去昔日在床上時的柔情蜜意。

我問汪醫生怎麼回事？鄭之龍一走，他反倒卡死在五官科。

"奇怪了，汪醫生卡死在哪兒干我何事？我和妳之間的事已了，妳走妳的陽關道，我過我的獨木橋，別再來煩我！"

醫院裏謠傳余主任的妻子看上一個小鮮肉，兩人打得火熱，搞得他心情大壞，難道謠言是真的？

" 我們之間的事還沒了，你忘了協議上的第三條：把崔媛媛調到體檢部。"我說。

" 那我不管，妳的事我已經做到仁至義盡，到此爲止吧！妳若想公佈不雅視頻，悉聽尊便，我就不信妳會做魚死網破的事！"

與一個禮拜前的膽戰心驚不同，余主任有自棄般的決絕，我問出了什麼事？

"不關妳的事，妳管好妳自己就行。"他突然想起什麼似，惡狠狠地看著我，" 回答我，汪醫生的床上功夫是不是很了得？否則無法解釋妳爲什麼會做吃裏扒外的事。切！女人全一個德行，賤！"

"閉上你的髒嘴，我和汪醫生是清白的，他的高風亮節不是你們這幫衣冠禽獸所能及。"

"呵呵！衣冠禽獸？內科馮主任算不算？現在也只有他能救妳的情夫，有本事別求衣冠禽獸，慢走不送。"

被趕出辦公室，整晚我心神不寧，三條協議只完成一條，偏偏我還拿余主任沒辦法，讓人如鯁在喉。

想到助理護士資格考試一結束，五月份上場的就是Post Graduate考試，離現在不過三個月，再怎麼著也得趕緊讓汪醫生到下一個科室實習，否則真要來不及了……

當我還在魂不守舍，忽聞晚班護士長的催促聲："Miss Cui,妳怎麼還在這裏？八號病房第七床病人正等妳換藥呢！"

我噢了一聲，趕緊上藥房取藥。

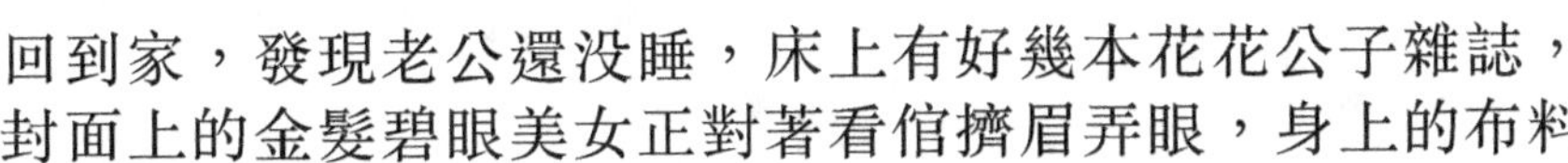

回到家，發現老公還沒睡，床上有好幾本花花公子雜誌，封面上的金髮碧眼美女正對著看倌擠眉弄眼，身上的布料一個比一個少。

"妳越來越晚回來了。"鄭之龍望了一眼牆上掛鐘後說。

"醫院的事說不準，你又不是不知道。"

說完，我走向衣櫃拿換洗衣服，臨下班才處理完一個大小便失禁的病患，全身髒得難受。

沒料到我一進浴室，鄭之龍也跟著進來。

"出去！今天沒心情。"我沒好氣地說。

"跟老婆親熱還得挑日子？沒這個道理。"

然後我被他強押著在淋浴房裏行周公之禮，而且在我尚未準備好的情況下長驅直入，疼得我眼淚直流。

“最近事多，除了做愛，我無處發洩。”離開我的身體後，他說。

不用他解釋，我也知道鄭之龍情緒不佳，他原先的計劃是醫院和私人診所兩頭跑，可以的話，還能把醫院的病患帶回自己的私人診所，等於挖牆腳，然而這個完美計劃卻在兩天前被打破，醫院院長在毫無預警的情況下請他喝茶，告訴他某個重量級人物舉報他的不端行爲，有物證（包括他收受藥商回扣及“偷竊”醫療器材），問他要自行引退還是交由醫療監控部門調查？

老公當場壯士斷腕，立馬提出辭呈，連辦公室裏的私人物品還是由我打包取回。

被請退後，鄭之龍滿腦子想的就是揪出那個背後使壞的小人，還讓我幫著找，壓根兒沒懷疑到我及余主任身上，讓我鬆了一口氣。

“其實你也没什麼好損失，名聲算是保住了，頂多缺了REQ的收入，但你有更多時間經營私人診所，亏不了多少。”我説。

“這不是錢的問題，而是感覺有股力量在蠢蠢欲動，讓我芒刺在背。”

我寬慰他職場上的角力很正常，要怪只能怪他鋒芒外露，還好現在遠離暴風圈，可以過幾天太平日子……

“説到太平日子，那個姓汪的大概以爲自己安全了。不行，得將他弄走，我人是不在了，但勢力還在，馮主任肯定會幫忙。”

這是繼離開余主任辦公室後，第二次聽到“馮主任”的大名。

“爲什麼……爲什麼你看他不順眼？他不過是個想往上爬的MO，連正式的醫生資格都還未取得。”

老公陰陰地笑：“怪也只能怪他長得太俊，我最討厭皮相好的男人，這個世界對他們太寬容，我得替醜人行道。話説回來，妳大概對他一直有非份之想，我可不允許自己被戴綠帽。”

原來長得好看也是原罪，真替汪致遠叫屈。

話不投機，我趕緊轉話題：“既然私人診所九點才開門，以後能不能晚一個鐘頭起床？我也能多睡會兒。”

“不行，業精於勤荒於嬉，我剛好趁這多出來的一個小時多做研究，醫學論文不能馬虎。”

這就是鄭之龍，一個在專業領域裏戰戰兢兢到近乎嚴苛的懸壺濟世者，卻在日常生活中施暴和縱慾。我多希望他只是個杏林學者而非變態，那麼我也無庸做“吃裏扒外”的缺德事了。

我特意提早半小時上班，下午三點半，馮主任殷勤地替我倒茶水。

“鄭醫生忽然辭識讓內科雞飛狗跳，尤其五官科，最近呼吸道疾病增多，走道裏都是排隊等看病的人。”

“我知道，汪醫生提起過。”

“汪醫生……提起過？”他投來好奇的眼神。

我趕緊把汪致遠三個月後有資格考試，但臨床輪轉一直卡在五官科一事告知。

“是汪醫生讓妳來求情的？”他問。

“不是，這是我的個人行爲。”

他呵呵笑，説我們鄭氏夫妻真有意思，一個要他將人往死裏整，另一個卻大獻愛心，他不知該聽誰的？

“別理我老公，他現在不在醫院裏工作，沒影響力了，你犯不著鞍前馬後。”

"醫護行業説大不大，説小不小，擡頭不見低頭見，搞不好哪天我需要鄭醫生幫忙，何況他是獲獎的名醫……"馮主任説得很慢，似乎在等我表態。

我嘆了一口氣，問他有什麼條件？

"我想再看一次妳穿低胸晚禮服的樣子，就妳跟我。"

"哪裏？"我有氣無力地問。

"我老婆剛回中國探親，家裏没人。"他答。

第二十七章／一錯再錯

你若問我爲什麼要一錯再錯？我也答不上來，好比洗頭洗到一半，總得洗乾淨吧？否則頂著一頭泡沫要何去何從？

馮主任答應我做完"那件事"，隔天汪醫生就能到眼科報到，一切順利的話，參加五月份的考試絕對沒問題，至於將我調到體檢部一事……只有院長和HR說得上話，這不在他的權力範圍內。

看來也只能走一步算一步了。

∼

我和馮主任約了下午一點見面，他從醫院溜出來，然後在離我家十分鐘步行距離的便利店接我。我拎了個大型紙袋（裏面是撩人的米色低胸晚禮服）偷偷摸摸地出門，路上不巧遇到相認的鄰居還得裝作不認識，好比諜戰大片。

在REQ的醫生群中，內科馮主任並不顯突出，我是説他長著一張大衆臉，一米七的身高，不胖不瘦的身材……除了身上的狐臭和油膩感之外，很難讓人有深刻印象，直到他將車子開上格蘭芝路上的高級住宅區時，我對他的評價才稍有改觀，原來他也是隱性富豪呀！

"那是萊佛士女子中學，看到没？"馮主任手指著右前方的黃色大樓，"如果不是爲了女兒，我們不會把房子買在'彭美華庭'，太貴了，每尺近三千新幣哪！"

接著他把豪宅的優勢介紹得巨細靡遺，宛如房產仲介，我因此知道這樓盤距離烏節路地鐵站和世界城購物中心只有八、九百米，往東是繁華商圈，往北是使館區，周邊除了本地名校萊佛士女子中學外，還有ISS國際學校、新加坡女子小學及英華小學等，Gramercy公園也近在咫尺……

"你女兒真幸福。"我説著應酬話。

"才14歲就有96公分的大長腿，臉也長得像她媽，漂亮得很，把萊佛士書院的男生迷得神魂顛倒，我不得不讓家務助理每天接送，好趕走那群蒼蠅。"馮主任繼續吹噓。

"還好這個點你的漂亮女兒不在家，否則就不好解釋了。"我冷冷地説。

"是，是，"他略顯尷尬，"現在家務助理也不在，我打發她到燕窩工廠拿貨，而且叮嚀她得盯著洗燕師把燕毛和燕頭都清洗乾淨，估計往返也要三個小時以上。"

他像交待什麼似的，在我耳中卻是即將巫山雲雨的告示。

晚班從下午四點到午夜零時，我和馮主任進入醫院大廳時剛好差一刻鐘四點，還好没遲到。我剛鬆了一口氣，忽然看到汪醫生往我們這邊走來，頓時慌了，五官科不是人滿爲患嗎？他怎麼有時間出外"溜達"？

"汪醫生，"馮主任向他招手，"正要找你呢！"

完了，就要東窗事發了……

“什麼事？”汪醫生看著馮主任，又轉頭看立在主任身後的我。

“明天調你到眼科，你在五官科待太久了，”馮主任拍拍他的肩膀，“小伙子不錯，加油！我看好你。”

他呵呵一笑後離開，留下我和汪醫生四眼相望。

“怎麼回事？”他問。

“什麼怎麼回事？”我的心跳得好快，“噢！那件事，你也聽到了，你被調到眼科實習，恭喜了，呵呵！”

相對我的“強顏歡笑”，汪醫生卻是一臉寒霜：“我問妳，馮主任爲什麼無緣無故調我離開五官科？妳……做了什麼？”

我答什麼都沒做，是他表現好，不關我的事，我什麼都沒說也沒做，和主任一起進醫院純屬偶然，踫巧在停車場遇上，他剛回家一趟……

越描越黑説的就是我，眼瞅著編不下去了，我趕緊藉口上班要遲到，拜！

～

一連幾天都沒看到汪醫生，我放下心來。

眼科部的主治醫生個個“慈眉善目”，他無庸連續值兩個班討某人歡心，這是好消息。

～

今晚我值大夜班，從凌晨到早上八點，辛苦不在話下。

“看來二月份我們基本睡不到一起了。”老公早餐桌上説。

“嗯！儲藏櫃裏有穀物，是你喜歡的牌子，如果吃膩了就到診所旁邊的食肆吃早餐，有油條、燒餅、豆腐腦等，晚上回來我煮好吃的等你。”

鄭之龍很滿意我的回答，他把雞湯細麵圇圇吞下肚，抹了一下嘴角後，起身準備上班。

之所以刻意討好老公是因爲爸媽今天下午到，他們來新加坡與我共度農曆新年，我希望到時他"賞臉"，別讓我下不了台。

鄭之龍走了之後，我到新加坡最高端的超市Market Place採買，近一年沒能承歡父母膝下，我感到內疚，所以想在食物上做補償。我挑了最新鮮的食材，還買了父親愛喝的五糧液，飄洋過海而來的中國酒在價格上貴出很多，但我不在乎。

回家後，該洗的洗，該切的切，眼看時間不早了，我脫下圍裙趕搭東西線地鐵至樟宜機場接機。

老公回家時，母親正將炸好的桂魚淋上熱氣騰騰的滷汁，吱吱叫的聲音，活像松鼠在哀嚎。

"我爸媽來了，"我接過他的公事包，低語，"快打聲招呼吧！"

鄭之龍面無表情地走過去喊了聲："爸、媽，你們來了。"

相較女婿的冷漠，我爸媽可是熱情洋溢，問他累不累？要不要喝口水？馬上就開飯了……

老公答不累、不渴，然後轉身提醒我吃飯時再叫他，他上樓去了。

"之龍怎麼了？很不高興的樣子。"母親一副戒慎小心的樣子。

"沒事，可能在診所受了氣。"我安慰她。

母親一下飛機就趕著將我手上的活兒接過去，頭髮亂了、滿臉油光，卻還關心自己女婿的心情起伏，我突然好想哭。

～

原本應該是和樂溫馨的一餐，卻被鄭之龍給破壞無遺。

「桂魚多少錢一斤？什麼？！三十新幣？妳也太不會過日子了。」

「怎麼不買葡萄酒？十新幣有一大瓶，這五糧液在新加坡可貴了，早知道就從中國帶回來，省不止一半的錢。」

「我們平常吃飯基本不超過三道菜，像這樣的‘宴席’絕無僅有。」

「剛開了家私人診所，貸了一大筆錢，也不知什麼時候能還完，借貸人是我們夫妻二人，所以不光是我個人的問題。」

……

真不知道鄭之龍是怎麼想的，偏偏挑這個時候談錢，讓爸媽胃口盡失，可惜了一桌好酒好菜。

「你……省省吧！不是剛買了個所費不貲的水晶吊燈掛在診所大廳嗎？」我沒好氣地反擊。

老公答那不一樣，病人進入高大上的診所，掏錢才會爽快，說到底這是投資，懂不？

聽到此，父親開口了：「我不知道你們的經濟狀況，看樣子小媛在這個家用錢要非常小心。你放心，我們這次來主要是家人團聚，伙食和住宿費多少會添點兒，只會多不會少。」

「爸，你說啥？」我急了，「來女兒家住還談錢，太見外了。」

說完，我望向自己的老公，希望他也表表態，然而他卻把眼光落在蠔油牛肉上，吃得津津有味。

“沒事，”母親對我微笑，“我們多年前買的股票漲了，每個月還有退休金，平常也沒什麼開銷，旅遊度假不也得花錢，哪有來女兒女婿家過得舒心？”

有了兩位老人的承諾，鄭之龍的態度一百八十度轉變，不僅勸我父母多吃點兒，還跟父親乾了好幾杯五糧液，整個人輕鬆許多。

~

我在廚房裏洗碗盤，母親幫著擦流理台和爐灶，只聽見嘩啦啦的水聲及碗盤踫撞的聲音。

“之龍對妳好嗎？”母親還是問了。

“好。”一答完，我的眼淚像斷了線的珍珠，啪啦啪啦地往下掉。

“要真過不下去就跟我們回家吧！”

母親說回“家”，我才發現在新加坡我沒有“家”，充其量只是住在一棟華美的宿舍裏，沒有愛和關懷，只有利用與折磨。

“回去不過是一張機票的事，但我不甘心就這麼灰頭土臉地離開。”我拭去淚水。

“唉！當時看鄭之龍老實巴交的，沒想到是隻披了羊皮的狼，早知道該多看看，妳舅舅的公司就有幾個不錯的小伙子……”

知道母親又要說些“事後諸葛亮”的話，我趕緊表示自己上大夜班，得走了。

“讓之龍送妳一程吧！”母親說。

“我向來自己打車。”

聽見母親在我身後長嘆一口氣，再也沒有比那個更無奈的了，唉～

第二十八章／年夜飯

再過兩天就是除夕夜，我好說歹說才得了連假，從除夕當天到大年初三零時，總算能和遠道而來的父母過大年，怎不令人雀躍？但……

"後天一早我飛巴厘島，幫我整理行李，大年初四回來。"吃完晚餐回到房內，老公說。

私人診所不像醫院全年無休，農曆新年是放假的，通常從除夕放到大年初四。本來想著老公有五天長假，我們全家能出外踏青，享受天倫之樂，沒想到計劃全被打破了。

"爲什麼？別告訴我出公差。"我冷冷地問。

"的確是出公差，我到巴厘島參觀製藥廠，爲以後的進藥做準備。"

"巴厘島有製藥廠？"我揚起聲來，"你怎麼不說伊拉克有時裝秀？"

鄭之龍冷哼一聲，說我是井底蛙，既短視又膚淺，他懶得跟我溝通……

"是呀！家花哪有野花香？想必Lucy不是井底蛙，既不短視也不膚淺，你樂得跟她溝通，而且是用身體溝通……"

"啪！"鄭之龍跳起來賞我一巴掌，"久沒打妳，皮癢了？"

老實説，我以爲再怎麼著，老公也不會在我父母來的時候打我，不看僧面看佛面嘛！沒想到他仍秉持一貫的作風，想打就打，毫不手軟。

"你乾脆打死我好了，打呀！"我跨前一步，"給你打！"

"妳以爲我不敢？"

當父母闖進來時，我已躺在地上捂著肚子喊疼。

"小媛，怎麼了？"母親過來扶我。

"媽～"還沒告狀，我已經淚流滿面。

爸開口了，聽得出來竭力想壓住怒火："之龍，小媛有什麼錯不能用說的，非得把她打倒在地？"

"你問問你的寶貝女兒做了什麼？男人在外工作容易嗎？動不動就疑神疑鬼，叫我如何安心工作？"老公説得理直氣壯。

我趕緊澄清自己不是無理取鬧，有誰大過年會出公差？怕是和小三雙宿雙飛，他和一個藥商代表已經不清不楚很久了……

"你們聽聽，這是什麼話？"鄭之龍轉向我，"崔媛媛，妳腦子有病，該看精神科！"

"夠了！"父親大喝一聲，"我自己的女兒清楚著，她不是胡亂編派是非的人，你肯定有不檢點之處。"

沒想到父親的"申張正義"換來的是我們仨同時被趕出主臥室。

"小媛，要不……"母親哽咽了。

"爸、媽，對不起，讓你們看到這麼不堪的一幕，我是如此不孝……"

我永遠無法原諒那個名義上稱爲老公的人，讓我們全家在應當歡樂的日子裏抱頭痛哭。

鄭之龍，我恨你！

除夕早上值完大夜班回家，剛好和拖著行李箱出門的老公擦肩而過，我們彼此沒有交談。

"小媛，快來吃早餐，媽給妳做了愛吃的大肉包，"她停頓了一下，"連之龍也吃了好幾個。"

母親的肉包在親友間是出了名的，皮薄、肉厚、汁多，但因那個冤家也吃了，害我頓時失去胃口。

"爲什麼給他吃？他還打妳女兒呢！"我很不滿，覺得自己被背叛了。

母親拉著我的手坐下，給我盛了碗豆漿，再從蒸籠裏挾了幾個熱呼呼的包子放在盤裏遞給我："吃！没放姜，知道妳不喜歡。"

我勉強拿起來入口，天呀！這麼好吃，簡直是人間美味。

母親看我吃得開心，清了清喉嚨後説："小媛呀！我和妳爸商量了，夫妻勸和不勸離，哪對夫妻不吵架？妳之所以生氣是認定之龍偷腥去了，但萬一他真的是爲這個家去打拼呢？難怪他會氣得打人……"

"媽～"我喊了起來，"你……你們到底站哪邊？我可是你們的親生女呀！"

父親本來坐在客廳裏看報，這時也加入談話："正因爲妳是我們鍾愛的女兒，我們才會委屈求全，如果不是爲了大局著想，我這把老骨頭肯定和那人拼了，但……妳有没有想過離婚的女人難再嫁？哪天我和妳媽上西天，妳身邊没個人照應，我們如何安心？”

“是呀是呀！”母親接棒，“而且今天早上之龍也説了，打人不對，他意識到自己的錯誤，只是礙於面子没跟妳道歉。”

雖然我有一籮筐的話要説，包括自結婚以來，挨拳頭已成了家常便飯，離婚是難再嫁，但也勝“伴君如伴虎”，還有還有，鄭之龍絕不是因公出差，没聽過度假勝地還有製藥廠……但這些我都不能説。

父母的思想很老舊，雖然偶爾有讓我回家的念頭，那不過是腦子一熱的結果，等冷靜下來就不是那麼回事了。

見我不言語，母親遞過來一個信封，説：“之龍很有心，他讓我們今晚找家餐廳吃年夜飯，別忙活了，這錢是他給的。”

我下意識打開來看，哈！虧他有心全換成2元紙鈔，看著厚厚一沓，其實才100新幣，折合人民幣五百元不到，這個數只夠上大排檔吃年夜飯。

“成，既然是他給的，我們就痛快地花掉，也算不枉費他的一番苦心。”我自嘲。

母親要我吃完早餐睡覺去，下午四點再叫我，但我睡不著，開始翻箱倒櫃，你若問我找什麼？我答：“老公的銀行卡。”

前陣子買診所的水晶吊燈時，商家説刷銀行卡可省3%，就在老公輸入密碼時被我“刻意”偷瞄到，現在只要找到卡即可……

没錯，我不介意當“家賊”。

鄭之龍爲了防止我多花錢，每月只給寒酸的生活費，如果有額外的開銷得另外申請，申請不通過就只能自掏腰包，而今天……這個理當家庭團聚的日子，他竟然想用100新幣堵住我們三人的嘴，門兒都沒有，非得讓他大出血不可。

我把想得到的地方都翻了個遍，依舊沒有銀行卡的影子，想必被帶走了。我很氣餒，原以爲他會像前幾次一樣，不小心把卡遺留在家裏。

下午四點，母親準時喚我。

"還想睡嗎？想睡就不吵妳。"母親小聲說，"對了，趕緊給之龍打個電話，他的銀行卡擱在兜裏，還好洗衣服前被我發現，否則……"

我趕緊跳起，搶過卡一看，果然是大華銀行卡，太好了！

老公有多張銀行卡和信用卡，小小的皮夾被撐得鼓鼓的，也許就是這個原因把其中一張卡給"擠"出來了。

"知道了，我會打給他。"我答，然後自然而然地收下那張卡。

"我看年夜飯還是在家裏吃了算，就我們仨，炒個菜很快的。"母親說。

我答怎麼成？她的女婿已經給錢了，不出去吃不合適，然後將她往房外一送："去化化妝，穿身漂亮衣裳，待會兒我們上頂級餐廳吃飯，嗯？"

第二十九章/植物園

新加坡人普遍喜歡外食，平均每月的外食金額佔亞太地區第一。到了重要節日，譬如農曆新年就更不在話下，各大餐廳的年夜飯早早爆棚，不光得提前預定，還被限制時段。這可不，我打了不下十幾通電話，皆被打回票。

"我看算了吧！家裏還有半塊叉燒及未開封的臘肉，我煮叉燒炒飯及青椒臘肉，再煮個筍片湯湊合著吃吧！"母親說。

這怎麼可以？一年中最重要的家庭團圓日卻吃得如此寒酸，父母還打老遠過來，怎麼都說不過去。我趕緊又撥打電話，這次是"鴻福軒"，一個平常就人山人海的中式餐廳，走的是高檔路線。

果然接線員跟我說抱歉，他家的預約早一個月前就滿了。我正想放棄，忽聞電話那頭傳來對話聲，大意是有客人因班機延誤來不了了……

"把預約給我吧！"我搶著說，"我們二十分鐘內能趕到。"

"可是……那是十人包間，有最低消費。"

"錢不是問題。"我豪氣地答。

～

我們才花十五分鐘就趕到"鴻福軒"，裏面已經人山人海。

"這麼多人，有位嗎？"母親皺緊眉頭問。

我要她別擔心，訂的是包間，在最裏面，没人跟我們搶……

"Miss Cui, 也來吃年夜飯？"

聽見有人喊我，我轉過頭去，發現是REQ的MO(全是從中國來的),總共五位，清一色是男的，包括汪致遠。

"你們怎麼在這裏？"我問。

答話的是小個頭的簡醫生，他説他們五個"老鄉"約了一起吃年夜飯，誰知道吃頓飯還得預約，他們已經被多家餐廳拒絕，看來得回家吃泡麵……

"吃什麼泡麵？跟我們一起吃吧！我訂了十人的大包間。"反正有最低消費，我樂得慷慨。

就這麼著，用餐人數從三人增至八人，一群人吱吱喳喳地進入包間。

～

五頭南非鮑魚八寶鴨、黃尾魚金槍魚撈生、乾炒蜜醬芝麻雞、藥軹蝦、香煎三文魚、銀魚炒飯、窩打春捲、西藍花炒臘肉、四川烤魚、家常火鍋，外加兩打啤酒及五扎鮮榨果汁。

"Miss Cui, 妳中彩票了？全點貴的，讓我看看自己皮夾裏的錢夠不夠付……"説話的是廣東腔很重的文醫生。

我答不用他們付，這單我買了。

話一落音，四位醫生齊齊舉杯謝我，除了汪致遠。

菜陸續上，啤酒開了十幾瓶，酒醉飯飽後，大家鬆懈了下來……

"你們都結婚了嗎？"母親問。

這五人當中有三人已婚，只有矮個子簡醫生及汪致遠未婚，於是母親將注意力轉向這兩人。

"老家哪裏？喜歡什麼樣的女孩？"母親問外在條件明顯比較好的汪醫生。

知道母親在想什麼，我提出抗議，要她別問私人問題。

"問問何妨？"母親睨了我一眼，"或許我可以幫他們介紹好女孩。"

"我已經有喜歡的人了。"汪致遠答。

母親因此流露出失望的神情。

"伯母若能替我介紹就太好了，我沒啥要求，不嫌棄我矮就行。"簡醫生搶著說。

母親的眼睛重新亮了起來，問他介不介意娶離過婚的女人？

"這……不合適吧？！我人雖矮，好歹是個醫生，應該配得上沒結過婚的女人。"

話題瞬間冷了下來，母親終於閉上嘴不再發問。

"吃！"父親接棒，"你們醫生平常很忙，吃沒吃好，趁現在補一補，有好的身體才能走更長遠的路。"

爲了這句話，醫生們輪番敬父親酒，只有汪致遠將父親的酒移開，遞上橙汁，說上了年紀的人要控制酒量……

結賬時不多不少近1000新幣，幾位醫生想塞錢給我都被我回絕了，包括汪致遠。

"這樣吧！明天輪到我休假，載你們出外逛逛，算是抵餐費。"

汪醫生一說完，其他四位都把錢給了"司機"，要他好好招待我們。

"太好了，有輛車到哪兒都方便。"母親喜滋滋地答。

我問汪致遠哪兒來的車？他答Avis網上就能租到，一天約一百新幣。

"那好，明天早點兒來，我們一起吃早餐。"我說。

過去幾天我值大夜班，加上老公每天在家吃晚飯，而我上班回來還得補眠，一天的時間被切割得亂七八糟，等於父母被迫宅在家裏，所以當汪致遠說要載我們出去玩時，我的心裏是歡喜的，不光爲了父母，也爲了趕走家裏的陰霾。

早上八點，汪醫生來敲門，母親笑盈盈地迎他進門。

"今天天氣好，是踏青的好日子。"母親說。

"是的，就怕待會兒太陽太大，還好植物園裏有很多樹，應該不致於太熱。"他答。

去植物園是父母昨晚做的決定，一來就在市區，一天可來回；二來散散步，順便活動筋骨；三來植物園免門票，再好不過。

我們四人邊吃著父親做的"崔氏蔥油餅"邊話家常，兜兜轉轉後，母親問汪醫生："你父母是做什麼的？家裏有兄弟姐妹嗎？"

知道她又要調查戶口，我趕緊說國外不時興問這個，没想到汪致遠主動交待自己的身世，還說平常喜歡攝影，待會兒幫我們拍照，他連專業照相機都帶來了。

"這個好，今年我们還没拍過全家福呢！"父親說。

新加坡植物園開放於1859年，這個位於鬧區旁邊的綠色寶

地滙集了超過兩萬種亞熱帶和熱帶的珍奇花卉與原始樹林，整個園區規劃得很好，環境優美、空氣清新，到處都是適合拍照的點。汪致遠拿起他的專業單反相機，咔嚓咔嚓地幫我們拍了好幾張。

"口渴了吧？！我去小賣部買幾瓶冷飲。"汪致遠把相機交給我後，轉身就走。

"多好的小伙子呀！如果當初看上的是他，妳也不用受苦了。"母親感嘆。

我答"當初"汪醫生還在中國的某個城市，何況他已經有喜歡的人了……

沒多久，汪致遠捧著汽水及冰棒過來，有我愛吃的榴蓮味。

"汪醫生，這邊坐，"母親挪了挪身子，空出個位置來，"這裏涼快些。"

我抗議自己和父親坐在凹凸不平的大石頭上，汪致遠卻能坐在平坦的花台上……

"吃人的嘴軟嘛！"母親轉向汪醫生，"你喜歡的女生是哪裏人？大過年怎麼沒約著見面？"

又來了，我要母親別再問私人問題（雖然自己也挺想知道答案）。

"她……住新加坡，今天……跟父母外出了。"

汪致遠真的有女朋友,還是新加坡人?這真是條大新聞，平常看他很忙，也不知是什麼時候認識的？

"我家小媛要有那個命就好了……"

"媽～"我喊了起來，"說什麼呀！讓人看笑話了。"

父親趕緊接口："老太婆，去前面的胡姬花園看看吧！妳不是挺喜歡花的？"

就在我們父女的通力合作下，總算成功轉移了尷尬話題。

第三十章／溫水煮青蛙

逛完植物園，父母說想看看海洋館。

新加坡的海洋館在聖淘沙島上，是世界上最大的海洋館，擁有 10 萬多個海洋動物，遊客們可一窺令人歎爲觀止的海底世界。

"妳的父母很有童心啊！"汪致遠說。

"的確，人家說'老小孩'，老人就像孩子，要哄著、疼著。"

"那麼待會兒上'海之味餐廳'，他們肯定喜歡。"

"海之味餐廳"設在海洋館內，算是整個新加坡最浪漫的地方，其神秘而憂鬱的藍色色調籠罩著整個餐廳，牆上有大片的玻璃窗，讓成群的海洋生物緩緩而過，說是置身海洋世界也不爲過。

果然父母對此大爲驚豔，嘴巴張得老大，大概不相信世界上竟然還有這麼夢幻的地方。

坐下後，汪致遠點了香煎魴魚、熏烤土豆泥，芹菜心、魚子醬、杏仁碎番茄凍、煎北極鮭、檸檬粗麥飯、仙人掌冰生蠔，燜牛肋佐松露醬、香煎鴨腿、炸麵包蟹等等。

父母一直說好了、好了、夠了、夠了、吃不完、別再點了……但做東的汪醫生卻不手軟，點了一道又一道，等呈上來時又是一番驚喜，因爲不僅擺盤漂亮，東西還好吃，配合周邊的美麗環境，這個新年晚餐實在太豐盛了，然而"一分錢一分貨"，結賬時我發現這一餐竟然比"鴻福軒"的十人年夜飯還貴。

"不行，不能讓你付。"我掏出老公的大華銀行卡，但被汪致遠推開。

"差也就幾十新幣，我不付，回去怎麼跟其他弟兄交待？"他說。

聽至此，我釋然了。

的確，其他MO給了他錢，總不能讓他背負私吞的惡名吧？！

回家路上，汪醫生問我何時上班？我答明天午夜。

"我休到後天，要不，我們上烏敏島玩玩？一天可來回，不會耽誤妳上班。"

我本來想回絕，但一想到過幾天父母就回國了，眼下我又即將上班，總得趁假期帶他們四處轉轉，好留下點兒回憶，況且"欠"汪醫生的錢也能在遊玩中以買這買那的名義歸還，否則如何兩清？

"好，明天見。"我答。

～

半夜起床找水喝，聽到客房裏傳來父母的對話聲。

. . . .

"這個汪醫生人挺好的，要多個女兒就好了。"母親説。

"多個女兒又怎樣？人家已經有女朋友了。"

"我看不是那麼回事，要真有，大過年不約著出去？我猜暗戀的成份居多。"

"暗戀就暗戀唄！老太婆管的事還真多。"

"這你就不懂了，暗戀表示還沒成，小伙子還單著，哎！若配咱家媛媛多好，鄭之龍這個王八蛋，根本就是隻癩蛤蟆。"

"妳少説兩句，小媛還是有夫之婦，這傳出去多難聽，省省吧！兒孫自有兒孫福。"

……

知道父母還在操心我的婚姻，我很內疚，結了婚也没讓他們省心，真是不孝！

～

早聽説烏敏島是新加坡最後的村落，一直有心前往一探究竟，可惜總被這事、那事牽絆而未能成行，經汪致遠這麼一提議，我終於有機會一睹廬山真面目。

開車到樟宜村時剛過八點，由於時間尚早，開門的店鋪不多，我們隨便找了家咖啡店點椰漿飯當早餐，味道還不錯。

吃完飯走到樟宜角碼頭乘船，是那種很古老的小船，在搖搖晃晃中，我們順利抵達對岸。

一上烏敏島，立馬讓人忘記城市的喧囂，很難相信新加坡還有這麼"鄉下"的地方，在這裏就該行走或騎自行車。考慮到要"環島"，我們租了自行車上路，天氣很好，陽光普照，沿路不僅看到山豬以及奇奇怪怪的植物，還經過一個穆斯林墳墓及眺望台。

就這麼騎騎停停，拍了多張照片後才往回走。下山時，風從耳邊吹過的感覺太舒爽，讓人從內到外都洗滌了一遍。

回到車上，我們繼續話家常，由於氣氛融洽，當汪致遠提到想念家鄉的紅燒肉時，母親立馬表示家裏有帶皮五花肉，現在才下午三點多，時間上來得及做晚飯，也不會耽誤我上大夜班……

"媽，也許汪醫生還有約會。"我趕緊阻止。

"没有，我没有約會，很想嚐嚐崔媽媽的手藝。"他答。

哎！話都説到這個份上，我只能任車子往Nassim Road駛去。

一回到家，母親馬上進廚房，父親則喊累，説要上樓躺躺，吃飯時再叫他。

諾大的客廳因此只剩我和汪致遠兩人，我爲他泡了杯熱茶。

"鄭醫生……不在？"他問。

"嗯！他……去巴厘島……參觀製藥廠……後天回來。"

"巴厘島……製藥廠……"他喃喃道。

我知道這回答很難令人信服，但恰恰是鄭之龍給的。

"你的臨床輪轉如何？"我轉移話題。

"不錯，眼科部的主治醫生都很nice, 有問必答，教會我不少東西……謝謝妳。"

我問他何以言謝？這事與我無關。

"與妳無關也謝妳，很少有人會爲我犧牲這麼多。"

汪致遠的回答讓人一頭霧水，他到底知道了什麼？

"你在這裏人生地不熟的，我們又同為中國人，別說犧牲，太言重了，算是抱團取暖吧！"

誰知汪致遠放下茶水，直言："媛媛，妳應該離開鄭醫生，他是泥沼，遲早會讓妳滅頂。"

聽他喚我"媛媛"而非"Miss Cui"，代表我們之間的情誼更進一步，讓我深受感動。

"我知道，這需要時間，老公又是脾氣暴躁的人，我若想走，怕有一番折騰。"

在新加坡，離婚對女性採取明顯的傾斜性保護，比如不管妻子是否有收入，離婚後前夫都必須支付贍養費直至前妻再婚或去世為止，而贍養費的支付標準是讓前妻的生活水平不會因離婚而降低。

鄭之龍已經離過一次婚，時不時還抱怨每月得"養"著不相干的人，我若提離婚，他豈不是又要大出血一次？哪有輕易放手的道理？

"妳若真想走總有辦法，譬如提出家暴證明。新加坡對家暴採零容忍，妳很容易能從不愉快的婚姻關係中解脫。"

我答非不得已不想走那一步，畢竟"面子"對我而言很重要，況且鄭之龍"正常"的時候對我還是不錯的，我不想將事情做得太絕……

"哎～家暴就是一步步踩著對方的底線而來，好比溫水煮青蛙，當事人往往不明白自己正在受苦，反而找各種藉口替對方開脫，我不想看到母親的悲劇再次重演，妳……好好想想。"

"會的，我會深思熟慮，謝謝你的提醒。"我答。

第三十一章／手舞足蹈

汪致遠說錯了，我不是不知道老公正一步步踩著我的底線將我逼至絕境，也明白自己正受苦著，之所以忍耐是因爲還未部署好，等時機成熟後必來個回馬槍，讓欺負我的人跪在地上求饒。

鄭之龍是在大年初四的晚上十點多進的門，那時我正收拾東西準備出門上大夜班。

"人哪？我剛談了筆大生意，回來連個拖鞋也沒有。"他立在門口咆哮。

老公的拖鞋一向擱在入口處，大概這幾天人不在，母親拖地時把鞋收進鞋櫃裏了。

"應該在鞋櫃內，你彎腰取就是。"我答。

"我偏不，妳幫我拿。"

"我趕上班呢!"

我走過去趿上平底鞋，一轉身被老公抓住，然後火速吃了他一個耳括子：" 翅膀硬了？把老公的話當放屁！"

爲了不驚動在樓上休息的父母，我委屈自己給他取拖鞋。鄭之龍趿上後還踹了我一腳，罵我動作太慢。

我忍住淚水對他説：" 我父母明天回國，能不能別吵？給他們留點兒好印象。"

" 這得看妳的表現，不是我説，妳最近像吃了熊心豹子膽，和我作對的次數越來越多。我警告妳，再這麽任性下去，妳有苦頭吃了。"説完，他逕自走向客廳。

我在原地沈默一會兒後，默默開門走向黑夜。

" 媛媛學姐，妳説愛人幸福還是被愛幸福？"問話的是清湯掛麵的護理員，幾次見面後，我知道她叫黃鶯，剛滿二十歲。

雖然出門前吃了老公一巴掌，心情很不好，但我還是回答了。

" 怎麽會無解？妳和學姐夫是公認的神仙眷侶，最有資格回答這個問題了。"她説。

我想了想，小女生對愛情很懵懂，有這類疑問很正常，遂告訴她有人覺得愛人幸福，另有人覺得被愛幸福，答案因人而異，能彼此相愛最好。

" 没錯，就像學姐和學姐夫一樣。"她笑嘻嘻地答。

噢！不，我對他從來沒有愛的感覺，若有，那也是不了解所帶來的假像，至於他愛不愛我……如果"打是情，罵是愛"，那麽他肯定很愛很愛我。

早上七點，還不到交接班，我卻看到寶兒的身影。

"家裏没吃的，特意來食堂吃早餐，一大早就吃湯包，滿嘴油膩膩的。"她解釋。

我啪啪啪地打著鍵盤，寶兒也没歇著，把最近發生的大小事都巨細靡遺地給交待了，包括汪致遠被調到眼科部一事。

"妳說怪不怪？五官科的新醫生還未報到就放人，害兩位主治醫生一天看一百多個號，連上廁所或喝口水都没時間，遑論吃飯，看Dr.Robinson和Dr.Thompson瘦得......"

我笑她太杞人憂天了，何況Dr.Robinson和Dr.Thompson一點兒也不瘦，兩人加起來近四百斤。

"哎呀！我是說跟以前比，倒是汪致遠這兩天有點兒發福，也許春節吃多了。"

"有種肥叫幸福肥，所謂'心寬體胖'嘛！"

寶兒説她不這麼想，一胖毀所有，如果汪醫生和她走到了一起，她會嚴格控制他的體重，讓男神的地位永遠屹立不搖。

"太遲了......"

話一説出口我就後悔，寶兒纏著我問爲什麼，儘管我答不清楚，別問了，她依舊像咬住獵物的狼，絲毫不放棄。

"好吧！告訴妳，汪醫生有喜歡的人了，還是新加坡人，妳......"

"不可能！"寶兒搶話，"這幾天我上早班，下班後都和汪醫生一起唸書，他很nice，一直輔導我的功課，若有喜歡的人，怎麼可能好幾天不約著出去玩？"

有那麼幾秒鐘，我懷疑汪醫生喜歡的人是寶兒，但再一想，寶兒不是新加坡人，她的父母也一直待在中國，與汪致遠描述的有出入。

"Well, 這是他親口説的，妳若有疑問可以向當事人求證。"

“親口？你們約了見面？”

我遂把這兩天發生的事坦白相告。

“哎！大過年若不用上班，我也能跟你們一起出去玩。”她很懊惱，好像已經從汪致遠的“女朋友疑雲”中抽身而出。

在機場免不了又是離情依依的場面，不同的是父母不再說些“吃飽穿暖，有空回國”之類的溫馨話，而是一昧地要我對丈夫順從，忍耐才能守得雲開見月明，等老公老了，他會知道髮妻的重要性……

“是呀！等他齒搖髮落沒力氣打我時，我的幸運日就來到……如果在那之前我沒被打死的話。”我心想。

“小媛，”母親拉著我的手，“要個孩子吧！有了孩子，男人的心就定下來，不會被外面的花花草草所迷惑。”

我無力地答知道了，然後催促父母進關。看他們離去後，我身體內的某些東西也被帶走，人好像成了空殼，恍恍惚惚的。

“鄭夫人……鄭夫人……鄭夫人……”

我一直走到機場六號口，那個“鄭夫人”的呼喚聲還不絕於耳，我心想這個鄭夫人還真耳背，不料右側肩膀被人點了一下，我轉過頭去，是個西裝筆挺的中年男士，很面生。

“請問是鄭夫人嗎？”他問。

我想了一下，回答自己的老公姓鄭，但我不認識他，他認錯人了。

“我也不清楚自己是否認錯人，但我的老闆讓我過來喊妳。”

我順著那人的目光望過去，看到一位身穿高爾夫休閒服的老人，他向我招了招手，原來是方淮安。

"是……是的，我是鄭夫人。"我承認。

"那麼一起過去吧！老闆的車停在地下二層。"他答。

方淮安的車子是1959年的凱迪拉克古董車，尾翼是經典的火箭造型，車身的顏色爲蘋果綠，還有個白色的頂篷，開在路上肯定拉風。

"這車是老闆從一年一度的蒙特雷汽車週中競價得來，花了1400萬美元。"方淮安的司機報料。

我倒吸一口氣，這價錢大概能買下一座小島。

"呵呵！把我賣了也賣不到1400萬美元。"我笑説。

方淮安倒沒在這個話題上打轉，他問候我的老公，我答鄭之龍已經離開REQ，開了一家私人診所……

"真可惜，他若在，下禮拜的體檢就能請他幫我檢查，最近老鼻塞加耳鳴，不知身體出了什麼問題？"

"放心，體檢部的醫生都是一時之選，尤其您是VIP客人，服務絕對是一等一。"

"哎！我喜歡的護士不在那裏，再好的服務也不過爾爾。"他嘆了一口氣答。

我想起"大番薯"説過的話，去年體檢部護士Miss Zhou在服侍完方淮安之後便離開REQ成爲他的私人看護，薪水不知翻了多少倍，儼然現實版的"麻雀變鳳凰"。現在方老闆説他喜歡的護士不在體檢部，難道指的是Miss Zhou？不對呀！他天天能見上面，何來遺憾？

當我"胡思亂想"之際，方淮安彷彿有心電感應，主動告訴我周護士離開新加坡到美國讀書去了，進修的費用還是他出的。

原來如此，看來替方老闆工作油水很多，不僅能把座駕從Honda換成路虎，還能遠渡重洋到彼岸鍍金，任誰都知道，留學的費用不會是筆小數目。

"體檢部是個美差，工作輕鬆還不用倒三班，我也想調到那裏去。"我有感而發。

"妳真的想到體檢部工作？"他問。

"是的，做夢都想。"

"小事一樁，我讓妳美夢成真。"他豪氣地答。

車子停在小區門口後，我和方淮安互留電話號碼，然後目視凱迪拉克呼嘯而去。

沒等桌上的熱茶冷卻，手機就傳來短信："對我而言，妳比凱迪拉克古董車還珍貴，哪裏能競拍？告訴我。"

看完短信，我喝了口茶水，意外發現茶味竟如此甘甜，以前怎麼沒發覺？

老公坐下來吃回國後的第一頓晚餐。

"Lucy懷孕了。"他邊吃邊說。

我愣了好幾秒後，問："是那個風騷女人Lucy嗎？"

"藥商代表就藥商代表，幹嘛給人家亂扣帽子？"

我吞了一口口水，艱難地問孩子該不會是他的吧？

鄭之龍兜了好大一圈，不外Lucy愛玩，不會是個好母親，但能怎麼辦？他已經四十多歲了，老婆又是隻不會下蛋的母雞……

剛結婚那會兒，我也期待有安琪兒降臨，所以完全不做防範措施，偏偏在頻繁的房事後肚皮依然無聲無息，鄭之龍遂將矛頭指向我，認爲是我偷偷服用避孕藥的結果。我把父母的生命拿來發毒誓，加上他翻箱倒櫃也找不到物證才勉強相信，然而下場是從此他便名正言順地指責我是隻不會下蛋的母雞，讓我百口莫辯。

"別做夢了，我寧願離婚也不幫別人養小孩，省省吧你。"我推開桌子離席。

一整晚我都在怪自己厄運當頭、所遇非人，就在自怨自艾中，我突然靈光乍現："崔媛媛呀崔媛媛，妳犯傻了？這是老公出軌的最佳證明，咬住這個迫他離婚，很快妳就能重獲自由身。"

想到此，我像中了頭彩似地手舞足蹈起來。

第三十二章/回到原點

上完大夜班回家，看見冰箱貼下有張老公留的紙條，他要我將藍色西裝褲拿去乾洗，又説最近很容易疲倦，叮嚀我買隻老母雞燉湯喝，末了，問我有沒有看到他的大華銀行卡？

看到"大華銀行卡"五個字，我的心喀噔了一下，怎麼把這事給忘了？

我把穀物倒入大碗裏，加了牛奶後，邊吃邊想：" 衣服送洗、燉雞湯、銀行卡......衣服送洗......巴厘島......Lucy......懷孕......"

老天！鄭之龍和小三旅遊完後回家，還理直氣壯地要求我燉湯及送洗遊玩時穿的長褲，而我還愣愣地發愁該如何解釋吃年夜飯花去的968新幣，簡直蠢得可以！

我把5新幣一大盒的Kellogg's推開，拿上老公的大華銀行卡出門血拼去。

~

濱海灣的金沙購物廣場面積很大，共有10層高，採用了全

183

玻璃的透明內飾，讓消費者能沐浴在陽光下購物。與其他購物廣場不同的是，它的地下一層有一條室內小運河，很像澳門的威尼斯人度假村酒店，兩岸同樣有奢侈品商店和餐館。

我買了LV的Cluncy手袋及Prada的殺手包，轉身看到某牌護膚品正在做促銷，什麼神仙水、大紅瓶、小紅瓶……等，我一出手就是兩盒套裝，只因銷售說買兩盒送一盒，結賬時才發現送的是一盒面膜。

大概我的臉色不太好看，銷售把我拉到一旁說悄悄話，告訴我來自迪拜的某家水療中心正在試營業，我的消費超過1000新幣，能獲得一張免費的面部護理券，然後很熱心地帶我前往，還好不遠，拐個彎就到。

接待我的人果然長著一副中東臉孔，能說怪腔怪調的英語，尚且達意。說好的給我做免費的保濕護理，話鋒一轉，提到她家新推出一款黃金面膜，還科普黃金自古以來便是美容聖品，其產生的微電流與人體電流基本相同，通過負離子作用能促進血液循環及刺激細胞生長，達到新陳代謝的效果……

我問多少錢？她答和美麗的容顏一比不算什麼，何況現在是試營業，所有療程半價。

想到今天就是來花錢解氣的，有什麼不可以？於是躺下，享受土豪才配享有的待遇。

付完4158新幣的黃金面膜療程後，我已經不再畏懼花錢，把魚子醬當零食吃還買了好幾件專櫃的當季衣服及鞋，甚至還買了一頂觀馬賽用的紫色幽蘭花禮帽，天知道我連賽馬場在哪兒都不清楚。

花錢解氣後，很快閒得發慌，是時候和小三談判，我約她在小運河邊的咖啡廳喝咖啡。

"没空，正上班呢！"她說。

"都六點了，上個鳥班？別怕，我不打孕婦。"

"妳……都知道了？"

我答非但知道，自己還被欽定當她孩子的養母，爲了這個任重道遠的安排，再怎麼著也得見見面討論討論……

剛掛上手機就接到老公的來電，他問我今晚的晚餐在哪裏？

"冰凍層有電視餐，放到微波爐裏加熱即可，再不然，下個餃子總會吧？"

"崔媛媛，妳一天到晚在家都做了什麼？連個晚餐也煮不出來？"

我要他別生氣，不過是一餐，大不了出去吃……噢！不，不能出去吃，待會兒有人送貨上門，他得幫我簽收。

"送什麼貨？"

我答我拿了他給的"精神損失費"買了幾樣小東西，順便預告待會兒請他的情婦吃飯，鮑魚及魚翅烏骨湯的花費不低，估計沒有一千也得八百……

"妳哪來的錢？"他問。

"你的大華銀行卡呀！傻子。"我哈哈大笑後掛上手機，同時爲了防止老公再打來，立馬關機。

請小三吃鮑魚、喝魚翅烏骨湯？我腦子進水了？門兒都沒有。

Lucy一坐下，我馬上替她點了最便宜的美式咖啡。

"我不喝美式。"她答。

"不喝也成，沒人規定談判一定得喝東西。"

"談什麼？"她將臉撇向一旁，"有什麼好談的？"

我看情勢不對，自己有所求，得來軟的，遂收起防衛的劍。

“妳肚裏的寶寶多大了？”我問。

“不知道，反正要打掉。”

想到這是鄭之龍盼星星盼月亮得來的骨肉，哪能說不要就不要？

“這事還得問孩子的爹。”我說。

“切，我都不清楚孩子的爹是哪位，問誰去？”

“妳什麼意思？”

Lucy在下一秒給出答案，原來她真的和老公上巴厘島遊玩（果然如同猜測），鄭之龍提議玩“水上飛魚”，Lucy以“兩個月沒來例假，可能懷孕”爲藉口，拒絕玩高危的水上活動，没想到鄭之龍自己對號入座，她倒没否認，畢竟孩子也有可能是他的……

這下子我懵了，原以爲是板上釘釘的事，現在卻是一團迷霧。

見我沈默，Lucy開口安慰：“孩子應該不是妳老公的，時間往前推算，另一位醫生更可疑，反正我不準備生下來，所以生父是誰不重要。”

“不，一定得是鄭之龍的，”我幾乎是怒火攻心，“拜托，別打掉孩子，妳早晚要生，倒不如趁年輕時生，身體恢復也快。”

Lucy像看怪物一樣地看我。

我深吸一口氣後，把已在腦海裏回鍋多次的計劃告知：**我無條件同意離婚，不要贍養費，她可以和鄭醫生組成幸福的三口之家……**

“我不明白妳這唱的是哪一齣？如果是行苦肉計大可不必，我和未婚夫就要結婚了，連酒席都訂好了。”

" 妳 …… 妳 跟 鄭 之 龍 不 是 來 真 的 ？ " 我 嚇 得 下 巴 幾 乎 要 掉 下 來 。

Lucy笑得花枝亂顫，她説這不過是婚前的浪蕩，根本没想過要跟張三或李四有任何結果，何況她的未婚夫要容貌有容貌，要學歷有學歷，要工作有工作，她已經打算金盆洗手，從此過上正常的家庭主婦生活……

怎麼會這樣？與我預想的完全不一樣。

"怎麼？鬆了一口氣吧？"她端起咖啡喝上一口，" 小三能做到我這樣不容易，一不要名分，二不要分手費，三連孩子都自己處理掉，妳呀！該知足了。"

哎！我寧願她要名分、要錢、要孩子，現在她什麼都不要才令人頭疼，害我又重新回到原點。

一進家門，我差點兒被堆在門口的大小紙袋絆倒。

"送貨員很盡責，交給我各個店鋪的明細，我按了計算器，一共是25188新幣，妳夠可以的了，厲害厲害！"

老公這個點還在家，有點兒出乎我的意料，不過我打算讓他更"如鯁在喉"。

" 我還做了黃金面膜療程及吃了點兒精緻料理，總共不到五千新幣，具體多少不清楚，你到網上銀行查得了。"

鄭之龍聽完氣得臉紅脖子粗，我隨時等候他出拳，没想到他只是要回他的銀行卡並且警告我没有下一次。

" 這不像你。"我皺起眉頭問。

" 要接受老公在外撒種的事實不容易，錢的事我不跟妳計較，但僅此一次，下不爲例。"他輕撫我的肩頭，" 放心，妳的原配地位不變，Lucy終究會成爲過往雲煙。"

～

好運没持續兩天，當我上完大夜班回家，剛一關上門，一個玻璃杯便迎面飛來，還好我反應快，讓杯子砸在身後的大門上，往下跌個粉碎。

"你……怎麼……了？"我嚇傻了。

"哼！我怎麼了？虧妳還問得出來，説！Lucy爲什麼打胎？妳到底對她説了什麼？"鄭之龍怒髮衝冠。

我反問他何不親自去問他的老相好？

"她把我拉黑了，電話不接、短信不回，只給了一紙聲明説孩子打掉了，還説要和別人結婚，從此不再與我有任何瓜葛。"

"這不挺好的？"

話一説完，第二個玻璃杯又擲向我，只是這次没那麼好運，杯子正中我的額頭，當場起了個大包。

"没想到妳是這樣狠毒的女人，巴不得我鄭家絕後，也成，除非妳能生出個一兒半女，否則就別想走出這個大門！"

第三十三章／脫離苦海

說來真可笑，因爲小三，我被老公強奸了，直到他再也舉不起來，才施恩般地放開我，而我渾身的骨頭早已散了架。

被施暴後，我以爲自己會一夜無眠，沒想到依然走入夢鄉。迷迷糊糊中，我聽到忽遠忽近的鈴聲，拿起手機接聽，是母親，她要我多保重身體，不要和老公硬來，以柔克剛才是正道……

掛上手機，我依然能聽到鈴聲，猛一張開眼，才發現剛剛是夢境，母親並沒有來電話。

"Hello."我含糊不清地説。

"Miss Cui, 還睡？太陽都下山了。"是早班護士長的聲音。

我問是不是明天排早班的事糊了？噢！不，我太討厭當夜行動物了，熬夜很傷身，我的臉上已經開始長痘痘，黑眼圈也很嚴重……

"別往壞裏想，剛剛人事告訴我，妳被調到體檢部，今晚不用上大夜班，明天直接到體檢大樓報到。"

"真……真的？"太過驚喜，讓我一度懷疑自己依舊在夢中。

"當然是真的，説也奇怪，體檢部不缺人，反倒我們住院部人手奇缺，妳一走，代表體檢部有個護士會過來，我想她恐怕不會太高興，搞不好背後問候妳祖宗八代……"

我呵呵一笑，説："還不致於這麼小氣吧？！"

掛上電話，我的心中冒起無數個幸福的小泡泡。

中國有句話"否極泰來"，西方也有句話"上帝關上門後，一定會另開一扇窗"，看來一點兒也不假，我的好日子就要來到！

～

洗了個戰鬥澡，讓全身充滿正能量，正想下樓，才發現門打不開。不會吧？！難道鄭之龍説的不是氣話，非要我生出個一兒半女，否則別想走出大門？

"喂！門打不開，你讓我怎麼煮飯？"我一通電話打給老公。

"呵呵！急了吧？！晚餐我上The White Rabbit 吃牛排，放妳假，不用煮了。"

我又喂了兩聲，才發現鄭之龍掛電話了。

這是處罰，肯定的，罰我殺了他的孩子及趕走他的情婦。天知道我根本什麼都沒做，這完全是Lucy的個人決定及作爲。

我焦急地在房內來回踱步，像隻無頭蒼蠅似的，就在束手無策之際，"媛媛學姐"的呼喚聲忽然響起。

對了，現在能救我的只有她。

寶兒值早班，此時應該快下班，我立馬打電話給她，邀她來家裏吃飯。

"好呀好呀！最近没一塊兒值班，挺想學姐的，不過我還得在醫院多待兩小時，沒辦法，有護理員生病了，大家得分擔工作。"

我答沒關係，我家吃得晚，又讓她打個電話給我老公，要他買瓶酒回家，因爲家裏沒酒了⋯⋯

"爲什麼妳不親自打？"

"因⋯⋯因爲⋯⋯哎呀！就是那麼回事，我們夫妻鬧矛盾，正冷戰著，妳是大家的開心果，有妳在，我們的感情才容易修復。"

寶兒一聽，很義氣地表示學姐的事就是她的事，放心，有她當和事佬，包管今晚我和老公人和解，很快又能甜甜蜜蜜地共浴愛河⋯⋯

掛上電話不到二十分鐘，鄭之龍就飛車回家，不僅打開上鎖的房門，還催促我洗手做羹湯，因爲貴客就要來家裏吃飯。

"還是三個菜？"我問。

老公想了想説多添兩個吧！來者是客，不能怠慢。

我在廚房裏洗洗切切，沒留意鄭之龍上哪兒了，待我放好碗筷才發現他已洗完澡，身上還噴了刺鼻的古龍水。

"嘖嘖嘖！這是怎麼回事？搞得像吃相親飯似的。"我挖苦他。

"書上説一個人對另一人的觀感在見面的13秒內就已決定，我得讓人留下好印象才成。"他邊打領帶邊説。

我第一次見有人在家裏吃飯還打領帶，説白了就是色心不改，今晚若是個男的過來用餐，他能穿條正式長褲就算不錯了。

寶兒抵達時已近八點，她不停地道歉，抱怨病人臨時出狀況。

"没事，快坐下，肚子餓了吧？"老公表現得很體貼，只差没替客人夾菜。

席間，寶兒果然不負所托，拼命拉攏我和鄭之龍，説我們是人人稱羨的神仙眷侶，她若有我的運氣，能遇上這麼好的老公，半夜也會笑醒……

"我真的有那麼好？"老公被捧得飄飄然。

"當然，人既聰明又多金，對學姐還溫柔，簡直好得不能再好。"寶兒繼續灌迷湯。

"是，没錯，"他點頭，"媛媛能嫁我是前世修來的福氣，可惜她不知足，不懂得感恩。"

我趕緊表示自己懂得投桃報李，只是工作忙又得倒三班，難免顧此失彼，還好今天得了個好消息，明天正式到體檢部報到，不用再輪三班，可以更好地照顧他……

寶兒聽了尖叫一聲，她説體檢部不僅工作輕鬆，還能認識名人及富豪，再好不過，她也想到體檢部工作云云。

"妳真的調到體檢部了？"老公仍有懷疑。

我告訴他是真的，衆所周知，REQ的體檢部是人脈中心，多少大鱷都在那裏體檢過，我若能認識其中一、兩位，對他的事業有利無害。

老公聽完不再説話，專心吃起桌上的雪菜毛豆。我知道他已入甕。

"媛媛學姐，哪天妳若飛黃騰達，可別忘了提攜一下妳的小學妹喔！"寶兒説。

"那當然。"我笑著回答。

也許在別家醫院，體檢部只能算雞肋，但在REQ不僅不是雞肋，還是隻會下金蛋的母雞，此話從何説起？

新加坡是繼紐約、倫敦、香港之後的第四大國際金融中心，也就是説在這個彈丸之地居住著很多富豪，他們想得到好的醫療服務完全可以理解，這也是REQ高級體檢部應運而生的原因，至於後來"醉翁之意不在酒"，吸引到全球有錢、有名望的人士前往則是附加利益，誰不想在體檢的同時也認識某個投行經理或公司老總？

由於服務對象的尊貴，REQ體檢部另外獨立出去，不僅在醫院主體建築物之外另建一座小樓，裏面也豪華到媲美五星級酒店。醫生、護士當然都是一時之選，也不知故意與否，從體檢部開始營業以來，在最前線服務的註冊護士清一色是未婚女子，而且顏質槓槓的，把她們往選美比賽一送，絲毫不遜色。

護士長以"體檢部首位已婚註冊護士"介紹我，引來訕笑。講話一結束，她把我叫到一旁，要我去見體檢部主任。

"爲什麽？"我問。

"大概歡迎妳來到這個大家庭吧！"

"別的護士新報到時也是如此嗎？"

那個已至不惑之年仍風韻猶存的女人想了想後，說："没有，不過我來體檢部不到一年，也許以前有這個慣例。"

謝過護士長後，我往主任辦公室走去。

主任從大辦公桌後起身，示意我坐在小型會客室的沙發上。

" Tea or coffee ？"他問。

我答皆不用。

待主任一坐下，我才發現他不僅長得好看，還有雙大長腿，有點兒像日本演員阿部寬。

難不成體檢部非帥哥美女不用？

"是這樣的，兩天前人事通知我要安插個人進來，因爲我們的VIP客戶點名要妳服務。考慮到這裏的護士都是經過層層篩選出來，爲了不落人口實，我們安排妳暫時在這裏工作，還好該客戶體檢只需三天，三天過後，妳還是重回妳的住院部，這就是我要説的。"

這消息無疑當頭棒喝，原來體檢部壓根兒沒看上我，我不過是做了一場春秋大夢。

"如果……如果在這三天裏我表現良好，有没有……有没有一絲絲的可能性讓我留下來？"我小心地問。

主任沈默許久後開口，語氣雖平靜，但字字句句打在我心上："我最討厭走後門破壞體制的人，妳既然能搭上方淮安，代表妳有手腕，何不模仿去年Miss zhou的模式，服侍完方先生就離開REQ，實在沒必要還留戀我們這座小廟，妳説是嗎？"

話説得讓人難受極了，偏偏我又無法反駁。

離開主任辦公室後，我知道自己已無退路可走，只能死死咬住那位老人，讓他帶我脱離苦海……

第三十四章/體檢第一日

和主任談話完沒多久，連新同事都還沒認全的情況下，護士長喊我喝咖啡。

"妳有沒有注意到新加坡有七成人口是華人，但受歡迎的飲品卻是咖啡而不是茶？"她遞給我一杯咖啡烏後問。

其實我早注意到南洋咖啡的製作方式與歐美咖啡不同，譬如咖啡豆要先炒過且將煉乳及砂糖置於杯底，再將滾燙的咖啡倒入等，也許這就是原因。

護士長說我的確觀察仔細，但還有一個主因，那就是早期移民新加坡的華人多做苦力，喝茶對他們來說是解渴用的，不如殖民文化中的咖啡雅緻。久而久之，若要優雅地喝飲品，首先想到的必是"咖啡"而非"茶"。

"又長見識了，護士長大概是本地華人吧？！"我問。

她答自己是婚後由福建移民至此，後來……後來離了，膝下無兒無女。

"I am sorry."

“没事，都過去了，聽説妳是鄭醫生的太太，久仰久仰。”

“他已經不在REQ上班，自己開了家私人診所。”

護士長問我爲什麼不在老公的私人診所幫忙？我答“距離産生美”，一個挑不出毛病的答案。

我們沈默地用著咖啡，我知道護士長在找一個好的切入點談今天的主題，所以靜靜等待她出招。

“方淮安……方安製藥廠的老闆指名要妳，我們REQ體檢部向來以無微不至的服務著稱，這點兒小事絕對會滿足客戶的要求，考慮到住院部需要像Miss Cui這樣的優秀護士，我們没理由搶人，所以……”

看來主任已把“消息”下傳。

“知道了，方先生一離開，我會重回住院部。”

護士長鬆了口氣，説我果然好溝通，待會兒她會請Miss Mundra 帶我熟悉環境及示範儀器的操作。還有，方先生明天到，今天我得去方家取客戶糞便及痰液，去之前請先約好時間，以免久等。

“爲什麼是今天取？”我問。

護士長答一向如此，只有尿液才取當天的。

“知道了，我會完成任務。”

帶我的MISS MUNDRA 是個好看的印度人，身材前凸後翹，妝化得很濃，身上有化不開的香水味。她很熱心地幫我融入新環境，還問我何時辦迎新？是不是這週末？她要帶她的男朋友過來，一個有六塊腹肌和人魚線的健身教練……

“ Sorry. I don’t think there is a chance for a welcome party.”我説我不認爲有開迎新會的機會。

"Why?"

我答因爲自己已婚，而且不夠漂亮。她呵呵一笑，説我真有趣。

顯然説實話没人相信，我也無可奈何。

和方家通上電話，接電話的人説一切準備好後會通知我去取。我一直等到太陽下山才得到確認的電話，趕緊跳上體檢部的專用座駕往荷蘭路駛去。

這輛奔馳S600是專門用來接送貴賓的，當它停在第十郵區的豪宅前時，我倒吸一口氣，幾乎可以斷定方家絕對不是小富小貴之家。

按下門鈴後，是個穿傭人服的菲律賓人開的門，她交給我一個小盒子，什麼話都没説。我有點兒小失望，以爲會看到方淮安本尊或見識一下他的豪宅，結果兩樣都没實現。

把檢體送回體檢部後，我走出大樓準備回家，時間：下午五點多。

"媛媛，妳怎麼在這裏？"

聽到熟悉的聲音，我轉過身去，是汪致遠。

"我調到這裏……幾天，你呢？怎麼也在這裏？"

"我……"

此時一個有著V型臉的護士從大樓裏跑出來，衝著汪醫生喊客戶正在大發雷霆。

汪致遠對我尷尬一笑，我要他趕緊進去，自己也得回家了。

" 第一天上班有没有認識人？"晚餐桌上老公問。

我答護士、護士長、主任以及幾名醫生全打過照面了。

" 誰問妳這個？我是指有錢、有名望的上等人。"鄭之龍喝了一口用石斑魚做的咖喱魚頭湯後問。

" 我是新人，今天只是熟悉一下環境，還没真正披甲上陣呢！"我答，没把自己只"代班幾天"一事説出。

" 妳得多用點兒心，對了，把我的名片盒帶著，見人就發一張，老公的事業就是老婆的事業，我好妳才有可能好，別忘了。"

我默默吃著飯，把鄭之龍的話當耳邊風。

與REQ的作息時間不同，體檢部是早上九點開始，下午五點結束，下班後除了值勤人員之外，轉由某酒店集團接手。没錯，這是度假式的體檢，就算晚上客戶想看歌劇表演也是小事一椿，分分鐘能拿到票，而且保證是好位置。

我一大早就上體檢部報到，但一直等到十點半才等來方淮安，他穿著Armani的深灰色運動服，人看起來很精神。

" 方先生好，"我迎上前去，" 讓我帶您到客房。"

" 妳好，等很久了吧？！"

我答等了一小會兒，並且伸手去提行李。

" 別，怎能讓女人提行李呢？"他望了身旁的中年男士一眼，" 放心，我的司機會效勞，現在帶我去客房，還是ioio房，對吧？"

" 是的。"我在前面帶路。

ＩＯＩＯ房有個大窗戶，能俯看一大片的綠草如茵和姹紫嫣紅。

"房間塗上新漆了，去年還是淺綠，現在是米色。"方淮安說完，在小客廳裏坐下，沙發是布藝沙發，有家的感覺。

我答不清楚去年的房間顏色，不過感覺米色還不錯，讓人心情舒暢。

"我没説這顏色不好，至少讓我聯想起我們第一次見面時妳身上衣服的顏色。"

我們初次會面是在鄭之龍的頒獎典禮上，我穿著一件Alexander MacQueen 設計的米色露背拖地晚禮服，頭髮高高挽起……

"那時妳一舉手一投足，顧盼生姿，美得不可方物。"他附加一句。

"您過獎了，我只是個普通的已婚婦女，和方太比，差多了。"

方淮安說他太太的確是校花，畢業於南洋女子中學，人也冰雪聰明，可惜那個年代的女子講求三從四德，她因此早早走入家庭，若放在今日，肯定讀出個博士來。

我想起那個胸部乾癟的女人，怎麼看都不像方淮安所形容的知性美人，氣質倒很接地氣，雖然一身的行頭很昂貴……

大概我的表情很詭異，方老闆解釋頒獎典禮上出席的是他的二老婆，大老婆長年吃齋唸佛，早已不過問俗事，現在方家的大小事都是二老婆在張羅，他們是在澳門賭場認識的，當時她是發牌員……

果然如同傳言所説。

"Well,現在是不是該填表格了？"他突然問。

我從臆想的世界回到現實，趕緊取出牛皮紙袋內的表格。

新加坡的體檢和國內不同，事前有不少問診表格需要填寫，包括身體基本狀況、病史、生活習慣、職業病風險等，甚至詳細到家族病史、近期服藥情況、平時抽不抽煙、一週大致飲酒量……等,也得逐一回答。

鑒於客戶的要求，我幫著填寫，最後再由方先生確認簽字。

"其實這是多此一舉，去年和今年沒什麼不同，把去年的表格拿來用即可。"

"怎麼會不同？去年您69歲，今年……"我住口了，真是的，哪壺不開提哪壺！

方淮安倒不以爲忤，他說自己的年齡的確大了點兒，但內心還住著一個小男人，看到年輕的美女依舊會動心……

"咳、咳……表格填完了，我交回去，您先休息片刻，待會兒就做檢查。"我站起身來。

"好、好、快去快回，我來體檢就是爲了看美女，可別讓我等太久。"他說。

第三十五章／寬衣解帶

我帶方淮安到更衣室更衣，那是一套兩件式的條紋病號服，上衣沒有鈕扣，而是在右腋下方打結，長褲則類似睡褲，鬆鬆垮垮的。

除了眼鏡外，任何首飾、手錶都不准配戴，於是我將取下的勞力士金錶及藍寶石男戒放進牛皮紙袋內封好，再請方先生確認簽字。

"東西會放在哪裏？"他問。

"我們醫院有保險櫃，也買了遺失險，放心，肯定不會給客戶帶來損失。"

他說他倒不在意勞力士，但那枚男戒對他的意義重大，可千萬別丟了。

就因爲這番話，將牛皮紙袋上繳後，我親眼見它被鎖進保險櫃內才離去。

～

Dr.Wood與方淮安當面核實問診表的內容後離開，我接著替客戶做基本的身體狀況測量，包括身高、體重、腰圍、血脂、血壓等。

"好了，接下來做超聲波檢查 。"我說。

超聲波檢查有四個項目，包括腹部、心臟、頸動脈及肝硬度，每個臟器的檢查都需要十幾分鐘以上的時間，醫生會反復要求被測者吸氣、呼氣、屏住呼吸、放鬆……然後拍攝很多組照片以供觀察。

做完超聲波檢查已近中午，我請方先生移駕到餐廳。供客戶用餐的餐廳在五層，窗外的景色非常迷人，天氣好的時候還能看到植物園內的天鵝湖。

"午餐有西式和中式兩種選擇，您要哪一種？"我問。

方淮安反問我會做何選擇？我答"中式"，因爲經過廚房時，我已聞到紅燒肉的味道，食慾一下子被勾起，油汪汪的五花肉，我愛吃極了。

"那麼要兩份中式，妳陪我吃。"

"不了，員工有員工餐廳，在地下一層，待會兒我到那裏用餐即可。"

"把護士長叫過來，我要投訴。"他忽然說。

什麼？第一天正式上陣就被投訴，真不知自己做錯了什麼？看方先生一臉正經，我只好灰頭土臉地把護士長請來，心裏很忐忑。

"我想請這位美麗的護士用餐，多出的費用加在我的賬單上，可以嗎？"方先生很有禮地詢問。

"這得問Miss Cui的意願，我們不勉強護士做不願做的事。"護士長不卑不亢地答。

話一說完，他們兩人的目光同時打在我身上。

和老男人吃飯讓人如坐針氈，本想一口回絕，但再一想，我只有三天的時間可以拉攏方淮安，不趁此時更待何時？

"那麼……恭敬不如從命了。"我答。

菜一道一道地上，除了紅燒肉，還有水煮牛肉、荷香雞、蟹黃豆腐及炒時蔬，加上冒著熱氣的台灣凍頂烏龍茶，很能撫慰饑餓的腸胃。

方淮安撿了一塊肥瘦相間的紅燒肉到我碗裏，道謝後，我將之囫圇吞下肚，嗯～真是美味極了。

"看來妳很喜歡吃紅燒肉。"他説。

"嗯！我無肉不歡，除了紅燒肉還喜歡吃蟹，我是吃蟹高手呢！"

方先生説那麼我應該到日本嚐鮮，那裏的帝王蟹、毛蟹和松葉蟹才叫個"極品"。

"我哪有這個福氣？老公一天到晚忙工作，即使有空也是帶小三去，豈有糟糠之妻的份？"

"家有貌美的妻子還到外面找小三，真是罪過、罪過。"

我舀了一匙豆腐到方淮安的碗裏，然後有意無意地説還是成熟男人識貨，懂得我的價值……

方淮安呵呵一笑，沒有接話。

我離座，想把牙縫裏的雞肉摳出來，沒想到在洗手間外聽到裏面兩位同事的對話。

. . .

"那個新來的噁心死了，我帶客戶到餐廳用餐，不過多待了幾分鐘，雞皮疙瘩因此掉了一地。"

"怎麼回事？説來聽聽！"

"就那麼回事，公然和客人打情罵俏，也不看看自己的身份，估計鄭醫生要丟臉死了。"

"呵呵！鄭醫生也不是什麼好鳥，雖然專業領域很令人欽佩，但私生活……嘖嘖嘖……"

……

在聽到更多蜚短流長前，我果斷離開。

～

回到餐廳，有兩個客人正和方淮安談話。我説過，這個高級體檢中心同時也是人脈滙集處，在這裏展開業務要好過數十天的披荊斬棘。

"Excuse me."看見我來，方淮安竟然退出談話，讓我覺得未來大有可爲。

"下午三點照胃鏡，您要回房小憩一下嗎？"我問。

"是該打個盹，年紀大了，不睡午覺不行。"他答。

～

幫方淮安蓋上涼被，再把空調調到適當的溫度後，我離開1010房到休息室喝咖啡，那兩個"大嘴巴"也在，微笑著和我打招呼。

我沒撕破臉，一個人默默坐在角落，邊喝咖啡邊思考。

方淮安和我想像的不一樣，原以爲他會是個老色鬼，沒想到卻是個孤獨老人。他想要美女相伴，更多是爲了填補心靈的空虛而不是共赴巫山雲雨，看來我得改變策略，從溫情下手……

"Hi，這裏有人坐嗎？"一個有著V型小臉的女孩問，我認出是昨天喊汪醫生去看診的護士。

"没人。"我答。

於是她坐了下來，不僅喝光端來的咖啡，還吃了好幾根能量棒。我問她中午飯吃了嗎？她答没有，因爲汪醫生爽約，害她餓肚子。

"妳指的是MO Wang嗎?"

"正是，昨天的香港客人很難侍候，我看汪醫生快招架不住就出手幫他，大概看在這個份上，他説今天中午請我吃飯，結果臨時出狀況，改成吃晚餐。晚餐也好，反正今晚我没約會。"

我忍不住問眼前的這個年輕女子叫什麼名字？她答Joyce, 是教母取的，因爲小時候的她雖然調皮，但有天真、可愛的一面，和誰都聊得來……

不用她説，我已經看出她是個活潑外向的人，没什麼城府，像一杯清澈的水。

"汪醫生是個好人，就是太一根筋了，不懂得變通。"我説，順便測測Joyce對他的看法。

"這樣才好，我不喜歡複雜。"

想到汪致遠喜歡的新加坡女人、暗戀他的寶兒再加上眼前的這位V型臉美女，一根筋的他還真招桃花呀！

我讓方淮安側臥躺好，再幫他蓋上毯子，接著醫生將內窺鏡管子慢慢放入他的鼻腔內，由於咽喉處比較敏感，雖然

管子很細，還是會讓人有嘔吐感，所以檢查的時候，我在方淮安的背部上下輕撫，以緩解他的緊張和不適，還用毛巾幫他擦口水。

好不容易做完檢查回到1010房，方淮安馬上喊口渴。

由於麻醉藥的作用，做完胃鏡檢查不能馬上吃東西，連水也不能喝，我遂提議用棉花棒沾水給他潤潤唇，他只能無奈接受。

潤完唇，方先生問我幾點能正常飲食？我答六點以後。

"妳陪我吃吧！我知道附近有一家好味道的墨西哥餐廳，他家的涼拌豬皮及甜油條是我吃過最好的。"

"不行，我得回家做飯，晚一分鐘開飯老公會過問。"

"要不，把鄭醫生叫來一塊兒吃。"

我答那更不行，鄭之龍很容易猜忌，一有風吹草動馬上對號入座，我已經吃了他不少拳頭。

"不會吧？那樣儒雅的人會打老婆？"

看來沒有證據，正義是不會站在我這邊，於是我脫下護士服，讓他看我身上的烏青，還好那些印記尚未褪去。

"這……這……"那老人嚇得不輕，當然有部份原因是不敢相信我會當著他的面寬衣解帶。

我很快穿好衣服，然後問他還需要些什麼，快五點了，我得下班。

"能到附近酒吧給我買瓶威士忌嗎？我不喝點兒酒不行。"他有些狼狽。

"好，但得等到六點以後才能喝。"

得到他的承諾後，我拿上他給的錢買酒去。

第三十六章／糖爸爸

把威士忌給了方淮安後，我問他通常幾點起床？他答他一向睡得淺，五點半即起。

見我面有難色，他問怎麼了？

"明天我得過來取晨尿。"

"小事，我會打電話讓前台來取，妳不用那麼早趕過來。"

把早餐送上桌後，我拿起包就要出門，老公問我幹嘛去？

"上班，我的客戶今晨得空腹抽血，我若晚去，他豈不是餓肚子？"

"還真鞍前馬後，該頒給'最佳員工獎'給妳。"

顧不上鄭之龍的冷嘲熱諷，我趿上平底鞋匆匆外出。

今天要檢查非常多的血液指標，包括各類腫瘤標誌物，加上餐後得測血糖，一共要抽15管，我都替方先生疼。

等抽血完畢，我帶他到餐廳用早餐。

"早餐有西式和日式兩種選擇，您要哪一種？"我問。

方淮安反問我會做何選擇？我答"西式"，因爲不喜歡一大早就吃乾飯配醬菜。

"好，就西式，兩份，妳陪我吃。"

我没反對。

西式早餐有火腿西多士、芝士烤腸、土豆泥、培根滑蛋和一大碗的布丁水果燕麥，果汁和熱飲當然是無限量供應。

用餐期間，方先生問起我的家庭狀況，我在兩分鐘內交待完畢，鄭之龍的部份只以"倉促之下所做的錯誤決定"帶過。

"您呢？除了大、小老婆外，有孩子嗎？"我反問。

"我没有後代，其實想開了也没什麼，上天這麼安排一定有祂的旨意，無庸煩惱。"

我又問Miss Zhou的近況？她的學習還好嗎？

"前陣子在加州，現在在哪裏就不清楚了，反正要錢的時候自然會出現。"

呃......這豈不是把人家當搖錢樹？方淮安怎麼看都不像傻子，這是怎麼回事？

見我沈默，那人好像聽到我內心的聲音，主動解釋："我已經日薄西山，有誰會想接近這樣的老人？所以只要能帶給我快樂、充實我的人生，我不介意用金錢交易。"

怎麼聽都像西方世界所説的Sugar daddy（糖爸爸），男方管女方的吃喝玩樂換來陪伴，雙方都清楚這樣的關係是暫時的，互取所需罷了。我呢？是不是在找糖爸爸？肯定不是，畢竟我有一份過得去的收入，那麼接近方老闆圖的是什麼？他是挺有錢的，但能否幫到我、助我脱離目前的處境？

“有什麼可以幫到妳？”方淮安突然一問，把我嚇壞了，以爲他有讀心術。

“沒……沒什麼要幫的，如果您用餐完畢，我們得測餐後血糖。”我說。

“好的。”他答。

早上除了血測還安排了五官、聽力和肺活量的檢查，做完已近中午，本來方淮安還想和我有午餐的約會，但湊巧在餐廳遇到熟人，我很識趣地退出，自己到地下一層的員工餐廳吃飯。

體檢部的員工餐廳比醫院總部好，雖然選擇性少了，但菜品卻提高了，連桌椅也從塑料換成沙發座，整個水平往上提高了不止一個檔次。

我很清楚自己不過是體檢部的浮雲，沒必要公關，所以挑了角落的位子坐，偏偏有人不願放過我。

“ Miss Cui, 昨晚我和汪醫生吃飯了，他還問起妳。”Joyce大喇喇地坐在我對面。

“妳怎麼說？”

“我說和妳不熟，只知道妳一來就有客戶指名要妳，讓其他護士很不滿，謠言四起。”

早知道女人間的撕逼很慘烈，沒想到我都這麼低調了，還是被流彈打中。

“愛怎麼說我管不著，我只管做好自己的工作。”

“聽說妳後天回住院部，是不是真的？”

連這個也傳開了？我無奈點頭。

“汪醫生要我照顧妳，怎麼照顧？妳才在這裏待幾天而已。”她嘆了口氣說。

聽到汪致遠還是眷顧我，一股暖流上心頭。

“不需要照顧，我已經是成年人了。”我答。

“我也是這麼告訴汪醫生，但他說別看我的外表很幹練，行事有時還像個孩子，所以能幫就盡量幫。”

“謝謝妳,真的不需要。”喝完最後一口湯，我打算撤。

“那麼妳可不可以幫幫我?我喜歡汪醫生，想和他有進一步的發展，妳能幫我美言幾句嗎？”

看她笑得一臉燦爛，我答好，有機會的話。

下午是重頭戲，核磁共振 MRI主要檢查大腦和頭部血管情況。

方淮安躺上機器後，平台升起，因爲檢查的時間比較久，我怕空調下會冷，遂幫他蓋好毯子，同時遞給他一個橡膠球，交待如果有不舒服，捏這個球就行，檢查的工作會暫停。

他表示了解後，我按下啓動鍵。

做完核磁共振，稍微休息後緊接著做上下腹部、胸部、內臟脂肪的螺旋CT，時間相對快一些，然後是照胸部X光片，正面和側面各拍一張。

“今天辛苦了。”我扶方先生離開放射室後說。

“哪裏，身體是自己的，該做的檢查還是得做，没人能替代。”

想到離用晚餐的時間還有半小時，我問他要先回房還是到休息室喝飲料？

“我想妳有話對我説，還是回房喝咖啡吧！”他答。

ＩＯＩＯ 房 有 個 小 型 的 家 用 咖 啡 機 ， 能 製 作 Espresso 和美式咖啡。

“給我來杯美式，加奶不加糖。”方淮安説。

我給了他美式，自己則來一杯意式濃縮，好集中精神。

“説吧！我聽著。”那老人像神燈裏的精靈，等著應允我。

“我……我想……陪伴您，也想……結束不愉快的婚姻。”

“所以‘結束不愉快的婚姻’是目標，‘陪伴我’是回饋，對嗎？”

既然他“直來直往”，我也没什麼好隱瞞，坦言鄭之龍若能輕易放過我，我也不用求他了。

方淮安思考片刻後説這件事比較棘手，可能需要一些時日，事成後我得答應陪伴他至少一年……

“我知道。”我低下頭去。

“放心，這不是情色交易，因爲身體原因，我和大小老婆已經多年無性生活了。”他説。

第三十七章/又見曙光

體檢的最後一天只安排骨密度檢測和醫生總結，前者的測量機器很大，會掃描全身上下的骨骼密度，著重點在骨盆及大腿部位。

"去年我的骨密度指標相當於五十歲的人，醫生還說我老當益壯，可以玩水上運動呢！"方淮安不無驕傲地說。

我趁機表示自己的骨密度指標大概在六十歲，因爲長期挨揍，骨架多少有些鬆散……

"嘖嘖嘖！鄭醫生怎麼下得了手？"他握住我的手，"像水蜜桃一樣多汁的女人，疼都來不及。"

此時的我應該推開他的五爪才是，但我卻回握住他瘦骨嶙峋的手，眼眶含淚地求助："救救我吧！"

雖然方老闆曾口頭答應幫我，但難保他一轉身就忘得一乾二淨，今天是體檢最後一日，我得加把勁。

果然女人的眼淚對某些男人來說很管用，我看他起身去取紙巾，並且爲我端來熱茶。

"謝謝！"我說，然後用紙巾拭淚。

"本來想緩個幾天再說，既然這樣，今晚妳回家打包行李，明天就上我家當我的住家護士。"

我没料到幾滴眼淚就把方淮安給收服了，好是好，可是我該怎麼跟老公開口呢？我陷入苦思。

"別想了，就說爲了藥廠投資案，妳打算深入虎穴和我打好關係。"

藥廠投資？我問這是什麼玩意兒？

"原來鄭醫生還没跟妳提呀！"他停頓了一下，"我的方安製藥廠計劃在印度另開個廠，打算採合資合作方式，有意向者不下十位，鄭醫生只是其中之一。由於他投資的金額過小，我還在猶豫，看來現在只能先給他希望了。"

一個製藥廠的成立可不是個小數目，老公竟敢斗膽加入，未免也太不自量力了。

等我知道他的投資金額高達一千萬新幣時，倒吸一口氣。

"他的私人診所還是我們夫妻聯名貸款買下的，他哪裏來的錢？"我說。

"也許鄭醫生另外有個小金庫吧！"方先生似笑非笑的表情讓人很難堪。

我答若是那樣倒還好，怕就怕他把我給賣了。

下午做總結，凡檢查過的項目都會在電腦軟件中展示，醫生會逐項逐條向客戶說明結果。

講解完畢，Dr.Wood詢問方淮安有什麼問題要問？

我以爲那老人會針對自己的身體狀況做更深入的交流，没想到他卻問了一個奇怪的問題—保存在精子銀行裏的精子能存活多久？

Dr.Wood煞有介事地回答最多十年，久了就不敢保證。

我還沒從詫異中驚醒，方先生壓低聲音對我說：「別驚訝，去年我問醫生人死後靈魂去哪裏了？」

聽他這麼一說，我呵呵笑，同時鬆了一口氣（老實說，我也不知道自己在緊張什麼）。

Dr.Wood離去時已近下午三點半，方淮安說他想和一些熟人打招呼，順便做做公關，「命令」我提早下班。

提早下班是不可能的，我也有事要做，譬如遞辭呈、與同事話別等，所以當我的未來雇主說「明天見」時，我轉身趕辦這些事。

體檢部早知道我做到今日，可能還巴不得我提早離開，所以出了體檢大樓後，我往總部走去。

人事喋喋不休地唸叨住院部人手不足，偏偏我在這時候提辭呈，太沒敬業精神了……

「針對這點，我無話可說，該怎麼處罰，我無異議。」

那個四眼田雞兼慾求不滿的老女人說違約金肯定得付，上個月的薪水就先扣住不發，工簽和保險也得停，等一切準備妥當，她會通知我簽字、付費。

「好，我等候通知。」

離開人事室後，我緊接著到住院部辭行，同事們直呼太突然，紛紛詢問方老闆給了多少月薪？我答不清楚，還因此被怨保密到家。

由於正值交接班時間，同事好奇過後很快作鳥獸散，晚班護士長趁機拉我至角落，說沒想到我是那個幸運兒，成了方淮安的新寵。

"大番薯"是有名的八卦王，我的回答得非常小心才行。

"其實我有任務在身，不是妳想的那樣。"我說。

"我能想哪樣？要身材沒身材，要容貌沒容貌，年紀還一大把，怎麼都比不上你們這幫年輕人。"她拍拍我肩膀，"放心，我一點兒也不嫉妒，這是妳該得的，哪天富貴了，可別忘了我。"

我還想說什麼，寶兒向我奔來，問我到底怎麼回事？辭職是真是假？

"是真的，即刻生效。"我答。

"妳怎能這樣甩下我不管？明天的考試叫我如何專心是好？"

我說這是兩碼事，即使辭職，我仍在護士崗位上，也沒離開新加坡，有空還是能約著看電影、吃飯。

"聽說妳被一個有錢老頭看上，他答應給妳雙倍的月薪，換成是我，大概也會跳槽。"

天哪！我人還在這，連自己都不知道薪水有多少，謠言已經自動幫我加薪了。

"沒那麼多……應該沒那麼多……"我試圖解釋，但總有"越描越黑"之嫌。

"別羨慕了，"晚班護士長開口，"趕緊做事要緊，早點兒做完還能看會兒書，這次若沒通過考試，還得等一年才能翻身。"

我站到"大蕃薯"那邊。

"那好，考完試我找妳。"寶兒説。

我特意在醫院大廳及眼科部稍作停留，以爲會踫到汪醫生，可惜人來人往，没一個是他，只好快快離去。

回到家，我趕緊忙活，由於打算明天離家（並且不再重入家門），我做了一桌子的好菜與老公告別。

"這是怎麽回事？"鄭之龍進門後毫無欣喜，替代的是懷疑與不滿，"妳知道我們家的規矩。"

"我當然清楚，若不是有喜事，怎麽可能惹你不高興？"我把最後的冬瓜排骨湯捧上桌，再奉上兩碗白米飯後坐下。

"什麽喜事？"鄭之龍也坐了下來。

我答先吃飯再説，但老公非要我講明白不可，我只好邊吃邊説，而且從旁入手。

"這幾天我服侍方淮安做體檢，他跟我提到你有意和方安製藥廠合作辦廠，你哪來的錢？莫非有個小金庫？"

"怎麽不早説方淮安體檢去了？要早説，我就派妳當説客。"他很懊惱。

"你還没回答我的問話呢！該不會錢是大風吹來的吧？！"

"哪兒來的風？房子可以做二次抵押嘛！"

聽完，我的心喀噔了一下，房子是他的，愛咋咋地，但該不會又要求我共同背債吧？！

"説什麽傻話？妳是我老婆，債務當然得背一半，只是方安製藥廠好像對我的合作案不感興趣，我以爲事情糊了，所以也没跟妳提。"

我想起我的計劃，趕緊重新燃起鄭之龍的希望之火，説一千萬新幣雖不多，但他的名聲夠響亮，方淮安也没完全放棄，只要推幾把，還是有希望……

" 能有什麼希望？請他們的高管吃了不少鮑魚、龍蝦，又讓我的行政助理安排上了好幾次夜總會，還是不肯鬆口，我的鈔票倒是因此花了不少。"

我説找小囉囉有什麼用？當然得直搗黃龍才行，然後我把方淮安雇我當住家護士一事相告。

老公聽完很生氣，他説新加坡就那麼點兒大，何必住家？頂多朝九晚五。

" 合作案是否迫在眉睫？不日夜奮戰哪能成？何況競爭對手的出價比你的多得多……"我竭盡全力遊説。

鄭之龍聽完皺緊眉頭，我知道他在思考，靜待他的決定。

" 那好，我把這個重責大任交給妳，妳盡快辦妥。事成後找個藉口離開，畢竟妳是有家室的人。"

我表面沈著，但內心早已樂開花。

" 當然，誰想和老人在一起呢？"我答。

第三十八章／方宅

劉禹錫在《陋室銘》中曾以"苔痕上階綠，草色入簾青"來描繪清新悠閒的自然環境，然而都市生活的快節奏卻剝奪了這種享受，人們只能住在高聳入雲的鴿子籠裏，勤快地往返都市叢林間。

新加坡也不例外，它是個已開發國家，其GDP甚至超越香港，到處是鱗次節比的建築物，唯獨第十郵局獨樹一幟，不僅有優越的地理位置、便利的配套設施、優質的教育資源、永久的地契……還因綠化覆蓋率高而成爲富人區的代表，很難讓人相信在寸土寸金的中心地帶，竟然還有鬧中取靜的慢節奏生活，其尊貴及稀缺性可想而知。

方淮安的家就在第十郵區。

～

吃完早餐，我要鄭之龍上班去，他卻執意載我一程，爲的是—如果老婆跟別人跑了，他還有個地方找。

車子行經荷蘭路和皇后路，沿途是茂密的綠林，清雅恬靜，最後停在一棟花木扶疏的豪宅前。

"媽的，這房子得值多少錢？光土地就不少吧？！"老公死盯著方宅，眼露傾羨的神情。

根據小道消息，方淮安在兩千年初買下這棟佔地約一公畝的紅瓦老屋，還因成交價破 1.5 億元而榮登當年的"別墅王"，更讓人咋舌的是不到兩個月的時間工程隊就進駐，把百年老宅推倒重建，成了今日以金色和黑色爲主調，加上大片單向反光玻璃的三層豪華居所。

"好了，你走吧！我自己進去。"我説。

"什麼時候回家？"他問。

"説不準，現在最重要的是把案子拿下，你才能高枕無憂。"

鄭之龍聽了很欣慰，他表示在緊要關頭才看得出誰是自家人……

聽他把我當成自己人，我噁心地想吐，趕緊下車，連再見都没説。

還是那個皮膚黝黑的菲律賓女傭開的門。

" This way, please."她對我微笑，態度比上回好太多。

我從恢宏的鐵柵門側門進入，右翼有個池塘，被白色的栀子花群環抱，那優雅的水中倒影很是靜謐；左翼有個茶亭，在悠閒的午後與親朋好友品評茶味，感受時光的流逝，應該是件愜意的事。

穿過錯落有致的長廊後，我來到中式古典風格的客廳，當看到大紅燈籠及繪有潑墨山水的漆器屏風時，我感到很新奇，時光彷彿一下子倒退百年。

叫 Alodia 的女傭請我坐下，待我坐定，才發現太師椅中看不中用，雖然外表看起來莊重嚴謹，但舒適感明顯不足。

" Tea or coffee? "她問。

我答茶，只因這氛圍適合喝回甘的中國茶而非歐式飲品。

在等待的同時，除了擺放在紫檀木花几上的黃蕊白瓣水仙花吸引我之外，池邊戲水聲也一直撓我耳朵，看樣子這個宅子不似先前想的寂寞冷清。

趁女傭爲我端來鐵觀音，我問方老闆在嗎？她答不在。

" Then who will I be seeing?"我問那麼我要見誰呢？

照我的想法，老闆既然不在，我應該被帶到房間安頓才是。

" Mrs.Fang wants to see you."她答。

聽到方太太想見我，我頓時沒了主意。女人天生敏感，我又懷著目的而來，她肯定能聞到不尋常的味道，這如何是好？

就這麼七上八下地等了數分鐘，終於等來那個平胸的方家二太（原本還期望來者會是校花級別的原配夫人）。今天的她穿著白襯衫加黑色條紋長褲，齊肩的髮剪成赫本頭，多了幾分幹練。

" 方……方太太好。"我站起身。

"坐，鄭夫人請坐。"她説。

我們兩人都在太師椅上坐下後，她問我鄭醫生可好？我答好，然後她開門見山地問我爲了什麼目的前來？

" 目的？"被人瞧見內心的秘密，我很不安，" 没……没什麼目的。"

"肯定有，有才正常，没有才讓人起疑，誰會想把大好青春浪費在一個老人身上？"

方家二太約四十歲上下，雖然和方准安是老少配，但頂多算是父女戀，我就不一樣了，妥妥的爺孫戀。

" 我來是爲了工作，没有別的原因。"我答。

方家二太就著紫砂茶杯喝了好幾口後，直言我不像周小姐一樣坦白，她一來就要車子、珠寶和現金，明碼標價。

我因此陷入兩難，如果開口要鄭之龍盡快在我眼前消失，外人不明真相，我就成了怪物（誰也不願家裏迎來不尋常之人）；如果像周小姐一樣要錢倒還容易些，方家不缺錢，看來在這方面也給得大方。

" 我……也想要有周小姐的待遇。"我給了一個比較安全的答案。

"呵呵！錢果然是利器，連鄭醫生的夫人也趨之若鶩。得，我會比照周小姐，給妳相應的回報，唯一的要求就是守口如瓶，這宅子裏發生的任何事都不許往外説，知道嗎？"

我點頭如搗蒜。

" 妳的房間在二樓，我讓Alodia爲妳帶路。"她説，同時代表談話結束。

~

我以爲房間會是中式風格，有架子床和窗花格，還好一切"正常"，床是柔軟的席夢思，家俱是西式的，連牆紙也帶粉紅色小花，很有少女氣息。

此時外面的嬉鬧聲更加清晰，因爲窗戶開著的緣故。我遂走向窗口往下一探，那是個約25米長的短池，雖然是標準游泳池的一半，但對家用而言已足夠。我看見清澈的水面上浮著一隻大黃鴨，有兩個身穿比基尼泳裝的洋妞正在戲水，説著不知是哪國的語言。

"看著像烏克蘭人，聽説那裏盛産美女，個個身材纖細、面貌姣好。"我心想。

離開窗口，我把行李箱裏的東西全拿出來各就各位，再把父母與我的合照放在床頭櫃上，算是把家暫時安在此處。

~

我讀著亦舒的愛情長篇小說《玫瑰的故事》，美麗的玫瑰經歷婚姻失敗，卻能在中年後重逢真愛，讓我覺得未來可期，畢竟自己還三十歲不到……

"扣、扣、"

" Come in."

來者是Alodia，她喊我吃飯，於是我閣上書下床。

這是第一次與方家人用餐，得給他們留下一個好印象，於是我從衣櫃取下藍白相間的連衣裙，穿在身上像個保守的中學女生。

走進餐廳，我才發現不止方家夫婦在，同桌的還有一對姐妹花，那是方才戲水的洋妞。原來她們是孿生子，有同樣的髮型和穿著，連臉上的雀斑數也一樣（我猜的）。

"快坐下，餓了吧？"方淮安問我，口氣很溫和。

"還好，不是挺餓。"我邊答邊坐下。

這是一張黃花梨大圓桌，上面還有個轉盤，方便取菜。

"開動吧！"男主人說。

話一說完，兩隻"金絲雀"馬上用叉子對食物進行攻擊，難不成她們聽得懂普通話？

方淮安給了二太太一隻鵝腿後，再依次給我和兩位洋妞，看她們毫無忸怩地接受了，我也安心吃起來。

席間除了那對姐妹太呱噪，被女主人訓斥之外，倒也風平浪靜。

飯後，方淮安說想吃紅毛丹和蜜釋迦，方家二太吩咐Alodia把水果端到我房裏。

"爲什麼是我的房裏？"我心裏犯嘀咕，但没說反對的話。

第三十九章／投桃報李

我的房間裏有個小客廳，但沙發與席夢思之間完全没有遮擋，所以感覺自己的隱私被侵犯，非常的不自在。

"都説房間會有住宿人的氣味，真的一點兒也没錯。當Miss Zhou在時，這個房間有柑橘花的味道，現在則是桂花香。"方淮安説。

我不知自己的身上是否帶有桂花的香味，但這段話的意思是：一、**Miss Zhou** 住過這間房。二、方老闆也同樣探訪過。

這是什麼狀況？我很迷惑。

"吃，可甜了。"他把蜜釋迦一扳兩半，給了我半個。

這種水果是我認爲最奇特的水果之一，不僅長相奇怪，吃起來還不容易，完全無優雅可言，還搞得一手黏乎乎的。

"謝謝！"我還是接過手。

"談談妳的童年吧！"他突然説。

我的童年？啊！我想起了那個水鄉古鎮，也想起了老冰棍、爆米花、踩影子、畫手錶、跳格子、小溪戲水……等。記憶中的童年痕跡如同牆上的塗鴉，即使年代久遠，依舊模糊地存在著，時刻提醒我那些不可複製、一去不返的美好時光……

方淮安説看來我有一個快樂的童年，他就不一樣，打從很小很小的時候起就開始養家，每天天一亮便與哥哥推著小車沿街叫賣嘟嘟糕。那是一種類似蒸糕的食物，用小圓盤裝著，馬來名是Putu Piring，意思是"分開的盤子"，內餡是椰絲或花生，由於販賣者會以"嘟嘟"響的喇叭聲代替叫賣，因而得名。

"您父母呢？"我問，順便遞給他濕紙巾擦手。

"我母親在家製作嘟嘟糕及看護更幼小的孩子，至於父親……他是街頭郎中，早在醫療技術沒那麼發達的50年代，新加坡有一種在街頭給人看病的職業叫Koh Yok，通俗點兒説就是'江湖郎中'，他們以傳統中醫爲基礎，造福了不少沒有能力看私人診所的平常百姓。"

我説難怪他現在"製藥"，從某方面來説也算是"繼承衣鉢"。

方淮安笑了笑，同意我的説法。

我們就這麼東拉西扯地談了近一個小時，然後我的老闆説他累了，想睡個午覺。

新加坡是熱帶國家，中午不打個盹的確受不了，我説連我都昏昏欲睡呢！

"那我們一起睡吧！"

我當他開玩笑，但方淮安來真的，他很快在我的席夢思床上躺下，還招手要我過去。

"不，我現在不睏。"我趕緊敬而遠之。

"不睏也陪我睡，我喜歡睡覺時旁邊有'香妃'陪伴。"

傳説在清乾隆皇帝的四十多位后妃中，有一位維吾爾族女子遍體生香，她就是聞名遐邇的香妃。

"我不是香妃。"我答。

方淮安不高興了，他説我住他家，領著他的薪水，該不會以爲月薪一萬新幣的工作只是測測體溫、量量血壓而已吧？

一萬新幣？我没問過薪水，萬萬没想到方家如此大方，幾乎是REQ給的近三倍（也許這個數是比照Miss Zhou給的）。

我好奇地問Miss Zhou也陪睡嗎？

"當然。"他答，樣子很坦蕩。

我躊躇了幾秒後，順從地在那人的身旁躺下。他握住我的手，閉上眼，没多久便打起鼾來。

方家的晚餐吃得早，六點準時開飯，此時桌上有麒麟鮑片、清燉鰻鱺湯、千層肉、七彩凍鴨絲、翻沙芋、蠔烙及粉粿。

"喜歡潮州菜嗎？如果不喜歡可麻煩了，我老公特別喜歡選料考究、刀工精細的潮州菜。"方家二太説。

我對潮州菜的感覺一般，談不上喜歡或不喜歡，只是留意到但凡以潮州菜主打的餐廳，標價都不便宜，讓人懷疑非貴價上不了菜單。

方淮安給我上課，他説潮州菜也有平民菜色，但傳入南洋後，餐廳改走"食材優先"的精緻路線，譬如：鮑參肚翅、燕窩、響螺片、老鵝頭......等等，導致現在只要一提起"潮州菜"便與"價高"劃上等號。

"潮州菜不錯，我喜歡。"我討好地説。

方家二太接話："那對雙胞胎就不一樣了，口味還停留在炒飯、炒麵、咕咾肉的層面上，給她們吃精緻料理太浪費，所以今晚我讓她們出去吃。”

我看到方老闆因此轉頭看牆上時鐘。

“放心，我交待她們十點前回來。”平胸老闆娘答。

我正奇怪那兩隻波斯貓上哪兒去了？原來出外用膳。

外國人無法欣賞中國的地方美食不難理解，像我也不見得全盤接受國外的地方特色菜，譬如鹽醃鯡魚、袋鼠肉、藍紋奶酪……等。

“希望她們能找到家鄉菜。”我說。

“沒吃到家鄉菜也無所謂，那兩人過幾天就回俄羅斯。”二太太答。

“原來是俄羅斯人，我還以爲是烏克蘭人，傻傻分不清，”我吃了一口鴨絲，“她們來新加坡幹嘛？”

突來的沈默讓人很忐忑，我說錯什麼了？

“Bepa和Tamapa是來工作的，和妳一樣。”半天，二太太蹦出一句。

～

“Bepa和Tamapa是來工作的，和妳一樣。”這句話在我耳邊回蕩，久久不散。

如果只是前一句倒還好，畢竟大部份的人都得工作糊口，但加上後一句就不那麼純粹了。雖然早知道“住家護士”不過是掩人耳目，但陪一個老頭兒“純睡覺”還是奇怪得不得了，如果我做的是“陪睡”的工作，那麼姐妹花做的又是什麼？

晚餐過後回到房間，老公給我打來電話，怕他囉嗦，我藉口幫雇主做腳底按摩，很快掛上電話。沒想到一語成讖，小說才看沒幾章，女傭就喚我做腳底按摩。

我說我不會腳底按摩，Alodia 一副“妳不會，誰會？”的表情，讓人很無語。

想到自己的月收入，再對照自己的工作內容，得，拿人錢財就得爲人辦事，我認了。

闔上門，我默默跟隨女傭上到三樓。

“Come in.”是二太太的聲音。

我轉開門把進入，麝香的味道迎面襲來，讓人很詫異。古代宮廷戲中，妃子若長期聞麝香味會導致流産，其真實性不可考，但那的確是一種令人不愉快的濃郁氣味。

相比味道，房內的裝潢好多了，如果說我的房間是簡約風，那麼主臥室便是法式宮廷風。瞧！厚重的波斯地毯、金箔塗飾的家俱、鼓型邊桌、大肚斗櫃、捲草紋窗簾、水晶吊燈、瓶插百合花……處處彰顯著浪漫的貴氣。

“妳來了正好，許久沒人幫我按摩了。”二太太的雙腳正浸在足浴盆內。

我左顧右盼找雇主。

“不用找了，老頭子不在。”

“可……可是我沒受過真正的訓練，怕按錯穴位反而不好。”

二太太説她不介意，只要舒服就行，難不成按錯穴位還會少塊肉？

話都説到這個份上，我只好拉來沙發凳，打算胡亂按兩下。

“Miss Zhou按得不錯，妳也上點兒心，別被比下去了。”她叮囑，説得好像替她按摩是件神聖得不得了的事。

我把茶几上的毛巾取下，將她的雙腳擦乾後開始按起來。

“輕點兒，別亂來。”二太太明顯不高興。

我也不高興，本來就不關我事。

"我説了，我没受過訓練。"我冷冷地答。

方家二太説有没有受過訓練是一回事，有没有心才是重點，我不喜歡她，所以才會馬虎交差……

"妳言重了，妳是我雇主的……妻子，我怎麽可以不喜歡妳？"

"嘖嘖嘖！瞧妳們這些女人，一個個全是心機婊，難不成妳還喜歡我？我可警告妳，別以爲老頭子看不出妳心裏想什麼，他精得很。"

不用她説，我早看出來，方淮安雖然表面大方，有商有量，但心裏一直有個算盤在，不是能予取予求。

"謝謝妳告訴我這些，我從没想過佔人便宜，投桃報李的道理還是懂的。"我説。

"怎麽投桃報李？牽牽小手、親親小嘴就算投桃報李？妳也太單純了！"

我表明女人的青春有限，把生命中最璀璨的時光奉獻出來，已是最好的回報……

"是呀！妳不過是簽了一年的賣身契，不像我，既没合法名份還把餘生全耗在這裏，就顯得不智，妳是這樣想的，對吧？"

"我怎麽想不重要，問題是妳怎麽想？像二太太這麽睿智的人，下棋肯定把接下來的好幾步都想通透了才是。"

她沈默了一會兒後，喃喃道："妳和前幾任護士不同，有頭腦也識大體，也許這次能行……"

"能行？什麽意思？"我問。

二太太笑而不語，她把腿收了，要我回房歇著。

"搞什麽？話説到一半，真要急死人了。"我心想。

懷著惴惴不安的心情，我離開二太太的房間。

第四十章/俄羅斯女郎

我的房間沒有衛浴，得到公用浴室去洗，等我洗完回房時，剛好看到雙胞胎姐妹上樓的身影。

"原來她們的房間在三樓呀！"我心想。

回到房內，我打開電風扇吹乾頭髮。沒辦法，即使是晚上十點，新加坡依然悶熱，開空調是一個辦法，但我通常會在夜裏開窗，讓空氣流通一下。

"嘟……嘟嘟……"是寶兒的來電，我接聽了。

"媛媛學姐，最近好嗎？我想妳了。"

早習慣寶兒的"瘋言瘋語"，我也配合演出，說自己想她想得睡不著覺……

"那好，爲了一解相思之苦，明天我去找妳。"

"不成，我現在住在雇主家，而且今天第一天上班，不好告假。"

"那更好，早想看看富豪之家長什麼樣，剛好明天公休，加上剛考完試，正好放鬆一下。"

我還是説不行，哪有把朋友帶進雇主家的道理？太不成體統了。

手機那頭的寶兒很失望，但没有死纏爛打，她轉而跟我要方淮安的住址，説去不成，從外面瞻仰一下也行，以後想念學姐時也好有個想像空間……

我嘴巴唸叨著她没事找事做，但還是報上地址，同時再三叮嚀她別做衝動的事，譬如爬牆進來……

"媛媛學姐，妳真幽默。"她大笑兩聲後掛了電話。

就這麽結束了？我還以爲她會跟我煲三個小時的電話粥呢！

我又吹了一陣子的電風扇，直到樓上有音樂聲傳來，那是一種緩慢的淺聲低吟，在這樣的夜裏更顯暧昧。

"是誰在聽音樂？"我站起來走向窗口。

方宅的主體建築物呈L形，我住的是南翼，面向泳池，東翼的寬度相對較窄，不到三十米。到底音樂來自我這邊還是另一邊無從分辨，更別提是從哪間發出的。

我皺著眉頭離開窗口。

於是在方家的第一個夜晚，我就這麽邊聽撩人的音樂邊走入夢鄉。

～

熱帶國家清晨五點多便朦朧亮，加上昨晚忘了拉上窗簾，被陽光喚醒後再也無法入睡，只好起來梳洗。

待我重新回到房內，窗外的水聲吸引我往外探去，原來是方淮安，他在晨泳，像隻緩慢的青蛙。

看一個老人游泳其實很無趣，但我硬是站在窗前良久，大概對自己的雇主感到好奇吧！

方淮安游了數個回合後上岸喝水，我得以看到他裸身的樣子，以近七十歲的老人而言，他算保養得不錯，沒有大肚腩，雙腿看起來也很結實。

他喝了一口瓶裝水後，轉身舉起瓶子向東致意。我伸長脖子想看個清楚，卻什麼也沒見著，莫非他向太陽致敬？這也太詭異了吧？

早餐吃粥。

我喜歡粥品，像是皮蛋瘦肉粥、及第粥、艇仔粥等，但方家吃的是白粥，加上配菜的顏色不怎麼討喜，我頓時沒了胃口。

讓我來告訴你桌上都有些什麼，除了酸菜、貢菜、烏欖、菜脯蛋、麻葉等奇怪的菜外，還有各種的醃製物，比如小海蟹，鹹薄殼，鹹蝦蛄，鹹血鉗等。

"這些是鹹雜，潮州話的意思是小菜，可好吃了。"我的老闆說，然後三兩下就吃完一碗粥，把碗一伸，讓 Alodia 再添去。

反觀二太太，今天的心情好像不咋地，從一上桌就擺臉色，四周圍因此彌漫著一股低氣壓。我反倒希望姐妹花在，多少能帶來活潑的氣息。

"怎麼？不喜歡吃粥？"見我遲遲不下箸，方淮安問。

我答潮州早餐看著很鹹，而成人每天正常的食鹽量應該控制在6克以下，若長期食鹽過多，會導致高血壓及骨質疏鬆，同時加重腎臟的負擔，中老年人尤其更要注意⋯⋯

"Miss Chui，妳大概不知道潮汕人多長壽，百歲老人比比皆是吧？"二太太冷冷地說。

"這我不清楚，但身為方老闆的私人護士，我有必要提出專業意見。"

方家二太呵呵笑，說讀過書就是不一樣，腦子都不會轉彎了⋯⋯

我想反駁，但被方淮安截了先：" 生死有命富貴在天，鹹雜的確鹹了點兒，但我們也不是天天吃，這樣吧！明天吃烤麵包，好嗎？"

見雇主都這麼低聲下氣，我還能說什麼？只好把不滿吞下肚去。

吃完早餐，我爲老人量血壓和體溫，還好都在正常範圍內。

" 血壓最好空腹前量，上午和下午各量一次。"我收好血壓計說。

"好，以後固定在早餐及晚餐前量，記得提醒我。"

見他起身，我問我的雇主上哪兒去？他答去公司轉轉，中午回來。

呃！差點兒忘了他是公司老闆，雖然樣子看起來像已退休。

做完例行的工作，我回房看小說，這個"住家護士"當得輕鬆自在，宛如度假，我正心中竊喜，没想到剛一坐下，女傭就來敲我房門，樣子很急切，話說得顛三倒四,我不得不請她重述一遍。

" Your friend⋯⋯Well, I don't know that's true or not. She is downstairs. I guess she has some trouble."Alodia 說我的朋友在樓下，看樣子有麻煩了。

我的朋友？誰呀？

懷著狐疑的心下樓，但除了打掃衛生的女傭外，誰也没見著，倒是聽到前院有人說話的聲音，我往外走去，看到大鐵門開著，方淮安的座駕堵在門口。

"媛媛學姐，妳來了正好，幫我解釋解釋，我說不清楚呀！"寶兒像抓住救命稻草似地呼喊起來。

我看見幾個男人將她團團圍住，那樣子像在收網捕魚。

通過七嘴八舌，我終於搞明白，原來寶兒不僅爬上了圍牆，還拿起手機對著方宅猛拍⋯⋯

"媛媛學姐，妳要相信我，我沒有惡意，只是想看看妳工作的地方，沒想到這宅子又大又美，心血來潮便拍了幾張照片，如此而已。"她說。

沒想到再一次一語成讖，寶兒真的爬牆了。

" Sorry, she is my friend."我只好硬起頭皮道歉，並且羞愧地承認來者是我的朋友。

" 不行，這是入侵行爲，何況還拍了照，不知目的爲何，怎可輕易放過？還是交給警察處理爲妥。"那個西裝筆挺的中年司機不買賬。

聽到要叫警察，寶兒嚇得腿軟，她指天發誓再也不敢了，請求放她一馬⋯⋯

"算了吧！"方淮安按下車窗，" Miss Cui的朋友就是我的朋友，若不嫌棄，留朋友一起吃個便飯。"

"他就是方淮安？看起來像慈祥的老爺爺，"寶兒環顧四周，"這個房間比我的大。"

我遞給她一杯茶水，問她最近可好？

"老樣子，每天做著端屎端尿的工作，什麼時候是個頭呦？活著真沒意思！"

我安慰她一番，說只要通過考試，助理護士比護理員的含金量大，沒那麼多髒活，薪水也多⋯⋯

“我也只能這麼想，要不然日子就過不下去了。”

然後她又告訴我新近醫院發生的事，不外一些雞毛蒜皮及女人間的碎言碎語。我也告訴她方淮安有兩個老婆，而且同住一個屋檐下，大老婆還没見著，二老婆倒是一副刀槍不入的樣子。

“小心別成爲人家的第三個老婆。”寶兒雖没指名道姓，但明顯是衝著我來的。

我老大不高興，説自己是有夫之婦，何況方淮安的年紀老得可以當我爺爺了……

“説説而已，妳怎麼就當真了？”

“開玩笑也得有個度。”我仍氣憤著。

此時窗外傳來戲水聲，寶兒馬上衝向窗口：“快看！有外國人哪！原來這宅子還有個泳池，早知道就帶泳衣過來……”

我也走向窗口，依舊是那兩個洋妞，她們穿著黃色比基尼，胸前的巨彈呼之欲出，而丁字型的泳褲設計也讓圓潤的屁股毫不忸怩地示人……

寶兒問我爲什麼洋人的身材可以這麼好？要胸有胸、要腿有腿，連腰也那麼纖細。

“那是婚前，婚後的洋女人很多都乳房下墜兼具水桶腰，身上的雀斑也多，像密密麻麻的褐色蟲子，而且老得快。”

“看來還是小骨架的亞洲女子經得起時間的考驗，對了，那兩個金毛是什麼來歷？”

“二太太説她們替方家工作，過幾天就回俄羅斯，應該是兼職性質。”

“是嗎？”寶兒望向那兩個美麗的胴體，“她們能做什麼呢？”

寶兒的疑問也是我的疑問。

第四十一章／東翼

黃花梨大圓桌上已擺滿了菜餚，看樣子是中國各地的美食大雜滙，有上海紅燒肉、四川麻婆豆腐、廣東燒鵝、客家梅乾菜扣肉、福建佛跳牆、東北大燴菜、還有一大盆的砂鍋螃蟹米粉。

"哇！你們吃得那麼好？光爲了吃，我也想待在這裏不走了。"寶兒嚷嚷起來。

"坐，崔小姐的朋友也一起坐。"方淮安招呼我們這兩個遲到的人。

"我叫寶兒，"她一屁股坐在男主人旁邊的位子上，"是REQ的護士，請多關照。"

"REQ的護士果然都是水噹噹的美女，來，給妳一杯鳳梨汁，鮮榨的。"

寶兒飲過主人遞過來的果汁後，當下決定替方家幹活，就爲了能再喝到那麼好喝的鳳梨汁。

"妳能做什麼？"老頭子問。

“很多呀！媛媛學姐能做的，我都能做；她不能做的，我也能做，譬如下腰、一字馬及劈叉等。”

我很反感寶兒的“自薦”，尤其還把我拖下水。

“哪天方家也整個雜技團好了。”二太太開口，一臉寒霜。

寶兒呵呵呵地笑起來：“想吃蝦不一定得買養蝦場，何況我不止基本功好，還有治癒的能力，能讓不開心的人立馬開心起來。”

“這麼厲害？那還需要心理醫生做什麼？雇一些小丑得了……”

“吃，這紅燒肉煨得好。”方淮安下箸，並給同桌的每個女人都來上一塊油汪汪的五花肉，藉以轉移注意力，好避開一場可能的風暴。

我看見俄羅斯女郎把紅燒肉撿出來放在空盤子上，也是，每100克的肥肉熱量約807千卡，而一個身材中等的成年女性每天只需2100千卡的熱量，也就是說吃一塊肥肉已經佔據一整天所需熱量的1/3，那不得在跑步機上待兩個小時才能消耗完畢？

然而寶兒不在乎，沒一會兒工夫便把五分瘦的肥肉給消滅殆盡。

“好！就喜歡好胃口的女孩，來，再給妳一塊。”方淮安果然又夾了塊紅燒肉到寶兒碗裏。

“太幸福了，從小到大，除了爺爺沒人這麼待我，今天看到方老闆就像看到自己的親爺爺，將來若有機會，我必承歡膝下，讓您享受久違的家庭溫暖。”

一句話又燃起二太太的怒火，她批評寶兒不會說話，什麼“久違的家庭溫暖”，說得好像這個家沒溫暖似的……

“得了，得了，跟個孩子計較什麼？”那老人又充當和事佬。

“你總是這樣，自己當好人，讓我扮黑臉，得，眼不見爲淨，我讓你和這些鶯鶯燕燕逍遙快活去。”

二太太很生氣地走了，讓俄羅斯金絲雀一臉茫然，不知究竟發生了什麼？

“吃，給你們每人再來一隻燒鵝腿。”男主人似乎又找到轉移注意力的藉口。

～

也許因爲來客人的關係，方淮安沒像昨天一樣用過午膳要我“陪睡”，事實上我不知他身在何處，這恰好給我一個說教的機會。

“妳剛剛的言行很不恰當，難怪二太太會生氣。”我說。

“嘴巴是我的，我才不管她生不生氣。”

真是任性得可以，我遂端出學姐的架勢，指責她這個，批評她那個。

“奇怪了，老頭子都沒說我什麼，旁邊的人倒說上話，我走就是，沒什麼大不了。”

她果真揚長而去，讓我很錯愕。

“寶兒是怎麼了？她一向唯唯諾諾，很少紅臉，尤其對我……”我心想。

～

日子匆匆過了三天，用過午餐我回到房內，正想著該不該給寶兒打個電話，那天不歡而散後，心裏挺掛念她的。

就在此時，敲門聲響起。完了，又是方老闆，我真的成了名副其實的“陪睡”丫鬟了。

然而門開後，外面站的卻是女傭Alodia，她說方太想見我。

真是討厭！說了不會腳底按摩還硬要我去，這不是爲難人嗎？

我心裏犯嘀咕，但没把氣發在不相干的人身上，只是告訴傳話者，兩分鐘後自己會上三樓……

只見Alodia慌忙擺手，她要我別上三樓，方太在二樓等我，然後手指著東翼的方向。

說來很不可思議，來方家近一個禮拜，我還未去過東翼。好吧！我承認由於好奇心的驅使，我曾"不小心"彎到那裏去。但入口處的中式木雕門緊閉，我推了兩下没推開，倒是從狹窄的門縫裏看到裏面有個柚木雕花長台、壁爐（裝飾用的）以及古董座鐘，牆上還有幾盞復古燈。

"多做尼？"一個女人走過來問我。

"没……没什麼，看看。"

問話的人是廚房幫工佩玖，年紀比我大上一輪，體型壯碩。

她嘴巴唸唸叨叨，說的潮州話我没全聽懂，只能胡亂猜，大概是要我別亂走動，省得惹麻煩。

我還未反應過來，她已拉開木雕門進入（真是的，我怎麼就只知道往裏推，不知往外拉？）。

由於自己是新進人員，加上佩玖的"警告"，我認爲多一事不如少一事，所以不再踏足東翼，没想到今日二太太約我在那裏見，正好趁此機會一窺究竟。

" All right, I will be there in a minute."我對Alodia説。

～

這一次我不再像隻菜鳥，很輕易便拉開木雕門，這才注意到裏面像座博物館，好似在中式老宅內硬擺進歐式風格的古董家俱，成了一種異樣的租界文化風情，讓人彷彿跌進時空隧道，穿越到那個動蕩不安的年代。

東翼和南翼相比，這裏顯然有低調的奢華，

上到二樓，幾支老式燈管散發出溫潤柔和的昏黃，照亮著飽經滄桑卻依然華美的舊物。不僅如此，頭頂的兩根橫樑上還有線條優美的古畫，地上鋪的則是實打實的柚木地板，一縷縷的陽光正從仿舊的直櫺窗照射進來……

"這讀照仔。"又是佩玖，她從其中一間房走出來，手裏拿著空托盤，告訴我正是這間。

"夏夏嘞。"我向她道謝，用的是我剛學會的潮汕話其中一句。

一進房我就怔住，在場者除了二太太之外，還有一個年紀雖大卻風韻猶存的女人。

"這是大太太。"二太太介紹。

"大太太好。"我畢恭畢敬地喊了聲，感覺自己像個剛進門的妾。

"好，坐。"那個手拿佛珠的女人說。

我在空了的椅子上坐下。

"其實方先生也想過來，我說最好不要，讓我們女人講講私房話。"大太太語氣平淡地又說。

私房話？我和兩個老女人能有什麼私房話好講？然而話到嘴邊卻成了："是的，女人說話，男人在場總是不便。"

我看見大太太緊接著對二太太點了個頭，後者馬上起身離開。

"二太太去哪裏？"我問。

"她去取個東西，馬上回來，妳先吃東西，這綠豆糕不錯，是在東興糕餅店買的。"說完，她夾了塊糕點到我的盤子裏。

由於不知她們的葫蘆裏賣什麼藥，我食不知味，只希望快快結束這場談話，好讓我回到安逸的小房間。

第四十二章/機密合同

"崔小姐，聽說妳老公是醫生，結婚多久了？"大太太問。

我答快一年了。

"也算新婚，年輕夫妻分開來住不妥當吧？"

"我……不算年輕，老公還比我大很多，他是二婚。"

"應該沒有孩子吧？否則妳也走不開。"

我無奈稱是。

大太太沈默一會兒後說他們方家也是，本來打算就這樣了，有沒有孩子命中注定，勉強不來，但自從知道方先生的心思後，她和二太太決定滿足方先生想要子嗣的願望……

我不太明白大太太的意思，這是要我幫找代孕者？我是護士，可不是仲介呀！

大太太說我誤會了，不是要我去找，而是希望由我擔任這個承先啓後的重責大任。不瞞我說，前幾個人選也是護士（因爲方先生有制服情結，尤其喜歡白衣天使），可惜她們不是受不了苦就是體質太差，還有獅子大開口的，簽完合同又要求加價，搞得烏煙瘴氣，要不是二太太説新來的這個看起來挺靠譜的，她幾乎就要放棄了。

"可……可是我是有夫之婦呀！"我太驚訝了。

"妳不也想擺脫這個婚姻？只要擺脫了就好，不是嗎？當然，簽合同前我們得確認妳的身體適合懷孕而且不會撼動這個家的穩定性，妳知道的，方先生已經有兩個老婆，再來一個就太擠了。"

我嚇得目瞪口呆，大太太竟然以爲我會對"三太太"的寶座感興趣，還有，我可不是生育機器，要生當然得跟所愛的人……

大太太反問我難不成想跟鄭醫生生孩子？

"不，當然不，我是説也許……也許以後我會遇到對的人。"我弱弱地答。

此時二太太推門進來，手裏拿著一個牛皮紙袋，她問我們是否談完了？

"崔小姐對這個提議不感興趣。"大太太説。

"那好，不勉強，"她收起牛皮紙袋，"妳現在可以收拾東西回家，12個月的薪水過幾天就會到賬，我們方家不小氣，所以也希望妳守口如瓶，別對外亂説。"

就因爲我不願當代孕媽媽就炒我魷魚？這也太狠了吧？

"我是方先生雇來的，只有他能辭退我。"我義正辭嚴地説。

二太太輕蔑一笑："他現在就在妳房裏睡午覺，妳可以走過去問他，如果答案有異，我趴在地上學狗叫。"

不，不可能的，當初説好他幫我解決燙手山芋，我則陪伴他一年，怎麼現在臨時變卦？

二太太説這還得怪我，没事把個小姐妹叫來，現在老爺子整天想著寶兒……

寶兒？No way，說什麼我也不信她會扯我後腿。

"二妹快別這麼說話，崔小姐恐怕要和朋友決裂了。"大太太轉向我，"妳的朋友未必挖妳牆腳，只是代孕這件事一波三折，我們希望快點兒定下來，加上方先生不反感寶兒小姐，所以妳若不願意，我們得執行B計劃。"

事情來得太快，我一時拿不定主意,說自己需要想一想。

"妳當然可以考慮，"二太太將牛皮紙袋遞過來，"這是合同，如果兩天之內還下不了決定請銷毀，我們會聯繫寶兒小姐做替補。"

我沒有回房（此時面對方淮安讓我難受），而是約寶兒下班後在醫院附近的酒吧見面。

趁著等人的空檔，我把合同拿出來瀏覽一遍，法律條文向來艱澀難懂，但我還是很快梳理好重點：

1、方家保證鄭之龍不再騷擾我。

2、生完孩子與方家再無瓜葛，不得以任何名義回來探望孩子或索要財物。

3、贈美國豪宅一棟，市價不低於八百萬美元，另給現金五十萬新幣。

4、對外不得洩露有關方家的任何信息。

當然，合同的成立還得基於我無遺傳性疾病及生理上的不育。

闔上合同，我嘆了口氣，這條件好得不能再好，何況我只是代孕，與方淮安沒有真槍實戰，說到底只是出租子宮九個月罷了。

要不要簽合同呢？我陷入兩難。

我已經喝得兩眼無法聚焦才等來穿藍色制服的寶兒，她的臉色緋紅，的確比我可人。

"渴死我了，"她將我的白開水一飲而盡，"待會兒還得加班，護士長讓我先吃飯去，我跑步過來的。"

"加……加什麼鳥班？眼看就要飛……飛上枝頭變鳳凰，有大把……大把的鈔票花……花不完。"說完，我喚服務員再開一瓶烈酒，順便給不喝酒的客人來一杯鮮榨果汁。

"虧妳還記得我對酒過敏，我以為妳不care我了。"

"什……什麼時候我……我不care妳了？"

"就剛剛，明明知道我是窮人還挖苦我，還有，妳總是需要我時才利用一下，不需要就棄之如敝履。沒錯，我是沒妳聰明也沒妳好運氣，但who knows，也許下一秒我就時來運轉了。"

沒料到寶兒是這麼想的，虧我還對她掏心掏肺。

"妳……妳就從來沒利用過我？也不想……想考試用的參考書還是我……我的，還有，若不是因為我……的緣故，妳能搭……搭上方淮安？別……做夢了！"

"搭上方淮安？什麼意思？"

看寶兒一臉無辜，難道我錯看她了？

"沒什麼，算……算我說錯話，自……自罰一杯。"我把服務員送來的威士忌斟滿，然後一飲而盡。

“這是幹嘛？”她把酒吧提供的花生堅果往我的方向挪，“還不快吃點兒下酒菜，空腹喝酒最傷身。”

“寶兒，”我醉眼朦朧地抓住她的手，“告訴我，我們……我們最終不會反目成仇，視對方爲不……不共戴天的敵人。”

“説什麼傻話？我們不過是小吵小鬧而已，怎麼可能反目成仇？看來妳真醉了，讓我護送妳回家。”

我嘴巴答不用，但身體軟綿綿的，要不是寶兒攙扶我，我一步都邁不開。

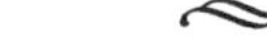

ALODIA 來敲我房門時，我才知道已經到了吃早飯的時候。

“ I don't feel well. Could you tell Mr. and Mrs. Fang I won't eat breakfast?”我以身體不適爲藉口，避開會有的尷尬。

然而如願躺回床上後卻再也睡不著，二太太給我的期限是兩天，我得盡快下決定才是……

這一想才憶起那個牛皮紙袋，昨晚寶兒送我回來，有否落下那個重要東西？

我趕緊跳起，可惜把整個房間全翻遍還是没找到。

“喂！妳有没有看到我的牛皮紙袋？”我一通電話打給寶兒。

“有，昨晚到了方家，一個皮膚黝黑的外國女人扶妳進去，關上大門後我才發現妳的東西在我包裏。”

“那好，我馬上過來取，半小時後見。”

“可……可是今天我換包包了，妳的東西現在在我家。”

Shit.這豈不是得等到太陽下山？萬一寶兒今晚又加班了呢？

“快，打個電話給房東，説我會上門取東西。”

“幹嘛這麼心急？幾張破紙而已。”

“妳……妳看了？”我嚇得幾乎拿不穩手機。

寶兒答沒看，牛皮紙袋扁扁的，要真有東西，也只是幾張紙頭罷了。

“没錯，就只是幾張紙，朋友交給我保管，我怕弄丢了不好交代。”

“既然這樣，中午我回家一趟，剛好昨晚打包的滷水鴨還剩大半隻，我們可以一同消滅它。”

“好。”

掛上電話，我走向浴室梳洗。

第四十三章/代孕媽媽

這個月寶兒上早班，中午用餐時間估計在11:30～13:00之間，那麼12點之前抵達她家即可。

在得到二太太的允許後，我徒步走向地鐵站。寶兒住在中峇魯市場附近的舊式組屋內，租的是三居室其中一間，房東是新加坡人，有個還在讀高中的兒子。

我以爲來開門的會是房東，沒想到卻是寶兒，身上的粉色制服讓人眼前一亮。

"妳……通過考試了？"我難掩興奮之情。

"嗯！今天一早公佈的，下個禮拜起生效。"她扯了扯身上的衣服，"護士長讓我把制服拿回家試穿，她說尺寸不合可以換。"

"好看，好看，很合身，恭喜妳了。"我上前給她一個擁抱。

"謝謝！"她答，然後輕輕推開我。

雖然我和寶兒都是保守的中國人，很會克制情感，但以我倆的交情，我不認爲寶兒會拒絕我。

“今晨我的喉嚨有點兒發癢，怕是感冒了。”她隨後解釋。

原來她還是那個善解人意的寶兒。

“多喝點兒熱檸檬水會好些，家裏有嗎？”

“有，待會兒泡。”她轉身把客廳沙發上的報紙移開，“坐，房東出去了，我把滷水鴨熱一熱，再煮個蛋花湯就可以吃了。”

我體貼地表示滷水鴨可以留著晚上吃，中午我請吃牛排，慶祝她當上助理護士……

“没什麼好慶祝的，工作還是一樣的忙與累，薪水是多了，但只夠買兩管叫得出名字的口紅，所以……還是省省吧！”她冷默地答。

這真是一頓冷得可以掐出水來的午餐，我問一句，寶兒答一句，我若不問，她便不答，屋子靜得連牆上掛鐘的滴答聲都能聽得一清二楚。

我很客氣地吃了一根鴨腿，喝了小半碗湯，然後起身：“我得趕著回去幫雇主測血糖，謝謝妳的午餐。”

直到走到門口，我才被寶兒喚住：“妳忘了妳的牛皮紙袋。”

“噢！謝謝，差點兒忘了。”我接過東西。

“是哪個朋友把牛皮紙袋交給妳保管？”她問。

“哪個朋友？……噢！新近認識的，説了妳也不清楚。”

“看來妳的朋友就要發了，八百萬美元的豪宅外加五十萬新幣，忍耐九個月就能換取後半輩子的高枕無憂，真是可喜可賀！”寶兒答。

回到房內，我把牛皮紙袋往桌上一扔，再把高跟鞋一踢，然後趴在床上像條死魚。

寶兒知道了，雖然合同上只寫著甲方是方淮安，乙方欄空白著，但明眼人一看就知道，偏偏我沒勇氣承認，只是打哈哈糊弄過去，把已經混亂的局面搞得更加複雜。

"怎麼辦？寶兒會不會向外說去？合同有保密條款，萬一鬧得滿城風雨，方家會不會不履行承諾？還有，若被鄭之龍知道我當了代孕媽媽，肯定又是一場腥風血雨……"我就這麼天馬行空地胡思亂想，直到敲門聲響起。

" Yes?"我開門，門外站著雙胞胎姐妹花。

" #@&$¥€………"

我沒聽懂，Pardon 了兩次。

" Bye!"兩姐妹齊說，然後走下樓去。

最後一句我是聽懂了，但她們去哪裏？回俄羅斯嗎？

晚餐桌上只有三人，但照樣有吃不完的菜餚。

"俄羅斯貓終於走了，謝天謝地，打從她們搬進來就有一股去不掉的狐騷味。"二太太說。

"吃，今天的菜做得好，牛腩煮出味道來了。"方淮安說。

"你總是這樣，一跟你談正經事就轉話題。"二太太不滿。

"好，那麼我們就談正經事，妳跟寶兒說讓她搬進來了沒？"

話一說完，一股低氣壓四處遊走。

" 說……說了，我讓崔小姐代為傳話，今天中午她們踫面了。"

二太太的回馬槍打在我身上，方淮安遂將目光投向我，我吞吞吞吐吐地表示寶兒剛通過考試當上助理護士，目前不想有變動，搬家的事還是緩緩再説。

"哎！自從那天……我滿腦子想的都是她，這麼可愛的女孩真恨不得24小時都能見到。"我的雇主無限感慨地答。

用完餐，方家夫婦到客廳看電視，我背著男主人杵在走廊不走，二太太只好起身向我走來。

"我幫妳腳底按摩，三樓見。"我壓低聲音説並且先行一步。

等二太太一進房間，我劈頭蓋臉地質問什麼時候她讓我傳話給寶兒？

"這不是重點，妳難道看不出自己失寵了嗎？方先生現在喜歡的是寶兒。"

"不可能，從喜歡到不喜歡總有個過程，哪能説翻臉就翻臉？"

二太太聽完大笑兩聲，説我還活在象牙塔裏，從喜歡到不喜歡當然有個過程，所以我還能待在這裏乾領薪水，但人終究要面對現實，現實就是我即將被取代……

"我決定當代孕媽媽。"我截斷她的話。

"真的？"

"嗯。"

"那麼明天先上姚醫生那裏做個檢查，確認沒有遺傳性疾病及不育後，我們再來簽字。"

除了點頭同意，我別無他法。離去前我問若簽了合同鄭之龍依舊不放過我，這如何是好？

"放心，他有把柄在我們手上，肯定會爽快放人，這點妳無庸置疑。"

～

走出房門，剛好和二太太的美甲師擦身而過，我心想畫個指甲不得要個把鐘頭？遂走向客廳。

此時的方准安正背對著我看新聞頻道，原來樟宜機場調高機場稅了。

"妳要一直站在那裏嗎？"他問。

我藉機走上前，並且佯裝對新聞感興趣："我不知道機場稅提高了。"

"何止機場稅，個人所得稅也提高了。"他答。

"聽說俄羅斯姐妹替方家工作，她們也納稅嗎？"我把一直以來的疑問以"納不納稅"做掩護提問。

沒想到方先生因此臉色潮紅，講話也前言不搭後語，一會兒說她們是方家的客人，再一會兒又說給了她們不菲的工資......

"她們是做什麼的？"我又問。

"瑜......瑜伽老師，噢！不，舞蹈......舞蹈老師。"

我問方先生學什麼舞？吉魯巴還是恰恰？

"我......我只看不跳。"

結合俄羅斯姐妹花的火辣身材、曾經聽過的曖昧音樂，再加上眼前男人不安的神情，我靈光乍現，原來她們是脫衣舞娘，夜夜對著老頭兒寬衣解帶。

"舞......舞蹈老師走了，您難不難過？"我問。

"有點兒，但很快又會有新老師來。"

"新老師該不會是寶兒吧？她可不會跳舞，而論護士資歷，我高過她，您也不需要兩名護士，不是嗎？"

方准安答寶兒會不會跳舞不重要，只要陪他聊天，讓他開心就行。

“二太太說我失寵了，您現在喜歡的是寶兒。”我豁出去了，就想知道他的真實想法。

“哪裏的話？我喜歡她也喜歡妳，只要是美女，我通通喜歡。”

原來兩位太太揣摩了上意又假傳聖旨，方淮安壓根兒沒讓我走，這讓我大鬆一口氣，再想到過去幾天的焦慮，我不假思索地告起狀來。

“太不像話了，把我說得好像是見異思遷、不守信用之人。放心，即使不做代孕媽媽，妳仍然能留下。”

有了雇主的保證，我安心不少，但……經過深思熟慮後，我還是決定接下這個承先啓後的工作，畢竟報酬很可觀，加上事成之後能換個地方重新開始也挺不錯的。

我把想法告訴方淮安，他很高興，說我一定會是個合格母親。

“不，母親是大太太和二太太，我只是出借子宮而已。”

方淮安一臉茫然，他說我不僅出借子宮還是孩子生物學上的母親，因爲大太太和二太太都已經停經了……

我倒吸一口氣，怎……怎麼没人告訴我這些？不，這交易絕對不能做，我不賣自己的孩子！

“妳上哪兒去？”方淮安在我背後喊。

“找二太太喝茶去！”我答。

第四十四章/原罪

今天美甲師給二太太做的是當下流行的法式甲，也就是在指甲前端畫出有如微笑般的圓弧形，底色是珠光質地，上面貼了幾顆水鑽，看起來很俏皮。

"二太太，我有重要事跟妳談。"

"說。"

我看了一眼美甲師，二太太馬上心領神會。

"章師傅，麻煩妳到門外稍等一下，我談個事兒，很快的，不會耽誤妳賺錢。"

美甲師遂起身，看起來不太愉快，走過我身邊還瞪了我一眼。

"人走了，有什麼事快說吧！"

"方……老闆說我除了出借子宮，還得提供卵子，這樣一來意義就不一樣了。"

"什麼意義？反正是人工受孕，又不是真槍實戰，如果卵子用他人的，還得費好一番功夫，對方也不知是龍是鳳，亂七八糟的我們可不要。"

"如果真用我的卵子，孩子無疑有我的一半，到時要割捨就不容易了。方家有的是錢，找個有顏有學識的女人提供卵子不是難事。"

二太太答是不難，我就是他們要找的人選，既提供卵子也孕育胚胎，唯有知道懷的是親骨肉才會上心，否則上東南亞隨便找個代孕媽媽易如反掌，費用還不到一輛小車的價格，他們何苦花大錢？

"但……"

"妳該不會以爲方家的錢好賺吧？既然我們能提供優厚的條件，相對的要求自然也會多。"

我不能說二太太錯，方家的確待我不薄，何況我是已婚婦女，不年輕，比我聰明貌美的大有人在……

見我沈默，二太太使出殺手鐧："如果不願意就算了，據我所知，妳的婚姻毫無質量可言，想讓我們替妳擺脫家暴老公不是難事，但非必要誰也不願把麻煩往身上攬，不是嗎？我再給妳一天的時間，如果仍三心二意，這件事就做罷，我們會另找適合的人選，譬如……寶兒小姐。"

"我……知道了，明天給妳答覆。"

躺在床上，我一會兒覺得爲了大局著想，這點兒犧牲不算什麼，況且孩子將成爲方氏企業的繼承人，前途一片光明；一會兒又覺得生他就得養他，怎能棄孩子於不顧？這會遭天打雷劈……

就這麼一夜輾轉反側，我失眠到天亮。

"崔小姐怎麼了？精神不太好的樣子。"早餐桌上，方淮安問起。

“她昨晚没睡好，一夜失眠。”二太太代答。

方老闆很好奇，問自己的二老婆怎麼知道？莫非有千里眼。

“没千里眼，倒有讀心術。”

他們兩夫妻一問一答，把我當隱形人。

“不好意思，我實在没胃口，你們慢用。”我起身，轉頭對二太太，“我出去走走，晚餐前會回來。”

直到離開方宅，我才算真正鬆了口氣。

想找個人說說話，顯然此時此刻寶兒不是適當人選，於是……

我跟汪致遠約了一起吃午飯，他現在在婦産科實習，忙得不可開交，所以我把吃飯地點選在離REQ不到五百米的咖啡館裏，一來人少可以避人耳目，二來簡餐上菜快，吃完他能馬上回醫院報到。

没想到原以爲會遲到的人卻比約定時間早到十分鐘，讓我很驚喜。

“真準時。”服務員走後，我調侃。

“有三床孕婦的陰道口開了四指，主治醫生要我趕緊吃飯去，否則得午晚餐一並解決。”

我笑說醫生都是鐵打的身體，而且還得練就絕食的功夫。

“不止醫生，護士不也一樣？真搞不懂爲什麼大部份的孩子都選在半夜出生，而且一窩蜂趕著同一時間，彷彿上帝就要關上大門似的。有一次忙不過來，我跟某位孕婦說忍住，別讓孩子出來，結果被罵得狗血淋頭。”

"哈哈！當然得罵，生產的痛可以達到十級，没經歷過的人不會知道。"

"説得好像妳經歷過似的，對了，談談妳的近況，在方家過得可好？"

"你……都知道了？"

他答當然，我走的那天流言四起，想將耳朵堵住根本不可能。

哎！這樣也好，不用話説從頭。

"那麼我簡單回答你的提問，方家答應幫我擺脱鄭之龍，而且給我美國豪宅一棟，外加五十萬新幣。

"什麼條件？"他問。

"條件……條件就是提供卵子和子宮，替方家完成傳宗接代的使命。"

話一説完，汪致遠將身子往後一靠，眼睛眨也不眨地盯住我："妳没答應吧？"

"我……不知道，還在考慮……"

"考慮個屁！這還要考慮？當然是拒絕。"他抓住我的手，"媛媛，妳到底有没有心？"

我甩開他的手，説我當然有心，否則不會快滅頂了還拼命探出頭來呼吸，他不是我，自然體會不到我的不易。

"妳不是我，妳也體會不到我的心痛，看妳一再沈淪，我真想抛開一切帶妳遠走高飛。"

"你……你……什麼意思？"

"我……就是那個意思。"

"Excuse me, chicken?"服務員適時送餐過來，我舉一下手，她把雞肉套餐放在我面前。

"Then beef must be for you."服務員接著把牛肉套餐放在汪醫生的桌上，"Enjoy your meal."

我們尷尷尬尬地用著餐，刀叉蹠撞的聲音聽起來很刺耳。

"我吃完了，"我用餐巾擦拭一下嘴巴，"你慢用，我先走一步。"

"等等，我還沒吃完呢！一個人吃飯很寂寞。"

我只好待在原位。

不知爲什麼，這頓飯汪致遠吃得特別慢，一小塊肉可以咀嚼半天，彷彿那是塊橡皮，嚼不動。

"妳喜歡方老闆？"他終於開口問。

"說不上喜不喜歡，他和公園裏做晨運的老人沒兩樣。"

"這樣也能上床？妳不覺得噁心？"

我說他誤會了，方老闆身體不行，要孩子只能靠人工，還好他把精子冷凍起來了。

"即使那樣，妳也是孩子的生母，方家打算把妳擺在什麼位置？"

"什麼位置也沒有，生完孩子直接送出國，從此一刀兩斷。"

汪致遠放下刀叉，神情非常嚴肅地說這件事得從長計議。

"來不及了，今晚我得回覆，如果say no, 我仍能留在方家，他們則另外找……找人。"

"這不挺好的？"他問。

我答他不懂，事情沒那麼簡單，如果我不入地獄，有人……有人會入地獄。

"什麼意思？有人？誰呀！"

" 我胡亂説的，你別往心裏去。Anyway，今天我得上姚醫生那裏一趟，如果檢查出我不育，情況又是另一種局面。"

没錯，我擔心的事不止此，結婚近一年，在没有任何防護措施下，我的小腹依舊平坦，老公説是我的錯，我没全信，但也不排除這個可能性。如果我真是隻不會下蛋的母雞，那麼連簽合同的資格都没有，一切又回到原點。

姚醫生原來也在我工作的公立醫院任職，我和他曾有數面之緣，後來他離開醫院開私人診所，算一算我們已經有兩年未見，還好他不知道我後來結婚了，否則恐怕要瞠目結舌。

" 妳 …… 真 的 是 妳 ， 我 還 以 爲 同 名 同 姓 。 " 姚 醫 生 依舊被嚇到。

" 是的，是我。" 我羞愧地承認，" 我是方家送來的第幾個？"

" 呃……記不清了，反正有好幾個。"

" 那我們……開始吧！"

第四十五章/人工授精

說我對汪致遠的表白無動於衷是騙人的。

回方宅的路上我一直說服自己別自作多情，雖然內心深處我渴望愛情，那種讓人捧在手心的感覺很美妙，但……這不包括"憐憫"及"移情作用"。

汪致遠曾說過他的母親也是家暴受害者，極可能他把對母親的愛轉移到我身上，說白了就是"戀母情結"在做祟。

"一定是這樣的，否則無法解釋他會對深陷泥沼的我感興趣。"想到此，我五味雜陳，不，畸戀必須扼止在搖籃裏。

爲了掐斷這一點點的可能性，回到方家後我直搗黃龍上到三樓，還好方家夫婦都在。

"我準備好簽字了。"我說。

"姚醫生還沒給回覆呢！"二太太說。

我告訴她今天下午我才從姚醫生診所出來，基本排除不育，至於基因檢測……今晚出結果。

"那麼等結果出來再說吧！"

“好的。”

我正要走，被方老闆叫住，他問我寶兒今年多大了？

“二十初頭。”

“屬什麼的？”

“不清楚。”

看我一臉狐疑，二太太索性開誠佈公，原來算命先生説老爺子今年犯沖，只有屬豬的人可以化解。

哈！都什麼世紀了，還相信江湖術士的胡言亂語，簡直太迷信了！

二太太答不迷信，算命的還説方家會一舉得男，孩子的母親屬龍，這也是他們看上我的原因之一。

“怎麼知道我屬龍？”我問。

“想知道總有辦法。”她答。

這可不妙，我在方家面前簡直赤條條，毫無隱私可言。

“那麼我相信你們很快會查出寶兒的屬相和喜好，包括她一天吃幾頓飯，刷不刷牙。”

大概我的口氣不太好，方淮安開口了：“没錯，我們是對妳的身家做了些調查，畢竟讓一個素昧平生的人進門有風險性。寶兒的生辰不難查，我只是一時興起問妳，別介意。”

“没事，我太小題大做了，請原諒。”老闆都開口了，總得給人台階下。

關上房門，我還能聽到二太太不滿的聲音：“真以爲自己得道升天了？有骨氣就別簽字！”

~

九點剛過，二太太差人讓我去她房裏，想必姚醫生給了滿意的答覆，她直接遞上合同，我沒有囉嗦，很快簽名蓋上手印。

"姚醫生説妳的卵泡發育正常，不需要藥物刺激，記得排卵日前三天到他那裏報到。"二太太叮囑。

我是註冊護士，知道人工授精的最佳時機分別在排卵日前72小時、24小時以及排卵後24小時。我的月經周期向來固定，下一次的排卵日應該在十天後，也就是説再過一個禮拜，我將接受第一次授精，這讓我感到害怕與惶恐。

啊！這個決定會不會是錯的？如果是，我該怎麼辦？

我躲汪致遠好幾天，來電不接、短信不回，没想到躲躲藏藏還是被逮個正著。

"你怎麼知道我會來這裏？"我問。

"姓姚的婦產科醫生不多，這個不難打聽。"

"厲害，你該轉行當偵探，Excuse me."

我想走，但汪致遠不讓，他説我一旦踏入診所，這輩子就注定活在自責與後悔當中。

"我知道自己正在做傻事，但我別無選擇。"

"怎麼會別無選擇？妳還有我呀！讓我們共同努力，一定可以挽回劣勢。"

想到他的"戀母情結"以及"移情作用"，我瞬間狠下心來斬斷情絲。

"聽著，我不相信你會帶我脱離苦海，何況我不喜歡你，甚至感到討厭，請你從此遠離我的生活圈，別再來煩我！"

"妳真這麼想？"

"我真這麼想。"

"那好，不打擾妳了，再見！"

看他遠去，我忽然有股衝動想喚住他，但張嘴卻發不了聲，只能眼睜睜看他越行越遠……

"妳是對的，讓他自由，妳也能得到解脫。"即使自我安慰，我仍心情鬱鬱，感覺錯過了什麼。

當方淮安的精子進入我體內，我感覺一切都完了，從此不再有春天。

"妳得躺2～3小時，以防精子流出。"姚醫生説。

我忽然憶起那個離去的背影。

"不，"我跳起，"我不做了，我後悔了。"

"妳去哪兒？"姚醫生喊。

"去找回愛情。"我頭也不回地答。

我跑了整整大半個新加坡才來到REQ，時間剛好過了飯點。

他在哪裏？對，婦産科，我得上五樓。

然而没等我抵達五樓，護理員黃鶯叫住我："媛媛學姐，妳怎麼來了？好久不見。"

"是……是好久不見，妳好嗎？"

"好，妳來找寶兒嗎？她和汪醫生在一起。"

我問是哪個汪醫生？

"汪致遠醫生呀！告訴妳，寶兒拼命想抓住他，一有空就往他那裏跑，也難怪，汪醫生是很多未婚護士心目中的男神，她若不趕緊拿下，恐怕夜長夢多。”

“汪醫生是很優秀。”我喃喃道。

“呵呵！還好媛媛學姐結婚了，不然寶兒又多出個競爭者。”

我要她別開玩笑，我和汪致遠只是……只是普通朋友。

“說的也是，如果連已婚者也回過頭來跟我們搶男人，這世界就亂套了。”

我意氣消沈地離開REQ，黃鶯說的沒錯，我結過婚，有什麼資格跟未婚者搶資源？何況汪致遠是如此優秀，他值得更好的。

“喂，姚醫生嗎？今天……很抱歉，請原諒我的任性，明天我準時上診所做第二次人工授精。”

放下手機，我伸手招來出租車，道出地址後，我疲憊地閉上雙眼。

第四十六章/MISS ZHOU

兩天後我没赴約，而是等到排卵了才去，不是我爽約，而是姚醫生臨時有事推遲了。

做完人工授精，我很配合地躺在床上不讓精液流出。

"兩個禮拜後回來測血HCG，看是否妊娠。"離去前，姚醫生對我說。

"如果没有呢？"我問。

"那麼就得等到下次排卵日再做。"

雖然注射的導管很細，姚醫生的動作也很輕柔，但整個過程並不令人愉悅，畢竟讓自己的私密處示人是件尷尬的事，即使對方是醫生。

"記住，少運動，飲食輕淡點兒，別胡思亂想。"他又加上幾句。

他怎麼知道我會胡思亂想？

"你肯定認爲我是個壞女人，爲了錢，什麼都能做。"我說。

"放心，我没那麼死板，道德只是華麗的外衣，只要不觸犯法律，我樂得自掃門前雪。"他推了推厚重的眼鏡框説。

姚醫生不知我已婚，背著老公和別人生孩子已經觸法，當然，我不會蠢得不打自招。

~

也許剛做完"不道德"的事，離開診所後，我竟然想起老公，不知他近況如何？

説來奇怪，剛開始到方家，鄭之龍時不時打電話問進展，又説家裏没女人很不便，連口熱飯都吃不上等等。在我曉以大義又建議他可以雇鐘點工之後，慢慢的電話少了，最近這兩天更是一點兒消息也無，不免讓我起疑，他……該不會生病了吧？

~

站在老公的私人診所外已有好一會兒，期間只見一名病患進出，用"門前冷落車馬稀"來形容再合適不過。雖然開業之初總有個低潮期，但我以爲像鄭之龍那樣的名醫無庸擔心，病患肯定會接踵而至，没想到少了大醫院當靠山，一樣得慢慢累積口碑……

"媛媛，真的是妳。"

聽到熟悉的聲音，我嚇得寒毛直立。

"我……我給你送水來。"

瓶裝水是來時路上我在便利店買的，已經喝了大半瓶，没想到老公絲毫不介意，一口氣喝光。

"渴死我了，銀行連杯水也没請我喝。"

"銀行？"

“我剛從銀行回來，妳來了正好，我有要緊事跟妳談。”

我以爲他會帶我進診所，沒想到是在附近找了家情調很好的咖啡館，他還鼓勵我點甜品吃。

“不了，一杯摩卡就夠。”

鄭之龍没囉嗦，點了一樣的。

“最近好嗎？挺想妳的。”服務員走後，他説。

我望了他一眼，不確定他是否來真的？

“還行，不好不壞。”我心存戒備地答。

他緊接著問我那件事進行得如何？有沒有希望？

我答老先生很精明，估計還要一段時日。

“得加緊了，銀行在催……”

“八字還没一撇的事你又貸款了？真不怕死！”

老公説他指的不是藥廠投資案，而是當初買辦公樓當診所貸了款，現在利息調高了，加上最近手頭有點兒緊，已經晚了十多天没交……

“診所生意看起來是不太好，但你手中多少有存款，問題應該不大。”

“存款……存款早没了，因爲……因爲前陣子上聖淘沙，所以……”

好呀！我一不在家又和Lucy聯繫上，真是色心難改。

“這回是幫Lucy買了鞋還是買了包？你替別的女人買單可真不手軟！”

“不是她，而是……家裏空蕩蕩的，我很寂寞，説到底也得怪妳！”

鄭之龍有把過錯推到我身上的"習慣"，早見怪不怪。

"隨便你怎麽説，反正繳不了款，上黑名單的人是你。"

"不止我，妳忘了當初的貸款是聯名貸。"

糟糕！怎麽忘了此事？我問他欠下多少？

"連同這個月得還款八萬多，還有，雲頂賭場也在催……"

"雲頂賭場？"我揚起聲，"你竟然跑去賭博？"

"我是被忽悠去的，仲介説我可以用她的信用額度玩兩把，後面的事簡直像惡魔上身，我控制不住自己。"

我打了個寒顫，問他"總共"欠下多少？他弱弱地答一白多萬新幣，其中十萬是成爲頂級玩家的費用。

太不可思議了，平常那麽摳的人，賭起來卻一擲千金，豪氣得很。

"抱歉，我幫不了你，我的薪水多少你很清楚。"

他忽然像即將滅頂的人，緊緊抓住我的手不放，要我一定得幫他，否則……否則他的照片就會出現在討債公司的頁面上，對他的個人名譽造成不可計量的損失。

"怎麽幫？"我冷冷地問。

"用信用卡還款最快，多申請幾張，我保證等錢一到位就能將窟窿填上。"他答。

如果我們夫妻的感情好，我兩肋插刀在所不辭，偏偏這個家風雨飄搖，我怎可能再深陷其中？

"不行，我的薪水不高，申請不到足夠的額度。"

"不試試怎麽知道行不行？走，現在就去。"老公拉著我起身。

～

在百得利路上，如果不是我喊肚子疼藉機逃跑，估計老公會帶我走遍新加坡的大小銀行，然而跑得了和尚跑不了廟，當晚鄭之龍就上門要人，我嚇得躲在房間裏，連大氣也不敢吭一聲，最後還是由二太太出面把人勸退。

鄭之龍走後，有人主動敲我房門。

"我跟妳老公説了，明天妳會回家一趟。"二太太説。

"什麼？我這一去還有回來的可能嗎？我們是簽過合同的，事情不該如此。"我急得跳腳。

"放心，都説好了，鄭醫生同意先分居，妳回去是簽離婚協議。"她進一步解釋，"新加坡有結婚不到三年不得離婚的規定，妳該不會不知道吧？！"

没想到那麼容易就解決長久以來的夢魘，感覺很不真實。

二太太笑説這可不容易呀！光説服鄭醫生上賭場就花了不少功夫，最後還用上美人計。

我一時怔住，這是怎麼回事？

經我詢問才得知方家雇了個漂亮的賭場仲介去引誘鄭之龍，没想到他是隻鐵公雞，去了幾次都是"小賭怡情"，爲了讓他"大賭傷身"還真的費了好大一番功夫。

"可是……那時我還没答應簽合同，也有可能我的身體不行，你們怎麼……"

"還不是方先生心腸軟，看到妳被欺負就急著想當護花使者，説到底是武俠小説看太多，把自己當成行俠仗義的俠客。"

事到如今，真不知該説什麼好，雖然早知道老公把錢看得很重，可是怎麼也没料到一百多萬新幣就能收服他，看來錢真是個好東西。

"謝謝！我會遵守約定，不讓你們失望。"

"最好如此，方先生想當大俠是方先生的事，但我不是慈善家，付出當然求回報，"她在我耳邊低語，"如果妳忘恩負義，我絕對有辦法治妳，好比……Miss Zhou。"

第四十七章/珠胎暗結

周小姐原是REQ體檢部的護士，後來被方淮安看上帶回方宅，最新消息是她到美國"留學"了，費用由原雇主承擔，這顯然是你情我願、皆大歡喜的事，怎麼到二太太嘴裏就成了恐怖事件？

然而我沒有"剝絲抽繭"很久，因為自己的麻煩事已太多，譬如明天簽離婚協議能否順利？老公會不會臨時變卦？這才是我需要煩惱的事。

約的是中午12點，連口飯也不讓吃，真是的。

沒想到一進門就被身繫圍裙的老公給嚇住，他不僅為我遞拖鞋、送茶水，還熱情地請我入座。看到桌上似曾相識的印尼炒飯、蝦片、沙爹牛肉（和我第一次上他家吃飯的菜色一模一樣），我的心喀噔了一下，這不像要談離婚，倒像是快樂大和解。

"我以為我是來簽離婚協議書的。"我冷冷地説。

“是要簽，但人總得吃飯不是嗎？來，快嚐嚐我的炒飯，加了好多葡萄乾，補血。”

我心有疑慮，但還是拿起叉子吃了幾口，他的炒飯一如既往的美味。

“好吃嗎？”他問。

“嗯！”

“我今天没上班，特地爲妳做的，妳喜歡就好。”然後他把他的荷包蛋也給了我。

這下子我完全没胃口了，鄭之龍肯定有所求。

“我吃飽了，”我站起身，“你慢用。”

“怎麼才吃兩口就飽了，是不是身體不舒服？”

我答是的，簽完協議，我想回家躺躺。

“那麼妳上樓眯一會兒，我不吵妳。”

鄭之龍竟然以爲我口中的“家”是這個家，真是滑稽至極！

“不，這裏已經不是我的家。你到底簽不簽？不簽我走了。”

我以爲我已經説得足夠清楚，偏偏老公的思路與常人不同。

“媛媛，做戲到此爲止吧！我感激妳替我行苦肉計，否則方家也不會出手相救。這樣吧！妳回去撒個謊，就説協議簽了，等錢一到賬，妳就搬回家，藥廠投資案我看算了，本來希望就不大。”

原來他以爲我以受難者的姿態博取方家同情，目的是爲解他的燃眉之急，實在把我想得太偉大了。

“方老先生看起來像傻子嗎？但凡事業做得這麼大的人，肯定不能隨便忽悠，你的小伎倆很快會被識破。”

“大不了還錢，過了這關，我會努力賺錢，很快就能還上。”

"不，不是這樣的，我不是行苦肉計，而是真心想離開你，請你……請你放過我，求你了。"

話一說完，一個巴掌搧過來，我立即眼冒金星。

"方家給妳施了什麼法術？我們一向過得好好的，要吃有吃，要喝有喝，我還給妳大房子住，妳還有什麼不滿意？"

我摀住臉說不滿意的地方多了去，有哪家老公會動不動打老婆？即使是條狗，也不能這麼打。

"說對了，我不打狗，因爲狗不會違背主人的意願，不像妳！"

"得，看來今天的協議是簽不了，我走了。"

鄭之龍立馬堵在門口，咬牙切齒地說："我就看妳今天出不出得了這個門！"

疼痛每幾分鐘就找上我，我想伸伸腿，無奈腳踝被膠帶綁在椅腿上動彈不得，再這麼下去，我會因血液循環不暢而導致腿部動脈硬化。

"我得上班去，妳乖乖待在家，想喊叫請隨意。"他說。

主臥室做過隔音工程，即使我喊破喉嚨也無人能聽見。

"有沒有想過方家會向你要人？"我問。

"要什麼人？妳是我明媒正娶的妻子。"

我聽了爲之心寒："好，就算不理會方家，雲頂賭場的賭債怎麼辦？你對付得了那幫凶神惡煞？"

鄭之龍一怔："這倒是個問題，嗯……我找他們老闆商量，也許能緩緩，妳不用擔心。"

擔心？我當然擔心，難道從此又要過上永無寧日的生活？

鄭之龍寧願負擔債務也不願放我走，這讓我感到憂心忡忡。

夜晚降臨，是吃晚飯的時間，方家人是否察覺有異？有沒有出動找人？還是從此將我遺忘？

我又等了許久，才等來明顯遲歸的老公，他逆光站著，我看不清楚他的臉。

"快！幫我解開，憋了半天尿了。"我說。

他走過來解開我身上的繩索和膠帶，我一自由，馬上飛奔至廁所，再回到房間時，他已不知去向。

下樓後，我發現鄭之龍坐在客廳裏，報紙擋住他的臉。

"我……回去了。"

"等等，簽了協議書再走。"

他放下報紙，我看到一張腫脹的臉，紅的紅，紫的紫。

"嘖嘖嘖！打架了？"我問。

"正確地說是被打了，没想到那幫人來真的。妳也算是找到好靠山，方家的車正在屋外等，簽完字馬上走，把門帶上。"

我把桌上一式兩份的協議書拿起來瀏覽一遍，没有贍養費，也不能帶走一屋一瓦，十足的不平等條約，但我不在乎，爽快地簽字。

"我……不會再回來，你……多保重。"我的離別情懷正在作祟。

"哼！像妳這種不要臉的女人，在我屋裏多待一分鐘都嫌髒，別再給我看鱷魚的眼淚，妳就安心當老頭子的禁臠，我咀咒你們這對奸夫淫婦不得好死！"

這是怎麼回事？我想進一步細問，但那個憤怒的男人大手一揮，像揮走一隻骯髒的蒼蠅。

我没囉嗦，拿起那份得來不易的協議書離去。

雖然知道解救我的人必定是大權在手的二太太，但我没料到她的動作如此之快，簡直是雷厲風行！

"跟我鬥？早著呢！"二太太輕蔑地説。

我要求還原事件始末，她答不過是付了點兒錢，没想到鄭醫生這麼不禁打，没兩下就投降了。

不，一定還有什麼，否則他不會如此決絕。

二太太說我果然冰雪聰明，所謂打蛇打七寸，鄭醫生聽聞自己的老婆答應替方淮安生孩子，並且已做了人工授精後，強烈表明不要不潔的女人，看來這次是鐵了心不要我了……

我忽然想起債務問題，如果這個没解決，鄭之龍在走頭無路的情況下依舊會回過頭來咬住我。

"妳放心，一碼歸一碼，我們方家是講信用的，債務問題肯定會解決。"二太太拿出手絹擦拭鼻頭上的油光，"妳也看到了，我們爲了妳的事操碎了心，可別做白眼狼啊！"

"一定，"我頷首，"非常感謝！"

"不用謝，保護生育機器是我的職責所在。"她似笑非笑地答。

二太太譏笑我是"生育機器"，但我不在意，如果孕育的過程有感情，那才是不道德的，我樂得當無感的機器。

這一天，我來到姚醫生診所做血測，它是通過測量女性血液中的HCG值來判斷是否懷孕，相比傳統的尿檢更加準確，誤差也小。

"中了嗎？"我問，心裏很忐忑。

"妳的血HCG已達到400IU/L。"姚醫生的目光離開測試紙，嚴肅地對我説。

"這麽説是懷上了？"我喃喃自語。

姚醫生没説"恭喜"，反倒問我想不想生？

這個問題已經在我腦海裏翻滾過無數回，如果不生，欠下的人情債如何還？如果生，肚裏的孩子畢竟是我的骨血，我害怕到時無法割捨。

姚醫生點頭表示理解，他説一般代孕媽媽不提供卵子，就是怕到時候做不到全然的放棄，方家的作法實在令人費解……

"哎！事已至此，多説無用，只能走一步算一步了。"我無奈地答。

第四十八章／大悲咒

對於我的成功懷孕，方家上下喜慶一片，我被簇擁著來到東翼，原來東翼三樓不僅有個佛堂還有方家列祖列宗的牌位。

"媛媛，快跟方家祖宗磕個頭，他們會保佑孩子順順利利地生下來。"大太太説。

我順從地跪下，磕頭完畢，方淮安、大太太、二太太也跪下，只見他們各拿著三柱香膜拜，嘴巴唸唸有詞，説的是潮汕話，加上音量小，我一句也没聽懂。

上完香，我們一起到一樓起居室喝茶，由於我是孕婦，要了玫瑰花茶，説是富含維生素Ｃ，可促進鐵質吸收，預防貧血。

"來，這個給妳，"二太太夾了一塊橙色的扁平物到我盤裏，"這蕉柑是著名的潮汕特產，能潤肺、降火氣，妳現在是一人吃兩人補，吃得下就多吃，可別盡想減肥的事，把寶寶餓著了。"

"二妹快別這麼説，萬一過胖就不好生了，"大太太面向我，

“放心，妳跟我一起住東翼，我會盯著妳吃，肯定營養均衡。”

“我跟大太太住？爲什麼呀！”我太驚訝了。

此時一直喜上眉梢卻保持沈默的方先生開口了：“大太太長年吃齋唸佛，會把福分帶給妳，況且在宗教氛圍濃厚的環境裏養胎，有助情緒的平穩。”

聽他這麼一説，我没異義，反正九個月轉眼就過了，我比較關心的是大太太吃素，這是否意味著我也只能吃草？

大太太笑了，她要我不用擔心，餐會分開來煮，餓不著我。

這大概是今天唯一的好消息吧？！我不禁鬆了口氣。

“東翼有五個房間，都在二樓，大太太佔一間，其他四間妳可任選，選好後告訴我，我讓家裏的傭人把妳的行李搬過去。”二太太説。

我的行李不多，就幾本書外加幾件換洗衣服，一個人拿也行，但衆人紛紛搖頭，他們説孕婦最忌拿重物，要我安心當甩手掌櫃。

“好的。”我接受他們的好意。

四間房大同小異，我選擇了書房。

“書房的床小，妳確定要這一間？”大太太問。

我點頭。

書房的床是輕搭紗缦的單人古典床架，小是小了點兒，但一個人睡足矣。

“那好，以後妳就住這間，有什麼事叫我一聲，我聽得見。”大太太説。

也許有人會認爲我傻，幹嘛不挑大點兒的房間？但只有自己心裏清楚，我是撿到寶了。

整棟豪宅裏最能體現平和、典雅的地方大概就屬這間書房了，瞧！書架上有成排成列的書籍，在幽暗的燈光下閃著神秘之光；寬大的書桌上不僅有文房四寶，還有象徵幸運的法國木鞋型書擋；書桌左側是一個酸枝木大衣櫃，既有簡約的英格蘭風格線條，又有中式雕花與立柱，妥妥的中西合璧。

再看格子窗外，幾株桂花樹正迎風搖擺，濃郁的花香瞬間沁人心脾，帶來芬芳的氣息。

想到自己每天都能在書香及花香中醒來，這是多麼愜意的事！我高興極了。

然而生活總有辦法潑你冷水，下一秒大太太便要我每天用毛筆抄寫《大悲咒》及唸誦咒文至少五遍。

"爲什麼？"

"抄寫及唸誦《大悲咒》能今生免惡死，來世得善生，所以爲了自己及肚裏的寶寶，妳一定得堅持下來。"她答。

我嘴巴應允著但心裏很抗拒。

～

大太太一向在自己的房間用餐，爲了我，屈尊降貴到一樓餐廳吃。

"其實我可以自己吃，您不用陪我。"我説。

"没事，一個人吃飯多可憐，我陪妳吃，順便講講話也挺有意思的。"她答。

然後我驚奇地發現桌上除了兩碗素菜、一碗湯是大太太的之外，其餘都是我的。

"這麼多，怎麼吃得完？"我皺著眉頭。

"妳不用全吃完，但每樣多少吃一些，營養均衡最重要。"

於是我吃了老醋黃瓜拌木耳、豬肝菠菜、蝦米芹菜、清炒西蘭花、黃豆排骨湯，又在大太太的督促下喝了半碗的八寶燕麥粥。

"每天下午佩玖會送燕窩或花膠給妳食用，都是些好東西，能補氣血，記得一定得吃啊！"大太太叮囑。

我能感覺自己就是一具生育機器，爲了得到好的製品，不得不張大嘴吃進各種據稱有營養的東西。如果我懷的不是方家的種，壓根兒就沒人會關心我有沒有吃、吃了什麼。

"對了，妳的《大悲咒》寫了嗎？現在背給我聽。"

"寫了嗎……嗯……會寫的……背……很長的……背不了……"

然後大太太開始唸：南無、喝囉怛那、哆囉夜耶，南無、阿唎耶，婆盧羯帝、爍鉢囉耶，菩提薩埵婆耶，摩訶薩埵婆耶，摩訶、迦盧尼迦耶……

我沒想到大太太來真的，原以爲只是口頭說說而已。

"好的，我盡量。"我低下頭去。

"不是盡量，晚餐時把功課交給我。"她說。

記憶中磨墨寫字還是小學時期會幹的事，沒想到二十年後我又重新拿起筆來，人生啊！永遠不知下一秒會是什麼。

《大悲咒》全文84句，共415個字，如果只是拿圓珠筆隨便寫寫，最多也就十幾分鐘的事，偏偏大太太要我使用毛筆，很是折騰人。

我將窗戶打開，讓空氣流通，再注水磨墨，然後在攤好的宣紙上寫下第一個字。寫著寫著，我紊亂的心慢慢靜了下來，一豎一橫一點一捺也不再無聊乏味，反而有作畫的樂趣，難怪有人説中國字本身就是個藝術品。

"扣、扣、"

"請進。"我説。

佩玖端來一個托盤，上面有冰糖燕窩、紅棗糕及各色水果拼盤。

"謝謝！"我的目光重新回到案上。

那個虎背熊腰走過來一探，説我寫得好，不像周小姐，她的字醜。

我一驚，差點兒握不住筆桿。

"周小姐也寫過《大悲咒》？"我問。

佩玖答是，書房原來沒有床，爲了周小姐，不得不把檔案櫃移到儲藏室，這才勉強空出一塊地來。

"這麽説周小姐也懷上了？後來呢？流産了？"

"不清楚，有一天周小姐忽然就不見了，連衣服也没帶走。"

我放下毛筆走向衣櫃，打開後問："這是她的衣服嗎？"

"惜啲，剹拐，紮墨灰晃栽嘚麗？"她一副不解的表情。

得到肯定的答案後，我心裏發毛，走得再匆忙也不可能不帶走隨身衣物，除非她還想著有朝一日歸來。

晚餐一樣很豐盛，而大太太依舊是兩菜一湯，連飯也只是小半碗。

飯後我把"功課"交上，她讚美我的字美。

"和周小姐比，誰寫得好？"我問。

"她……你們的字各有各的美，難分軒轾。"

"周小姐爲什麼没有妊娠成功？"

大太太答可能跟個人體質有關，她看我很健康，這次應該没問題，不用擔心。

"她人呢？在美國？爲什麼没帶走隨身衣物？"

"隨身衣物？妳大概看走眼了，我們方家没有她的東西，即使有也全部銷毁，因爲她不可能再回來了。"

"可是我明明……"

大太太截斷我的話，她要我默背《大悲咒》給她聽。

"嗯……南無、南無喝囉怛……怛那、哆囉……哆囉　南無、阿唎……阿俐……摩诃薩………薩……"

"崔小姐，看來妳没背好，我認爲妳應該回房把功課做好，妳認爲呢？"

大太太很默然地上樓去，留我一人面對一桌的剩菜剩飯發起愁來。

第四十九章／偶遇汪致遠

我就這麼發呆了好一會兒，直到佩玖過來收碗盤。

"佩玖，今天下午妳的確看到周小姐的衣服在我房裏，對吧？"我問。

"惜啲。"她點頭。

還好我沒出現幻覺，那麼就是大太太沒搞清楚狀況囉！嗯……這也不無可能，畢竟周小姐跟我一樣只是個過客，不是方家重要的人。

謝過佩玖後，我起身回房做功課，《大悲咒》像道符咒綁住我手腳，一天沒背好，一天不得安寧。

我把準備高考的衝勁拿出來，不過415個字，小菜一碟，然而真正實行起來卻有難度，由於不了解字義，加上句子又拗口，著實花了我好一番功夫，還好上床前我已勉強能背出，想到明天大太太滿意的表情，不禁沾沾自喜。

當我打算換上睡衣就寢時，衣櫃裏周小姐的衣服又落入眼底。以前不知道那些小一號的衣服是誰的，礙於禮貌一直沒跡，今天佩玖證實衣服是周小姐的，而大太太也明確表示那人不會再回來，這勾起我的好奇心。

我把衣服一件件拿出來，都是些質量很好的短衫、短裙和短褲，色彩多爲萍果綠，加上衣服上的淡香水味道，我很快在腦海裏勾勒出一名青春洋溢的活力女孩。

眼看吊掛的衣服全無可疑之處，我把它們通通歸位，至於抽屜裏的內衣褲……我匆匆瞄了一眼便闔上，誰會對別人的貼身衣物感興趣？我又沒有戀內衣癖。

取出自己的睡衣後，我關上衣櫃的門。

"早！"我坐了下來。

"怎麼了？一副無精打采的樣子。"大太太問。

昨晚爲了背《大悲咒》，我灌下一整壺的黑咖啡，背是硬背下來了，後遺症則是換來整晚的輾轉反側及頻尿，可説是得不償失。

"昨晚沒睡好，老做惡夢，夢裏有個穿綠衣的女人向我招手，手裏還抱著個啼哭的娃兒。"

我以爲自己開了個不大不小的玩笑，誰知大太太當真了，她的臉瞬間慘白，像被抽乾了血液。

"大太太，您怎麼了？"我問。

"没什麼，吃粥！冷了不好吃。"説完，她低頭認真吃食起來。

與其他地方不同，潮汕人一日三餐都能吃到粥，粥水是他們的主食。

我喜歡粥品，但不喜歡潮汕人吃粥配的鹹雜，還好現在桌上沒有這些鹽漬物，而是一般的熱炒，大概考慮到我是孕婦的關係吧？！

今晨我的胃口很好，吃了不少，反觀大太太，一塊豆腐乳兼涼拌菠菜都沒吃完。

飯後我問她要不要聽我背《大悲咒》？

"待會兒吧！"她起身，"我不太舒服，先回房躺躺。"

說要回房躺躺的人，我卻發現她上三樓佛堂唸經去了，木魚敲擊的聲音很規律，像首梵樂，但稍嫌急促些。

～

《大悲咒》抄到一半，佩玖就來敲我房門，她說大太太要她陪我上植物園走走。

"不用了，我待在這裏很好。"我答。

"奏搭，歹台台拐不搞橫。"

知道大太太可能會發火，我不想挑戰她的底線，遂收好文房四寶，隨佩玖出門去。

都說孕婦需要經常走動，生產時才好生，但在大太陽底下步行又是另外一回事，簡直就是酷刑。

"佩玖，幫我買瓶冷飲。"我很快躲到樹蔭底下大喘氣。

她答大太太沒給錢，我只好自掏腰包讓她買兩瓶，一瓶給她。

沒多久她捧來兩杯涼茶，雖然我挺不喜歡藥草味，但口乾舌燥下，我呼嚕呼嚕地一口氣全喝光。

"了哈。"佩玖把手中喝到一半的涼茶遞給我，大概以爲我的肚裏仍有一盆火。

“不用，我不渴了，我們還是回去吧！”

佩玖搖頭，她說做法事沒那麼快。

法事？什麼法事？我想起早上自己胡謅過的話，難不成就爲了那個穿綠衣的女人？這也太搞笑了吧？

“我沒看過做法事，趕緊走，也許還趕得上。”我興致勃勃地說

然而佩玖依舊搖頭，她說大太太曾耳提面命做完法事才能回家，因爲怕做法事的過程中傷到孕婦及肚裏的孩子。

哎！真是自做自受，難道今日要整天曝曬在陽光下？

見我意氣消沈，佩玖建議我去看場電影，聽說剛上映的《阿凡達》挺不錯的。

“好，聽妳的。”

從電影院出來，夜幕已拉開，我滿腦子都是納美族人的怪異臉孔，真害怕會影響我肚裏孩子的長相。

“可以回去了吧？”我問。

還沒等來佩玖的回答，一個男人向我走來，我緊張地說不出話來。

“他惜雖？”佩玖問我來者是誰？

我答一個……朋友，並要她先行離開。

佩玖很爲難，她說大太太會不高興。

“那我不管，我是代孕媽媽，不是犯人，依然有人身自由。”我不客氣地答。

待人走遠，這次換汪致遠問我：“她是誰？”

“方家廚工。”

“她很擔心妳的樣子。”

“當然，因爲我是孕婦。”

談到尷尬的話題，我們彼此都沈默下來。

“妳……寶兒好嗎？”還是他先開口。

寶兒好嗎？怎麼問起我來？我已經十天半個月沒見到她了。

汪醫生喃喃自語怎麼會？同在一個屋檐下……

我問什麼意思？原來兩天前寶兒離開REQ，成了方家的又一名私人護士。

不對，方家曾要我探探寶兒的意願，被我找了個藉口回絕，以致她完全不知道方老闆曾投來橄欖枝。

“無緣無故，怎麼就……”

“因爲……她向我表白，被我給拒絕了，後來她向醫院辭職，聽說去了方家。”他答。

“爲什麼拒絕？”

“妳難道不知道？”

這叫我如何回答？與其攀高枝被看輕，倒不如先灑脫地說不。

“我……配不上你，你有更好的選擇，何況……何況我已經懷上別人的孩子。”

“妳別模糊焦點，行嗎？告訴我，妳對我有感覺，像我對妳一樣。”

“我……沒有……有……但……”

“什麼都別說，”他的手指輕觸我嘴唇，“我已經得到我要的答案。”

∾

我渾渾噩噩地回到方家，一路上沈浸在戀愛的甜蜜中。

"妳回來了。"大太太站在二樓樓梯口問。

"嗯！"

"到我房裏。"她命令。

真倒霉！一回家就被逮到背《大悲咒》。

"好。"我無奈地答。

第五十章/第一次產檢

"南無、喝囉怛那、哆囉夜耶，南無、阿唎耶，婆盧羯帝、爍鉢囉耶，菩提薩埵婆耶，摩诃薩埵婆耶，摩迦......摩......摩尼......迦........耶......耶......"

"崔小姐，看來妳沒背好。"大太太直言。

我像個沒做好功課的小學生，羞愧地低頭認錯並且承諾馬上回房背《大悲咒》。

"等等，那人是誰？"

"誰？"我一頭霧水。

"今天在電影院遇到的男人。"

沒想到佩玖是個大嘴巴，一回方家就說嘴。

"他......他是我以前的同事，踫巧遇見，所以談了會兒話。"我解釋。

"聊天能聊三個多小時，恐怕不是普通朋友。"

"什……什麼意思？難道我沒有見朋友的權利？"我喉嚨發乾地質問。

大太太要我別誤會，我當然有見朋友的權利，只要對方不是男的……

這又是什麼意思？我請她明說，猜來猜去很累人。

"那好，我就開門見山地說，Miss Zhou 在懷孕期間遇到真愛，没知會一聲便把胎給打了，事後毫無愧疚還不斷索取，威脅不給錢就對外報料，帶給方家不小的麻煩。"她答。

原來還有這段插曲，我趕緊給大太太吃定心丸，請她放心，我答應過的事一定辦到，不捅簍子。

"看得出妳是個實在的人，但很多情勢不是自己控制得了，譬如……愛上一個人。"

我感覺大太太若不是有火眼金睛，就是有讀心術，我的那點兒小心思在她面前無所遁形。

"就算愛上一個人，我也不會打胎，畢竟這是條生命。"我答。

"好，我相信妳，妳可以回房去，我也得做晚課了。"

回房後，我看見牆上貼了許多鬼畫符，搞得我人心惶惶，再發現周小姐的衣服全不翼而飛，我不淡定了，難道他們認定我夢中的女人是周小姐？都說只有冤死的人才會有怨氣，這麼說……她死了？

想至此，我嚇得不輕。

"南無、喝囉怛那、哆囉夜耶，南無、阿唎耶，婆盧羯帝、爍鉢囉耶，菩提薩埵婆耶，摩訶薩埵婆耶，摩訶、迦盧尼迦耶……"

慌亂中，我竟唸起《大悲咒》，希望能如大太太所言：今生免惡死，來世得善生。

隔天吃完早餐，一個年輕女孩過來敲我房門，我認出是打掃東翼衛生的馬來人Stella，她說二太太找我。

"I know. Thanks."

關上房門後，我往南翼走去。

"坐，身體好嗎？三餐吃不吃得下？"她問。

我答懷孕初期尚好，目前沒有不適。

"睡眠呢？"她又問。

"還可以，如果不做惡夢的話。"

"聽大太太說昨天已經請人洗過了，應該沒問題，如果還是睡不好，那就再洗一遍。"

我趕緊阻止，表示昨晚一覺到天亮，不需要洗了。

"那就好……對了，那人是誰？"

"誰？"

"昨天在電影院遇到的人。"

沒想到佩玖不僅告訴大太太，連二太太也說了，真是個特大嘴巴！

"他是我以前的同事汪醫生，踫巧遇見就聊了會兒天。"我答。

二太太和大太太的想法一樣，她說能聊三個多小時的人恐怕不是普通朋友。如果話至此，我還不致於發怒，但她接下來暗指我是白眼狼，吃在嘴裏看在碗裏，養人不如養狗……

誰能吞下這口氣？

“沒錯，汪醫生不是普通朋友，是男朋友，怎麼了？”我反擊。

“那麼我只好將妳禁足以絕後患。”

“開什麼玩笑？我就不信方家會囚禁我，”我起身，“我現在就去找我男朋友！”

我下樓，經過中式古典風格的客廳，打開實木大門，走過長長的走廊，彎過池塘、花園及茶亭，眼看雕花大鐵門在望，我忽然慢下腳步，難道今天真要去找汪致遠？這不在我的計劃內呀！

“ Miss Cui, please stay.”我看見方家的警衛向我走來，“ Show me your permission.”

然後我才知道二太太剛下令沒有她的批准，我一步也不能離開方宅。

我不信，硬闖，那個人高馬大的警衛竟開始跟我玩影子遊戲，我向左，他向左；我向右，他也向右，完全不讓我有機會鑽空子。

完了，真把我囚禁起來，以後還有好日子過嗎？

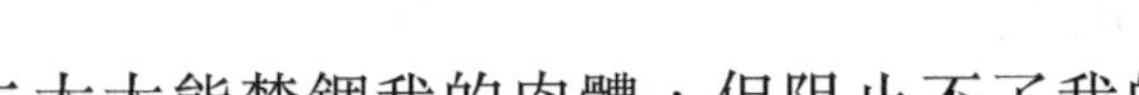

二太太能禁錮我的肉體，但阻止不了我的心，還好手機沒被沒收，我告訴汪致遠我被禁足了。

“不管怎樣，妳需要產檢，我讓姚醫生打個電話。”他說。

“你讓姚醫生打電話？你們……認識？”

“別多問，見面詳談。”

果然隔天吃過午餐，大太太便轉告我下午四點到姚醫生那裏做產檢，佩玖會跟我一起去。

想到那人的大嘴巴，若再度見到汪致遠豈不鬧得雞飛狗跳？

不行，絕不能讓她跟去。

"我不需要人陪，自己去就行。"我説。

"那不好，産檢很重要，我們也想知道寶寶健不健康。"

我藉口佩玖在廚房做事，身上的油煙味讓我作嘔，懷孕已經不易，不想再雪上加霜。

"哎！看來只能由我陪妳去囉！"大太太説。

"不，不麻煩，寶……寶兒可以陪我去。"我靈光一閃。

"想必妳也知道寶兒搬進來了，那好，妳確定要她陪？"

我用力點頭，然而事情比我想像的要複雜多了。

我讓Stella去喚寶兒過來，等了近一個小時，她才姍姍來遲，哈欠聲連連。

"天亮才睡下，現在正睏著，"她環顧四周，"這就是妳睡覺的地方？我還以爲豪門孕婦再怎麼著也有個五十平米的大房間，看來妳在方家的地位不高呀！"

没有比被閨蜜取笑更難受的了，別人可以看輕我，她不可以，我一向待她如手足……

寶兒輕蔑一笑，問我何時正眼瞧過她？還不是把她當丫鬟使喚，連當代孕媽媽這麼大的事也瞞她，更別説爲了得到方淮安的專寵而阻止她進豪門，説穿了就是"防火防盜防閨蜜"，噁心透了！

我能感覺自己的臉頰發燙，那是一種被揭開面紗的難堪。

"聽著，我能理解妳的不高興，但事出必有因，合同有保密條款，我不能違約。還有，方家是個大泥沼，我不願妳也深陷其中。"

“免了吧！爲了攀高枝，甩掉自己老公的人會是什麼好貨色？我怎麼没早看穿妳？”

我没想到寶兒對我的誤會及恨意如此之深，只好揭穿鄭之龍家暴的事實。

“哈……哈哈哈……連鄭醫生那麼好的人也被妳形容得如此不堪，嘖嘖嘖！妳的內心到底有多黑暗？”

聽她這麼一説，我徹底放棄了。

“行，妳請回吧！我另外找人陪我產檢。”

“請神容易送神難，反正我已經被吵醒，看看妳的產檢報告也無妨。”她答。

知道寶兒和汪醫生的過往，我發了條短信，請他回避。

第一次產檢不外基礎檢查及建卡，趁著等報告之際，姚醫生以幫做問卷調查的名義支開寶兒。她一走，汪致遠就進來，滿面春風。

“中彩票了？瞧你高興的樣子。”我説。

“是高興呀！因爲看到妳和……寶寶。”

我很納悶，他會對方准安的孩子感興趣？

汪致遠以“孩子都是天使”的模棱兩可答案帶過。

“看樣子你認識姚醫生，什麼時候的事？”我問。

他答兩人在一個醫學座談會上認識，因爲都喜歡籃球員科比，感覺很投緣。

“難怪他會幫你把我約出來，你付給他多少好處費？”

“談錢傷感情，我們是互助互利的合作關係。”

"合作？合作什麼？"

他忽然變得神秘，不僅左顧右盼還拉我至診室的最角落，壓低聲音說："媛媛，答應我，無論聽到什麼都心平氣和不發火，好嗎？"

我點點頭，心裏七上八下。

第五十一章/行走的火藥庫

"那天妳說討厭我，讓我遠離妳的生活圈，我因此難過了一整天，隔天硬拉姚醫生出來喝酒，順便問起妳的情況。他答妳不配合，做完授精就跑掉了，還說去找回愛情，讓我感覺又有了希望。"

"那是……"我想說些什麼，被他阻止。

"就在妳原定做第二次授精的那一天，我被姚醫生叫出去，才得知他有了大麻煩。由於前幾次的授精沒有成功，方淮安儲存的冷凍精子只剩一管，他格外小心，沒想到在解凍的過程中，管子因不明原因爆裂，少數存活的精子根本不夠量，做也是白做，他正愁不知該如何向方家交待。"

我想起姚醫生那日的確爽約，改成排卵後再做。

"可是後來我明明做了第二次授精……"

此時汪致遠的表情豐富透了："那是……那是我的精子啊！"

我驚訝地摀住嘴，這消息來得太突然也太震撼，我竟然和他有了結晶，還是在完全不知情的情況下……

"媛媛，這是最好的結局，不是嗎？"他問。

"不，不是的，第一次授精時我雖不配合，但精子畢竟導入了，所以寶寶還是有可能是方淮安的。"

汪致遠説這也是他必須得到我同意的原因，他希望我能在妊娠滿8週時通過陰道穿刺取絨毛的方式進行DNA檢測，屆時就知父親是誰。

"我……我……你……你……爲什麼？"

"還問爲什麼？妳和別人生孩子讓我嫉妒，這是上天給予我們最好的機會。"

啊！我何德何能得到一位優秀男子的眷顧與愛情？

"如果……如果檢查結果顯示孩子不是你的，又該如何？"我問。

他答如果真是那樣，他希望我終止妊娠離開方家，世界這麼大，總有我們的棲息地。

我頓時陷入兩難，出爾反爾不是我的作風，還有，萬一孩子是汪致遠的，難道把他生下來交給方家養？當中牽扯的問題太多，不是"一走了之"能解決的。

"別擔心，走一步算一步，上天自有安排。"他安慰我。

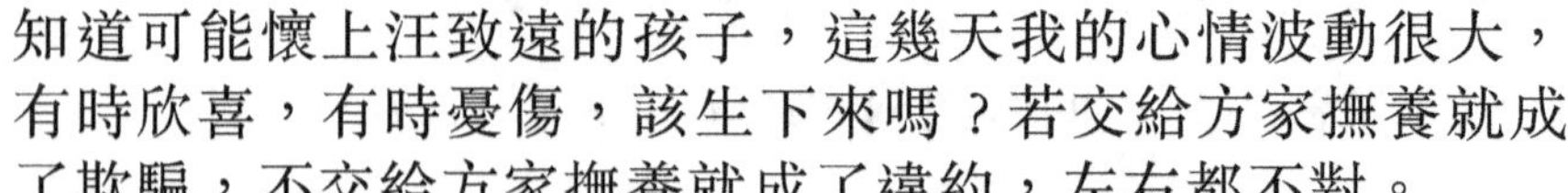

知道可能懷上汪致遠的孩子，這幾天我的心情波動很大，有時欣喜，有時憂傷，該生下來嗎？若交給方家撫養就成了欺騙，不交給方家撫養就成了違約，左右都不對。

"怎麼了？菜不合口味？"大太太關心地問。

"嗯！大概天氣熱的關係。"

佩玖過來收碗盤時，我聽到大太太吩咐她準備綠豆涼糕給我當下午茶，讓我心存感激，衆所周知，綠豆解暑。

下午四點，當我抄寫完《大悲咒》沒多久，佩玖捧來下午茶，除了綠豆涼糕外，還有一小碗的紅棗枸杞燉燕窩。

佩玖解釋本來涼糕有五片，燕窩是滿的，但都被蔡小姐給截足先登了……

蔡小姐？蔡寶兒嗎？呵！連吃的東西也跟我搶，我無語了。

"知關，撈班核歡喘資娘仔。"她説。

雖然知道佩玖喜歡搬弄是非，但這次我沒懷疑，方淮安的確喜歡寶兒，距離喜歡我也不過幾個月的差距。

見我不作聲，佩玖似乎找到新樂子，竭誠地告訴我更多內幕，譬如俄羅斯女郎走後，寶兒每晚大跳豔舞給老闆看，直到清晨才回房，二太太因此氣得頭上冒煙，好幾天都臭著一張臉，受苦的莫過於他們這些下人，全被當成出氣筒……

還有這回事？

我問那個夜夜笙歌的女人現在在哪裏？佩玖答泳池。

時間往前推一個多月，那時戲水的是金髮碧眼的雙胞胎姐妹花，寶兒則在窗口對她們的胴體品頭論足，物換星移，現在的水中美人魚變成了寶兒，身上的比基尼連我看了都面紅耳赤。

趁她從水中探出頭來，我諷刺："沒想到妳的身材這麼有料，裹在護士服裏簡直暴殄天物。"

"妳不知道的事還多著呢！要不要我一一向妳報告？"

"好呀！洗耳恭聽。"

她上岸後，從白色躺椅上取下浴巾，邊擦乾身體邊望著我笑。

"What?"我問。

"我說妳的胃口也太小了，只爲一棟房子和少量現金就出賣自己，換成我，肯定要大的。"

"呵呵！我畢竟還有要的資格，不像某人已淪爲夜場的脫衣舞娘，誰贏誰輸，不明擺著？"

我拿針刺她，就等著她發火，好曉以大義，没想到她只是冷笑一聲，然後大搖大擺地離去。

好個不受教的東西！

生氣歸生氣，冷靜過後，我發覺還是自己不對，誰會對明顯有敵意的人擺好臉色？我得來軟的才行。

主意一打定，我約寶兒明天喝下午茶，地點在我房裏。

因爲吃的是"和解飯"，我特意向廚房多要了幾份甜品，還到花園採了幾朵怒放的花，就爲了讓談話的氛圍好一些。

"怎麼吃的都是東南亞的糕點？"她用叉子戳了戳娘惹糕，"粘乎乎的，好噁心！"

我把布朗尼遞過去："吃這個，記得妳喜歡巧克力口味。"

她把東西往外一推，說她現在不喜歡了，人的口味是會變的。

"那麼喝茶，水果茶養顏美容。"

"我討厭鳳梨的味道，像屎一樣。"

知道她是故意惹我生氣，我放下身段，掏心掏肺地請求她別和我對立，這宅子裏真心的朋友不多，何苦再樹立敵人？

"妳也知道真朋友不多？早幹嘛去了？這世界就是壞人當道，好人注定要吃大虧。"

從過去的談話中，我知道寶兒對我的隱瞞很介意，又懷疑我曾阻礙她上升的管道，這些都可理解，我也解釋過了，不明白她爲什麼還是糾著不放？

"如果妳要的是一個道歉，那麼我鄭重跟妳説聲對不起，讓我們再回到從前，好嗎？"我説。

"回不去了，我現在就要這麼活，以傷人爲樂，失去多少就要拿回多少，這才解氣，才算公平！"

～

沒有得到寶兒的諒解讓我心情鬱悶，夜深了，我藉著唸誦《大悲咒》平復低落的情緒。

"嘟……嘟嘟……"是汪致遠的來電，我按下接聽鍵。

" Guess what?"

" What?"

" 我通過Post Graduate考試了，現在是合格的住院醫生。"他的聲音帶著喜氣。

爲了這場考試，汪醫生吃了不少苦，如今苦盡甘來，怎不令人雀躍？

" Congratulations! 我真爲你高興。"我説。

"我想見妳，讓我們慶祝一下。"

想到自己被二太太禁足，我猶豫了。

"別擔心，讓姚醫生再打個電話即可。"

"即使得到許可，我也無法單身赴約，方家上下都是眼線。"

"這樣啊～"他停頓了一下，"讓寶兒跟來吧！我也能藉機與她和解。"

"這樣好嗎？她現在像行走的火藥庫，我怕……"

在汪致遠的再三保證下，我最終接受他的提議。

第五十二章/我不是壞女人

我不知道寶兒住哪間，只是想當然爾地認定她必是住在我的"舊居"，然而……沒有，就在不知所措之際，我再度聽見樓上傳來的曖昧音樂，趕緊直搗三樓。

三樓的房間有好幾個，除了二太太住的那間，其他對我來說都像潘多拉的盒子，彷彿一打開就有成群的妖魔鬼怪迎面而上。

我尋著魔音來到一扇暗紅色的房門前，薩克斯風正在吹奏careless whisper，那種類似人聲的呢喃讓我的身體無端地燥熱起來。

寶兒在裏面嗎？我能想像一個曼妙的身軀正對著七旬老翁恣意搖擺……

這還是我認識的"學妹"嗎？我用力閉上雙眼，感覺難受極了。

"崔小姐。"

聽見有人喚我，我嚇得離開房門好幾步。

"幹嘛呢？"身穿銀白色晨褸的二太太問。

" 没 ， 没 幹 嘛 ， 看 看 ， 噢 ！ 不 ， 不 是 ， 我 睡 不 著 ， 到 處 走 走 。"

"睡不著喝杯熱牛奶。"

我懦懦稱是，然後慌張地走開，直到下到底層才鬆了口氣。

" 真 是 的 ， 被 抓 現 行 ， 丟 臉 死 了 ！ "我 心 想 ， 然 後 攬 頭 望向三樓。

方宅的南翼設計是中庭挑高，所以我能清楚地看見各樓層，當那身銀白色袍子緊貼著暗紅色房門時，我嚇到不行，原來"偷窺"是人的本性，不止我有。

～

大太太說姚醫生讓我再上診所一趟，約的是下午六點半。

"知道了。"我答。

" 這産檢的頻率也太高了，還有，診所不是開到六點嗎？這時候去豈不趕上休診？"大太太喃喃自語。

我解釋也許今天的病號多，沒什麼好懷疑的。再説，方家的寶寶如同晨星般珍貴，多一次檢查就少一份擔憂，可見姚醫生是個負責任的好醫生，感謝都來不及……

"我也就這麼一説，怕妳舟車勞累，妳可別放在心上。"

我笑説沒有的事，接著詢問回來的路上能不能和寶兒去吃頓飯？我們姐妹倆好久沒出外走走了。

"没問題，我跟二妹說一聲，讓她放行。"

～

"搞什麼？診所都關了，姚醫生也真是的，讓我們白跑一趟。"寶兒嘟著嘴抱怨。

之所以約六點半完全是爲了配合汪致遠的下班時間，反正謊言終究會被拆穿，我索性開誠佈公，告訴她今天沒有產檢，而是爲了慶祝汪醫生通過Post Graduate考試所撒的謊言。

"通過了？哼！算他運氣好。"她說。

然而等男主角一到場，寶兒又是不一樣的嘴臉。

"恭喜！你真厲害，我爲你高興。"

雖然寶兒臉上的微笑有一絲絲的勉強，但禮數到了，汪致遠也順勢表示感謝，同時問她想吃什麼？他請客。

"怎能讓你請？你是懸壺濟世的醫生，我巴結你都來不及。這樣吧！今晚吃法國大餐，我請客！"她豪氣地說。

位於濱海灣金沙的Waku Ghin是家米其林二星餐廳，坐擁無敵海景，讓客人在品嚐美食的同時還能欣賞新加坡無與倫比的天際線及海灣風景。

我們被帶到繭式包廂，說白了很像吃鐵板燒，座位沿著大鐵板展開，只有五把椅子，除了一對早到的白人情侶外，我們包辦剩下的三個座位。

西裝革履的服務員遞過來燙金的菜單，看到上面的數字，我倒吸一口氣，這不是普通中產階層能負擔得起的價格，我擔心寶兒的口袋。

"這家的海膽及魚子醬是特色菜，我們叫來嚐嚐吧！"她說，臉上的表情很平靜。

我們還未表示任何意見，寶兒便伸手叫來服務生，擅自點了漬牡丹蝦配海膽、蛋羹、魚子醬、帕爾瑪火腿、黑松露三明治、生蠔、意大利麵、芥末和牛等，還開了一瓶八二年的拉菲。

現在的問題已經不是一個月的工資能不能打發，而是我們三人今晚能不能走出餐廳大門，衆所周知，八二年的拉菲是很貴很貴的。

"我不能喝酒，妳也是，咱們還是把拉菲退了吧！。"我給寶兒台階下，但顯然她不領情。

"既然妳不能喝，我和汪醫生喝得了，當上正式醫生多不容易，肯定得喝好酒慶祝，是吧？"寶兒對汪致遠示好，還將身子緊挨著他，像藤蔓找到依偎的大樹。

當服務生送酒來時，汪致遠額外爲我叫了一碗熱湯，因爲我是孕婦，不能吃生海鮮，而寶兒點的食物以冷食居多，大概只有意大利麵及蛋羹能入口。

"你對媛媛真好。"她説。

寶兒一向喚我"媛媛學姐"，第一次聽她直呼我名還真有點兒不習慣。

"那當然，因爲她是孕婦。"汪致遠無畏地答。

"如果我也懷孕，你也會對我好？"

"會的，孕婦是重點保護對象嘛！"

我們邊吃可口的食物邊話家常，氣氛不錯，没有劍拔弩張。飯後甜點是精緻小蛋糕，配上英式紅茶，爲這不菲的一餐劃下完美的句號。

買單時，寶兒掏出信用卡，面不改色地在賬單上簽字。

"讓妳破費了。"汪致遠説。

"哪兒的話？我跳一場舞得到的小費就不止這個數。"

"跳舞？"汪致遠很迷惑的樣子。

我將話岔開，問現在是不是唱歌去？他們一個小王菲，一個北大陳奕迅，不唱歌太可惜了。

"好呀好呀！好久没唱歌了，今晚讓我們唱通宵。"寶兒興致勃勃地呼應。

然而唱没兩首就悲劇了，不能喝酒的寶兒此時滿臉通紅，身上像有跳蚤，抓個不停。

"早警告過妳不能喝，這下好了，長酒疹了吧？！"我氣急了。

汪致遠要我別説了，到藥房買氯雷他定吃吃就没事。

"那個藥……孕婦能吃嗎？"寶兒問。

"孕婦？"汪醫生望向我，"妳也長酒疹了？"

我否認，然後他回答寶兒的問話："孕婦不能吃抗過敏的藥，只能塗抹藥膏，但收效甚微。"

"那麼……我還是用藥膏吧！"寶兒説。

我問這是什麼意思？難道……

"我的例假一向很準，這次晚了一個禮拜，不怕一萬只怕萬一，不是嗎？"她答。

我們到24小時營業的藥店買驗孕棒，當我看到只出現一條對照線時大大地鬆了一口氣，也有餘力發火："妳是怎麼了？自棄到這種程度，方淮安大妳整整五十歲，妳知道獨自帶孩子的辛苦嗎？"

我的"關心"並没有爲自己帶來善果，寶兒冷哼一聲："別五十步笑一百步，自己又高尚到哪裏去？妳之所以生氣是因爲我差點兒影響到妳在方家的地位，而非老少配。"

面對指控，我氣得説不出話來。

汪致遠試著當和事佬，然而寶兒根本聽不進去，還說經過這麼一折騰，害她忘了買過敏藥，要我們等她一下，她馬上回來。

寶兒跑回藥店，汪致遠轉而安慰我：“她還年輕，口無遮攔，妳別往心裏去。”

“告訴我，我不是壞女人。”我執著地要一個答案。

他答我當然不是壞女人，充其量只是一時糊塗，這有本質上的差異。

“那麼跟我來。”

“去哪裏？”他問。

我没回答，逕自走進小巷裏……

第五十三章/STELLA

新加坡有兩百多萬的打工仔從事建築及其他製造業，他們遠離家鄉及妻子，加上年青力壯，生理需求十分旺盛，若不解決這方面的問題很可能造成性犯罪，所以新加坡政府特別在芽籠設立紅燈區，但因發放的牌照有限，根本不夠用，於是私設的紅燈區便如同雨後春筍般拔地而起，好比現在，站街的小姐分站兩旁，只要有獨行的男士經過，她們便一湧而上。

我們屏住呼吸前行，那些女人投射過來的眼光,已經設定我們是妓女與買春客的關係。

"媛媛，妳到底要去哪裏？"汪致遠壓低聲音問。

"開房。"我答。

∽

在床上是騙不了人的。

有愛的性能讓人更放鬆，也更願意配合；無愛的性就像玩一個玩具，玩完就扔，不會在乎妳的感受，連該有的前戲也很馬虎。

我很高興通過性，知道汪致遠很在乎我。

"我們不應該做，這樣對寶寶不好。"他說，然後在我的肩胛骨上咬一口。

"好，不做，聽你的。"我轉身背對他。

然而汪致遠心口不一，第二次做的功夫比第一次還足，他毫不吝嗇地在我乾燥龜裂的土地上灑下傾盆大雨，讓雨後開出希望之花。

～

回到方宅已近午夜，我聽見門口警衛給大太太打電話，完了，東窗事發了，然而直到上床都相安無事，讓我不禁懷疑剛才的一幕是否真實發生過？

隔天早餐桌上，大太太問我產檢的結果如何？

我擡頭觀察她的表情，像無波的平靜湖面，我不知道該不該扔塊石頭擾亂它？

"很……很好。"我答。

"那就好，昨晚見妳很晚沒回家，我還有點兒擔心，沒事就好。"

由於大太太的關心與信任，我主動告訴她離開診所後，我和寶兒去吃法國菜，飯後看新上映的《阿凡達》，納美族人的長相很奇特……

昨晚沒看電影，我把前幾天和佩玖看過的電影拿來充數。

"噢！是嗎？大概年輕人都愛看電影，我已經好幾年沒看了，連電影院在哪裏都不知道。"她說。

看來大太太對我的行蹤沒有懷疑，我大大地鬆了口氣。

因爲大太太佈下的功課，我的毛筆字越寫越好，頗有瘦金體的架勢。

“雅死。”佩玖站在我背後讚美。

“我也覺得不錯，”我轉過身去，“今天吃什麼？”

佩玖答桃膠皂角米燉銀耳及紅棗糕。

從數量看，寶兒並沒有染指我的下午茶，她……還好嗎？

被人放鴿子的滋味不好受，我決定負荊請罪。

“妳不必貓哭耗子，我不需要同情。”寶兒坐在床上，她的臉、脖子和四肢都起了大面積的不規則形紅疹，看起來挺嚇人的。

“吃藥了嗎？”我上下打量，“看起來不管用。”

她憤恨地瞪著我，要我別做戲了，汪致遠不在現場，做了也是白做。

寶兒像座活火山，不論我從哪個角度切入都能成功點燃。

“看來我是熱臉貼冷屁股，妳……好自爲之。”

我起身，還沒走到房門口，後腦勺被扔過來的枕頭擊中。

“妳和汪致遠昨晚背對我幹了什麼好事？怎麼沒個說法？”

如果寶兒能好好說話，我還不致於口不擇言，偏偏她不好好說話，我也變得不理智。

“我和他做了不可描述的事，咋地？”

“果然和我想的一樣，你們這對狗男女！”

寶兒罵得越兇，我越不買單，挑釁地問她打算告訴大太太、二太太還是方老闆？

"那樣就不好玩了，我要慢慢凌遲妳，等著瞧！"她答。

等待是場漫長的煎熬，我每天正常的起床、正常的吃飯、正常的睡覺，但內心波濤洶湧，害怕DNA檢測的結果。不論孩子是誰的，擺在眼前的道路都難行，一眨眼，也到了揭曉的日子。

因爲無法信任佩玖和寶兒，我找來什麼都不懂的Stella作陪。到了診所，我給她50新幣，讓她上附近的商場逛逛，她歡呼一聲說早想買《海賊王》的漫畫，這下子能買十本，太開心了。

要Stella陪我產檢是迫不得已的事，我知道她還未成年，與其說她保護我，倒不如說我保護她，但現在我也保護不了她，早早將她支走，因爲害怕她聽到隻言片語後回去說嘴。

我躺在床上叉開腿，讓姚醫生取陰道絨毛。

"多久出結果？"我問。

"加急的話，24小時。"

"不急，你慢慢來。"我感覺自己還没準備好，能拖就拖。

姚醫生說我不急，他可急了，如果結果是方淮安的倒好，如果不是，他就頭大了。

"既然明知有百分之五十的機率惹上麻煩，爲什麼還讓汪致遠上場？"我問。

"不瞞妳說，我被汪醫生感動了，他希望通過這個方式留住妳。"

"哎！我已是殘花敗柳之身，不值得人憐惜。"

"別妄自菲薄，愛情沒有好與不好，只有合適與不合適，好比兩塊拼圖，各自完美但拼不起來又有何用？"他答。

話說得沒錯，人生這麼長，誰能保證沒有個差池？我是走錯一步，有個已婚的烙印，但當愛情來敲門，我也有開門的權利，不是嗎？

我開始思考接受新戀情的可能性。

～

姚醫生要我回家等消息，如果是方淮安的，他答Green; 如果是汪致遠的，他答Red.

"不，不，剛好相反，如果是方淮安的答Red; 如果是汪致遠的答Green。"我急急地說。

也許潛意識裏，我希望孩子是汪致遠的，所以選擇"綠燈"，至於善後......那是以後的事。

～

我在候診室等了半小時，依舊沒等來Stella的身影，打她手機又不接，該不會回方宅了吧？真是的，我人還在這裏，她倒先回去了，小孩子就是小孩子，太不靠譜了！

懷著些許的無奈與失望，我獨自回方宅，然而一直到用過晚餐，Stella依舊杳無音訊，此時緊張的氣氛開始彌漫整個宅子，我成了第一個被詢問的人。

"我......我......今天檢查的時間比較久，我怕她無聊，所以給她50新幣逛商場，約了下午五點在診所見。"

"都這時候了，她還沒回來，可別遇上壞人，她才14歲，阿彌陀佛。"大太太雙手合十。

Stella才14歲？雖然臉上帶著稚氣，但她的身高比我高，我還以為她起碼17歲。

"若真那樣，對她家裏就不好交待了。"方老闆皺緊眉頭。

二太太想的比較實際，新加坡禁用童工，若不是看Stella家窮，人又勤快，方家是不會知法犯法，這下好了，攤上大事了。

"對……對不起，我這就去找。"

二太太忙拉住我："妳也幫幫忙，懷孕還到處亂跑，妳這是要讓我們都睡不好覺嗎？"

"可是……"

"妳就別自責了，"方淮安接口，"我看還是報警吧！一個女孩子這麼晚還在外面，怕出事。"

我們這廂急得像熱鍋上的螞蟻，Stella那廂卻無事似地走進來，看見我們都在，喊了聲："Good evening."

"Where are you going?"二太太氣急敗壞，"We worry about you so much."

Stella嚇到了，期期艾艾地表示原本想買幾本漫畫，没想到新加坡的漫畫如此昂貴，索性就待在漫畫店裏看，没想到一看就忘了時間，還因叫了東西吃，連打車的錢也沒有了，她是徒步回來的。

知道Stella安全後，二太太雖有不滿，但嘴裏唸叨幾句就讓她回房去，看來這次的風暴就這麼過去，真是萬幸！

第五十四章／東窗事發

方老闆的員工娶兒媳婦，請了廚師到家裏"辦桌"，原本今晚
要一同出席婚宴的二太太卻被YH集團的總裁夫人抓去打
牌，方淮安形單影隻，大太太希望我能接下這個任務……

"可是……我没有名份呀！"我説。

"就説是方先生的侄女吧！没人會計較這些,妳也知道參加婚
宴最好成雙，員工請老闆出席就更不能怠慢。我吃素，婚宴
上大魚大肉的，即使刻意分開來煮，也難保不會沾上葷腥，
所以還是由妳去最好，潮汕人辦起桌來很豐盛，剛好替
妳補補身子。"

我不喜歡這類的場合，建議還是由寶兒代爲出席爲宜，她年
輕有活力，比我受歡迎。

"那孩子毛毛躁躁的，出席公開場合恐怕欠妥。再有一點，
方家素來好客，來此做客無任歡迎，但若想紮根於此……這
個家就太擁擠了。"

不難聽出大太太很擔憂寶兒是衝著方家三太太的寶座而來，
也難怪，過去往來的鶯鶯燕燕都擺明了"過客"姿態，唯獨寶

兒不一樣，她的到來不是爲了生育（這個已由我代勞），那麼圖的是什麼？不免讓人懷疑其動機。

"知道了，我會盛裝出席。"我答。

我穿上紀梵希的紅色小禮服，再戴上大太太借我的珍珠耳墜及綠瑪瑙項鏈，總算有點兒貴婦的樣子，不致於失了方家的臉面，然而到了現場，我不免爲自己的慎重其事感到不值，這哪是我想像的豪宅家宴？不過是戶外臨時搭建的遮雨棚，底下擺了數十張大圓桌及塑料椅，連廚房也是就地生火，十足的克難。

相較於我的格格不入，方淮安倒挺"入鄉隨俗"的，不僅給了大紅包不說，還跟參與的人稱兄道弟，很會籠絡人心。

"妳怎麼也來了？"我問穿得比我還隆重的寶兒。

"因爲妳在這裏呀！"她笑得一臉燦爛。

在方淮安的介紹下，我和寶兒都成了他的侄女，正待字閨中……

"大伯，你真是貴人多忘事，我是未婚沒錯，但媛媛已經懷上了，不算待字閨中。"寶兒當著衆人的面，很不客氣地讓我出糗。

如果眼光能殺人，我已被無數道投過來的匕首給千刀萬剮、血肉模糊了。

"咳、咳、我是懷孕了，孩子的父親在REQ上班，人還長得好看，是很多小護士眼中的男神。"我解釋。

說完，匕首成了禮花彈，我接收到從四面八方投來的羨慕眼神，除了寶兒之外。

"REQ是私立大醫院，能當上醫生娘是幸福的事，恭喜！"婚宴主人說。

我們被安排和新郎、新娘同桌，可見方淮安身份之尊貴。與
簡陋的硬件比，廚師的廚藝好太多，呈上的都是新鮮上乘的
食材，輾壓很多大餐廳。

"吃，没什麼好招待的，都是些鄉下食物，別客氣啊！"新郎
官的母親説，喜悅之情溢於言表。

看著滿桌的菜餚，我頓時傻眼。

新加坡的海岸線長達兩百餘公里，各色海産琳瑯滿目，潮汕
食物又多取自大海，所以山珍少、海味多，瞧！潮州生醃、
海鮮炒米粉、珍珠花菜牡蠣湯、酸梅泥猛、蠔仔烙、姜蔥炒
花蛤、冰鎮黃鱔片……

"怎麼了？没胃口？"寶兒問。

"不是，我怕吃了過敏或拉肚子。"我是護士，知道孕婦最好
少吃海鮮。

"那就等著餓肚子吧！"她將滑而韌的血蚶肉連著殼和汁水一
起吸入，再"噗"地吐出殼來。

我想起從前的姐妹情誼，我們總是約著一起上食堂吃飯，寶
兒會爲遲到的我佔位及買飯，怕我吃不夠，還會端來湯湯水
水，什麼時候這種親密的感情變得薄如紙片，
比陌生人還不如？

"如果可以，我想回到從前，與妳一起吃五新幣一碗的叻沙
或肉骨茶。"我有感而發。

寶兒的回答無異打了我一巴掌，她説自從吃過1500新幣一個
的北海道甜瓜後，她發誓再也不吃骯髒的路邊攤及便宜
的粗食……

我嘆了口氣説："哎！原來是生活拉開了我們。"

"不，是妳拉開了我們，"她用力扯下鯽魚眼珠塞進嘴裏，"
多虧妳跟汪致遠嚼舌根，我才知道原來一向敬重的姐姐是條
毒蛇，妳隱藏得真好。"

"什麼意思？"

寶兒沒回答，因爲新郎新娘開始逐桌敬酒，我也站起來以茶代酒，應景地説了些吉祥話。

～

寶兒恨我，非常非常地恨，這絕不僅僅因爲我曾有過的隱瞞，一定還有別的原因。

我想起汪致遠，他肯定知道些什麼，不待我問，他已打電話過來。

"媛媛，明天我想見妳。"他説。

"我也有話問你，對了，別讓姚醫生再打電話，産檢太過頻繁，容易讓人起疑。"

掛上電話，我才煩惱起該用什麼藉口溜出方宅。

～

我跟大太太説想買幾件內衣，原來的……太小了。

她瞄了一眼我的胸部，很快放行，我正慶幸自己的腦子轉得快，沒想到在雕花大鐵門前與正要外出的二太太撞個正著。

"崔小姐，上來吧！我送妳到烏節路買內衣。"她搖下車窗説。

烏節路是新加坡有名的購物街，猶如日本的銀座。

"謝謝！不用了，我正好散散步，活動一下筋骨。"

我和汪致遠約在上次的酒店見面，説是爲了避人耳目，但我知道他和我一樣，非常渴望對方的擁抱。

然而霸道的二太太豈能容許別人説不？她堅持送我一程，我無奈上車，心中叫苦連天。

～

我拿了好幾件F罩杯的內衣進更衣室，落地鏡前的我，乳房腫得很大，彷彿即將爆裂的瓜果。

"紅色的不適合妳，"二太太忽然拉開布簾走進來，"看起來很風騷。"

我雙手護胸，要她趕緊出去。

"我是關心妳，怕妳買錯內衣。"她伸手捏了捏我的胸脯，像捏水果攤上的西紅柿，"没錯，看起來是真懷上了，這年頭還得提防作假的人。"

我怒不可遏，要她馬上出去，再不出去，我叫人了。

"別氣，妳有的，我也有，没什麼好稀奇！"

她離開後，我馬上換下內衣。

～

二太太説我脾氣大，説不得，也罷，她還趕著去婦聯會開會呢！

謝天謝地，就等著她消失好赴約。

我抵達酒店時，已比約定的時間晚了兩小時，汪致遠説鐘點房只有三小時。

"那還等什麼？"我打開前襟的鈕扣。

完事後，汪致遠問我今天怎麼來晚了？

"二太太堅持跟我到內衣店，趕都趕不走。"我躺在汪致遠的懷裏説。

"她是不是起疑了？"

我答應該没有。

“扣、扣、”敲門聲忽然響起，我頓時寒毛直立。

“没事，大概時間到了，酒店過來問我們續不續？”

汪致遠從浴室抓來浴巾裹住下身，然後去應門，没想到……

“抱歉！我以爲裏面住的是崔小姐。”

聽到方淮安的聲音，我嚇壞了。

“崔小姐？没有，這裏没有崔小姐。”汪致遠的聲音打顫著。

“没有就好，如果你遇到一位孕婦，請轉告她到酒店大廳見我。”

“孕婦？會……會的。”

關上房門，我和汪致遠像兩隻喪家犬。

“怎麼辦？”我的心撲通撲通地跳。

“別擔心，我和妳一起去見他。”

我想了想，還是自己獨自面對好些，方老闆雖是見過世面的人，但也好面子，我得顧及他的感受。

汪致遠走後，我在房裏又磨磨蹭蹭了半天才鼓足勇氣下樓。看著樓層越來越往下，我的心也越来越低落，不知電梯門後等待我的會是什麼，心裏很忐忑。

第五十五章／春風又綠江南岸

"媛媛，我待妳不好嗎？"方老闆問。

"好，很好，太好了。"我的頭低得不能再低。

"那爲什麼......"

我很快答因爲我戀愛了，我愛上汪醫生，他讓我期待每一天的到來，懂得欣賞花開花落，食物從此也有了滋味......哎！說這些，他是不會懂的。

"我雖是耄耋老人，但也曾年輕過，知道戀愛的甜美，但我們是雇傭關係呀！妳來上這麼一齣，我不免懷疑妳肚裏的孩子是誰的。還有，會不會像周小姐一樣把孩子打掉，轉身和情夫雙宿雙飛？"

"不，我不會把孩子打掉，畢竟那是條生命。"我趕緊表忠心，而且因爲過於羞愧，竟紅了眼眶。

方淮安隨即給了我紙巾，還叫來果汁和水果盤，他說懷孕的女人要多補充維他命C......

生平最怕人來軟的，如果地上有洞，我肯定鑽進去。

見我平靜了些，方老闆開門見山地表示他不在意當別人的跳板，但在意被欺騙，還問我他看起來像傻子嗎？

我急得又快哭出來，重申全是我的錯，千刀萬剮也難辭其咎……

"當然是妳的錯，我們會盡快安排姚醫生做DNA檢測，如果……二太太恐怕不會太高興，妳得有心理準備。"

我無語了。

方老闆是好人，但絕非沒有原則的"老好人"，這可不，客套話一結束，他很快"在商言商"，只是……"二太太恐怕不會太高興"這句話是什麼意思？

"嘟……嘟嘟……"手機鈴聲劃破寂靜，看見來電顯示，我趕緊掛掉。

真是的，姚醫生早不打晚不打，偏偏挑這個時候打，嫌局勢不夠混亂嗎？

"誰打來的？"方老闆問。

"不認識，大概打錯了。"

沒多久，手機短信提示音傳來，看到"春風又綠江南岸"的詩句，我煞白了臉。

"妳怎麼了？一副驚慌失措的樣子。"他問。

"沒……沒什麼。"我拿起橙汁喝了一大口，又吃了好幾片梨及香瓜片，總算才安撫住內心奔騰的馬匹。

"看來妳很喜歡這裏的水果，我再叫一份。"

儘管我答不用，他還是轉身吩咐服務員再來一盤……

姚醫生以隱晦的方式通知我懷上的是汪致遠的孩子，讓我

又喜又悲。喜的是我終於沒在歪路上越走越遠，悲的是我竟然讓方家失望了，這該如何是好？我左右爲難。

"昨天買了幾件內衣？"早餐桌上，大太太問。

"沒買，那些內衣都太……風騷了。"

"咳、咳、"大太太捂住嘴，"大概現在流行這個吧！聽說昨晚妳和方先生出去了。"

我期期艾艾地答是，路上偶遇方先生，約了一起吃晚餐又坐了會兒摩天輪。

新加坡的摩天輪比英國倫敦的"千禧眼"還要高30米，坐在裏面可把風光綺旎的濱海灣及高聳的大樓都盡收眼底，視野甚至遠及馬來西亞及印尼的部份島嶼。

之所以約方淮安坐摩天輪並不是因爲骨子裏的浪漫情懷在作祟，而是想在只有兩個人的密閉空間內告訴他"噩耗"，也許滿天星斗及萬家燈火的美景能起到緩衝作用，然而直到下到地面，我還是沒敢開口。我如何告訴他孩子不是他的？又如何告訴他冷凍精子全沒了，他這輩子不可能再有子嗣？

"上回我坐摩天輪還是剛安裝沒多久的時候，"大太太跌入回憶裏，"方先生帶我去的，那風景可真美，有朝一日我想再坐一回。"

"走！擇日不如撞日，待會兒我們就去。"我提議。

大太太想了想，左右沒事，遂點頭答應。

在方先生面前說不出口的話，我選擇向大太太坦白，她是有信仰的人，應該不會輕易動怒。

"所以妳懷的是情夫的種，而我們方家注定沒有下一代，因爲冷凍精子已全數作廢，妳說的是這個意思嗎？"大太太問，聲音粗巴巴的。

"是……是的。"我打著哆嗦。

大太太將目光投向纜車外，眉頭緊鎖，我等著她表態，大氣不敢吭一聲，數分鐘過後……

"妳、姚醫生、汪醫生都是有罪之人，把我們方家當猴耍，太不可原諒了。"她說。

很少看到大太太如此生氣，想必是踩了她的底線。

"我知錯了，任何責罰都願意承受，只求您轉告方先生，我實在沒勇氣說出口。"

"說是一定會說，出了這麼大的紕漏怎麼可能不說？我不知方先生會做何反應，但二太太肯定不會讓妳好過，妳要有心理準備。"

這是第二次我從方家人嘴裏聽到要我有心理準備的忠告，到底是什麼懲罰？都二十一世紀了，難道還會家法伺候？

我一整天都心神不寧，尤其聽說方先生和大太太午飯過後臉色凝重地一起出門。

"他們去哪裏？莫非是向姚醫生興師問罪去？"我心想。

找不到人商量，我一通電話打給汪致遠，他知道我懷上他的孩子後，很是高興。

"奇怪，姚醫生怎麼不通知我呢？"他問。

"也許他想知道下一步我怎麼走，畢竟出來的結果不是他想要的。"

"也對，他是心思縝密的人。"

我問汪致遠現在該怎麼辦？方氏夫婦大概找姚醫生算賬去了。

“別怕，我這就趕去。”

“別去，免得禍及池魚。”

“兩位老人怕什麼？我正好求他們成全我倆。”

我還想説什麼，但他已先一步掛上電話，再打，無人接聽，我急得在房內來回踱步，正尋思該不該出門攔截時……

“儂台台造漏。”佩玖説二太太找我。

這時候找我肯定沒好事，我藉口受風寒，躲在屋裏不願出去，沒想到她主動上門來。

“這麼巧，挑這個時候生病。”來者冷嘲熱諷。

“二太太請坐。”我把唯一的座椅讓給她，自己則坐在床上，“今天一早喉嚨發乾，頭很痛，應該……應該是生病了。”

二太太説生病得治，她馬上帶我看病去。

我答不用了，自己睡個覺就好……

此時房內忽然闖進兩名大漢，橫眉怒目的，看著好嚇人。

“妳若聰明就乖乖跟我們走，不聰明就等著被五花大綁，我讓妳選。”

聽二太太這麼一説，我只能選擇當聰明人。

“帶上幾件換洗的衣服，手機別帶，帶了也沒用。”她説。

第五十六章/飛越杜鵑窩

我們一行下到底層，經過中式古典風格的客廳時，看到寶兒正抱著IRVINS的鹹蛋黃薯片咔滋咔滋地咬，這是今年新加坡最火的零食。

"你們去哪兒？"寶兒問，嘴角還有薯片殘渣。

二太太答我生病了，她帶我去看醫生。

"不會吧？昨天不是才和汪……"寶兒趕緊踩刹車。

原來是她，這下子我終於知道是誰向方老闆通風報信的。

寶兒避開我傳遞過去的憤怒眼神，表示天氣熱，還是到泳池泡泡爲宜。

"記得待在水淺的地方，免得被水鬼抓走。"我憤恨地説。

"妳還是擔心妳自己吧！泥菩薩。"她反將我一軍。

"這是要去哪兒？"車子開出皇后道，我問。

“給妳介紹個朋友。”二太太氣定神閒地答。

車子行經車水馬龍的街道後，往兀蘭的方向開去。

“這是要去馬來西亞嗎？我可没簽證。”我心想。

見車子在跨海大橋前轉彎，我鬆了口氣，没想到……

“妳該不會想把我送來這裏吧？！”當我看到Institute of Mental Health 的閃亮招牌時，立馬有想跑的衝動。

“説了給妳介紹個朋友。”二太太依舊不重不輕地答。

這所精神科醫院劃分了幾個區，有以年紀分的，如：兒童、青少年、成年及老年；也有以嚴重的程度分，如：輕度、中度及重度；另外還有以治療的過程分，如：諮詢、檢測、復健及輔導等，看得我眼花繚亂。

“ We came here to see Miss Zhou.”二太太對前台説。

周小姐？前REQ體檢部的周護士？她不是在美國留學嗎？

懷著疑問，我跟著來到某區走廊左側的一個房間，通過門上的玻璃，我看到裏面約二十平米大小，有空調及衛浴，採光不錯但窗上有鐵欄桿，一個留妹妹頭的纖細女子坐在被褥凌亂的床上。

“ 她是……”

“ 方先生的前私人護士，跟妳一樣。”

“ 怎麼……”

“ 她勾搭上一個小奶狗，還把方先生的孩子給做掉，我讓她在此反省一下。”

我的眼光重新回到房門上的小玻璃窗，房間內的周小姐雖然身穿淺藍色的病號服，容貌依然美麗，有巴掌大的小臉、白皙的皮膚、精緻的五官……只是那對大眼睛稍嫌空洞了些。

"這家瘋人院的要價可不低，我一點兒也没虧待她，讓她住在高級病房裏。"

我没想到二太太還有臉説這個，簡直恬不知恥。

"太殘忍了，即使她做錯事，妳也無權將她囚禁於此。"我義憤填膺。

"我可没打算將她終生囚禁起來，只是關著關著就瘋了。這樣吧！妳進去問她要不要離開醫院？如果想離開，隨時能走。"

二太太拿出鑰匙開門，我還未問她怎麼有鑰匙，背部被人用力一推。

"喂！開門，"我拼命敲打，"這一點兒都不好玩，快放我出去。"

然而二太太完全聽不見，她和兩名大漢很快消失在走廊盡頭。

這可怎麼辦？

我的腦筋快速運轉起來，對了，手機。

"喂喂！"我一通電話打給汪致遠，氣餒的是手機那端傳來無服務的語音提示。

"没用的，爲了防止病人和外面聯繫，整棟樓的牆體用了特殊材質，手機在這裏根本收不到信號。"那個坐在床上的女人説。

"妳……妳没瘋？"我問了個連自己都覺得莫名其妙的問題。

"我當然没瘋，要不要我背九九乘法表給妳聽？"

"不用了。"

我們彼此沈默了一會兒後，她忽然輕輕哼唱起經典的英文情歌《My Love》。

．．．

THE ROOMS ARE GETTING SMALLER

I wonder how

I wonder why

I wonder where they are

The days we had

The songs we sang together

Oh yeah .And oh my love……

我讚美她的歌聲宛如天籟。

"我遇到一個很會唱歌的男人，和他比,我差多了。"

聽她這麼一説，我想起汪致遠，他也有一副好歌喉。

"那個會唱歌的男人現在在哪裏？"我問。

"我不知道，本來他和我一起，然後……血……好多好多的血……像河一樣流過……裏面有一個寶寶、兩個寶寶、三個寶寶、四個……"周小姐邊數數邊扯下自己的頭髮，一根、兩根、三根、四根……

我嚇得倒退好幾步，直到抵住房門。

"開門呀！"我轉身拍打門上的玻璃，"我不要跟瘋子在一起，開開門呀！"

我的聲音在走道間回蕩，没多久，從四面八方傳來回音，有字正腔圓的普通話，也有不知來自哪國的模仿聲，全喊著："Kaimen, Kaimen, Kaimen……"

"完了，真的來到杜鵑窩了。"我感到絕望。

據說杜鵑習慣把産下的蛋放在別的鳥窩裏，孵化後的杜鵑會把同窩的小鳥扔出去，由於這種行爲既殘忍又令人不解，所以人們常把杜鵑和瘋癲聯想在一起。

此刻的我正是那隻不明就裏的無辜小鳥，四周圍都是等著將我鏟除的杜鵑，我該怎麼辦？

"救救我呀！汪致遠。"我心吶喊著。

男護士來送餐時，我抓住他的臂膀："聽著，我是正常人，不應該在這裏，我要見院長，拜托了。"

"放心，這裏的人都是正常人，没一個是瘋子，"他低頭看食物，"今天的晚餐有鳳梨蝦球，酸酸甜甜的，很開胃。"

我一怒將盛食物的托盤打翻，轉身就逃，被眼明手快的他反手抓住。

"妳不是想見院長嗎？我這就帶妳過去。"男護士説。

院長没見著，我被帶進黑濛濛的小屋裏。

"像妳這種病人，只要一電擊就會乖，但妳有孕在身，不宜電擊，所以只好委屈妳了。"男護士關上房門後，不忘給我希望，"一旦妳平靜下來，就不關小黑屋，知道不？"

他走後，我細細打量自己的所在之處，房間不到五平米，窗戶只有一本雜誌大小，入夜後，光線全靠屋外昏黄的路燈，難怪叫小黑屋。

我在房內焦躁地來回踱步，眼下的我無疑成了籠中鳥，越掙扎著出去，只會頭破血流。不行，我得按遊戲規則走，先做小伏低再謀對策，否則瘋了的周小姐就是我未來的模樣。

靠著曾經背誦過的《大悲咒》，我度過漫漫長夜……

我被強烈的饑餓感給喚醒，從昨天下午至今滴米未進，也許我能忍受，但肚裏的寶寶可不行。

" Excuse me. May I have something to eat?" " 我敲門討吃的。

沒多久，一個長形麵包從門上的小門遞送進來。顧不得手髒，我抓起就啃，原來法棍這麼美味，以前怎麼沒發現？

" You, get out." 一個胖得令人喘不過氣的女護士忽然開門，很不客氣地要我出去。

我要她等等，自己正吃著東西呢！

女護士一個箭步上來，將我手中的麵包扔地上，我像被搶走心愛玩具的孩子，怒不可遏。

沒等我發威，昨天的男護士衝了進來：" 快，院長要見妳。"

院長要見我？這是怎麼回事？

我趕緊起身。

第五十七章／自欺欺人

說要見院長，男護士卻帶我走向停車場。遠遠的，我看見方淮安的凱迪拉克古董車，蘋果綠的車身此時更顯清新。

司機打開後座的門，我坐了進去。

"讓妳受驚了。"方老闆說。

"沒有……有……"

司機問老闆是不是回方宅？

"去吃肉骨茶吧！寶寶需要補鈣，嗯？"他對我微笑。

我吃了大塊排骨、紅燒豬腳、鳳爪腐竹、炒芥藍、加了油條的米線，又喝了馬蹄水解膩，把胃給撐大了。

"妳的胃口真好。"方淮安說。

"是的，從昨天下午餓到現在，當然胃口大開。"

“那可不行，有寶寶的人得按時吃飯，這可是方家的骨肉啊！”

我放下即將入口的佳餚，轉頭直視我的雇主。

“我問過了，答案是肯定的。”他説。

看方老闆篤定的眼神，我感到深深的迷惑，難道我誤會姚醫生的詩句了？

“別愣著，趕緊吃。”他將一塊油汪汪的豬腳放進我盤裏。

我用紙巾擦了擦嘴角，聲稱自己吃飽了（真是的，聽到晴天霹靂的惡耗後，誰還吃得下？）。

“既然吃飽就回家歇著吧！天氣熱，正好睡個午覺。”方老闆説。

一回到方宅，我立即被二太太迎進客廳，她讓女傭奉上今年台灣的冠軍茶“東方美人”，聽説一斤要價兩萬多新幣。

“免了吧！我品著不出好茶或壞茶，別浪費那麼貴的茶葉了。”我冷冷地説。

“哪裏，妳不喝，肚裏的寶寶要喝，他是我們方家的種，肯定金貴。”

不到一天的工夫，二太太變臉變得好快，讓我感覺很陌生。

“我累了，有什麼話請説。”

“昨天的事……忘了吧！對妳、對她、對任何人都好。”

這個“她”不是別人，指的正是可憐的周小姐。

我問二太太打算怎麼處置瘋掉的人？紙包不住火，周小姐的家人肯定不會坐視不管。

“這就是麻煩之處，周小姐是孤兒，這世上還有誰會要一個瘋子？”她握住我的手，“媛媛，我錯了，現在唯一能彌補的就是讓她在一個相對安全的地方度過餘生，妳説是吧？”

我抽回自己的手，問方先生和大太太是否也知曉此事？

"大概知曉一二，但方家口徑一致，對外都説周小姐在美國留學。"

呵呵！果然"不是一家人不進一家門"，就這麼把一個風華正茂的女人給毀了，還絲毫没有愧疚感，我感到極度噁心。

"周小姐也算……幸運，能遇到你們，否則就要餐風露宿了。"我起身，"抱歉，我睏了，先行一步。"

躺在床上，我很快入眠，睡夢中，一個無臉的男人躺在血泊中，周小姐擁著他呼天搶地，讓人鼻酸。

我從夢中驚醒，想著還好懷的是方家的種，否則汪致遠恐怕也有滅頂之災……

"等等，都過了一天，他怎麼也没來個電話？"我一急，趕緊起床找手機，這才發現原來没電了。

插上電源後，我立馬打給汪致遠，可惜無人接聽。對於醫護人員而言，這再正常不過，總不能一邊給病人上藥一邊和他人講電話吧？！

放下手機，我才開始憂慮。汪致遠以爲我們有了愛的結晶，如今反轉，我該如何告訴他懷的不是他的孩子？他會不會因此傷心難過？

哎！我終究還是走在歧路上，無語。

日子又回到原來的軌道上，佩玖照例在三點一刻爲我端來下午茶，她説四紅補血粥是二太太熬的，看她站在爐灶前忙東忙西，很是辛苦。

我拿起勺子舀了一匙，原來是用花生、紅棗、紫米、紅豆煮成的甜粥。

"拿走，看了想吐。"我捂住口鼻。

佩玖一時拿不定主意，我遂作嘔吐狀，她只好趕緊端走。

打發走"二太太的好意"，我拿出文房四寶寫《大悲咒》。若說來方宅有什麼得益之處，大概就是學會背誦這個"今生免惡死，來世求善生"的經文，它讓我紛擾飄浮的心得到安置，不再像隻無頭蒼蠅。

一直到佩玖來收碗盤，大太太還是守口如瓶，我不得不開門見山。

"妳要我如何回答？方先生説什麼就是什麼。"她打馬虎眼。

這個答覆很可疑，我問姚醫生怎麼説。

"他能怎麼説？方先生不舉已很久了，即使⋯⋯也因患上睾丸生精功能障礙而無法取精，還好前些年曾留下幾管冷凍精子，想著再怎麼著，總有一個能成吧？！沒想到⋯⋯哎！造孽呦！"

我很迷惑，到底我懷的是不是方家的孩子？

大太太答學佛的人不打妄語，讓我去問姚醫生。

"好，我明天一早就去，請大太太放行。"我立馬説。

她只能無奈點頭。

有了上回的教訓，我讓Stella在候診室等我，自己單獨面對姚醫生。

“很好，孩子看起來很正常。”他給我紙巾擦拭肚皮上的啫喱。

“聽你這麼一說，我放心了。”

“記得多吃蔬菜水果，少食油膩，還有，放鬆心情，這個很重要。”他邊說邊在鍵盤上飛快地打字，大概在寫病歷。

“昨天……方老闆……你怎麼說？”我還是問了。

姚醫生停止打字，轉頭直視我：“Green是汪醫生的，Red是方淮安的，這是妳說的，怎麼反倒問起我來？”

“既然如此，爲什麼……”

姚醫生說還是去問我的雇主吧！也許他有不一樣的解讀。

大太太要我問姚醫生，姚醫生要我問方老闆，被人踢皮球的滋味並不好受。

離開診所後，我很消沈, Stella問我是不是有壞消息？

“ Yes, very very bad.”我承認。

她安慰我一切都會好的，如果還是覺得不安，可以到聖安德烈教堂做禱告，神會應允我所求，每當不開心時，她都是這麼做的。

St.Andrew’s Cathedral 是新加坡最大的教堂，其潔白的哥特式建築非常莊嚴肅穆，很多新人在此舉行結婚儀式。

我想了想，還有哪裏比教堂更合適說話？

“ Yes, I need to pray in the church.”我說自己正需要禱告。

爲了不讓方家人起疑，我要Stella千萬保密，因爲大太太是佛教徒，我如果去拜耶穌，她會不高興。

“ Don’t worry. I won’t tell anybody.”她笑嘻嘻地答應。

～

汪致遠拋下病患前來與我見面，他說如果帶的MO招架不住就得趕回醫院去。

原來通過考試的他已是主治醫生，現在也帶起新人來了。

“好，我長話短說，孩子是……你的，但方老闆説是他的，讓我一頭霧水。”

汪致遠嘆了口氣：“這有什麼不明白的？以假充真唄！妳想，方先生的冷凍精子没了，左右不可能有子嗣，與其面對失敗，倒不如自欺欺人。”

“他們能自欺欺人，難道我們可以假裝不知情？”我問孩子的爹。

“媛媛，這是個兩難問題，身爲父親，我當然有義務養育自己的孩子，但這樣一來，妳就不好向雇主交待了，我……反正聽從妳的決定。”

汪致遠將燙手山芋扔回給我，讓我有些許不快，但他能做什麼？他什麼也做不了，不是嗎？

“好，我想想，畢竟是自己捅的簍子。”

“媛媛，別誤會，我……”

我要他什麼都別説，他的心思我懂的。

“哎！如果那天驗孕棒顯示寶兒懷孕就好了，她能得到她想要的，妳也能脱身。”汪致遠説。

“没用的，方老闆患上睾丸生精功能障礙，這輩子算是求子無望了。”

説完，我和汪致遠都沈默了。

第五十八章／接棒

由於提到寶兒，我問汪致遠是否曾對她説過什麼？自從她搬進方宅後，處處與我做對，除了白色謊言外，我想不起哪裏得罪她了。

看汪致遠欲言又止的樣子，我知道有事不對勁，在我的一再盤問下，他終於承認爲了擺脱寶兒的糾纏，説了不該説的話。

"你到底説了什麼？"我問，心裏七上八下的。

原來汪致遠曾暗示他們兩人不合適，但寶兒完全聽不進去，只是一昧地表示會爲他而改變。他想了想，長痛不如短痛，直言自己是睡眠淺的人，聽説寶兒會打鼾，他可不想日日頂著兩個黑眼圈上班……

寶兒的確會打鼾，而且"驚天動地"，這是護士站公開的秘密。

"就爲了這個恨我？未免也太小題大做了？"我很不解。

"她……她還問是不是妳嚼的舌根？我没回答，只是重申兩人不合適，可能她因此對號入座，認爲是妳從中做梗。"

"你……哎！"我已無話可說。

"嘟……嘟嘟……"汪致遠的手機響了。

他接聽，三兩句話便掛斷。

"抱歉！MO招架不住了，我得趕回醫院，她……"汪致遠看了一眼正在讀聖經的Stella，"回去會不會說嘴？"

"放心，待會兒我會告訴她，你向我傳教，反正她聽不懂普通話。"我答。

～

大太太問我什麼時候開始對基督教感興趣？她很開明，只要是勸人行善的宗教，都好。

原來Stella也是個大嘴巴，讓人始料未及。

"呃……就是接觸一下，目前沒什麼想法。"我答。

"妳若要上教會，我不反對，帶上Stella，她是基督徒。"

這下子我知道Stella爲什麼要透露口風，她想上教會，但一個月兩次的休息日對她而言太少了。

"好的，聽聽聖經也不錯。"我順水推舟。

沒想到這麼輕易就換來一週一次的自由身，簡直太棒了。

～

"聽説妳信教了，大概身上的罪孽深重，趕著去洗滌吧？！"我在花園裏散步，寶兒冷不防出現。

自從汪致遠告訴我發生在他倆之間的事後，我曾試圖從寶兒的角度看自己，沒錯，的確是心機婊，完全不顧姐妹情誼。如今的她時不時潑我冷水，未嘗不是一種宣洩，如果不曾真心付出過，也不會如此耿耿於懷。

“我是罪孽深重，需要每週向上帝懺悔一次，同時也爲妳禱告。”

“干我何事？別再假惺惺了，最恨妳這種表裏不一的人。”她邊說邊扯下海桐灌木上的白花，彷彿跟它有仇似的。

都説沒有無緣無故的愛，亦沒有無緣無故的恨，我不想繼續誤會下去，直接告訴她想和解，任何條件都接受。

“把汪致遠還給我。”她說。

“除了那個，其他都行。”

“除了這個，其他我都不要。”

我問果真如此，那麼她來方家又爲哪椿？

“爲了讓妳不好受，妳不能既有很多錢還擁有汪致遠，如果真是那樣，這世界就太不公平了。”

我答錢財可以放棄，問她是否感到平衡了？

“不能，妳至少擁有我得不到的愛，我有什麼？雖然方老闆目前對我有求必應，但難保有一天他不會喜新厭舊，到時候自己就是隻破鞋。”

寶兒是在暗示我什麼嗎？

“莫非妳有當方家三太太的念頭？”我問。

“妳怎麼可以有如此可怕的想法？”她很驚訝，“方淮安對我而言不過是台取款機，我窮怕了，不想再待在社會最底層。”

我陷入苦思，寶兒的三觀出現嚴重問題，但也正因如此，給了我逃離困境的契機。

“妳願不願意幫助我和……汪致遠？我懷的是他的孩子。”

寶兒的表情複雜極了，既憤怒又有些許的難以置信，

“妳好大的膽子，竟敢在老虎頭上拔毛，也不怕方家發現實

情後將妳就地正法。”她說。

“方家人不僅知道實情，還打算將錯就錯，把別人的孩子當成自己的來養，我若推波助瀾，事情就簡單多了。”我答。

寶兒的表情更複雜了，她說看樣子我不想“睜一隻眼閉一隻眼”，那麼和汪致遠隱姓埋名、遠走高飛，有何不可？

“不，我想要一家三口能光明正大地走在路上，而不是像驚弓之鳥似地躲躲藏藏一輩子。”

也許是“一家三口”四個字刺激到她，寶兒皺了皺眉頭說：“讓我好好想想，事情全趕一塊兒了。”

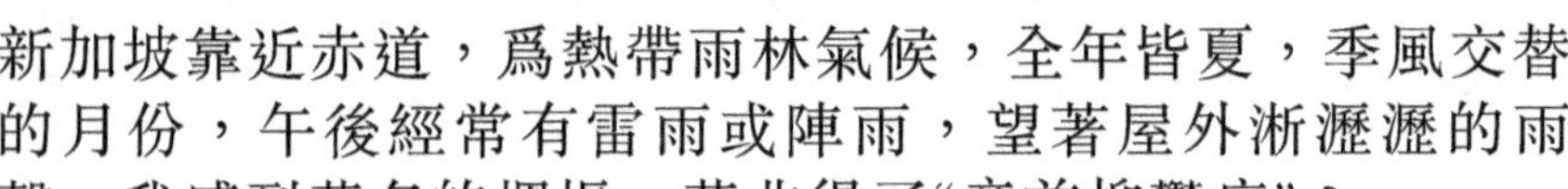

新加坡靠近赤道，爲熱帶雨林氣候，全年皆夏，季風交替的月份，午後經常有雷雨或陣雨，望著屋外淅瀝瀝的雨聲，我感到莫名的惆悵，莫非得了“產前抑鬱症”？

三點一刻，有人敲門，想必是佩玖送下午茶來，我走過去開門。

“端午節快到了，廚師包了好幾串粽子，我迫不及待拿來與妳分享。”寶兒捧著銀托盤走進來，口氣好得讓我感到詫異，以爲曾有的不愉快未曾發生過。

“粽子是甜的還是鹹的？”我問。

她答廚師包的是娘惹糕，甜鹹味皆有。

娘惹粽是新加坡特有的粽子，餡料是將上等瘦肉與香甜爽口的冬瓜條混炒，鮮而不膩，鹹中帶甜，巧妙地融合中國和馬來兩地的飲食特色，很有熱帶風情。

雖然不難吃，但我還是比較喜歡福建的燒肉粽，有蝦米、香菇、滷蛋、花生、紅燒肉……等。

寶兒說她亦有同感，吃娘惹粽有點兒像吃異域的食物，少了家鄉味……

來新加坡四年多了，四周圍雖然有很多華人，但彼此總像隔著一重山，怎麼也無法完全融入，只有寶兒和我是道道地地的同鄉，人親土也親。

"寶兒，我很高興妳回來。"我有感而發。

"我一直都在呀！"寶兒把娘惹粽裏的冬瓜條挑出來，"妳看，像不像肥豬肉？"

"我倒覺得挺像妳的小指頭。"

寶兒驚呼一聲，過來捶打我，我們又像從前一樣打鬧。

趁著教友在唱聖歌，我和汪致遠很有默契地走到教堂外。

"妳說寶兒願意接棒是什麼意思？"他問。

"就是……她願意生一個寶寶給方家，但當初應允給我的房產和現金必須轉交給她。當然，由於生理原因，方准安現在取精困難，所以這個寶寶注定和方家沒有任何血緣關係。"

汪致遠說捨棄身外之物不成問題，我們都有一技在身，不怕餓肚子，但寶兒爲何要淌這混水？

"每個人都有追求的目標，她現在追求物質，我也不好說什麼，畢竟她要的愛情沒了。"

汪致遠想的比較深，當初方家如此大方是建立在孩子與他們有血緣關係的基礎上，現在我懷的是他的孩子，方家忍氣吞聲來個"自欺欺人"也是不得已之舉，寶兒若要接棒，就是把那層窗戶紙給捅破，方家未必樂意。

我想了想，他分析得没錯，遂說："我這就回去探探口風。"

第五十九章/DR.HOWARD

我的計劃是先跟大太太談，如果她同意，事情就成功一半了，然而還未走進東翼，我就聽見劇烈的爭吵聲。

"給幾分顏料就開起染房來，妳這個不要臉的X貨，給老娘洗腳都不配！"二太太的聲音像鑽石劃過玻璃。

"別像瘋狗一樣亂咬人，錢是老頭子給的，妳叫嚷什麼？"寶兒也不甘示弱。

"錢雖是老頭子給的，但賬是我在管，妳買買衣服，到處吃喝也就算了，現在竟然買起珠寶來，卡地亞是妳這種來路不明的野雞戴的嗎？不行，今天我就讓老公把妳的副卡給咔嚓掉。"

寶兒冷哼一聲說左右不過是個妾，還好意思"老公，老公"地喊。

"我至少還是被承認的妾，妳呢？算什麼？別以爲老頭子摸妳兩把就飛上天，像妳這種貨色，要多少有多少，在下一個脫衣舞娘取代妳之前，趕緊抓緊時間得瑟吧！"

我刻意咳嗽兩聲，好平息雙方怒火。

二太太用力闔上賬本，没好氣地説：“另一台碎鈔機也來了，妳們聊，我得工作，這一大家子的開銷可不是讓大風給吹來的，總得有人負重前行才成。”

她走後，寶兒氣到不行，大顆大顆的眼淚往下掉。

“別哭，人在屋檐下，哪能不低頭？”我無奈地説。

“方家還缺錢嗎？我不過是刷了條手鏈，兩萬新幣不到，她就這樣侮辱人，太可恨了！”

兩萬新幣約十萬元人民幣，無怪乎二太太會發火。

我可以順著寶兒的思路走，和她一起罵耀武揚威的人，氣是解了，但治標不治本，同樣的情景還會一再出現。

“能怎麼辦？形勢比人強，她雖然不是方淮安的原配，但方家大小事都歸她管，連老頭子也得敬她幾分。妳就低調些，省得方老闆真把妳的副卡給收回去。”

寶兒嗚咽著問我二太太説的可是真的？方淮安跟她只是玩玩？

我以爲寶兒早已熟知遊戲規則，她的問話讓我感到詫異，難不成她以爲“提款機”會對她動真情？

“妳心中難道没有個點數？那對俄羅斯姐妹花最後不也走了？”

寶兒哭喪著臉，我安慰她這本來就是“各取所需”的交易行爲，方先生算不錯了，給“跳舞老師”這麼高的收入……

“妳真以爲扭扭屁股就能掙這麼多錢？我是手口並用地幫他達到高潮。”

頃刻間，我腦海中那個清純如小白兔的可人形象轟然崩塌。

“妳……何必呢？好好的一個人……”我喃喃道。

“剛開始只爲了氣妳，和妳互別苗頭，没想到越走越遠，最後就成了這副模樣……哎！算了，還是實話實説吧！我是被金錢給俘虜了，以前即使做死，月工資也達不到兩千，現在隨隨便便就能吃好、穿好、用好，誰還會苦巴巴地老實工作……反正我是這麼想的。”

我說既然如此，我把棒子交給她正好，九個月後她會有大房子還有五十萬新幣的現金，省著點花，一輩子都不愁吃穿……

寶兒直視我好一會兒，像要把我生吃活吞。

“What?”我問。

“妳真覺得夠？萬一我長壽或者遇上一個不長進的老公，那點兒錢就只能塞牙縫。”

“什麼意思？”

“意思是我不想當妳的替代品，我想單幹，以前答應的就此作廢，當我沒說。”

我嚇壞了，責備她怎能說話不算話？

“我也是剛剛福至心靈，這還得感謝二太太的利口，否則就錯過大好機會了。”她面帶喜色地說。

~

寶兒單方面“毀約”，讓我很不爽，斷不可能主動找她。我不找她，她也沒來找我，加上我住東翼，她住南翼，我們就這麼彼此僵著。

第一次感覺不對勁還是從佩玖嘴裏聽來，她說方老闆和二太太大吵一架後，開車帶走寶兒，已經好幾天沒見到那兩人了。

這倒稀奇。

沒想到一個禮拜又過去了，那兩人還是沒回家，大太太問我能不能給寶兒打個電話？

“好，待會兒打。”我答。

“妳没問理由，莫非知道些什麼。”

“這還用問？年輕女孩愛玩，旁邊又有個幫忙買單的人，肯定樂不思蜀。”

“若是那樣倒好，怕就怕事情不單純。”大太太説。

飯後我打給寶兒，問她在哪兒？她答墨爾本。

“妳上那兒幹嘛？”

“玩呀！廢話！”

我要她趕緊回，大太太在找老公。

“知道了，順利的話，兩個月回。”

兩個月？這是公然挑釁大太太與二太太。

“妳是否綁架了老先生？”我問。

她哈哈大笑兩聲後掛上電話。

我的肚子越來越大，手指腫得像一節節的小香腸，連戒指都拔不出來，不得不上珠寶店請專人剪開再重鑄。

“把它還給鄭……我買個新的給妳。”汪致遠説。

我喋喋不休地抱怨，忘了戒指是鄭之龍當年求婚送的。

“對……對不起，我會還回去的。”

藉著一週一次上教堂的名義，我和汪致遠得以見面説話，也算是上帝給的恩澤。

爲了轉換尷尬的氣氛，我説九月出生的不是處女座就是天秤座，真希望寶寶是愛美的天秤座，而非吹毛求疵的處女座。

“追求完美有什麼不好？我就是處女座。”他答。

我吐了吐舌頭：“真是的，哪壺不開提哪壺。”

“不光是妳，一般大衆對處女座多少有誤解，其實有毅力的人才會追求完美，再說了，12個星座中，處女座最有孝心。”

聽他這麼一說，我想起他那位被家暴致死的母親。

“能不能問你個問題？問過後，這輩子我絕不再問。”

“呵呵！如果妳想問我有多少存款，恐怕要讓妳失望了。”

汪致遠知道這不是我要問的，他之所以這麼説，更顯內心惴惴不安。

“算了，還是別問。”

“問，話説到一半讓人如鯁在喉。”

於是我問他是否把對母親的愛投影在我身上？否則難以解釋他會選擇各方面條件都不好的我……

由於久久聽不到他的答覆，我的心跌至谷底。

“我知道了，你不用回答。”

我轉身想走，被他從後抱住：“聽著，妳是我這輩子唯一想擁抱的人，就算妳長殘了、變老了，我愛妳如昔。”

聽完我淚如雨下，轉身投入他懷裏。

啊！我是如此幸運，在茫茫人海中遇到一個心性如此契合的人，他不在乎我那不堪的過去，給了我重生的機會。

正因如此，我暗自下決心一定要帶走我們的孩子，不讓愛我的男人有一絲遺憾。

～

寶兒來敲我房門時，我才知道她回新加坡了。

"給，澳洲的保健品，吃了對寶寶好。"她把瓶瓶罐罐堆在我桌上，有魚油、蜂膠、鯊魚軟骨、羊胎素......等。

"謝了，也不知道孕婦能不能吃，得問問姚醫生。"

"甭問了，Dr.Howard説可以吃。"

Dr.Howard? 我問這誰呀？

寶兒露出謎之微笑。

第六十章／離婚

我問 Dr.Howard 是何方神聖？寶兒答是世界知名的男科聖手。

"他該不會讓方淮安重振雄風了吧？！"我又問。

"這有難度，Dr.Howard能做的只是實行外科手術解除輸精管梗阻，順利完成取精。"

這就怪了，姚醫生也算新加坡數一數二的名醫，他做不到的事，澳洲醫生卻做到了，讓我不禁懷疑其真實性。

"是嗎？如此一來又多了幾管冷凍精子。"

"是呀！所以我把它帶回來了。"她答。

冷凍精子是將收集來的精子加入保護劑後，儲存在零下100多°C的液氮中，裝液氮的桶子有半人高，我問她是如何攜帶過海關的？

"人肉快遞唄！哈哈！"她笑得花枝亂顫。

"妳該不會……"

“Yes，快向我恭喜吧！”

我張嘴卻發不了聲，寶兒直接懷上方淮安的孩子，還有比這個更令人震撼的嗎？

“對不起，把妳嚇到了，”她捂住嘴吃吃笑，“這是最好的結局，不是嗎？比懷上阿貓阿狗的孩子更有底氣。再告訴妳，方老闆說了，生一個給一千萬新幣，生兩個給兩千萬，以此類推。”

這豈不成了生子機器？她是護士，不會不知道生育是項大工程。

寶兒說她當然清楚，不會傻到一再將肚皮吹大。實話說，Dr.Howard爲了一勞永逸，一次性放入數個受精卵，如此一來，她生多胞胎的機率就大大提高了，想到那些白花花的銀子，半夜都會笑醒……

我看著那個笑得一臉滿足的寶兒，她才二十歲初頭就一腳跨過人生應該奮鬥的黃金時期，直接享受多數人工作一輩子也得不到的財富，這是福還是禍？

“恭喜，這下子我也能功成身退了。”我說。

突然丟了工作，但我不遺憾。

“媛媛學姐，方老闆說答應給妳的東西一分不少，妳就安心留在方家待產吧！”

寶兒又喚我“媛媛學姐”，看來是盡棄前嫌了。

“好的，替我謝謝他。”

我没完成任務，但仍得到回報，怎麼看都不對勁，像方家這樣精明的人家，怎麼可能做“損己利人”之事？果然没兩天就找我簽新合同，這回是保密合同，凡有關方家大小事，對外一律守口如瓶，否則……

得，這也在情理之中，我大手一揮，簽了。

～

由於“真貨”降臨，我肚裏的“假貨”受冷落也在意料之中。大太太雖然對我一如既往，但傭人們就不一樣了，變臉變得比翻書還快，叫都叫不動。

反觀寶兒，妥妥的“母憑子貴”，不僅搬到面積大一倍的房間內，而且“軍令如山”，即使半夜想吃芽籠的梧槽豆花也吃得到，讓我好生羨慕。

然而有失必有得，在方家不受待見，但我的行動自由多了，沒人管我何時外出、見了什麼人，大概他們更希望我“人間蒸發”，只是礙於顏面，不好做得太絕。

“妳若不開心，我們另外租房住，只是我白天上班，留妳一人在家，挺不放心的。”汪致遠說。

他和兩位男室友合租在中峇魯老街區的“飛機樓”裏，房間小又陰暗，廚衛還共用，很是不便。

我不是沒想過搬家，但如同汪致遠所說，白天我一人在家，萬一有個差池，如何是好？

“我看我還是待在方家直到分娩爲止，對了，美國的工作有消息嗎？”我問。

“還沒收到回覆，再等等。”

方家答應給我的房產位於芝加哥郊區，據說光土地就有好幾個足球場大。我和汪致遠一致認爲換個地方重新開始挺好的，他想的是從此遠離高強度的工作，我想的就不一樣了。

新加坡有“結婚三年不得離婚”的規定，除非一方有家暴、嫖妓或變態性行爲。雖然以上三條鄭之龍都當仁不讓地給囊括了，但爲了保護他的顏面，我們皆同意先分居再離婚，然而我還是擔心夜長夢多，萬一鄭之龍反悔，又回頭纏住我怎麼辦？那麼躲到美國便成了當前最好的選擇，頂多時間一到再飛回來辦手續。

“嘟……嘟嘟……”我從床上掙扎著坐起，一接聽，卻是久違的恐怖聲音。

“我想見妳。”鄭之龍説。

我以“不方便”三字回絕。

“我就在方宅外，既然妳不方便出去，那麼由我進來吧！”

“別……”我趕緊阻止，“我們約個地方見面。”

鄭之龍約我回“家”見面，想到上回被他甕中抓鱉給囚禁起來，這回我堅定拒絕，約他在“查理布朗咖啡店”見面。

查理布朗是史努比的主人，店內牆上有他及露西的圖片，一男孩一女孩，很是活潑可愛。我選擇那裏是因爲鄭之龍尚未看過我大肚子的模樣，若在有童趣的環境下見面，多少能沖淡尷尬的氛圍。

“Hi.”鄭之龍没在第一時間認出我來，我只好主動打招呼。

“妳……”他上下打量我，“坐吧！想喝什麼？”

我答隨便，於是鄭之龍到櫃台點了果汁和三文魚雞蛋厚多士給我。

“看樣子妳快生了，預產期什麼時候？”他問。

“九月。”

“九月？九月好像是處女座，我比較喜歡摩羯座，若是男孩就更好，既穩健又有執行力。”

我問他何時開始對星座感興趣？他答自從知道自己當了爸爸，孩子又是摩羯座男孩起……

我驚到不行。

“也許我們本來就不應該在一起，妳瞧！一分開我們都開枝散葉了。”鄭之龍樂呵呵地説。

我問孩子的母親是誰？

“她是我到廣州參觀醫院時的接待人員之一，我們曾在一起數日，最近她告訴我有了身孕，做過産檢，是個男孩，預産期在明年一月。”

消息來得太突然，我原以爲我一直無法懷孕的癥結在他，没想到……

“恭喜了。”我言不由衷。

“媛媛，”他突然抓住我的手，“我們離婚吧！對方父母説若不出示離婚證明，他們將帶女兒去打胎，我已經四十好幾了，要個孩子也不容易。”

我抽回自己的手：“可是……”

“我知道新加坡那個可笑的離婚規定，要不，妳就承認自己有異於常人的性需求，這樣一來我們馬上能離。”

我難以置信鄭之龍在最後關頭還不忘利用我，真是下作小人！

“你説這話倒提醒我你曾做過的缺德事，要離婚可以，你得承認自己有家暴、嫖妓及變態性行爲，三者缺一不可。”我起身，“我反正不急，你慢慢來。”

～

鄭之龍約我三日後在法院“訴訟”離婚，他承認所有的罪狀及解除之前的“聯名貸”，而我不求償也不要求贍養費。

由於没有涉及錢財，程序走得很快，當手上拿到那張離婚紙時，我竟然不可抑制地慟哭起來。

“別哭，”鄭之龍壓低聲音，“讓人以爲妳不想離。”

天知道這一路走來我有多麽不易，我是喜極而泣呀！

"你說的對，"我拭去眼淚，"離開你我應該開懷大笑，該哭的是你未來的新娘子。"

我的"前夫"聽了，臉上青一陣紫一陣，而我挺起腰桿，高傲地離去。

第六十一章／三胞胎（完結篇）

把好消息告訴汪致遠後，我走遍三個商場才鼓足勇氣與遠在中國的父母微信通話。他們一聽說我離婚了，還是淨身出戶，很是擔憂。

"這社會對離婚婦女並不寬容，還好妳有個護士的工作在，一時不致於捉襟見肘。"母親說。

"爸、媽，我離職了，因爲……因爲我懷孕了，預產期在兩個月後，孩子的父親是汪醫生。"

由於害怕父母看到我因懷孕而浮腫的臉，我特意選擇語音通話，然而此時的我多麼想看看他們的表情，藉以判斷他們是喜亦是悲？有沒有生氣？會不會感到失望？

"他怎麼想的？對妳是否真心？"

隔著那麼遠的距離，我還能感受到母親的憂心忡忡。

"他有結婚的打算，婚後我們想搬到芝加哥。放心，世界各地都缺醫護人員，我們很容易就能找到工作。"

我没告訴母親我在芝加哥有棟十幾個房間的大房子，甚至還有個小湖供垂釣，怕她問我餡餅打哪兒來的？

“媛媛，”説話的是父親，“妳擺脫那個惡魔，我們爲妳高興，妳等著，我們這就飛過去幫妳辦婚禮，妳肚子大了也需要有人照應……”

知道父母接受我的“一意孤行”後，我有隱隱的快樂，像喝完水，發現水杯還是滿的。

掛上電話，我決定走路到REQ,親自告訴孩子的爹應該找婚慶公司了，還有，得租個大公寓準備迎接岳父、岳母及新生命的到來。

～

還没坐完月子，汪致遠就帶回來一個好消息：芝加哥州立醫院給了他 **offer,** 並且答應幫他辦綠卡。

“太好了，是不是？”我對著襁褓中的嬰兒，“爹地找到工作，我們就要搬家了。”

兒子似乎能聽懂，咿咿呀呀地附合著。

～

在一個風和日麗的下午，我剛餵完奶，母親推門進來說有朋友來訪，還是個孕婦。

“那是我的好友，快請她進來。”我説。

寶兒進來時剛好與抱著兒子的母親擦身而過，她還逗弄小東西好一會兒。

“妳兒子長得像妳，還好。”她説。

“什麽意思？説得好像我老公其貌不揚。”

寶兒要我別誤會，誰不知道汪致遠是潘安再世？她是怕自己陷入萬年魔咒中，老子愛不上，結果愛上小子……

"妳真逗，坐吧！"我指著最靠近的座椅，"最近好嗎？"

"不太好，肚子裏有三個，夜裏常翻來覆去睡不好覺。"

寶兒真的懷上多胞胎，而且謝絕醫生的提議，三個全留下。

"多子多孫多福氣，何況還有三千萬新幣等著妳。"

會這麼說是因爲寶兒曾經不止一次告訴我她的花錢計劃，首先當然是瘦身，當她又美美地出現時，鐵定殺到烏節路瘋狂大採購，一改過去二十幾年的寒酸氣。

"說來奇怪，本來我對肚裏的孩子很無感，但隨著時間的推進，我漸漸有了感覺，常常幻想他們可愛的模樣。當胎動屬害時，我還會告訴寶寶們別打架，待會兒給他們吃好吃的。"

我呵呵笑，問她吃的可是一式三份？否則又有的打了。

"可不是嗎？方家現在把我當豬養，恨不得將碗口粗的管子伸進我嘴裏，24小時不間斷地輸入食物。"

"太誇張了，又不是養鵝肝，"我上下打量她，"妳的肚子雖大，四肢還算纖細，生完肯定能瘦下來，到時拿上方淮安給的錢到處買買買，也算了了妳的夙願。"

"怎麼辦？我反悔了，三個白胖小子多可愛，真不想把他們留給方家，我要自己養。"

我勸她別輕舉妄動，一個小小孩能讓一個家庭雞飛狗跳，何況三個？再說了，養孩子不用錢嗎？我家王子一個月的奶粉錢就要五、六百新幣，遑論其他。

"好啦！知道了，我也就這麼一說，妳倒婆婆媽媽起來。"

我們又交換一下新近發生的瑣事，她告訴我方家來了個新的脫衣舞娘，年紀有一些，喜歡濃妝豔抹，小腿上還有靜脈曲張，看來方淮安的品味越來越差了……

我則告訴她汪致遠在芝加哥找到工作，一個月後得打包上路。

“這麼快？以後我可不可以去找妳？”她問。

“當然可以，從新家的每個房間看出去，景色都不一樣，任君挑選。”

我們就這麼拉拉雜雜地談論及計劃著未來,像兩個不諳世事的少女。

~

“今天下午兩點，保姆會上門面試，可別睡過頭了。”早餐桌上，汪致遠不忘提醒我。

“知道了，已經調好鬧鐘。”我答，哈欠聲連連。

雖然家裏雇了阿姨及園丁，但獨自一人照顧孩子還是有些力不從心，所以Luke一斷奶，我們便積極尋找保姆，既要負責盡職，又要會說普通話，Dr.Johnson因此介紹了個人選，聽說以前是幼師，我們很快約了時間見面。

“走了，愛妳。”老公吃完我準備的愛心早餐後起身，然後在我的臉頰上小啄一下。

從我家到芝加哥州立醫院有一百多公里的距離，他得早早上路，好避開交通高峰期。

老公走後，我喚阿姨收拾，自己則端起咖啡到陽光房看報。

最近靜極思動，想找個Part-time的工作，不爲錢，只爲了不與社會脫節。就在瀏覽徵人廣告時，我意外看到一則醒目的國際新聞標題【代孕媽媽帶走三胞胎，七旬老翁一夜白頭】。

“嘟……嘟嘟……”手機響了，我接聽。

“崔小姐，近來可好？”是方家二太太。

“很好，什麼風讓妳想起我來？”

“寶兒生了，三個都是帶把的。”

這麼快？而且三個都是男孩。

“方老闆肯定樂壞了。”我說。

她答那自然是，方家上下喜氣一片，光打賞用的紅包就派出去好幾千個，可是……

聽二太太說“可是”，我忽然緊張起來，不會吧？！

“可是寶兒拒絕餵母乳，而且瞧著心情很低落，怕是得了產後抑鬱症，妳能飛來看她嗎？”

知道寶兒有情緒病，我很擔憂，趕緊答沒問題。

“機票錢由方家支付。”二太太補上一句。

“謝謝！我把家裏安排好，即刻啓程。”

掛上電話後，我走到客廳放音樂，聽說聆聽莫札特的作品能讓人頭腦清晰，還因此有了“莫札特效應”一說。

我邊聽《G大調回旋曲》邊思考該如何開導寶兒，希望在面試的保姆到來前能理出個頭緒來……

《完結》

【看不夠嗎？B杜的《愛上比佛利》正等著您，以下是前三章，先睹為快。】

《愛上比佛利》

第一章/演員夢

比佛利山莊（Beverly Hills）位於美國洛杉磯，距離聖莫尼卡海灘不遠，不僅全年都能曬到著名的加州陽光，還能享受從太平洋吹來的清爽海風，有"全世界最尊貴的住宅區"之稱，是財富與名利的象徵。

既然尊貴，當然離不開購物，羅迪歐大道是比佛利山莊最馳名的時尚街，兩側有眾多的奢侈品店及高檔的餐館、酒吧、畫廊⋯⋯等，讓人在大飽眼福之際也能一窺富人的消費世界。

就在一片繁榮景像中，我徒步從豪氣逼人的四季酒店轉彎走兩百米，那裏與"富麗堂皇、窮奢極侈"截然不同，好比現在，我正走進平價的"莫先生的中國漢堡店"（Mr.Mo Chinese Burger）。

"萌萌，這麼早就收工了？"櫃台後一個胖墩墩的中國婦人說。

"運氣不好，今天又没戲了。"我唉聲嘆氣地答。

"別難過，機會總會有的。"說完，她遞給我一個臘汁肉夾饃。

我給了她三美元，然後坐到角落狼吞虎嚥起來。

沒錯，在中國賣三塊錢的白吉饃夾肉，到了美國揚眉吐氣，身價翻了六、七倍。雖然心疼，但與動輒上百美元一餐的西餐比，還算經濟實惠，所以吸引了不少食客。

說起這家的店主人莫太太，我一週總要見上幾回，言談間，我知道她有個洋氣的名字叫Molly，和莫先生於十年前來到洛杉磯，什麼苦活、髒活都幹過，只爲求個溫飽，可惜命運多舛，沒兩年莫先生就得了肝癌，把好不容易攢下的幾萬美元悉數花光，還欠下一屁股債。那陣子Molly消瘦不少，一逮到人就訴苦，感嘆時不我與、造化弄人，漸漸把四周圍的人都給趕跑了，畢竟誰的生活都不易，沒人有義務當告解的神父。

擦乾眼淚後，孤立無援的莫太太決定與命運抗爭，Mr. Mo Chinese Burger就是這樣開起來的，藉以紀念她那因病早逝的丈夫。

我三兩下把中國漢堡吞下肚，拍拍衣服上的餅屑，起身。

"今天到我妹那兒嗎？"Molly問。

"嗯！Monica今天到有錢太太家收貨，臨時叫上我。"

Monica是Molly的親妹妹，兩人的年紀差上一輪，她在羅迪歐大道上開了一家二手奢侈品專門店，平常店裏有兩個韓國妹紙幫忙，當人手不夠時會叫上我，雖然是兼職性質，時薪又不高，但在實現演員夢之前，不失爲雞肋。

"等等，"Molly把兩個肉夾饃放進紙袋內交給我，"告訴Monica用的是半肥瘦的後豬腿肉，她會喜歡。"

"沒問題。"我愉快地答。

這已經是這個月第四次讓我當免費送餐員，但我一點兒也不介意。Molly不知道自己的妹妹正值減肥期，碳水化合物一律免沾，我因此成了最大的受益者。

"嘻嘻！今天的晚餐有著落了。"我心想，樂不可支。

~

我一走進以老闆娘的名字爲店名的二手店，就被Monica往外推："快，來不及了，LP的總裁夫人三點鐘要出門，我們得趕在她離去前打聲招呼。"

"這個LP該不會是加州最大的電影製作公司吧？！"

"怎麼不是？我跟他們做生意已經不下數十回，熟悉到保安看到我的臉就主動放行。"她邊答邊往外走去。

Monica的車是黃色布加迪威龍，以每月三千美元的代價從二手車行租來。

"想在這裏生存就得開好車，否則連乞丐都不鳥你。"Monica曾對我說。

以一個開店老闆娘的收入，買一部代步工具不成問題，但……布加迪威龍實在太貴了，她只好以租代買。

"那個……今天不開車嗎？"我問。

我明明看見黃色跑車就在眼前，Monica卻視而不見。

"今天貨多，我租了房車。"她往一輛奔馳維特斯系列的九人座房車走去。

"爲了載貨而另外租車，划算嗎？"

"當然，賠本的生意沒人做。"Monica 信心十足地答。

~

"喏！那棟灰的以前是麥當娜的，後來賣了2800萬美元……紅屋頂的是貝克漢姆和維多利亞的房，他們的大兒子布魯克林和科洛拍拖時，我看過一次他們一起走進豪宅的背影……噢！那是賈斯汀.比伯在18歲時買下的，呵呵！我18歲時還在想牛肉麵要點大碗還是小碗，人家已經購入千萬房產……這個是湯姆克魯斯的……那是華裔婚紗設計師王薇薇的……"一路上Monica不遺餘力地向我介紹屋子的主人。

對我來說，那些童話般的城堡宛如歐美大片，可望而不可及。

見我沈默，Monica問我今天試鏡的結果如何？我答再一次糊了，自己的英語不行，又長著一副亞洲臉孔，除非演的是裹小腳的女人……

"那也不無可能，如果《末代皇帝》重拍，妳一定拿得到角色。"她說。

真不知是褒還是貶？亞洲題材的電影或電視劇在好萊塢算小眾，若有重拍的經費倒不如拿去拍怪獸或外星人。

"也不一定得等到那時候，我現在已經放低姿態，群演也成，若有一、兩句台詞更好。"我笑呵呵地答。

話說得雲淡風輕，實際上我已經付不起合租的費用，淪落到住在房車內。

你若問我混得這麼差怎麼不回國？哎！說來話長，在國內我學的是表演，畢業後跑了三年龍套，好不容易得了個女四的角色，那高興自不在話下。誰知導演醉翁之意不在酒，約我到酒店討論劇本，一進房間便動手動腳，我竭力反抗，抓了他一臉，可想而知，最後連個啞巴的角色也沒撈著，連夜被踢出劇組，更慘的是我的裸照隨後就到，那些不高明的合成技術差點兒讓我得了抑鬱症。考慮再三，我決定到美國找機會，沒想到美國也這麼難生存，這下子就更不能回國了，因為沒臉呀！

" Here we are."Monica說我們到了。

果然如同她所言，豪宅保安主動打開電閘門。

"好……好大啊！"我嚇得目瞪口呆。

之所以說好大是因爲從入口處看不到盡頭，彷彿進到公園內。

"誰說不是呢？"Monica意味深長地一笑，然後腳踩油門。

第二章/ELSA

"待會兒看到總裁夫人可別直呼其名，要稱Madam, 富貴人家都很重視稱謂。"Monica提醒我。

"知道了。"

車子沿著坡度不大的車道蜿蜒直上，整個園林被劃分成若干幾何形地塊，到處是開闊的草地及修剪整齊的樹籬，花壇則種有玫瑰及冬青，偶見新穎的雕塑小品。

"這棟房子原來是個英國佬的，所以房子外觀及花園都被設計成都鐸復興式莊園，誰知Elsa購入後決定來個混搭，花了五百多萬美元把屋內打造成摩爾式建築風，讓初次造訪者多少有些不適應，彷彿剛吃了傳統的英式下午茶，緊接著又來上一口阿拉伯烤全羊。"

"呵呵！我喜歡英式下午茶，也愛吃烤全羊，口味能瞬間轉換，毫無勉強。"

"嘖嘖嘖！不愧是演員，見人說人話，見鬼說鬼話，簡直是條變色龍。"

講到變色龍，Monica才是個中翹楚，她若說第二，沒人敢排第一，與自己的姐姐Molly相比，一個是老實巴交的勞動人民，另一個則是趨炎附勢的牆頭草。偏偏虛比實吃得開，當Molly還在爲3美元一個的肉夾饃勞累時，Monica早已憑藉轉賣二手奢侈品在西木區買下華麗的penthouse，能俯瞰整個加州大學洛杉磯分校。

"喏！那棟就是。"Monica努努嘴。

看過近萬平米的生態園林後，一座典型的都鐸風格英式別墅赫然在目，有急坡屋頂、高煙囪、大格窗、拱門以及由印第安納石灰塗抹的外牆。

車子停妥後，Monica看了一眼車內時間顯示器，說差一刻三點，希望Elsa還在，而且有好心情。

"爲什麼非得有好心情？我們不是來搬貨的嗎？"我問。

"這妳就不懂了，Elsa要賣的是已退流行的產品，我的火眼金睛就是要把不在名單上的精品找出來，逢主人心情好，我就撿漏了。"説完，Monica下車走向那棟深色豪宅，後面跟著一臉茫然的我。

" Please come in."腰繫白色荷葉邊圍裙的女傭開門後說。

走進屋內，我看到巨型的巴卡拉枝形吊燈從圓頂天花板垂掛下來，地上鋪著純手工編織的波斯地毯，牆面有大面積的拼花布紋織物，到處可見鑲有植物、幾何、阿拉伯書法紋樣的器具及裝飾物。猛一看，大紅、水藍、深紫、橙黃、松石綠……讓人目不暇給。

" This way, ladies."女傭又說。

雖然我對屋內設計感到好奇，但我們直接被帶到二樓的某個房間內，錯過一覽全貌的機會。

" Good afternoon, madam."Monica對著一個身形略爲豐滿的女人行屈膝禮。

在西方禮儀中，女性會向社會地位高於自己的人行屈膝禮，落到今日，這個習慣早已不多見，只剩歐洲皇室還保留著。

" 這位是……"宛如女皇的人注意到我，而我也注意到她 原來是會講普通話的華人。

" 她是新來的助理，叫衛萌萌。"Monica介紹。

我有樣學樣，也來個屈膝禮，並且遵循Monica的叮囑喚她Madam（夫人）。

" 長得挺水靈的，" 她上下打量我，" Well, 時間不多了，開始吧！"

我們跟隨她走進一個大到像高檔精品店的衣帽間，女主人的手指彷彿仙女棒，凡點到的, Monica便要我取下，很快我懷裏的東西便小山也似的高。

" 快放到門外的長沙發上。"Monica提醒我。

我就這麼來回跑了十幾趟，直到Elsa喊停。

" 今天就這麼著，天氣熱了，這裏的東西也該騰出位置給當季新款。"

" 是，是，"Monica點頭如搗蒜，" 回去整理完畢，我會發個明細過來。"

" 沒事，我一向信任妳。"

就在Elsa轉身前，Monica趕緊說繡花的橙色花呢包、帶亮片的帆布旅行包以及盧加洛太陽眼鏡早過時了，另外，Christian Louboutin 的紅底鞋鞋跟有半個指甲蓋大小的漆掉了……

" 拿走拿走，我趕著和朋友見面呢！"女主人大手一揮，像揮走什麼骯髒的東西。

" 謝謝！慢走。"Monica對著離去的背影深深一鞠躬。

～

雖然豪門貴婦的衣服都有專人負責清洗，但爲了賣相好，回店的路上通通被我們送進乾洗店，至於皮具……我將它們一一塗上防霉隔離精油及皮包潤澤精華液，再用塑料袋密封好，一個個全上了展示櫃。

"萌萌，妳可以走了，路上小心。"Monica說。

我看了一下時間，晚上九點。

韓國店員早在三個小時前就已下班，因爲美國勞工部規定工作時間超出每週40小時的員工可領取加班費。Monica爲了省下那1.5倍的支出，留下我這個便宜的"黑工"不難理解，只是我得加緊腳步，房車露營地離公交站牌有一段距離，我可不想在車少人稀的道路上走那麼一大段路。

～

在國外，利用房車旅行非常普遍，我的直屬學姐和她男友在辛勤工作五年後也決定加入行列，只是交通工具克難了點兒，是用麵包車改裝的，不過裏面應有盡有，不僅安裝了隔音、隔熱板，還DIY了儲物空間，通上電路和水路後，連廚房也有了。

"萌萌，要不要吃拉麵？"我一回到房車內，正吃著麵的學姐衝著我喊。

"好呀好呀！晚餐只吃了兩個冷掉的肉夾饃，餓死我了。"

"去，"學姐推了正在打遊戲的男友一把，"萌萌肚子餓，記得打個雞蛋。"

"切，就我命苦，遊戲打得正好……"

我趕緊說不用了，自己其實沒那麼餓。

學長立馬丟下遊戲機去煮麵，還說我若不乖乖把麵給吃了，今晚學姐會罰他不准上床……

啊！我何其有幸在最困難的時候遇上兩位貴人，如果不是他們正好旅行至此，我恐怕就要住進臨時收容所，與流浪漢生息與共了。

“萌萌，妳有沒有想過一個禮拜後怎麼辦？我們……我們也該上路了。”我正吃著麵，學姐忽然提起煩心的事。

“放心，今天的試鏡很成功，導演說有個華裔女醫的角色特別適合我，估計很快會開機，我馬上就有錢租房子住了。”我笑得一臉燦爛。

“真的？那太好了，”學姐看著學長，“如此一來我們也能安心離開了。”

當燈熄了之後，只有窗外的月亮還醒著，我蜷縮在兩人硬座上，怎麼也睡不著。

離我一步之遙的學長和學姐已經沈沈入睡，鼾聲雷動，他們不知道我連群演的機會也沒得到，現在只靠Monica給的微薄薪水在苦撐著，而下學期的學費又迫在眉睫。如果不繳學費就拿不到學生簽證，沒有簽證，我立馬得回國，一環扣一環，壓得我喘不過氣來。

“也許……也許明天環球影城會給我好消息，那位經理看起來很和善，這次應該沒問題。”我給自己打氣。

第三章/李奧

我已經在社區大學上了兩個多月的課，意思是《美國文學史》也已經上了兩個多月，在這段時間裏，我主要和馬克.吐溫打交道。

他的作品我只看過《湯姆歷險記》，一直以爲他是童書作家，沒想到老師說他很"毒舌"，是美國批判現實主義文學的奠基人，善於黑色幽默，年紀越大越顯語言暴力......

呃！我還以爲《湯姆歷險記》中那個調皮搗蛋的小男孩是作者原型，連帶把馬克.吐溫也給美化了。

下課前，老師提醒我們兩週後交報告，想針對馬克.吐溫做研究也成，但切記別把上課內容全給寫進去，以往有學生照本宣科，一律低分。

真是糟糕！我原本想當"搬運工"，把老師說過的話一五一十寫下以表忠心，沒想到他"六親不認"，叫我如何是好？尤其剛在"環球影城"覓得一份短期工，薪水不錯還提供三餐，什麼都好，就是每天得站八個小時，這意味著我得逃課，如今得知兩週後交報告，還不准"人云亦云"，真要愁煞人！

考慮再三，我還是決定去賺這1200美元，畢竟沒有了麵包，什麼都是浮雲。

～

影城的工作從明天開始，我以爲至少今天能當好學生，沒想到下午一點半Monica發來短信，我才得知金小姐和尹小姐中午不知吃了什麼髒東西，兩人上吐下洩，現在店裏只剩她一人。問我能不能現在過來？

知道又有收入，我回覆馬上到，然後趁老師轉身寫白板之際，偷偷從後門溜出去。

～

奢侈品太貴，讓很多有品味的中産階級和白領小資轉身投向二手名店。饒是如此，一些看上去十分普通的東西也要好幾千美元，連最不起眼的鑰匙扣、小銅鎖也標價一百多，看到這些數字難免讓人氣餒到懷疑人生。

我剛服務完一個買禮物哄女友開心的"成功人士"，在下一個客人進門前，我走到Monica身邊。

"忙什麼？妳已經坐在這裏快一個鐘頭了。"我問。

她答正在列Elsa的貨物明細，錢也得滙出去。

我看了一眼清單，乖乖，剛剛賣給"成功人士"的愛馬仕包售價兩萬八千美元，Monica卻只付給Elsa四千，連零頭都不到。還有，巴寶莉的羊毛格紋圍巾在店內賣一百五，清單上寫的是三十，只夠在叫得出名字的餐廳點上一碗奶油蛤蜊湯。

"妳做的是一本萬利的買賣呀！"我說。

Monica聽完輕蔑一笑，她答二手店的經營方式有寄賣和回購兩種，一般業者傾向寄賣，因爲賣出才需給錢，傭金也多，高達30%；回購就不一樣，賣不出去等於囤貨，當然得把價錢壓低。

"可是也太低了，利潤能達80%以上。"我竟打抱不平起來。

"我承認給Elsa的價錢低，但一來她不在乎，甚至感謝我將'垃圾'帶走；二來我的服務好，能上門取貨且付款及時，這也是我和她一直合作愉快的原因。"

哎！這叫周瑜打黃蓋，一個願打，一個願挨。

我聳聳肩，正想回到工作崗位，一低頭，不巧看見昨天收購回來的Christian Louboutin紅底鞋正被Monica踩在腳下，難怪她這麼熱衷上比佛利山莊，甚至不惜花150美元租下奔馳房車。

∽

好萊塢環球影城是一個以電影爲主題的遊樂園，在這裏可以參觀電影的製作過程及回顧經典的影片片段，它甚至還有專屬的購物區—環球城市大道，而我……從今天起將在這裏工作兩個禮拜。

我在演員更衣室裏換上戎裝，再紮起馬尾，這位家喻戶曉的巾幗英雄代表果敢堅忍，我得嚴肅對待，別出糗。

" Mulan, this is your husband ."經理喚我木蘭，還鄭重介紹我的"丈夫"。

在動畫片裏，花木蘭最後和李翔將軍"有情人終成眷屬"，沒想到影城真的給我配了個肌肉男。

"Hi."他對我微笑，然後伸出手臂，" Let's go."

我的"老公"大概以爲我會像新娘子似地挽著他的手出場,偏偏我不配合，逕自向外走去。

來環球影城的遊客多半是親子，不止小孩，很多大人看到

cosplay人物也很興奮，我和"李翔將軍"非常有默契地做到來者不拒、有求必應。

"妳去哪裏？"李翔將軍問。

"時間到了，回休息室。"我答。

經理說每工作兩小時，演員能休息二十分鐘，但也只能在休息室裏待著，絕不能穿著戲服到處溜達及做出"不合身份"的事，譬如《冰雪奇緣》中的"安娜公主"就曾經在園內大喇喇地吞雲吐霧，遭到小朋友家長的投訴……

回到休息室，那裏人來人往，吵雜的聲音好比菜市場，雖然有熱飲及小點心供應，但我如坐針氈，因爲老煙槍太多了。

"空氣很不好。"我的"老公"說，然後遞了塊蛋糕給我。

"不吃，謝謝！"

他問是不是哪裏得罪我了？

"没有的事，我是演員，保持好身材是我的職責，即使喝咖啡，我也從來不加奶和糖。"

"光管住嘴没用，還得邁開腿，我就每天上健身房，風雨無阻。"他說。

"有那個錢我就不來這裏擺pose了……對了，你怎麼也來此工作？"

"我大學學的是戲劇，戲劇系學生畢業後很自然會來好萊塢碰運氣，可惜我的運氣不好，到現在還在打游擊。"

知道他也是學表演的，而且同樣混得不好，我的心忽然與他靠近許多。

"妳呢？"他問。

我三兩下把自己的過往給交待了，當然跳過那個不美麗的"性侵未遂"。

“ 有夢想最美，堅持住，我是李奧，”他伸出手和我握了握，“ Nice to meet you.”

“ 我是衛萌萌，請多指教。”

因爲和他握手，我注意到他手腕上戴的是瑞士浪琴錶，實際上那是名匠系列情侶錶中的男錶，Monica的店內有售，一對約五千美元，還是二手價。

“ 你戴的是浪琴錶。”我說。

“ 好眼光，路邊攤買的，五十美元不到。”

李奧不知道我在二手名店兼職，雖然不致於馬上分辨出正品或A貨，但是不是地攤貨可一眼就能判斷出，他的錶……絕對不止五十美元。

“ 這麼便宜？哪天帶我去瞧瞧。”我說。

“ 没問題。”他答。

作者介紹

在異國的背景下加入纏綿悱惻的愛情故事是B杜小說的一大特點，她的文筆清新、筆觸詼諧、畫面感很強，讀完小說有種看完一部愛情偶像劇的感覺，特別適合懷春少女及對愛情有憧憬的女性閱讀。

B杜創作了一系列異國戀情N部曲，包括《法蘭西情人》、《東瀛之愛》、《新西蘭之戀》、《英倫玫瑰》、《愛在暹羅》、《情定布拉格》、《獅城情緣》、《愛上比佛利》、《夢回楓葉國》、《早安，歐巴》……等作品，歡迎關注。

ALSO BY B杜

狮城情缘（简体字） Love in Singapore (simplified character version)

《愛上比佛利》 Love in Beverly Hills

《法蘭西情人》 Love in France

《新西蘭之戀》 Love in New Zealand

《愛在暹羅》 Love in Thailand

《情定布拉格》 Love in Prague

《英倫玫瑰》 Love in England

《東瀛之愛》 Love in Japan

《早安，歐巴》Love in Korea

《夢回楓葉國》Love in Canada